MACHINE MAGE

MACHINE MAGE

IN MY DEFENSE BOOK TWO

J. Drude

Podium

To Lily and Jude
You're not old enough to read these yet,
but I still want you to know Dad loves you very much.
Maybe someday I'll have the words to express just how much.
I'll keep trying.

Cover design by Diana Franco Campos

ISBN: 978-1-0394-9743-6

Published in 2026 by Podium Publishing
www.podiumentertainment.com

Podium

MACHINE MAGE

PROLOGUE

Hey guys,

  If you're reading this letter, something's probably happened to me. Either I'm hurt or I'm dead or I forgot to pick this thing back up after we won. If it's the third, then definitely stop reading and burn this immediately.

And if I'm just hurt, isn't it a little early to go picking through my things, especially if you're being so thorough as to look inside the spare turret barrel under the cot? You found it, though. Good on you, I guess. Consider a career in law enforcement or as a foster parent or something.

But I'm guessing the real reason you're here is because I'm dead.

Okay, since I'm dead, let's get this out of the way: I'm not from this planet. I'm not even from this universe. And, as those of you thinking ahead will have probably guessed, I'm not a monk, either.

I'm human.

I was dumped on Ralqir a few months ago as a sort of crash course in how to be an Exotic or what you guys call a "practitioner." I woke up in a forest somewhere south of here with no idea where I was or what I was doing, but the monsters that lived in that neck of the woods sure knew what to do with me. I was hunted, driven like an animal, and all I could do was run.

Until I fell into the not-so-tender care of the Stone Heart goblins, that is. Once they, shall we say, "took me in," they put me to work and gave me an opportunity to practice my new Exotic mojo, but my problems followed me there, too. My monsters became the goblins' monsters, and most of my captors were killed. Despite how the Stone Hearts had treated me, I still feel bad about that.

Once I escaped my cell, I fell in with a traveling group of Miur led by a nobleman named Traylo Jassin. He was on his way to Eclipse and took an interest in me after finding me on the side of the road. While I was grateful for the ride, I once again got the distinct impression my attendance was mandatory. Jassin's the one who gave me the monk cover story, by the way. He knew I wasn't what I said I was, and he didn't want the guards at the gate asking questions.

Don't take this as my trying to put any blame on the man. I lied to you all about being part of your church. There's no getting around that. I just thought you should know what brought me here.

After that, you probably know the rest. The Church asked me to get to the bottom of the plague, and—if there was nothing else to be done—purge the infected. I met up with you guys, and we all got stuck in the Undercity together while the world went to hell. Now I'm just trying to put things right.

As of right now, while I write this, we're gearing up to go out into the city to rescue those folks at the western gate.

Trix, you're probably working with our interns on food and ammo production. You're great with people, by the way, and we won't have been able to pull this off without you. I hope you know that.

Sissa and Samila, you're mending your armor. In fact, I can see you right now across the room as I write this. Did you know that you both bite your bottom lips when you're concentrating? Well, you do. You're both the head and the heart of our little team, and it gives me some comfort to spend these last moments of calm with the two of you here.

Geddon, I have no idea where you are as I write this, but you said you had something to take care of before the battle. The sisters tell me you're probably monopolizing a bathroom somewhere, grooming your mane, picking your teeth, and flexing in the mirror. You're gearing up for what you believe to be your final battle. I hope my plan to save your life doesn't inconvenience you overly much.

Yes, I plan to save all of your lives. I know it sounds presumptuous, but I do.

The odds aren't looking particularly good, the way I see them. The plague has infected most of the city now, so everyone who used to live here is either now dead, one of them, or *both*. I never asked any of you about Eclipse's former population, but if I had to guess, I'd have put it in the hundreds of thousands. That's a lot, considering there's only five of us.

I have a trump card, though. The infected—the Scourge—they hate me. *Seriously.* They hate me with such a fiery passion it would rival your sun for intensity. Whenever they catch a whiff of me, they fly into a fury. I'm counting on that to make my little plan work.

No, I didn't plan to die, Sissa. Despite what you may have thought of me, I didn't have a death wish. I was just trying to give you all the best chance I could give.

I hope you all made it. You're good people, and your home needs you right now.

Ryan Kotes - Alien

Letter, recovered in year 1308 TB amid the ruins of the ancient
city of Eclipse by the Order of Reclamation, Third Expedition

CHAPTER ONE

Force Some Honesty

My eyes fluttered open, the dream I'd just been having dissolving into wisps and vague impressions of motion and color that my conscious mind didn't have the language to understand. Now that it was gone, I felt an emptiness like I'd forgotten something important.

I was in a plain room constructed of the Spire's characteristic smooth stone, windowless and undecorated. It was small, just enough space to stand up and take two short steps before running into a wall or three steps out of the door near the foot of the bed, which creaked and cracked as I shifted my weight.

Given how heavy I was, I wondered if I would now have to be extra careful about where I slept for the rest of my life. Hammocks were definitely out, as were most cots. Those things weren't made for a guy as heavy as I was, or, more accurately, as dense. My metal parts, combined with a high Body score, seemed to have given me all the problems of an Olympic strongman without a proportional size adjustment. I'd probably end up sleeping on the floor more often than not. At least I wouldn't feel sore afterward with my Exotic-level recovery.

The sheets scratched and crackled as I sat upright. They peeled away from my skin and clothes—clothes I didn't recognize—to reveal patches of the otherwise-white sheets that were brown with dried blood and yellowed with dried sweat.

I reached up to rub the gunk out of my eyes, surprised to find a bandage over one of them and a big bundle of white cloth tied to my scalp. There were a lot of bandages all over me, actually, from head to toe, including a big one that wrapped all the way around my stomach. All of them were now more rust-colored than their original bright-white. The sheer amount . . . Was I really that hurt?

I thought back to the battle, remembering vivid flashes of violence and snarling faces. My body didn't feel cold like it used to, but I shivered nonetheless.

Thoughts mercifully turning back to the now, I gingerly peeled off the bandage around my wrist to find clear, unblemished skin underneath. Exotic healing was no joke.

I'm never going to get used to this, am I? Maybe if I ever do, that's when I should start worrying.

Just then, a whiff of something savory hit me, which I tracked to two bowls sitting on a table next to the head of my bed. No steam came off them, and a quick check with my fingers told me they'd been there for some time. My stomach gurgled, regardless. I took up the first bowl and grabbed a spoon with a shaky hand.

I must have been in here for a good while, considering how hungry I was and the dryness of my mouth, not to mention how weak I felt. How long had I been out?

It was so quiet and still. I wouldn't say I missed the sound of the guns, but their absence did trigger an unease in me that was hard to pin down, a sort of unsettled feeling akin to my first few days on Ralqir, when I had to acclimate to its strange atmosphere and the fact that its air didn't move as I was used to back home.

If there weren't any guns firing now, what was holding back the Scourge?

The guards, probably. My friends. They shouldn't have had to, though. They couldn't heal like I could. They didn't have a System repairing their body until it was good as new even if they were ripped apart.

I frowned into my bowl.

That was what had been bothering me. If my guns weren't working, I wasn't helping. The Scourge-Touched were coming, and others were doing the fighting for me. That would not do in the slightest. The longer I stood still, the higher the chance someone else had to pay the price in my place.

Still, the soup was delicious—some kind of salty vegetable blend with dark broth and chunks of some kind of starch that I couldn't quite identify as potato. Too gritty.

I'd fully cleaned the bowl before I knew it, and I was on to the next one. As I'd become accustomed to doing when I was idle nowadays, I opened up my status screen to check on things and was immediately bombarded with notifications. They stacked one on top of the other, each seeming to blink in and out of the foreground of my vision like they were vying to be the first in line for my attention, but all they were doing was threatening to make me go cross-eyed. With a thought, I cleared them all away and started filtering by category.

Level Up!
You are now Level 16.
Max HP +10
Max MP +10
+1 Attribute point.
Achievements awarded this Level:
Spirit of the Warrior: You gained 51% of your Experience this Level from defeated foes as a non-combat Class. [+3 spirit]

Doing Your Part: Some of your creations have been used against agents of the Scourge. [+200% Experience awarded for new designs next Level]
Ambitious: You have defeated a foe above your Level. [+1 to lowest Level Ability]
Rift Hunter: You gained 51% of your Experience this Level from Nemesis-tagged foes. [+1 to all Attributes]
Reversal: You gained 100% of your Experience this Level from Nemesis-tagged foes. [+3 to highest Attribute]
Mass Slaughter: You have defeated more than 1,000 foes this Level. Combat-related Abilities and Skills gain power 50% faster for the next Level. [ERROR: Ability:Volatility:class_mismatch]

My Level-Up notifications, though numerous, weren't surprising, but seeing all of my achievements laid out like this felt so strange and humbling. They all looked generally akin to one another, with the exception of Level 11, which had labels like Big Spender, Inventor, Soulful, and the like. That made sense, given all the time I had spent in the lab during that Level. The rest were all fighting-flavored.

Reversal was a new achievement, and it was understandable that I hadn't gotten that one up until this point. Gaining 100 percent of a Level just from fighting a specific type of monster just wasn't normally achievable at my level of skill and with my Class's limitations. It probably wasn't feasible for even the combat Classes.

The achievement itself was what people referred to as a "snowball condition," where a small victory quickly turned into a series of larger and larger victories over time. The fact that my highest Attribute was Spirit made leveraging the influx of points more difficult, though. It was a weird Stat, and I wasn't entirely sure how it worked. I imagined if Body had been my highest Stat during the fight, the bonuses could have kept me going for a long time as the Levels rolled in, increasing my HP and giving me little Endurance boosts on into forever.

Of course, if I were a Body guy or a combat Class, I probably wouldn't have had so much Experience flowing in as I had in the first place. Yesterday's fight had been a culmination of a lot of time, preparation, and experimentation—stuff I couldn't have done if I weren't what I was. Automation was a powerful thing, something I'd do well to remember when I felt like whining over having gotten a non-combat Class.

I checked my character sheet to see what had changed and, upon reading it, I nearly fell out of the bed.

Ryan Kotes - Level 16 (?) Animator (Uncommon)				
Type:	Artificer (Common)	Abilities:	Shape 9 (Transmute)	Devouring Grasp 5(?)

Class:	Animator (Uncommon)		Consume 5 (?)	Volatility 3
Core:	Engine (Unique)		Iron Grip 4	Imbue 4
HP:	220/220		Trigger 4	Automate +4
MP:	186/186		Tempered Channels 3	Knife in the Dark 22 (?)
Attributes:		Skills:	Climbing 7	Unarmed Combat 5 (?)
Body:	40		Running 5 (?)	Stealth (Gray Man) 11
Mind:	33		Conduit 5 (?)	Split Mind 9
Spirit:	77		Spear 4	Deception 5 (?)
			Disguise 1	Sword 6 (?)
			Pistol 4	
		Affinities:	Goblinoid F	Limestone E
			Iron E	Cobalt E
			Steel F+	Deep Lead E
			Magnesium F	Nickel E
Free Attribute points: 0			Mendau Wood D	Copper F

Spirit: 77

My Spirit Stat had *doubled* overnight. That was—I had no idea what.

The other Stats had climbed significantly, as well. I let my eyes travel down the screen, looking over the values. I had a number of question marks on the page now, with milestones reached in lots of Skills and Abilities, and their associated prompts seemed to jump out at me when I gave them even the slightest bit of attention. I ignored them, though. I just wanted to get the big picture right now.

Knife in the Dark: 22

What the actual hell?

Knife in the Dark had been something like . . . three? . . . maybe? Before yesterday, that Ability had been one of my lowest, but now it was far and away the largest value in its category. The last time I'd used it I—Constance, forgive me for being an idiot.

The whole point of taking Knife in the Dark was to conduct an experiment. I wanted to see how much "me" my turrets retained when I Automated them, since they were essentially using a ton of my mana. The verbiage on the ability boiled down to, "If a target isn't paying direct attention to you, do bonus damage," and I'd wanted to see exactly what that meant. My first test had been on the wretchwyrm under the city, but I hadn't been in a position to think about it after it happened. There'd just been too much going on, what with me poisoned and breathing from an air tank in funky sewer water and all.

I went back to check the logs from yesterday.

Scourge-Touched Undead takes 18 Damage. (15 base, 3 Knife in the Dark bonus) (Piercing)
Scourge-Touched Undead takes 21 Damage. (18 base, 3 Knife in the Dark bonus) (Piercing)
Scourge-Touched Goblin takes 15 Damage. (12 base, 3 Knife in the Dark bonus) (Piercing)

The amount of messages just like this could have filled entire volumes. My head spun at the sheer amount of it.

Every time my turret had shot a monster, I had been using Knife in the Dark and getting the bonus Damage. It was no wonder the Ability had leveled up so quickly. I had eight turrets out there putting holes in the Scourge. Each magazine held about 900 rounds, 900 attacks, not to mention those emplacements with extra magazines and someone to feed them . . .

That meant I had to have used Knife in the Dark at least ten thousand times in the span of a few hours, and the System counted each and every one of them as progress toward the next Level. That was, in a word, ridiculous.

Oh, I'm going to exploit the hell out of this.

First, though, I needed to get to my workshop. No, scratch that. I needed to find out what was going on, then get to my workshop. No, I needed to know if everyone was okay, what was happening outside, how our supplies were holding up. Then it was workshop time.

With a brief flash of magic, I summoned a nail from my Spatial Storage and saturated it with mana so that I could Shape. The nail was small, and my mastery of my mana was better than it used to be, making the process a breeze. Soon a tiny razor edge had appeared on the nail's head, which I used to cut off my remaining bandages. Had this still been my first day doing this, that little trick would have left me sweating and drained. Now, with all my advancements, I almost didn't have to think, and it took seconds.

A quick check of the doorknob told me it was locked, so I set about re-Shaping my nail into a crude key—not an exact copy of an actual key but just flat enough to fit inside.

More Shaping, this time shifting the nail's matter until it fit all the tumblers in the lock. Then I gave it a turn.

Bingo.

click

Free at last, I snatched up the second half-full bowl of soup and reached for the door handle only to have it slam into my open palm, bending it backward painfully.

"Gah!" I yelped, pulling back and shaking my hand to work the feeling back into it.

Jassin's gaunt, almost-skeletal head reached into the room, followed shortly by the top of his set of black scholar's robes. He didn't open the door all the way, opting instead to lean in through the gap like he was just checking in on me.

"Ah, you're awake," he said, not seeming surprised in the slightest to find me up. He did, however, sound a bit short of breath. There was also a reddish hue to his pale skin and a sheen of sweat barely visible on his forehead. His slicked-back salt-and-pepper hair looked a bit disheveled, too, some strands of it hanging from his Miur antlers in a most peculiar way, almost as if he had run to get here.

"Jassin. Uh. Yeah," I replied, still trying to get the pins and needles out of my hand.

"Eloquent as ever, my boy," the Miur lord replied. "You're looking well. I see you enjoy wearing bandages as much as I enjoy sabbaticals."

I looked down at the pile of dirty cloth on the floor. "They needed changing."

He smiled at that and shook his head. "Unbelievable. When I saw your injuries, I was understandably cautious, but when I spoke to your Holy Church comrades, they all said something along the lines of 'Yes, he does that,' and dismissed my concerns out of hand. I didn't believe them right away, but now I see your Abilities are most extraordinary. Your legend is going to shine even brighter if word of this gets around."

There was a tight feeling in my stomach. "My friends, are they—"

"All fine. Do not worry," Jassin said placatingly as he stepped all the way into the room. "They are well taken care of and are probably more tired of being thanked for their heroic deeds than by their regular duties."

I sighed in relief. That was one worry off my mind. Wait—

"Did you say 'my legend?'" I asked. "I have . . . a legend?"

"Oh, yes. The guards that witnessed you at the gate—the talkative ones, at least—are abuzz with tales of the one-man army, the Rising Sun of Eclipse. They whisper your name with reverence as if you were a martyr. Your intestines were hanging out of you when you dragged yourself up to the doors, you know. They've been making toasts in your honor, thinking you succumbed to your wounds. If only they knew."

Blinking, I tried to wrap my head around that thought. The Rising Sun of Eclipse.

Right. If only they knew.

Jassin didn't choose his words lightly. I knew that even from the brief time we'd spent together on the road. He wasn't that type of man.

"So, I was just leaving . . ." I probed, leaning over and peering out of the open door. The hallway beyond called to me with its fresh air and people to see.

Jassin nodded. "I gathered that, but doing so right now would be unwise. It would be more prudent to keep you out of sight until it is time."

My metal hand twitched at my side.

"Until it's time? What time? Why?" I asked cautiously.

"Mostly for your sake, some for theirs," Jassin answered. "It is important we discuss something before you decide whether you want to go out there."

I looked around the room—at the bare, solid walls, ones Jassin probably thought were nice and sturdy, hard to break. "Someone locked my door by mistake," I said, letting a little ice trickle into my voice. "Strange that. I think I've proved that I'm here to help, right?"

"And there it is. It took you all of—what? Eleven sentences?" Jassin said with a sigh. "You're 'here to help.' The way you say it, so casually like you're dying to divulge your secret and cast us into ruin."

"No, I'm not divulging anything," I argued. "Dying or otherwise. I just want to get back out there."

"Before you do that, I feel the need to impress upon you that you must use care in your words *and* your actions. The secret you have in your possession could rip our world apart, and, intentionally or not, you broadcast it to all who know how to listen." He said it so matter-of-factly, like it was the most obvious thing in the world that I should be locked away and kept in the dark. Like I could hurt others simply by existing.

I raised a dubious eyebrow. "From where I'm sitting, I don't think I'm even in the top-five most dangerous things on this planet, Lord Jassin. The monsters outside count as just one, by the way. I'm pretty sure of that by now. The main point is that my machines are game-changers. They'll keep your people out of harm's way. No secret I have can offset that."

"Ah. I see." Jassin considered with a series of thoughtful nods. "We are coming to this issue from different perspectives. You see an army of angry monsters outside and believe them to be Ralqir's greatest threat, and maybe from your perspective, they are. I will admit that flesh-hungry hordes of indeterminate origin are cause for concern. However, from my perspective, *you* could do far more *lasting* damage to Ralqir than the mindless beasts that now lay siege to this place, and you wouldn't even have to lift a finger."

"How?" I asked indignantly.

"By just being who you are, Ryan."

Ominous, cryptic statements about *me*—a subject on which I was more than qualified to be the world's leading expert—were fast becoming my least favorite aspect of my new life. "I don't understand," I said between gritted teeth.

"Then let me help you understand. That is why I'm here," Jassin replied.

I looked to the door, specifically the lock from which my nail/key-lockpick still protruded. "Funny. You only came when I was about to escape."

Jassin sucked air through his teeth, taking a moment to mull that over. "Your point is taken," he finally said, an apology in his eyes. "But I have also been managing the defense of this school while you slept. I could not be here when you woke. The ward I placed on your door was meant to inform me if someone tried to enter, but, instead, it warned me you were trying to leave. I knew of no other way to keep your secret intact and simultaneously perform my duties. I apologize. I also want to take this opportunity to thank you. It should have been the first thing I did upon entering this room, but I failed at that. You had no reason to fight for us as you did, but you saved us regardless—at great risk to yourself, no less. That speaks to the strength of your character. Again, thank you."

I could feel the "but" coming down toward me like a meteor. Jassin didn't keep me waiting long.

"Be that as it may, if you go out there and mix with my people, you will sow the seeds for centuries of hell, despite your intentions. You are unwittingly reckless with your secrets, and it could potentially destroy millions."

I spread my arms out wide, fuming. "How?! Look at me! I'm just one guy! I kept my identity a secret on *your* request, and I've been doing fine so far, all things considered."

"Been doing fine, you say," Jassin mocked, putting his hands on his hips. "Have you? I have spoken with your 'friends' from the Undercity, the innocents you rescued, as well. They sing your praises until the light burns us all to ash, but ask them who you are or anything personal and they become quiet as mice, almost as if they have something to hide. Their stories can't stand up to more-than-casual scrutiny."

At that I could only shrug. "Sounds like a normal response to interrogation to me. Besides, they don't know anything," I said.

"They have questions about you, Ryan. They might not know *what* you are, but they suspect you are not what you seem. Yet still they protect you," Jassin mused, pausing to look pensively at the floor. When he spoke again, his tone was a bit more gentle. "I imagine that was something you earned rather than something asked for, but they are betraying themselves and their loyalties when they vouch for you. It is not something you should put them through."

I opened my mouth to say something but stopped. The lies I was forced to tell my friends—they hurt, yes, but I hadn't considered what I was implicitly asking of the others, even if they didn't fully believe what I told them. I'd kind of hoped we'd just moved past the expository part of our relationships already. Did they not ask anything more of me because they trusted me or because they didn't want to hear the non-answer they knew I'd give?

"They seem like good people, loyal companions, but if you are as careless among others as you are with them, your secret will come out," Jassin warned.

"Would that be so bad?" I asked, my voice just above a whisper.

"Yes!" Jassin hissed, his eyes flashing and the vein in his forehead popping out. He took a step back, closed his eyes, and breathed as he fought to get himself back under control. He looked exhausted at that moment, the lines on his face more pronounced than before, his eyes sunken, skin hanging off his bones like he'd aged years in the span of a couple of weeks.

"That is what I have been trying to impress upon you, Ryan. Your origins must be kept a secret, but—" He steepled his fingers and frowned in contemplation for several seconds before finally continuing. "Despite appearances, I am also unwilling to imprison you like others have."

"You have a strange way of showing th—"

"Here is my proposal," Jassin interrupted, holding up a finger. "You do not have to believe me forever. Believe me for an hour," he implored me. "Just one hour. Then you can decide if you want to thrust your presence out onto the world, damn the consequences. Let me show you why I ask this of you, and, as a bonus, it involves leaving this room." At that, he turned slightly in the direction of the door.

I followed the gesture with my eyes, trying not to let the carrot part of the Miur lord's offer obscure the stick. I wanted a nibble of that carrot first, to make sure it was real.

"What did you plan to do with me once we entered the city?" I asked pointedly.

Jassin's face assumed the perfect amount of restrained embarrassment. "To keep you safely away from other practitioners and to have this very conversation. That plan hit a very nasty snag, I'd say."

"I'm not stupid, Lord Jassin," I said. I had points in Mind now, so it was technically true . . . probably. "We could have had this conversation in private on the road, but you decided to string me along until we had reached your university. What exactly was your plan for your captured human?"

Jassin's expression darkened at the casual mention of my species, and he reached behind him to shut the door. The door latched closed with a nearly inaudible click.

Then the Miur lord stepped closer, speaking in a low, dangerous voice, almost in my ear. "What would you like me to say? That I'm one of the very few privileged people in the world who even knows what a human *is?* That I would have liked to get you into a lab where I could take you apart and put you together again over and over to see precisely what the Dark Lord saw? What if that had, indeed, occurred to me? Would that change things? Would having a villain in your story help you internalize your position? Would that make it simple enough for you?" His hard eyes flashed, and his nostrils flared.

I'd touched a nerve, apparently. Good. I wasn't going to get honesty from a mask. He'd been telling me half-truths the entire time I'd known him, and I was done accepting that.

Shaking my head, I leaned in to make sure he knew I wasn't intimidated. "I wasn't looking for simple. The truth would have sufficed."

"Good" he spat. "If you ever discover a simple truth, I advise you to distrust it immediately. If it will help you understand, my position as Headmaster is only the most recent in a long line of tasks assigned to me by my queen, Ryan. I am a . . . specialist of sorts, you might say, one of her favored. She has asked me to be many things over the years. All of them, without exception, required a complete rearrangement of my life and a new skillset to be mastered. For each role, I studied—sometimes for years—to become what was needed, and I did it without reservation. I slipped into my role as an actor slips into theirs—deeper even, just so that I may better serve."

He paused, his eyes focused on something far away—a memory, perhaps. "This role, however . . . *Headmaster.* It required nothing from me at all. In fact, it was one I would choose to do even if my queen no longer had need of my services. Scholar. Teacher. No more dirty taverns or blood-soaked decks. No sabotage, knives at my throat, or dismembering of corpses. This was going to be my reward for years of service, and I planned to relish every single moment of it."

Suddenly, he was back with me. His eyes bored into mine, the intensity of them making me want to look away, to get some breathing room, but I didn't allow myself that reprieve. I wasn't backing down. Not yet. Not when he seemed ready to be candid for once.

"It was strange, actually." He breathed. "Not having to be someone else. I didn't even know what I *was* anymore after so long. I was still coming to grips with the strangeness of it when the universe dropped, unannounced, a potentially world-ending extradimensional creature—a living, breathing legend—into my lap."

Jassin sighed and closed his eyes, the picture of weariness. He reached up and rubbed one of his temples as he calmed himself.

"A young man, not a devil. When I realized what you were, it was too late. A different me would have done what was needed without hesitation or remorse, but that wasn't who was in the carriage that day. It was just Trayalo Jassin. He did not have it in him to kill the boy he'd just met," he admitted tiredly. "Now we're living with that decision, you and I."

We stared at each other in what was maybe the first truly honest moment between us since the day we'd met. The man looked like he was carrying a great deal, the weight of an entire world, on his shoulders, and it was killing him.

I could understand that.

I broke first, swallowing the ball of righteous anger that had been building inside of me. "Well, thanks for not killing me. Would have been a shame to die without knowing why," I said. "You're proposing a field trip, then, Headmaster? I assume at the end of it, I get to find out why everyone wants me dead or worse?"

My reluctant agreement seemed to relieve him, somewhat. He stood up tall, straightened his shoulders, and put on a cool-but-professional smile.

"If you classify walking down many, many flights of stairs as a field trip, my boy. Also, to your other question, yes," he said.

"Perhaps I could use the exercise," I allowed. I wanted out of this room, and if that was going to come with answers, I was on board with that.

Jassin nodded slightly, turning to leave before thinking better of it and holding out a hand, which I nearly ran into in my haste to leave.

"Sorry. I nearly forgot. First, we need to get control of . . . all of this," he declared with an energetic flourish that seemed to encompass the entire room.

"What?" I asked, looking around to see what the man was talking about.

"Your aura. I mentioned it before, if you'll remember. We need to get your aura under control."

"How about we stop pretending I *should* know anything about my aura, and you tell me?"

"Yes. Of course. Zero knowledge. I suspect your previous story about your absentee master was true, in a way. Your aura is your field of influence, an external manifestation of your magical presence. Right now it is on display for all to see. When we met, it came across as annoying and rude, but now . . . it's like standing next to a whirlwind. I could feel it before I even entered the square yesterday, and I guarantee other practitioners are having a much harder time than I."

"A hard time?" I asked with a raised eyebrow. "Is having an aura bad?"

"No. No. We all have them, but we restrain them, a simple matter of holding it within. It becomes almost second nature by the time you've had your Dominion for longer than a few years. My practitioners, however—the ones who are still alive and functional after our ordeal, that is—are students, only now barely coming into their Dominions. Your aura is . . . disruptive for them."

"I'm not doing anything to hurt anyone—"

"Nothing like that, Ryan. No. It is your *presence* that is disruptive. When we met, I thought it was residual magic from the creature you slew or perhaps a flaw in your spirit, but your aura has changed in quality since then. It is hard to describe to a layman. Let me see . . . Imagine a terrible storm, violent and destructive, but no matter how hard you try, you cannot perceive it with your senses. You know it is there. The wind whips at the grass. Houses tumble by. Ancient trees are uprooted and cast down. The *effects* are plain to see, but *you* cannot seem to bring your mind to *process* the storm. That is the type of aura you have. Distracting, to say the least. Discombobulating for other practitioners. If you were any other student, I would place you in a centralized location in the Spire and have the new practitioners hone their skills in your proximity. It would be an excellent way to train their focus. However, I must work with what I have right now, and I need my students at their best."

"Fine," I replied with a shrug. "What do I do?"

"Hold this." He indicated a sack hanging from his belt. "It should mute the effects somewhat. Are you healthy now, Ryan? Have you healed fully?" Jassin asked.

"Uh. Yes. Pretty sure I'm intact."

"Unbelievable. Very good. I apologize for how unpleasant this may be."

Jassin took the sack and opened the cords on top, upending it to dump some-thing round, cold, and dark into my hand. It numbed my skin instantly.

"Quellstone?" I asked rhetorically. I knew what it was. I just didn't like it. Quellstone was in my top-five least-favorite stones, a real contender for the title if things kept going as they were.

Jassin squinted at me, moving his eyes over my face, down to the stone, and back, leaning slowly from side to side as if trying to see from many different angles.

"Better have another," he said, after some thought.

Out came another piece of quellstone. I noticed Jassin himself didn't seem to want to touch it. He was careful to dump the pieces directly from the bag into my hand.

Again, Jassin squinted at me.

Then, with a frustrated sigh, he emptied the bag into a heaping pile in my palm, eight stones in all.

Jassin shook his head. "Unbelievable. This will just have to do. Keep those next to your skin and think small thoughts while we walk."

"Small thoughts," I grumbled, my hand already aching with the unnatural cold. "No problem."

CHAPTER TWO

See the Future

Jassin was right about the number of stairs we'd need to take to get to where he wanted to go. Apparently, my room (read: closet) was near the top of the Spire, even above the observation deck where we'd surveyed the city and set up Trix's gun emplacement.

Jassin walked in front, leading me downward.

The question was, why up here? Angol had told me that the practice room I'd been using as a workshop was shielded to protect the rest of the school from spooky magic stuff. Shouldn't that have contained my aura? I was willing to bet it should. That meant Jassin put me up here to minimize my aura's effects on his people but probably also to hide me. It was possible that no one other than Jassin knew exactly where I was. Then there was the locked door. Was it entirely for me or were there others he wanted to keep out?

I stared at the man's back as if it would give me some clue as to his motives. Unsurprisingly, it gave me nothing.

While we walked, I glanced at my status screen from time to time. The amount of choices was staggering. I probably just needed to start at the top and see what was there.

Consume is now Level 5!

Upgrade Paths available:

Mass Upgrade: Increased mass limit of material able to be Consumed. Mass Upgrade will continue to grow as Consume gains power.

Efficiency Upgrade: Consumed material is converted to energy more efficiently and knowledge of material is gained more quickly.

Reservoir: Energy gained from Consumed material may now be given form instead of processed. Conversion process has a 50% efficiency rate. Only one Reservoir may be active at a time.

Passive Consumption: Engine may now passively draw energy from the

> environment around you, increasing your mana regeneration. Active activa-
> tion of this ability is significantly more powerful.

Well, damn. Those all looked useful. It would be nice to have an easy choice as my first. I would have to assume that any upgrade I gave my Consume would at least partially translate to my Devouring Grasp, so I had to take that into account.

> Devouring Grasp is now Level 5!
> Upgrade Paths available:
> Strength Multiplier: Strength Multiplier of Devouring Grasp is increased to +100% x E (where E = current MP/s value of Engine)
> Breach: Sacrifice Status Effect: Engine to increase kinetic force of Devouring Grasp by Engine's total value.
> Magivore: Devouring Grasp may now be used to Consume external, structured, magical phenomenon in a limited capacity. Type of mana Consumed retains high ratio of original type.

I didn't have access to a Ralqir calendar, but it had to be Christmas morning somewhere. I wanted it all, and I wanted it now. However, I would have been lying to myself if I didn't admit that Devouring Grasp having two Upgrade Paths that had to do with just how hard I could grip things was kind of disappointing. Oh, yes, I knew they were both powerful, given how many times the ability had saved my life, but they were too similar for my taste.

What needed to happen was synergy, a situation where I could use these two things to help each other. I'd just been using Devouring Grasp as the attack version of Consume, but I didn't *have* to do it that way. I could make both abilities more than what they were, together.

> Magivore: Devouring Grasp may now be used to Consume external, structured, magical phenomenon in a limited capacity. Type of mana Consumed retains high ratio of original type.

Yeah, I was choosing that one. I could grab harder some other way, some other day. What's more, I had a practitioner right in front of me whose intentions I wasn't sure of. Could be useful if only to knock down hostile spells when they started flying my way. How it worked . . . well, I guess, I'd find out.

Which Consume ability would complement it the best? Mass and Efficiency would probably let me get more mana out of every Devouring Grasp, which would be amazing. Efficiency would likely cut down on materials I would have to Consume and keep me from having to spend time and/or money getting materials to burn, saving me a mountain of stuff in the long run. But I hadn't run into that problem yet. I kept finding more and more good stuff to Consume, and my issues were more about getting the Engine-burning right than getting material at all.

That made Reservoir an attractive option, with Passive Consumption a close second. Reservoir wouldn't even be on the short list if not for Magivore being my pick for Devouring Grasp, though. Reservoir was basically a much-worse version of Automate, in that it let me store mana in an object but didn't let me do anything with it like Automate did. Tempered Channels and its nerfing of my ability to process foreign mana saw to that.

But what if I never had to have the foreign mana inside of me at all? Reservoir could allow for that. Maybe I could find a way to use weird mana types outside of my body, maybe as part of a construct.

I finally made my choices, bidding goodbye to some pretty cool options. Maybe I'd see them again someday. I had my doubts, though. When I hit ten in Stealth, all of my skills seemed to vibe with my chosen Upgrade Path, in a way. It would probably be similar for Consume.

By the time I was done we were near the ground floor, where we took a left turn and made our way farther into the interior of the building, past a heavy set of doors Jassin had to use one of those magical keys on a chain to get into, though this one wasn't on a ring like the guard captain had used. Jassin kept his on a chain around his neck and held it up to an otherwise-unremarkable spot of bare wall.

An unseen lock disengaged with a click, and Jassin pulled the doors open, stepping inside and holding them open for me. The room beyond was bare and cube-shaped with another set of doors just like the first directly in front of us.

It's an airlock.

"Shut the door quickly, please, and we'll get this over with," Jassin ordered.

I found myself reaching back and grasping the handle of the open door without even thinking. I stopped.

"What are we getting over with?" I asked.

"It's a security measure. Once you close the door, we'll be in darkness, but I advise you to close your eyes nonetheless."

I gave him my best skeptical look. "Did I mention I hate all this vague talk?"

Jassin sighed in exhaustion. "This room cleanses every being going in and coming out. It is not a design of the Dark Lord but of those that came after. There will be a brief moment of darkness and then a flash."

"That's it?"

"Of course that isn't it. If I tried to explain the entire thing to you, you would need to study years of theory to understand it. I only told you what you need to know to get by. I am simply asking for one hour of trust, Ryan. Can you still manage that?"

In answer, I shut the doors. Despite them being stone, they felt surprisingly easy to move and well-balanced. I heard the lock reengage once they were closed.

We were cast into absolute darkness. I stayed where I was, feet apart, muscles tensed, waiting for whatever it was to happen. The quellstone was beyond freezing in my hand by this point, cold to the point of biting numbness.

The world flashed white, so bright it was like a physical blow. Even through my closed eyes, it was absolutely overwhelming. My head smacked into the door I'd just closed with a *thwack*.

Spots danced in my vision and the world swam. I reached out with my hand to make sure the area in front of me was clear.

"You did close your eyes, yes?" Jassin asked from somewhere in front of me.

I nodded as I tried to blink the sensation away.

"Hm. Perhaps you are sensitive to it. Concerning."

Once my eyes healed, we were moving again, this time through the second doorway and onto another stairwell. We were in a cylindrical tube with glossy black walls, except for the stairs where we stood, which stuck right out of the side of the outer wall like they'd been grown there. Toward the center of the room—out of reach but just barely—a central pillar stabbed downward into the darkness and seemed to go on forever.

Jassin handed me the sack from his belt. "Here. You do not need the rocks anymore."

I hurriedly put the quellstones back where they came from and made a move to hand it back to him, but Jassin was already moving down the stairs, deeper into the tube.

Shrugging, I made the whole sack disappear into my Spatial Storage. You never knew when you might need soul-sucking rocks.

Down we went. We hadn't come into this room from the top, though. The stairs stretched upward as well, way up until I had to crane my neck to see the end of it. What really caught my eye, though, was the central pillar. It was the same black stone as the outer walls, but it wasn't perfectly smooth and featureless like the wall we hugged. It seemed to flash and sparkle erratically as we plodded down the stairs, the lights subtle and just rare enough to where I'd chalked it up to my imagination at first.

Out of the corner of my eye, I saw shapes intermittently forming in the flashes—symbols of some kind—but they were gone before I could focus on them. I tried to catch a couple by staring at the pillar as I walked but to no avail, as if even the slightest turn of my head or movement of my body ruined the angle so I could no longer see what had attracted my attention in the first place.

"What is this place?" I asked.

"The Spire, Ryan. The true Spire."

"You are insufferable with that cryptic language, you know that?"

Jassin laughed at that. "Apologies. Over the years, I have made it a habit to only give what information is truly necessary, especially as it pertains to sensitive subjects such as this. This central pillar goes all the way up to the observatory and all the way down to the base of the Spire. Farther, actually. It is the central pillar upon which the Dark Lord's Dominion spell rests."

"I've heard a bit about that," I mused, recalling the snippets of history I'd gotten from Trix. "The entire city is part of the spell, right?"

"Correct. The Undercity, the roads, the moon . . . They are all one grand ritual that draws in power and once shaped it to the Dark Lord's purpose. The Spire is the foundation and focus of that design."

I blinked. If the System had any sense of humor, it would have given me a Stunned status effect. "I'm sorry, did you say the moon?"

"Yes."

"The moon is part of the spell?"

"Yes. One part."

"The whole moon?"

"Yes. What do you not understand about this?"

I could feel my eyebrows crawling up my forehead. "I just assumed the ritual was to anchor the moon here or something, give the Dark Lord some shade during his retirement after the Purge. The scale is . . . just . . ."

"I did tell you to think small thoughts, Ryan, but that was when we were trying to suppress your aura."

I could hear the smugness in the man's voice.

"Very funny," I said. "Are you really going to hold it against me that I didn't factor entire moons into the equation?"

"When there is a giant moon suspended above you all day every day, yes. With that in mind, tell me. What are your thoughts?"

"Sure. Uh . . ." I paused, gathering the scattered bits of knowledge I'd acquired in my time on Ralqir. "Starting with the questions: Why is the moon stuck over Eclipse? What does it do for the spell?"

"Good," Jassin said. "Those are good questions, and you probably already have the answers. Continue down that line of thought."

"The moon must do something magical, because it's not actually about the shade."

"Correct."

"You have an observatory on top of the Spire, don't you?"

"Yes."

"Who built it? You or the Dark Lord?"

"Ah. I think you've got it or at least the beginnings of it. The observatory is of the Dark Lord's design, always aligned with the moon. Keep going . . ."

Jassin did seem to be having fun teasing the connections out of my brain. I was glad *someone* was enjoying themselves, at least.

"Is that moonlight shining through the central pillar?" I asked.

"No, but close enough."

"The moon is . . . a filter? I saw all the different colors of aurora out there during the day, like the moon has a magnetosphere or something like it. Does it do something to the light to make it useful?"

Jassin made contemplative noises down below me. "Hmm. Close. Do you know how lenses work, Ryan?"

I went with the simple explanation. "They bend light."

"Good. Think of the moon as a lens."

"Where I'm from, lenses are supposed to be transparent."

"Anywhere else, that would also be true. Not here, though."

"But to what end? The Dark Lord literally moved the heavens to make this happen. What does it do?"

Jassin was silent for a few heartbeats, and all I could hear was our footfalls on smooth stone.

"Right now, it is the only thing protecting Ralqir."

"From what?" I asked.

Jassin didn't answer. We'd reached the end of the stairs, and he was already ducking into an arched entrance. I followed him through.

Into an office.

The walls were made of warm-colored wood, oiled and lacquered until they shined. Skylights overhead cast soft, yellowish light that gave the impression of it being a sunny afternoon outside, even though we were far underground. Elaborate carpets covered the floor in reds and yellows, and they softened our footsteps as we came farther into the room. A simple, sturdy, wooden desk sat in the middle of the floor, tall enough to work at while standing. A fireplace crackled in the corner, well away from all the wood and carpet, and a single chair sat next to it a comfortable distance away.

Shelves climbed up the wall to our right, all the way to the ceiling, which was about twenty feet high or so. There were no books or tools on them. Instead, resting at regular intervals on every shelf were silver, four-clawed stands that held smoky crystal spheres.

Jassin saw me gawking.

"Phylacteries. The Dark Lord did not trust his memories to paper," he said.

"Not just that," I explained. "It's so—I don't know—"

"Not what you expected?" Jassin asked.

I nodded, drifting over to the shelves and the phylacteries. I approached one, feeling the desire to reach out and touch it, but I wasn't stupid (or at least I was trying not to be).

I looked back at Jassin.

"It is safe," he assured me. "For the untrained, they simply speak to you or maybe show you an image or two. If you want to dive deeper, it requires practice."

"They speak to me? Like they know I'm here?"

Jassin gave me a non-committal wobble of his head. "In a rudimentary way. They sense you and determine the best way to communicate their information clearly—that is, if they want to. They aren't always in the mood to cooperate. The Dark Lord was a willful being."

It hit me then. I'd seen one of these before. It had caught fire and screamed at me, way back in the mockvine cave. I pulled up the appropriate logs, the messages I'd received when I was looting the place and had run into something I couldn't store like the rest.

Vost'ralixal.

I mumbled the name aloud as I read it in my log, tasted it on my tongue.

Jassin was suddenly at my side. "What did you say?"

"Vost'ralixal," I repeated. "Before we met. I found a . . . uh . . . one of these, and the System labeled it Vost'ralixal."

Jassin frowned and bit his lip. "The pages of history continue to turn. You humans . . ."

"It's a name, then?"

Jassin nodded. "It has long been suspected, but there has been no proof that this was the Dark Lord's name. It explains much, however. Vost'ralixal was a study in wasted genius, the youngest born of a minor house who would never have been allowed to rise due to his station. His holdings were nearby, across the river. I would very much like to know where you found a phylactery outside of this place, Ryan." He paused, looking up at the crystal balls like he was currently recategorizing everything he knew about them. "But our hour is almost up. We had an agreement. Come. It is just this way."

Another heavy stone door led to another set of stairs going down. This place, as a contrast to the office, was clean and colorless, just black-on-black.

We finally were at the bottom of the big cylinder. The floor was a flat, smooth surface like the walls. The room was tall, easily fifty or sixty feet high, and the central pillar that we had been following for so long came down only halfway to the floor, terminating in jagged lines. Where the stone pillar stopped, a shaft of pure, white light shined down in a perfect vertical ray so intense that it all but engulfed the single shape in the center.

I stepped closer, tilting my head to get a better angle.

On a plinth in the middle of the incandescent shaft of light was a vaguely humanoid figure. It had two arms and two legs, one head—the usual stuff—but its body seemed to have something against the concept of symmetry. It was grotesquely muscular but in the oddest proportions, bulges upon bulges stacked on one another seemingly at random like a bad drawing of a bodybuilder done from a child's description instead of actual experience.

Its chest was deep and wide, shoulders so round they came up around the thing's neck until it probably couldn't turn its head anymore. The legs seemed shorter than they should have been but I'd seen trees thinner than these calves. It had no genitals that I could see, just more muscle. Sharp, exposed bones jutted from its joints and out of the sides of its ribs.

The face, though . . . The face was bulbous and misshapen. The mouth split vertically as well as horizontally, and it had teeth to fill out both. Eyes—many,

many eyes—that ran across the thing's entire head and down its neck to its shoulders blinked independently as they squinted into the light.

Its skin was a mottled contrast of flowing white and black that seemed to shift like globs of heated oil in water. The black morphed and changed, seeming to grow before my eyes, flowing through the creature's body along its arms and legs to disappear into the chest. As it did so, the muscles would flex and bend in response. Smoke rose out of its pores, and as it tried to move, different parts of its skin burned away in the harsh light only to be regrown nearly instantly.

I found myself drawn to that dance of color and the burn. I didn't know why. I just needed to see it, know what it was. It felt, at once, disturbing yet so familiar.

As I approached, I could hear the creature's strained breathing, the leather-band pops and cracks as it flexed against its restraints—silvery barbed metal that pierced right into the skin at the wrists, ankles and neck and writhed along with the creature. Where the skin was broken, black fluid coagulated and . . . *moved*, seeming to defy the law of gravity, trailing up into the air as if it were a living thing. That is, before it caught fire and burned down to nothing in a flash of intense heat, only to start the process again.

The smell—old sweat and unclean flesh—was so familiar, yet there was something else there too. Sweetness, rotted meat, tar, aged putrescence.

My mouth filled with saliva, and I turned away to be sick.

"What is it?" Jassin asked.

"The smell . . . I don't know."

"There is no smell. The light cleanses all of it, even the smoke."

My stomach spasmed, but I marshaled myself before I could lose all of my stew. It was a close call.

Then I turned to find I was within arm's length of the burning light.

"Stay back. It's deadly," Jassin whispered now that we were so close to the thing. "Contrary to popular belief, the moon does not shade us here in the Glade. Instead, it collects the maelstrom's light, even when our side of the globe is in darkness."

Another piece clicked into place. I cleared my throat to get some strength back into my voice. "And the moon focuses all that collected light here, through the observatory," I guessed.

Jassin nodded in affirmation. "Observe how it changes, the taint that spreads through its body. The light counters it somehow. Purges it. Any other being that stepped into that circle would die instantly, but this creature has been inside of it for centuries. It cannot die or be killed—not by any means we possess."

I held my hand up to my nose, trying and failing to keep it together. Now that I'd noticed it, it was all I could do to push past the revulsion I felt.

"What is it?" I asked.

"A lens of another kind, or, if you ask the Church, a fulcrum. The mechanism the Dark Lord used to create Dominion Magic. Magic, you see, is a primal force, wild in its natural form. Only those with extraordinary natural talent could shape it back when the Dark Lord was simply Vost'ralixal, and he coveted this power more than anyone has ever coveted anything in their lives."

"Cryptic. Jassin—"

"I am getting to it. Vost'ralixal's life changed when he happened upon a being of nearly limitless potential. Something not of our world. Not only did it have access to powerful magics but its magic was ordered, structured, and logical—a completely foreign concept to us at the time. When he asked the visitor how it was able to accomplish this miracle, it said: 'My people hold dominion over the stars.'"

"And this thing is what he found?"

"Yes. He captured it when it was weak, locked it away, and . . . experimented." The way he said it, I could tell he didn't want to elaborate. I didn't ask. I probably wouldn't understand anyway. "The Dark Lord learned much from his guest. Enough to usher in a new age and rule the entirety of our world."

"Your Dominions. They all come from that?" I asked.

"The knowledge comes from the Dark Lord's notes, recovered after his death, centuries after his rule ended."

I still couldn't fit all the pieces together. "So, he learned everything he could from our friend here and got his wish. He had everything he wanted. Why did he purge the planet?"

"He found out too late that the power he siphoned from his captive was tainted—a taint you can observe here. Its presence became a wound in our world. One that festered. His captive grew beyond his control, and his undead servants turned against him. The Dark Lord was a prideful man, however. He did not enjoy the idea of failure."

I nodded in partial understanding. "So he magicked you to the Bera Maelstrom, where the light could purge the infection."

Jassin's voice grew quiet, as if saying the words was transgressive in and of itself.

"Judging by what is happening now, it appears the infection was only dormant. And now, you visit us again."

"Wait—You can't be serious." I paused, peering at the thing on the plinth, how misshapen it was—mutated and mutilated. It seemed impossible.

Still, it all fit. The Scourge-Touched goblin conveniently at my insertion point so long ago. The constant glitching Nali was going through despite her failsafes . . . "Void corruption," she'd called it. The way brightsteel, the Crusaders' weapon of choice, reacted to my mana. The wires down below in the Undercity that were constantly being Shaped. The dragon—how it said my people's power was evil, insisting my "dark passenger" would overtake me someday.

Oh, shit! My sensitivity to the light.

It all fit.

I activated Detect Cobalt.

The barbed restraints that held the creature down wrapped around its bones, wound around the plinth, reached down into the floor, and spread wide in branching patterns that resembled the roots of a tree. Roots whose barbed shape and composition were particularly familiar to me.

I'd found the other Animator on Ralqir! I'd found it, and it was showing me my future. I—No, *we* Exotics, were touched. We were Scourge. Carriers, maybe, or something worse. We brought the infection with us wherever we went, spread it, and they hated us for it.

"I am sorry, Ryan," Jassin said, like he was giving me my last rites.

With the utterance of my name, something changed. Every single eye the creature possessed turned my way in that moment. Other eyes I'd not noticed flowered open on the creature's arms and chest, straining against the light but ultimately turning my way as well. Each focused their individual gazes on me, their misshapen pupils pulsing and vibrating out of sync with one another.

My body went rigid. My lungs seized, the air inside them thickening and refusing to move. I felt . . .

I awoke what felt like mere seconds later back in the Dark Lord's office. Jassin was over me, his fingers prying my eyelids open. He had just slapped me and he did so again, the sting bringing me all the way back to the waking world.

Jassin shouted in my face, "Ryan! Ryan!"

"Y—Yes! Ow! Stop!"

Jassin, heaving for breath, flopped down next to me with shaking hands. "I'm sorry. I saw the connection form between the two of you, and I feared the worst."

"A connection?" I coughed. "Wh—"

A message flashed on my screen, demanding my attention:

Ephelir (Level ???) has challenged you.
Stakes: Experience, Death.
Do you accept? Y/N

CHAPTER THREE

Break the Machine

I didn't think you'd be content with being a prince in a tower," Samila chided over her cup of tea. The blue-scaled dragonkin daintily brought the cup up to her lips to have a sip, expertly dodging the ridged collar on her breastplate. Everyone was suited up today, except for me, of course. My armor had to be recycled after my little skip through the square.

"I'm not a prince in a tower," I insisted. "I'm working."

"Working on making yourself irrelevant," she replied.

Trix, not willing to have my good name besmirched in such a way, chimed in, turning away briefly from the set of bubbling beakers and tubes where he had been concentrating. His brown fox fur stood on end, even under his robe, giving him a portly look, and the air around him crackled and popped with static. "Brother Ryan is as brave as they come, Sister. If I know him, he has good reason to spend all of his time hidden away in his room. Brother Ryan, not to complain, but why am I doing this again? I look silly."

"It's electrolysis," I told him. "I need lots of oxygen, as pure as I can get it, and you can use the magic jewelry thingy."

"It tingles in unfortunate places. Are these hieroglyphs I see?"

I shrugged, sparing a short glance over at the copper amulet he was holding. "I'd have to ask the goblins I got it from."

Trix made a face I couldn't interpret. "I'm guessing this blood is theirs, then. It's not even dry."

"Oh, uh, sorry," I said sheepishly. "I'm not sure. Maybe a little of mine, too. I can get you a cloth or something to . . . uh . . . better address your concerns. Samila, I'm working here because I'm backed into a corner, and I need to find a way out."

The corner I was backed into was more like a Rube Goldberg machine of destruction and death, but I didn't want to get into the details.

Not only was I trapped and under siege by a limitless tide of monsters that wanted to kill me, but also by my aura and how it played havoc with other practitioners—practitioners we needed for the defenses.

Apparently, I was also trapped by my secrets. If my true nature were to be discovered, the Church and the monarchy would want me dead, for fear of someone finding a way to send Ralqir back to where it belonged, somewhere where the light didn't outright kill you. Other factions would use me to do what the Dark Lord did, only better this time. Then there were the crazy people that would worship me. Wars would be fought over my fate, and I wouldn't have a say in any of it.

Let's not forget there was the tiny problem of the supremely powerful former-human locked in the basement. It had almost killed me with a look. That was a fun Sword of Damocles that had been hanging over Ralqir's collective heads for a long, long time, too.

The Church—and, by extension, my friends here—literally worshiped the maelstrom's light, seeing it as a holy force for good, and they were even partly right. Currently, it was the only thing keeping the world from ending. If the creature in the basement somehow got out and shook off its suntan, I got the feeling things would go badly for everyone, not just the people on Ralqir.

The problem was that the taint-purging maelstrom light was deadly to everything other than the Mendau trees. They loved it.

The worst part, though, was I was trapped by time, so to speak. Stuck in neutral, because I had no idea what the influence of the System was doing to me as I gained Experience. It had to be a gradual thing, the corruption of the self, or else people would notice as they changed, but I couldn't help but look at all the Experience notifications I was receiving while I worked and feel a sense of dread.

The System was altering me in more ways than I realized, and there was no way to tell how much.

What a damned mess.

I needed a new factor I could use to change things—something I hadn't thought of yet—because, as things stood, it sure as shit wasn't looking good for anyone involved.

My mana flowed into the Trigger on my new magazine design, but a more accurate term would be "tank" or "reservoir." Once my mana entered the Trigger, what was once a head-sized balloon of steel slowly shrank down to its other, much smaller form. The Trigger nearly tapped me out on mana, but I had some Mendau Wood right there to bring me back to the double digits again.

Letting the construct gradually do its thing, I swiveled on my stool and turned to check on the bundle of damp cloth sitting next to me on the table. Slowly and with great care, I isolated one of the tiny fibers that streamed off the back of it and traced it to the end before splitting it down the middle with my little work knife, observing the way the inside of the strand glittered as the mana made contact with it.

Willing Edge [2 MP/sec]

On a tiny knife like this it didn't take much to encase the whole thing in a sheath of mana. My new sword ability was supposedly meant to preserve the integrity of your blade at the expense of your MP—something I would have found particularly useful in the last battle. I'd gotten some use out of it in the workshop, preserving the atomically sharp but fragile edges of my tools, but I was more interested in other applications. My machines could use my Abilities now. How much mana would it take to sharpen a whole projectile or even just the tip? Not much, I'd wager. Magical armor-piercing bullets? Yes, please.

I placed the split end of the fiber in a clear jar next to the unaltered control one and triggered the low-powered Automation pebble I had wrapped up in the bundle with the larger part of the mockvine bulb. There was a muffled *fwoomph!*, and both test jars lit up with purple light. The intact fiber—the one I hadn't cut—produced a straight beam that strobed rapidly on and off for a full second before it went dark. Meanwhile, the split fiber jar flashed only once, then slowly faded away. I observed how the ends of the fiber retained some of the glow before the energy was fully spent. The water never rippled or bubbled, meaning none of the kinetic or thermal energy was transferred. I checked the wording of the logs again.

Mockvine Fiber Bundle: Fibers gathered from the remains of an Ancient Mockvine. These fibers perform many duties while they are alive within a specimen, carrying nerve signals, nutrients, sunlight, and mana to all parts of the plant. With age comes sophistication, and mockvines are no exception to this rule. These fibers are of the highest quality and conduct complicated patterns of mana nearly instantaneously over long distances.

Okay, so the bulbs work as repeaters, but they need intact fibers and water.

Samila pointed to the now-smaller metal ball on my bench. "Is that shrinking? I could swear I see it shrinking."

"It's shrinking," I replied distractedly.

Geddon's curiosity was piqued. The big man got down on one knee next to me to watch the metal ball do its thing, his thick mane invading my work area and forcing me to lean away. "You can do that? Can you grow them, too? I wouldn't mind a bigger sword."

I blinked, finally registering his misunderstanding and forming the words to dispel it. "What? No. Unless you give me more metal to work with or something. This was hollow on the inside, see? The mass doesn't change."

Geddon's face scrunched up as he thought this over. "So . . . it's . . . smaller *and* the same?"

"It's part of the new design. Hang on." I scooped up the construct now that it had shrunk down to something about on par with a baseball. Then I gave it a little tap with my metal fingers.

Solid. Stable. Good.

I knew the walls had thickened significantly on the inside, like I did with my air tanks, and the contents would now be under extreme pressure, the oxygen compressed down to almost nothing and mixing with the other substances. The Automated stirring mechanism hummed quietly in the stem.

Shaking my head to rid myself of the vision I had of one day tapping on one of these and having it explode in my face, I walked over to my new turret design—a taller, sleeker model with a slender barrel and several of my new compression bulbs attached to the back of the action—and I carefully inserted the final magazine. The activation-sequence Trigger engaged with a click.

Science time.

"Okay. Go over it again," I said, retreating from the turret to get behind one of the anti-explosive barriers in the workshop. Everyone else slowly ambled over to join me there.

Geddon spoke first, eager to tell his story again. Every time he did, he seemed to add more embellishments, more pantomime, but I didn't mind. I just needed the timeline, really.

"It was dawn on the day of our heroic victory, and we had just reached the cusp of the battle we were meant to descend upon. The light shone off our enemies' claws, and the song of steel rang out from the lines of beleaguered guardsmen—"

"The turrets were duds," Samila interrupted. "We set them up like you asked, up high. We picked a roof where they could blast the creatures down below without risk of hitting our people. But we flipped the switches, and they wouldn't fire. They just turned back and forth like they were looking for something to shoot, even though the enemy was clearly right there."

I nodded. "Right, and then?"

"The brave dragonkin sisters did something that made me proud. They suggested a full charge, despite not having your machines on our side. Their bravery almost brought a tear to my eye. However, I am not one to leave such mighty weapons behind where the enemy might find them, so I put your turret on my back once more. It resisted being moved at first, not wanting to stand still, but I am irresistible." Geddon grinned, flexing his sizeable, armored biceps.

"It was taking a long time, and Sissa was getting pretty pissed," Samila interjected.

"Indeed," Geddon replied, holding up a gauntleted finger. "I insisted, however. I even went so far as to pack up Sister Samila's turret, too. The weight didn't bother me overly much, given my prodigious strength."

"I admit, I didn't have as much faith as he did," Samila added, unashamed. If she felt the need to spare my feelings, she didn't show it. "I told him to leave the turrets behind. They were just going to slow us down."

"Good thing I didn't!" Geddon bragged. "It was glorious! We unsheathed our swords, strapped on our shields, and charged with the rising sun into the waiting jaws of death!"

"The creatures spotted us after the first or second kill," Samila continued. "Then they were all over us. That's when the turrets started to do their thing on the big man's back."

"Blood! Brains! Tissue! Shredded organs festooned my armor and my weapons!" Geddon gesticulated wildly, flinging imaginary guts all over the room and making surprisingly convincing gunshot sounds with his mouth.

"He laughed like a madman and spun like Death's own handmaid to hear the guards tell of it," Trix added. "They had to be convinced our people weren't some new breed of enemy."

"So the plagued had to be close to the turrets," I considered.

"Almost within sword range," Samila replied, with a helpful outstretched arm to indicate distance.

"Alright. Take this." I said, handing Samila a scrapped table leg. "Throw it in front of the turret once I step out of the room."

Summoning my sack of quellstone, I dumped the contents into my hand, feeling the cold seep in through my skin. Just as Jassin had suggested, I focused on how I felt at that moment: diminished, or perhaps "lesser" was a better word. It wasn't a great feeling. I hoped I could rid myself of it if I ever got control of my aura.

Then I stepped outside and shut the door.

After a minute or so, someone knocked on it, hard to let me know it was okay to enter again.

I came back in to find the scene unchanged, unfortunately. The scrap wood was on the other side of the room where the turret should have been able to see it and engage. Not good.

"Was that supposed to tell us something?" Samila asked.

"Just confirming a theory," I replied, slowly walking forward toward the active turret.

"And are you still confirming it, or are we safe to come out now?" Samila asked from her hiding spot.

"Still working. Probably safer if you stay behind the barrier."

"What's going on, Brother Ryan?" Trix asked.

I stepped closer, past the workbench. *Nothing.* I took another step. Now I was close enough to reach out and touch the turret's leg.

Experimentally, I slipped two of the quellstones back into the sack.

The action was instantaneous. The turret snapped into line, aiming directly at the piece of scrap wood. There was a purple spark at the end of the barrel, and a jet of orange flame shot out of the end with a *fwoosh!* The heat on my face would have been alarming if not for my superhuman range of pain tolerance nowadays. Setting yourself on fire a couple of times tended to recalibrate your pain scale a bit.

As it was programmed to do, once the turret doused the target in sticky, burning Pex oil mixture, it fanned back and forth to cover the entire area, a good twenty-degree rotation that expanded the pooled inferno.

I stood there, watching the machine work.

Once the area was ablaze and the turret stopped spewing its payload, I reached up and turned it off.

Geddon's curiosity got the better of him first. "So, did you just solve the problem, or am I meant to wear one of those on my back for the next battle?"

"I've always wondered how my doodads perceive things," I said as I stared into the flames. "They don't have eyes or anything. Turns out, they're using my aura."

"This new turret of yours is safe, I take it?" Trix asked, rubbing his arms and watching the other end of the room burn. The smoke never thickened or spread around the room, though. It seemed to pass into the ceiling and disappear like the solid matter wasn't even there. They really had designed this room for everything.

I could only shrug. "Safe" wasn't a word I would use to describe anything I did.

"Why didn't they work for us?" Samila asked.

"I'm willing to bet you were on the edge of my area of influence, or just slightly out of it. The turrets couldn't 'see' anything until they got close enough to touch. Then they did what they were supposed to do."

"And thank the Light they did." Geddon laughed. "I've never had that much fun in my life. It was a sad moment when the enemy lost their will to fight."

"I wouldn't say they lost it," I argued. "I had plenty of company the whole time."

"Sissa is never going to forgive you for that, you know," Samila stated matter-of-factly.

I reached up to re-Shape the turret's fuel bulbs closed again before disengaging them from the housing. "And I guess I have to live with that," I said. "And she gets to live with it, too. Just glad she's alive to hate me."

"I didn't say she hates you," Samila argued. "You hurt her, though."

I turned back to give her my best incredulous look. "She hurt me, too."

"A minor black eye that healed in minutes."

"It's not just that. It's emotional damage." I brought a hand to my chest to emphasize the point.

"The way you keep going on about it, I believe you," Samila replied dryly.

"For all she knew, I was still recovering from grave injury, and the first thing she did was deck me. That speaks to a willingness to really hurt."

Samila shook her head in pity. "I'm going to tell her she made you cry."

"Who's crying? Nobody's crying," I argued. "I'm building flamethrowers in a magic Faraday cage—"

"Ones we cannot use until you get your aura under control, apparently," Trix interrupted. "I don't think a guard would touch your new turret for even a year's worth of pay. I feel the ends of my fur curling up even from here. I still think it's time you rejoined the battle, Brother Ryan."

Samila piled on, as well. "Short and Poofy is right. You're hiding. Work on your aura and stop hiding from my sister."

I frowned, remembering the frustration of my previous failures. "I'm doing the stupid exercises Jassin gave me," I grumbled.

"Have you considered doing them better?" Geddon asked. "I happen to be very good at exercise. Perhaps you need a trainer."

"We miss you, Ryan. *All* of us," Trix said. "We hate to see you locked away, no matter your reasoning. No need for you to be locked away anymore, not when the enemy is on our doorstep."

Simila went in for the kill. "Listen, Monk, if it helps, we're not just asking because we like your company. There's a war council coming up, and we're not invited. We're outside their chain of command."

"So much for the hero treatment," Geddon mumbled under his breath.

Samila leaned in conspiratorially. "According to our man on the inside, it's a big operation. They're going to do a raid. Multiple fronts. One is headed for Riverside to grab as much food as possible for everyone here. The other is headed for the drawbridges. We think they're getting ready for a mass evacuation via the river. The only problem is, we still have people at the southern gate. The Church, I mean. Our people."

"They're not going to leave them behind, are they?" I asked skeptically.

"No," Samila said with a head shake. "Probably not, anyway, but they are using them as a means of taking pressure off their forces until they can accomplish their missions. I can see why they're doing it, but—"

"But . . ." Trix continued for her, " . . .seeing as how they're not using us, maybe we can add something to the plan. Remind them that we are fully capable of meeting our problems head-on."

"You want to just show up to the war council?" I asked. "And expect them to let you in?"

"Nope!" Geddon boomed. "The Rising Sun of Eclipse is showing up to their war council."

I considered the pros and cons, briefly. I wasn't getting anywhere in here, and my problems were all closing in while I stood still. There was danger in what my friends were proposing, but I was quickly becoming convinced something needed to change. I was stuck in a complex trap, but the thing about complex machinery was that it only took a single failure in the right place to turn it into a paperweight. If I still wanted to save Ralqir, I'd need to find that failure point.

"Sure," I said, unbuckling my tool belt. "I guess I can play the hero."

CHAPTER FOUR

Clear the Way

Clusterfuck. I never truly appreciated that word up until now. But I'd never been in the middle of a major operation before, so I had no real way of knowing how they were supposed to go. However, the amount of running back and forth, gear being taken off and put on, pissed-off sergeants, and last-minute inspections, all happening at the same time, dispelled a lot of illusions for me about how smoothly big military groups ran.

People dashed to and fro, carrying things, dropping things, shouting to one another. Formations were called together, broken apart, and reformed elsewhere. Beleaguered students with clipboards trailed behind officers, hastily flipping through pages of checklists.

And at the center of it all, Jassin, flanked by Garret, his master-at-arms. They floated from group to group solving problems, changing group compositions, and keeping the runners running to get everyone what they needed.

The two didn't come near my group, however. Jassin never even glanced my way, which came as no surprise. We'd had our talk. I knew the stakes. Now it was up to me to decide how to proceed. He was going to treat me like my cover was real, meaning disinterest at best, mild hostility at worst.

When we'd shown up to the planning session for the war council, the man slipped into the latter role like he'd practiced it, but we got the go-ahead for our part of the plan in the end. Our participation would cost the regular army nothing and gain them the use of my machines. As far as everyone except Jassin was concerned, there were no downsides to allowing us a spot in the operation. Sissa had hammered that point home repeatedly. I just stood there and did my best approximation of dark and mysterious.

We were underground, somewhere between three and ten floors below street level. The Spire got grander the lower you went, flaring outward until its base was two or three times as wide as the above-ground portion, and more spacious too. This place we were using as a staging area gave me the impression of a converted warehouse or storage room. It was tall and broad, with even flooring, big barn doors, and empty shelving hastily shoved to the perimeter of the room to give the military more space to maneuver.

"Glad to have you with us, Rising Sun," a stocky man carrying a pike against his shoulder said as he hurried by, tossing a hasty salute my way and not waiting for a response. I did my best to make encouraging noises as I waved back at him, but I wasn't sure if I pulled it off. I wasn't handling this "legend" thing very well, and I wasn't getting any better at it, even after all the practice I'd had in the halls as of late. No one warned me that being famous was an awkward thing where people recognized you and respected you despite your never having met.

I pulled my borrowed cloak tighter around my shoulders, not quite ready to cinch the hood yet but wanting to seem like I was preparing myself just like everyone else was, if only to get them to stop looking at me like I was an example to follow.

"He's not even armed. No armor, either. Takes balls, it does," I heard someone say.

"Maybe more of him's metal than we see there," someone else replied. "If you take my meaning. Eh? Eh?"

"I take it just fine. Just wasn't prepared to think about it like that. Saw him crush an Undead's head with that hand. Hate to see what he could do with the other bits."

Was it too late to fake my own death?

"Did you really have to give away my turrets?" Geddon whined for the third time. "I'm going to miss the *thunder*." The big man emphasized that last word with clenched fists and looked wistfully upward as if reminiscing about the boom of the guns.

"The Riverside crew are going to need them," I replied, relieved to have someone I knew to talk to instead of trying and failing to not be noticed. "They're a known quantity, and we know they're effective without me there to feed them. Relax, I've got the new ones."

Geddon's mouth turned down in a textbook cringe. "That's what concerns me. Those just don't have the . . . impact of the loud ones. There's still time to switch, you know."

"Our brother doesn't want to catch fire, Brother Ryan," Trix admitted on Geddon's behalf.

Trix, like me, didn't have a whole lot of gear to put on or adjust, so he stood to my side, watching all the other dramas play out. He carried his new Kotes' Carbine (patent pending), covered with a makeshift sling and a belt of extra mags over his shoulder. That didn't stop him from picking up some of the nervous energy in the room, though. Every once in a while, I saw him stroking the weapon, untying and retying the straps on the cover to make sure the rifle was still there. It wouldn't have surprised me to hear him whispering to it as well, so intense was his love for his new toy.

Even now, without any outside stimulus, I saw one of those vulpa full-body shudders take hold of him.

We're going to have to talk about that sometime.

At the mention of fire, I rolled my eyes. "For the love of—No one's catching fire this time, and I still brought a couple of the ballistic turrets. I just don't want to use them until we're all set up. More effective that way," I assured them. In reality, I wasn't entirely sure how the Scourge-Touched shared-consciousness worked or how strategic its thought process was, so I didn't want to reveal that card until we were dug in. Would they recognize my old turrets? If so, would they come running, thinking I was there?

"Besides, they spit metal at or above the speed of sound, deafen you, and run hot enough to char skin. How are you okay with having that on your back and not the new stuff?" I asked Geddon.

"It's the aesthetic. Also the accuracy." Geddon said, mumbling the last part and throwing a dubious glance over my shoulder as if he could see into my Spatial Storage.

I wasn't about to let my new babies be insulted like that. "The new ones hit their targets, too."

"And then some," Samila quipped quietly under her breath.

I grimaced and wobbled my head side to side, pained to admit they were, in totally immaterial ways, correct. The new turrets were awesome, though. Everyone would come around eventually.

"Okay. One in ten isn't a great success rate, but they make up for it in volume."

"Sounds like only a slight improvement over Geddon's proficiency on the range," Sissa stated, emerging from the crowd of bustling soldiers to enter our circle. A slightly taller and sharper version of her sister, she, like the rest of the Church guards, was already strapped into freshly polished and repaired plate and chain mail, carrying her helm under one arm and resting her other hand on the pommel of her sword. I observed the patches on her chain and the scuffs on her gauntlets. I could have done better work than that, but I'd not been asked. The elder dragonkin sister was still a little angry at me.

Sissa turned to me to give me a look. "You are going to stay with us this time, I presume?"

I tried to not look guilty but failed. Still, I'd gone over the last battle in my head time and again, and even knowing how much of their trust I'd squandered, I'd do it all again if given the chance.

"That's the plan," was all I said.

She raised an eyebrow ridge. "Is it, though?"

There was a long, meaningful pause.

I left it alone. It was going to take time to build trust again, and it wouldn't happen any faster if I insisted on having the last word.

"Our guide should be meeting up with us shortly," Sissa announced, finally turning to address everyone else.

"We have a guide?" Trix asked, tilting his head to the side. "Since when?"

Sissa shrugged. "I'm as surprised as you are. I thought we'd use the smugglers' key and be on our own again like always, but apparently, Headmaster Jassin has access to some unsavory sorts. Riverside rats, most likely."

"It's not doing much for my civic pride to know that the university knew the smugglers' tunnels so well and had a plan to use them," Geddon said.

"And had people familiar enough with them to act as our guides. Probably criminals," Sissa agreed with a nod.

"That'd be me, then," someone said from behind me.

We all had different reactions in that moment, when Corporal Fidus Bole sauntered out of the crowd to sidle up to us. The man had a new look—bearded, dressed down, and a little gaunt—but his voice and his demeanor belonged to the same man I'd fought down in the Undercity.

His guard-issue armor seemed to have been scrapped for a set of form-fitting black leathers, and his truncheon swapped out for a pair of short swords. A quick flash of Detect Steel told me there were knives behind the man's belt and at his wrists just above fingerless gloves with steel-reinforced knuckles. His unshaven face still managed to look strikingly roguish, helped along by the smug grin he had plastered across his face.

Sissa hissed. I mean, she *literally* hissed in the man's face.

Geddon put his hand on his sword and took a challenging step forward, ready to throw down.

Trix scrambled up my cloak to perch on my shoulder so he could be eye level with the man, and I heard the click of the charging handle of his gun locking into place from within the leather cover.

As for my reaction, I was already halfway between the rest of the group and Bole, looking back and forth between my comrades and the corporal like there was a tennis match being played in front of me.

Samila, in contrast to us all, got very small, tucking herself into the back of the crowd, well away from her sister. That was interesting.

Bole smirked, looking from face to face, pausing for a lengthy time on Sissa before he said, "Good to see you all again. Especially you, darling. Feel like we've been missing each other for a while now." His tone of voice could have greased pistons.

Sissa shook her head slowly, her expression morphing from disbelief to something hotter—volcanic, even. She looked back at her sister, nostrils flaring wide as if she were ready to breathe fire. Could dragonkin do that? I hadn't asked.

"*This,*" she hissed. "This is your man on the inside, isn't it? This is our source?"

Samila, for the first time since I'd met her, looked ashamed. She wouldn't meet her sister's eyes. In fact, she wouldn't look up from her own boots.

"You've been speaking with him the entire time? You ran cover for him? How long?" Sissa asked.

Samila again didn't answer.

Then Bole did the worst thing he could possibly do at that moment. He spoke.

"Don't be so hard on her, Siss. We're all on the same side here. You'll want your best man round for this one, trust me."

Sissa's blade was out and up against Bole's neck before anyone could react . . . Anyone except Bole. I'd forgotten how fast he was. He didn't react the way you might expect to a sword coming to end your life. He didn't pull his own blade. Instead, he lifted his chin and stepped 'into it, dragging his jugular across the edge all the way from the point toward the hilt.

The blade ran down his unshaven skin. The hair parted. A centimeter from the sword splitting the man's skin, Sissa's wrist bent and changed the sword's angle, giving ground until they were eye to eye, the sword between them. Bole just stared at his attacker, unafraid, that stupid grin still on his face. Triumphant.

Sissa bared her teeth. If looks could kill, Bole would be dead twice over.

The corporal had scored a point, however. He'd just gambled and won. Bole had been banking on the fact that Sissa was better than himself, and he was demonstrating that he could do all sorts of nasty things with that knowledge.

The two of them stood like that for a full second before Sissa pulled away and sheathed her sword in one motion. Her armor hid it, but I thought I saw the hint of a shudder pass through her body.

"Keep up, don't get in our way, and we'll get along fine, 'best man,'" she stated tersely.

Bole bowed slightly. "Your wish is my command, my lady blue," he replied.

With one last glare for her sister, Sissa turned on her heel and stormed off into the bustling crowd. Samila put out a timid hand, but her sister recoiled, yanking her arm away and not stopping until she was gone from sight.

"So," Bole began as if he hadn't a care in the world, "how's everyone been? Hello, Monk. So, you're a hero now, eh? You cut a better figure *without* hair, if you ask my opinion."

I ignored the barb, sparing a look for the rest of my friends before taking a cautious step toward the man, leaning into polite-conversation range.

"Bole, I see you're alive," I observed.

"Never waste a day or pay in full," he replied. It sounded like an idiom, something culturally significant. I let it slide past.

"Last time we spoke I asked you to get everyone out," I remembered. We'd sent him with the civilians to escape the Undercity back when this debacle started.

"Not to worry. I did just that. If a man sets himself on fire, then gives you a quest, you get it done, especially if you were gonna do it anyway. The trip through the tunnels was smooth, but the dead were up our asses soon enough. Came out in Riverside just ahead of 'em, and we had to live for a couple weeks on a boat in the middle of the channel."

"Everyone?" I asked.

Bole feigned indignance. "Yeah. Is that so hard to believe?"

"Absolutely. One hundred percent," I answered honestly.

Bole leaned back and clutched at his chest. "How dare you. You don't even know me, Monk."

"You did try to kill me for a minor slight."

He snorted. "Yeah, that was great. But I consider the two of us square now. Had some friends in the guard—that lot you helped out of a tight spot earlier. Good job. Are we just gonna stand around talking, or are we doing this?"

An hour later, the six of us stood next to the familiar, solid quellstone wall that I'd come to associate with exits from the smugglers' tunnels. This one was at the top of some stairs, and all of us crowded together as close to the wall as we could get without touching it. Geddon stood at the front, with Trix tucked directly behind. Sissa and Samila stood on opposite sides of the stairs pressed up against the stairwell's walls, trailed by Bole and myself.

"If we're in the right place, we'll come out in a basement," Bole whispered softly. "Stairs are on the left. The locked door leads to a loading ramp that should be facing the South Gate. The idea was to crate things up and slip into traffic after the inspection point. The gate's a bit of a run, though."

Sissa turned to us all, her face stone. All business. "We come out hard in the basement, then gather at the stairs. Force the door, then we move."

Figuring I was far enough from the Spire now, I reached into my shirt and scooped out the quellstones, making them disappear into my Spatial Storage again. I instantly felt warmer and more healthy, more *here*. As I'd been taught, I let my mind drift into that place that was out of focus, the one Jassin said I touched with my magic in that moment between being suppressed and being fully open. I didn't see anything with my eyes, but I did feel something happening there now that the quellstone wasn't trying to kill me—an expansion, like I was at the epicenter of a slow-motion explosion . . . but a good one. Then the feeling was utterly gone. I sighed in frustration.

I brought the hood on my cloak up and slipped on my cloth mask in preparation for the fight to come.

Sissa spot-checked all of us, nodded, then pulled the key necklace out of her armor to wave it at the wall. The bricks click-clacked aside, folding into one another until they melded into the wall, and then we were moving.

We stormed into a basement, just like Bole had said. Crates and casks were everywhere. Lots of them were broken open, while others were intact with a solid layer of dust on their tops. Particulates floated lazily in the air, illuminated by sunlight streaming in through the doorway up above.

Clear.

At Sissa's signal, we gathered at the stairs and charged up them, Geddon shouldering the door at the top aside and nearly taking it off its hinges.

We burst into morning daylight, its radiance blurring my vision momentarily after having been so long underground.

Bright blue sky. Huge flaming moon. Deep shadows all around. Then blurry shapes resolved into closely packed wooden buildings to my right, a stone wall to my left, muddy cobblestones making up the road. Straight ahead, through the mouth of the alley, I could see the big wooden gates that I'd entered a long time ago, shut now, and the giant arch above with parapets that overlooked the glade beyond.

It was maybe a block and a half away.

Between us and the gates, predictably, were plenty of Scourge-Touched. Packs of sickly dark and pale bodies padded on bare feet from one building to the next, ducking into doorways and back out again. They clambered up gutters, leapt to windowsills, hissed, and howled at things they saw.

Beyond them, a makeshift barricade of overturned wagons, scrap lumber, and sharpened stakes was jammed between two buildings, effectively blocking the alley and our way to the gates. Smoke billowed up from behind it.

We were in the right place.

I got the nod from Sissa and went to work.

This turret was a tall one, about a foot higher than myself once it was set up, with thin, multi-jointed legs that ended in hooks. On top, I affixed a circularly packed bundle of long barrels, twelve in all, to a boxy containment housing with a circular hatch on the bottom for me to be able to reload the thing. I didn't need to Shape-weld the pieces together, since it wasn't going to have any recoil to speak of, so the whole setup process took maybe thirty seconds, with me summoning a piece at a time from my storage and fitting said piece into place manually. I felt every one of those seconds, though. Curious eyes were all around, and it would only take one to bring the whole city down on us.

"You're using one of the blinky ones?" Geddon whispered. The guy's voice wasn't made for whispering, but he gave it the old Geddon try. That is to say, forcefully and with zero subtlety. It sounded more like he had a cold than anything else. "I thought we were setting things on fire," he continued.

I shook my head, pulling on the fastener to secure the barrels snuggly into the box housing. "Fire is for later. Everyone, remember what I said."

"We remember," Sissa assured me. "Now focus and get it done."

Finally, I slipped the specialized, Automated glow rod into the ammo housing, making sure it was in contact with the smart card before closing the hatch and securing the clasp. Instantly, the hooks on the turret's feet contracted with a quiet *crack!* as the stabilizer hooks dug into the cobblestones.

Good luck flipping this one, you little bastards.

"Done. Ready," I called quietly.

Sissa got beside me and began the countdown. "Three, two, one. Go."

I triggered the activation sequence with my mind—a simple Trigger that unleashed all of the Volatility mana in the core in a series of sequential mild explosions, not nearly hot nor forceful as the grenade version of this spell, of course. I didn't want to blow up my own turret. Instead, all of that energy was dispersed over time and through generous ventilation holes in the back of the turret housing with a quiet *fwoosh!*

The new turret went on an absolute rampage. The Trigger rod shot energy through all of the turret's systems, activating its rotator joints and its targeting programs. The turret, fully powered now, tracked and fired non-stop. Purple beams of concentrated light blasted out from its twelve barrels simultaneously, laying into the Scourge-Touched and raking silent death across the scattered monsters (and a lot of the alleyway) with ruthless vigor. All the while, searing white sparks flew out of vents on the back of the housing, bright enough to blind.

Wherever they were touched by the light, the enemy simply fell apart.

The violence had no associated sound—not that could be heard above the background noise of the dead city, anyway, except for a faint sort of *thrrrrrrup!* as *something* scored hundreds of hits in under a handful of seconds. I wasn't sure what it was that did the hitting . . . I was still working on that. I just knew that it was there based on experimentation and the System.

The mockvine bulbs and fibers, it turned out, weren't very good for burning things or activating Triggers in my machines, or at least not any better than the basic stuff I could make. What they were very good at was conducting mana, light, and all sorts of stuff the plant had used when it was alive. "Signals," the System had called them.

Though the heat and explosive force of Volatility normally did the heavy lifting when it came time to kill things indiscriminately, I'd discovered that the mana and light, components of the spell I'd written off as mere byproducts of blowing things to pieces were also considered part of the attack by the System's standards. Not much of the attack, but they did, indeed qualify.

So, after some experimentation, I determined that if I put a Volatility-charged rod next to a heat-shielded mockvine bulb that acted as a repeater, I could conduct said light and mana down the fibers and put on a pretty fantastic light show with the resulting signals.

The cool thing was that the mockvine bulbs repeated the signal they were getting perfectly and multiple times to multiple fibers, meaning the wild mana and purple light were getting repeated and sent down a dozen different paths every time the bulbs received them, and every single one of these copied flashes of fun retained the same level of Attack in the System, qualifying them for the bonus Damage from Knife in the Dark.

Meanwhile, every hit lit up their victim, and I became aware of them like I did when using my Detect Abilities, except not. This feeling was fundamentally different.

I brought my Combat Log up to confirm what I was seeing.

You hit Scourge-Touched Undead for 3 Damage. (0 base, +3 Knife in the Dark bonus)

Scourge-Touched Undead is marked.

Scourge-Touched Undead is cursed.

Scourge-Touched Undead takes 3 Damage. (0 base, +3 Knife in the Dark bonus)

Scourge-Touched Undead takes 1 Damage. (0 base, +1 Marked bonus)

Scourge-Touched Undead takes 1 Damage. (0 base, +1 Marked bonus)

Scourge-Touched Undead takes 1 Damage. (0 base, +1 Marked bonus)

Scourge-Touched Undead takes 3 Damage. (0 base, +3 Knife in the Dark bonus)

Scourge-Touched Undead is marked.

Scourge-Touched Undead is cursed.

You hit Scourge-Touched Undead for 3 Damage. (0 base, +3 Knife in the Dark bonus)

Scourge-Touched Undead is marked.

Scourge-Touched Undead is cursed.

Scourge-Touched Undead takes 1 damage. (0 base, +1 Marked bonus)

Scourge-Touched Undead takes 1 damage. (0 base, +1 Marked bonus)

Scourge-Touched Undead takes 1 damage. (0 base, +1 Marked bonus)

Scourge-Touched Undead takes 1 damage. (0 base, +1 Marked bonus)

Scourge-Touched Undead takes 1 damage. (0 base, +1 Marked bonus)

Scourge-Touched Undead takes 1 damage. (0 base, +1 Marked bonus)

It went on like that. Hundreds of attacks per volley.

They did very little Damage on their own, but the bonus ate away at flesh and eventually sawed through bone, given there were enough strikes.

And there were an absolute shit-ton of them. Every volley happened in a blink, and there were multiple blinks per second, making this thing an absolute buzz saw.

The two upgrades I'd selected for Knife in the Dark were already proving their worth.

Mark: A successful Knife in the Dark attack marks an opponent. Marked opponents take more Damage from additional attacks and are visible to you.
Curse of Obfuscation: Opponents struck by Knife in the Dark are now Cursed. Cursed opponents are now less likely to detect you and your actions.

The alley was awash in purple laser lights. The gun's aim was absolutely terrible, since I didn't know a thing about lenses, making this iteration of "laser turret" a bad choice if I wanted to defend a strongpoint, but it did wonderfully for clearing an area of all living things.

Scourge-Touched fell apart, reduced to piles of minced, vaguely organic puddles. Wood splintered and fell to dust. The cobblestones and any exposed stone supports fared just fine, however. Whatever Knife in the Dark was using, it seemed to only work on organic materials. Where the light touched inorganic stuff, strange, oily, multi-colored smudge marks covered the affected area. Instead of heat, like you'd expect from a laser, this was entirely bonus Damage, a classification that was strange and unqualified, defying explanation no matter what queries I made of the System.

"Weird Damage," I was calling it for now.

The turret stopped firing after a handful of seconds, the barrel sagging down to point at the ground as the power rod spent its last and the housing chamber hissed. The metal box clanked and popped under the stress of all the heat. Whether it was glowing or not, I couldn't tell in this light, but I suspected the temperature was nearing that level. I disengaged the release to let the expended rod fall to the cobbles with a *clang*, and with one smooth motion, I summoned another charged rod and jammed it into place, ready to fire again.

When I looked up, everyone was staring at me, mouths open, the collective sentiment a mix of horrified fascination, awe, and healthy disgust. I shrugged sheepishly, then summoned my sword in preparation for the next part of the plan. Did they have war crime tribunals here? If so, I'd need to be long gone before they could put one together.

After just a couple of seconds of hesitation more, Sissa ordered the charge, Geddon slipping in front, with Trix riding on his shoulders. The rest of us fanned out behind them, the Sisters and then myself and Bole in as much of a wedge formation as the alleyway would allow.

After ten or fifteen clanking steps, a trickle of curious Scourge-Touched began to poke their heads into the alleyway. A bunch of their own had just died, and if their collective consciousness worked like I thought it did, they'd know there was something here that needed killing. They streamed in and scattered, inspecting it all, crawling over the remains and looking for the cause.

A singular Baned turned our way, affixed its stare on us, and howled.

Trix let out a squeak and fumbled for his rifle, pulling off the cover. It was a short, carbine type weapon I'd made for him—about the size of a large pistol for a human but with a butt stock and a longer barrel that put it squarely into long-gun territory, at least for a vulpa. It didn't have the power of one of my turrets, only shooting tiny needle spikes of iron as ammo, but it had almost no recoil and very little report.

THAP! THAP!

Trix, it turned out, was a natural marksman . . . a marksvulpa . . . a *shootyfox*. Two Scourge-Touched, including the one that had started the alarm, went down in less than a second, and Trix didn't stop there. He let the lead fly. Every shot hit, most of them producing instant kills with tiny, nearly invisible holes blossoming from targets' heads and chests.

I hadn't tested the gun enough to determine by sound whether it was on full auto, but it might as well have been. Trix deftly tracked targets and filled them with daylight before they could even think to get in our way. All the while, he kept doing his signature tremble, but it didn't seem to affect his aim.

Soon, though, the word was out and the alley was wall-to-wall enemies—more than Trix could handle. Thankfully, we had Geddon to roll over them like a boulder. The massive Leori came through with force, bowling handfuls of the Scourge-Touched aside at a time, his sword chopping down and maiming or outright killing all it fell upon. Samila and Sissa were just behind him. Their swords flashed. The Scourge-Touched, already stunned and wounded, never had a chance to get to their feet.

My sword was already in my hand, and it did what it did best. Honestly, there wasn't much I needed to do in the back of the formation aside from finishing off those I could and staying close to the dragonkin sisters. My new sword model wasn't anything fancy, but it was sharp on both sides and stabbed just fine. I made sure to preserve my edge while I could, though.

Willing Edge [2 MP/sec]

Scourge-Touched crowded in, pounding out of doorways and jumping down from windows to land in the alley with us. I skewered one in the throat and followed up with a reverse slash across another's eyes, almost before I could even process they were there.

We kept moving. To stop meant getting bogged down and overwhelmed. I couldn't help but observe how much less painful this was with a team. Maybe there *was* something to this whole working-together thing.

Bole was next to me, slashing and stabbing on his own, every strike landing on something vital. He moved fast and accurately, with a confidence in his body and proficiency I lacked. There was a rhythm to it, too. Nothing that came up against him survived more than two moves, and those two moves happened almost too quickly to perceive.

I hugged the wall slightly to look beyond Geddon. We had maybe half a block to go. The alley was filling up fast, though. Too fast.

Gradually, our momentum stalled as the road flooded with opponents, but true to his nature, Geddon never stopped pushing and plowing through them, trusting us to have his back while he devoted everything he had to muscling his way to the goal.

Attacks were coming more frequently from the rear now, and Bole and I were forced to backpedal to defend ourselves. That's why I didn't notice we'd arrived at our destination until it reached out and touched me. I nearly impaled myself on a sharpened stake that the rest of the party had dodged. Luckily it caught me in the metal part of my shoulder, the tip of the spike snapping off and catching in my cloak.

Unfriendly faces and bared teeth pressed in around us, and we quickly went from being surrounded to being practically smothered. Our armored folks got to the edge of our half-circle and kept the baying creatures back while the rest of us worked on figuring out a way to get over the barricade.

There was a shout from behind the barricade, muffled but intelligible. It was one of those wordless calls—all vowels and harshly pronounced stops. Sissa answered something back that sounded like "*BOLTA!*" Again, no translation from the System. Probably a code.

Whatever they'd communicated back and forth, it must have worked. A length of coiled rope hit me in the back of the head, and arrows started to whistle in the air above us.

"Duty and mercy!" Sissa shouted, putting her will behind the call to help us get through this next part. That golden feeling suffused her words as they had in the Undercity, and the battle came into razor-sharp focus. I felt my blood quicken and hair stand on end.

At Sissa's direction, a panting and sweating Geddon fell back and tied the rope harness around himself, tugging on the end to request getting pulled up. Trix hopped onto the big guy at the last second and used the spent Leori as an impromptu sniper perch, squeezing off rounds from Geddon's chest as they rose out of my view.

I didn't watch them go all the way up, stepping into Geddon's place between the dragonkin sisters to help hold the line. Then I heard something wet gurgling behind my back and turned to find Bole there, skewering a Returned with both of his swords, wrenching the blades out hard enough to spill the rest of the Undead's guts onto the ground. He caught my eye and flashed that grin of his.

I didn't have the mental bandwidth for this right now. I was busy batting at reaching arms and dancing in and out with my sword while the shield-users took the brunt of the real punishment.

There was the sound of the rope smacking on wood behind me.

"Next!" Geddon bellowed from above. Trix's rifle barked again and again, starting to wipe out the Scourge-Touched closest to our flanks.

Bole went next. Then Samila. She shook her head at first, not wanting to leave Sissa but I shouldered my way over to get into her spot, giving her no choice in the matter.

Our circle had shrunk to just a few feet of breathing room. Full sword swings were impossible now, but the monsters didn't seem to have the same suicidal urge as the last time I'd fought them. They responded to my attacks as I expected a pack of rabid animals might, shrinking away from the dangerous point of my sword but never giving too much ground, always attacking where I wasn't paying attention.

An interesting data point for later.

"Time!" Geddon shouted. "Get out now!"

That was the signal. He had spotted something. The alleyway was about to become very, very popular. Sissa and I couldn't see over the press, but we had to trust Geddon to let us know when things were going to be too much for us.

"Get on the rope," Sissa ordered.

"Now! Trouble coming!" Geddon roared.

Not waiting for permission, I grabbed Sissa by the waist and yanked her back to the rope. Then I grabbed the end with my prosthetic and triggered Iron Grip. There was a momentary resistance to what I was doing I could feel through her body, but it only lasted all of a half-second. Then she was swinging with her sword and bashing with her shield to keep the creatures at bay while I did my best to hold on.

Our feet left the road.

The Scourge-Touched swarmed underneath us, leaping up to slash at us. One of them latched onto my leg and tore into the calf.

"Sissa!" I called.

"I know!" she said. "Up! Up!" she called to the rope-pullers.

"Sissa!" I shouted, hoping she remembered what I'd said before we started. "Look now! Look at the turret!"

I triggered the next volley. Being on this side of the carnage was a different experience. The strobing lights danced over the entire alleyway—a fire hose of purple beams, indiscriminate, seemingly infinite in number. Intellectually, I knew that every beam I saw had another four or five behind it, too fast to perceive from this distance with the naked eye. The general direction of the light tracked back and forth, bathing everything in that familiar purple.

There was a moment, a collective breath from all of us—Sissa and myself, the horde. Everything stopped for a heartbeat. Then a tipping point was reached.

The enemies at our feet liquefied in slow motion, starting at the back of the crowd and surging to the front.

I didn't dare look away from the turret to observe the process, though. Neither did Sissa. One lapse in attention would be an opportunity for Knife in the Dark to mark us. Then we'd be in a world of hurt.

Sissa and I continued to stare at the turret as it dispensed death, neither of us daring to blink, though I was pretty sure we probably didn't have to take our concentration on it so literally. We just had to be paying direct attention to the turret to not be affected. Sissa would probably have been fine with the armor she wore, but we weren't going to take any chances either, not with our precious eyes and faces exposed to the world.

Then the alley went suddenly dark. I blinked tears out of my eyes, scanning the area to see if anything was left alive.

Rainbow beef stew.

The thought came and went, and I was glad to see it go.

I saw some movement, but nothing that went beyond a pathetic crawl. Nothing that could run or jump. *Good.*

We crested the top of the barricade and Geddon got us up the rest of the way, letting us drop on the uneven wooden surface that looked like it was composed of doors and scavenged chests.

Sissa squirmed, spinning around to look my way, her eyes wide. She reached up to wipe black blood off my forehead with her sword hand.

"Ryan. You can let go now," she said.

Oh, yeah.

I let go of her waist, nearly sending her tumbling down, before turning away bashfully, suddenly very interested in what was going on in the yard beyond the barricade upon which we stood.

Church guards hustled everywhere, fully armored, swords in hand and battered shields at their sides. Our barricade wasn't the only one clogging up the streets that led into the gatehouse area. They'd piled up an impressive amount of garbage to create their fortifications, and they were manning those makeshift battlements as best they could.

The enormous gates themselves were shut and barred, making up the back wall of the camp, and the black city walls on either side of the gate were manned by crossbowmen and spears alike.

What surprised me, however, were the goblins. They were everywhere. They ran over the yard, carrying indeterminate objects and throwing them on the giant bonfire in the middle of the half-circle made up by the fortifications. Others carried spears and ran alongside Miur and bow-legged guardsmen whose species I didn't know the name for. Others shot arrows from crude bows up and over the wooden barricades as a guardsman directed their line of fire. Still more sat next to the pyre, sharpening lengths of wood with tiny knives and burning the ends to temper the points.

Suddenly, my view was blocked by a gaggle of . . . children. Goblin children. Lots of them. Where had they come from?!

"They have lots of stuff!" one said in a high, squeaky voice, in the goblin tongue.

"We can take it! A Baned eats my dad's spear yesterday." replied another.

"But they have swords. Does your dad use a sword?"

"No."

"Tie a sword to a pole and you have a spear," yet another voice suggested.

"True. True. Maybe one of the little ones!"

An older child—taller, well-muscled, and mohawked like a warrior—shoved his way to the front of the gaggle, pushing the smaller ones aside, and meanmugging at the crowd with impressive attitude. He turned to each in turn and stared them all down, forcing them to shrink away.

"No," he growled, in a manner that was probably intimidating to other goblins, but which to me just came off as cute. "They keep their stuff."

"Awwwww," came the collective moan from the rest of them.

The big kid wasn't having it, though. "Come on," he said. "We take them to the Big One."

"Yay! The Big One!"

CHAPTER FIVE

Eat a Curse

The children pressed closer, their little black eyes wide and innocent, but I saw more than one who made to grab for stuff that wasn't theirs. I headed them off as well as I could.

"Hey! We're keeping our weapons. And who's this 'Big One?'" I asked in Goblin myself.

A voice emerged from the crowd, not so much from an individual kid, but from multiple kids rolling over one another with their own excited jabbering until all I could do was pick out the collective sentiment. "Ooh, it speaks! Can we buy your sword? That's a good sword. I can tell."

"Stop it!" the larger kid scolded, reaching back into the crowd to cuff one of them on the head. "We take them to the Big One. That's it."

I did a quick check on my companions. No one had been swarmed by little green things with sticky fingers yet. The two groups were standing at a moderately respectful distance from one another, but Trix was dangerously close to the edge of the barricade, staring at the carnage down below, his hands clenched tightly around his rifle. No part of him was still. He was shuddering violently.

"Trix?" I called tentatively, but the distressed vulpa didn't look like he'd heard me.

"Trix!"

He started, nearly fumbling his rifle and losing it over the side. Then he looked around, bewildered and wild-eyed.

"Are you still with us, buddy?" I asked.

Trix opened his mouth to answer but shut it again almost immediately, choosing instead to nod. Samila squatted down next to him and ruffled his hair, saying something to him I couldn't hear over the racket.

"Big One! Big One!" The little goblin shouts had turned to chants now that they were all on the same page. I stood on my tiptoes to try and find the older kid who had calmed them before. No dice.

Sissa was staring at me, the obvious question on her mind: *Why do you speak Goblin?*

"I'll explain later," I mouthed to her.

"Who is this Big One?" I asked the children.

"You know their tongue, sir?" A Miur with short antlers, the beginnings of a beard, and a lot of ragged holes in his armor asked as he coiled our rope around his forearm. He must have been the one who had come to our rescue. "Command will be happy to hear that. The little ones just kind of do what they want, and we've just counted ourselves lucky they want to help for now. Some verbal communication between us wouldn't go amiss."

"I know *some*. Where might Command be?" I asked.

"Over that way," the guard said, pointing at a boxy building with a canted roof butting right up against the city's giant outer wall.

"The Big One! The Big One!" the little goblins collectively shouted again.

I retried my previous question. "Who is this 'Big One?'"

"Don't know. He's big."

Right. There's the language barrier, and I'm talking to kids.

"He got a name?" I asked.

"Probably."

I sighed and looked to the rest of the party, but, of course, no one else understood the conversation. Trix was on Samila's shoulder now, a thousand-yard stare on his face, but at least he wasn't going to get lost if we started moving.

"Guess we're going that way," I said, pointing to the guard building.

"Big One!" The energy level was climbing. These kids must have been surviving on energy drinks and rock candy.

I started climbing down from the barricade, having to slip down between handles that used to belong to some kind of cart, then sliding with the loose debris that my weight had knocked loose until I was on solid ground again.

Now that I was on street level, the semicircular yard these people had made their home painted a bleak picture. Tired faces stared at me from all around. Beleaguered guards sat on stools around little campfires that littered the cobblestone square, though none came close to the wooden ramparts. Wouldn't want to trap yourself in an oven of your own making. None of the guards were entirely intact, either—or at least their equipment wasn't. People were missing gloves, helms, or entire boots. Chest plates were dented or torn. Shields were missing edges or entire halves.

The goblins seemed the liveliest of the bunch, hustling back and forth in lines and carrying furniture, doors, loose stones and the like on their backs like ants, and bringing them up the precarious climb to the top of the ramparts to deposit them with uncharacteristic care.

An older goblin in a ragged shirt stood at the top of the construction area, yelling at them all while bending down to make minor adjustments as to where the garbage was being placed. Was I looking at a goblin engineer, or was he just too old to do the manual labor? Whatever he was, he was in charge but not universally respected. Before I'd passed, at least two of his workers gave the old goblin the finger, which he returned with double the enthusiasm he put into the rest of his work.

I saw why the bonfire wasn't very popular with the guards. It was hot, it produced a ton of rancid smoke, and then there were the blackened bones, teeth, and other, unidentifiable things littering the pit in which the bonfire burned.

"Nice setup. They better give thanks to the Light every chance they get. Lucky bastards," Bole said quietly.

Sissa hissed at him again. "Shut up, Bole. Not one more word."

Bole rolled his eyes but didn't offer any more commentary.

I looked questioningly at Samila from where her sister couldn't see. She leaned over to whisper to me. "Their gear looks like it's been through it, but they're all healthy and well-fed. Odds are good they've got a healer or two tucked away along with a stash of food. Better than most have fared through this."

"Wouldn't a healer drain their food?" I asked.

Samila shook her head. "No. Not a Church healer. Trix isn't one of those."

"What is he, then?" I asked, leaning forward a bit to check on him. He was just staring straight ahead and holding on tightly to his weapon as Samila acted as his legs.

"A rarity," she said. She looked like she wanted to say more, checking over her shoulder to make sure the vulpa wasn't listening, but then she thought better of it. Probably for the best. The little guy had good ears. "Ask him yourself if you really want to know," she said before clamming up again and falling back in line behind her sister.

We made our way to the building next to the city wall and entered through an empty doorframe whose door appeared to have been forcefully ripped out, probably used in the building of the barricade. The little goblin children paraded into the building in front of us, still believing themselves to be our captors but also really excited to get into the place for some reason.

The kids all gathered around a . . . well, it *was* a Big One! A big man, to be more precise. A familiar big man in what used to be white robes last I'd seen them, now dirty and ragged. Bishop Kolash, the hulking, slightly damp frog man (a "Rahn," I think he'd called himself) stood in the center of a circle of occupied sickbeds, one hand raised in the air, the other resting on his staff. His midnight-black skin had a sheen of moisture that reflected the light from the windows oddly, and his wide-set eyes were closed.

A low, humming song suffused the room, seeming to resonate with something deep in my soul. It reminded me of family dinners, rides with Mom, straight As on my report card, and Christmas afternoons, all at once. Golden light surrounded the bishop and everyone within ten feet of him. All of the people gathered around were wounded, most bleeding from their extremities, but they all seemed to rest easier as the song progressed. The skin of those that didn't have fur looked increasingly less pale, as well.

Sissa put a hand on my arm to stop me from getting closer.

"Better to not," she whispered.

"He likes to sing alone. Where did your sword go?" one of the goblin children whispered in my other ear. How the hell did she get up there?

"It hides. This the Big One?" I asked.

"The Big One. He's very big."

I had to agree. He wasn't Geddon-big, but he was still impressive, if more Frog Santa Claus than Incredible Hulk.

Sissa looked from me to the kid on my shoulder. "What are they saying? Also, you speak Goblin?! What else are you hiding?"

"They say this is the Big One. They were supposed to bring us to him. We can't go further right now, though."

Sissa nodded. "Glad the goblins could be taught that much. Don't want to step into an already-active ritual. You wait for it to—"

The bishop's song reached a crescendo, deepening in its tone and resonance. His voice broke or maybe expanded, and suddenly, I could feel it pass through me like a shockwave, burning and crackling all the way and absolutely overloading my nervous system until I saw (and tasted) *yellow*. I mostly stayed on my feet, but it was a close call.

Damn, that was much worse than the first time he'd hit me with one of those.

I looked around to check on everyone else. My friends all seemed . . . better. *Refreshed.* Bole, however, was conspicuously absent. Had he even entered the building with us?

The song was over. Two of the wounded soldiers already had their feet over the edges of their beds and were putting on their previously soiled clothes. Their wounds were entirely gone.

Wow. This really was a breed apart from Trix's magic.

"Brothers and sisters, it gladdens me to see that you have survived our great trial thus far," the bishop croaked as he hobbled toward us, his staff making heavy *thumps* on the wooden floor as he went. He was leaning heavily on it—much more heavily than when I'd first met him. "It is good that you have come now. We have need of strong sword arms and tempered resolve."

He waved his arms over his head gently, making shooing motions at the gathered crowd of green children. "Go on then, little ones. Go find somewhere else to play. Go."

The goblin kids took the hint. I almost didn't feel it when the tiny goblin girl jumped down from my back to be swept up in the river of hyperactive green bodies heading out of the door.

"Your Holiness," Sissa began once the noise died down, "it is good to see you alive, as well. We come to you with news. There is a large contingent of survivors and enlisted people in the Spire, and they would have you and our people come join them. They have a plan to get everyone out of the city."

Kolash's shoulders relaxed slightly, and he let out a long sigh. "Thank the Light for that. We run short on supplies and people. The infection worms its way into our ranks every day, and we cannot always be vigilant enough. The best we have been able to do is quick healing for the wounded. The rest is up to fate. What would you have us do, Sister Sissa?"

"We have a way to get our people to the Spire, through the smugglers' tunnels," Sissa said. "From there, it is a nearly direct route to safety. Headmaster Jassin offers a place for us all and a way out."

The bishop made a displeased sound in the back of his throat. "The Plagued will not make this an easy thing. We, too, had the idea of fleeing the city. We lost half of our flock, and now the enemy wear familiar faces when they come for the rest of us."

"They wear—Are the living turning as the Returned did?" Sissa asked.

Kolash shook his head mournfully. "Not yet. The goblins insisted we burn the dead, theirs and ours. At first we did not see the purpose behind it, and we had no way to ask for an explanation. Their queen, however, was adamant, so much so that we allowed them to burn their own but kept ours in repose in one of the empty barracks."

He stared into the middle distance for a few long heartbeats as he recalled difficult memories.

"Would that we had heeded their warnings. There was a raid two nights after our failed escape—not in overwhelming numbers, mind you. At least, that is what we thought. The Plagued, however, took our honored dead below, and now we see them again from time to time, come back to haunt us. It has been . . . disheartening."

"There were never any bodies," I observed quietly. In the Undercity, even in the places we were sure there had been a slaughter, there were never any bodies. I had just assumed the Scourge had been eating the living. Everything had to eat, right? Apparently not in this case. Or at least not everyone that died was food. The Scourge-Touched must have been recruiting.

"Quite so, young man" the bishop said, turning to me.

So the dead could be "touched" as well. What did that mean? The Returned were already dead. That made some sense. As for goblins, I'd not heard of any live ones getting turned; no infections. To hear the Stone Hearts tell it, their people were always taken or outright killed. *Interesting.*

"Your Holiness," I ventured, "have you had a chance to examine a living example of the plague? A goblin, perhaps?"

"*Glorp!* Yes," he replied with a hint of trepidation. "Why?"

"So . . ." I began. I had a theory cooking in my head somewhere, but it wasn't done yet. " . . . they were alive in the conventional sense? They aren't like the Returned?"

"In the early days of the plague, all of them were more or less alive. Quite mad but technically alive." He punctuated his sentence by reaching out and putting a heavy hand on my shoulder. His tone was grave. "You have insights, I imagine."

"Maybe," I answered. My mind was working hard, taking the pieces and rearranging them to try and make sense of them all. "There has to be some common thread here. But I can't yet put my finger on it." What was it that united them? Blackish blood? Maybe. Once they were too far gone, they didn't speak. There was that too.

"Perhaps you could start with explaining how it happened to you." the bishop said.

He had me there. I was a data point on living infection, but that was useless because I was different. I got my infection from the Sys—

Every thought in my head came to a calamitous, crashing halt.

What did he just say?

His countenance fell until the corners of his mouth hung well and truly past his bottom jaw. "I'm sorry, young one," Kolash croaked. He sounded genuinely sad, like he was giving me my last rites.

Oh, no. Kolash was one of the only people in the city who could detect the Scourge, and I, as of recently, just got an *unhealthy* dose of Experience and Stats through the System. I was more Scourge now than I had been last time we'd met.

Everyone I cared about turned toward me, worried expressions all around.

My mouth had gone dry, and my throat tightened until I could barely breathe—not because this was a revelation for me. Of course I was infected. Apparently, all Exotics were infected. That was Item No. 4,025 on my list of impossibly complex things to fix in the near-future.

What upset me was that I'd planned to tell them all eventually, once I figured out how to confess to the whole human-thing without causing some worldwide religious schism, but now this giant frog man had taken a portion of that truth I wanted to share and just slapped my friends in the face with it. It was just another breach of trust I would have to reckon with later.

If I didn't act soon, I wouldn't have any confessions left to make . . . or friends to make them to.

I reached up and took off my mask.

Kolash's eyes widened in shock. "Brother Ryan. *Grop!* I did not realize it was you. A true tragedy. I had hoped you were still out there and working to save us. I am very sorry." Resignation dripped heavily from his words.

Sissa reached over and grabbed my arm, squeezing so tightly it hurt. "Ryan? You—You don't look surprised." She breathed.

I shook my head, guilt sealing my lips.

Sissa pulled on my arm until we were facing each other. She stood tall to try and look me in the eye. "How long?" she asked.

"Why didn't you tell us?" Samila cut in, stepping forward to flank her sister, her tone quietly accusatory.

"Because—" I started, but Kolash cut me off.

"Let go of him, Sister," the bishop ordered. It didn't sound like something said in my defense, though. It was something else.

Sissa did let go, but she looked confused, as if she'd done it by reflex.

At the edge of my awareness, I felt something then—a tingle in Kolash's hand, a current of unpleasant warmth flowing into my skin. The air around me quivered in anticipation, and then some kind of tipping point was reached. Something seized me from the inside, took a hold of my body, and squeezed. Stabbing, electrifying pain ran down my arm and burrowed into my chest.

"How did it happen, Brother Ryan?" Kolash asked. "Did they take you? Do they speak to you? Do they tell you to do things in the dark?"

I shook my head in answer, suddenly very dizzy. My vision blurred, and I felt my muscles go slack. There was motion out there, along with disembodied voices.

"What is this? What did you do?" Sissa demanded.

Samila sounded even more alarmed. "Ryan? Look at him. He's—"

"It is as I feared. He is too far gone. Do not touch him."

"What?"

"He was just fighting alongside us! We need him!"

"He will turn on us. It is only a matter of time."

The world was out of focus. The System was nice and clear, though.

Status Effect gained: Cursed [-10 hp/sec]

" . . .a purge of his body. It will buy him more time if he lives."

"No! Take it back!"

"I will not. I will not have a being as dangerous as he is turning to the side of the enemy. He, of all people, would understand."

My thoughts were slowing down, grinding gradually to a halt as my world dissolved into fire. I knew this much, though. The bishop had cast a spell on me, and I couldn't remember the last time I'd taken a breath.

I felt my body shudder as a bead of sweat dripped down my nose.

Come on. Breathe. It should be easy. Just breathe!

Kolash was purging the Scourge from my body. Unfortunately, the Scourge was a part of what I was—an essential part.

Suddenly, my limbs lost their battle with gravity, and I fell to the floor, face first with a *whomp!* Concerningly, I didn't feel the impact in the slightest.

"Ryan!"

"Do *not* touch him, unless you wish to join him. The infection is insidious."

"Your Holiness," Trix squeaked. "This is extreme. Brother Ryan has—"

"He has done his best but failed his mission. We can only bid him farewell now."

"I thought you said he could pull through?" Sissa sounded irate, bordering on full-on panic.

"No one has done so yet, but if his spirit is strong enough, he may. Understand that we do this because it is necessary. We cannot allow the infection to walk among us. We have lost too much already." Kolash didn't sound, at all, like he held out much hope.

Inside of me, I felt the bishop's spell cling to me. Then it blossomed, folded out from itself, and latched onto my soft tissues, my arteries, my channels . . . and systematically began to destroy them. Blue-tinged me-mana (my personal "flavor" of mana that I seemed to produce naturally) haplessly flowed through the cursed area of my body but never escaped, dissolving into nothing as the curse snared it all. The tempered walls of my mana channels cracked and split like dry wood.

My entire body burned.

Tempered Channels is now Level 4.

"He's dying! Let me help him!" Trix's voice.

"Sacrifice, Brother Yik'i'trix. This is how we have survived thus far as a people. We cut out the infected flesh so the body may survive."

"Ryan!"

I was burning to death from the inside.

Scoured.

Purged.

With a final desperate effort, I gasped a single shallow breath, then lost track of why I'd done so. The edges of my vision darkened. Then . . .

I stopped breathing altogether.

I missed having a heartbeat. It had been a good way of making sure I was still alive.

Not your best move, System.

The world around me went out of focus, then melted away like old film in a hot projector.

Fog swept in. More like smoke, really, billowing up to obscure the physical and cloud everything else, a byproduct of the burning furnace inside of me that was using my life as fuel. In the smoke, however, there were some things that didn't fade as everything else had.

Little blue motes—tiny, bowl-shaped things that glowed against the backdrop of the dead world—drifted sluggishly upon nothing. Still. Stale.

That didn't seem right. So strange to have everything so fixed. It felt like the motes should be moving.

Like me. I should be moving. It's weird that I'm not moving. Why am I not moving?

I wasn't sure why I wasn't moving. Something was happening. Something important I'd forgotten.

I poked one of the little glowing motes mentally, a sort of numb, fumbling slap from my fading consciousness. I should have been concerned about that . . . the fading. Emotion was hard to conjure in this place, however.

The little blue thing quivered in response to my touch.

There were more of them, too, not just outside of my body. The motes were in me, clustered in greater numbers, too many to count. The blue motes bobbed through my mana channels, a lazy, cool river of life that illuminated what they touched . . . No, it wasn't illumination. I wasn't using my eyes. Whatever the motes touched, I could feel, touch, smell, hear, and see all at once. Perfect knowledge.

Not everything, though. The metal of my prosthetic pieces was a notable exception. Those were as cold as a dead star.

As I watched, the motes flowed throughout my body, bringing soft blue light to all they passed through. That is, until they reached my shoulder. The bishop's curse was a cluster of golden shards of light with razor-sharp edges that cut and ripped as they darted through my soft tissues. They swarmed my blue motes with angry zeal, attached to them, brought them down, and burned them to dust.

Hey. I needed those. I needed . . . my mana. That was my mana, and my mana was me.

My attention swerved toward my status.

HP: 50/220

My mana had to flow.

Needed to flow.

Or I would die.

A problem to be solved. I liked those.

The first step was to get things moving. There was an emptiness within me that called for it. The curse was killing me by starving me of my mana, and I was critically low already. I focused on the vacuum it left as it destroyed me—the hollowness. I reached out and swept one of the motes inside. It seemed eager to go, like it, somehow, knew I needed it there. *Success.*

So I gathered another, then another. I gave the new additions a place to go, paths to take.

Move. Move together.

They did. Sort of. They drifted through me mostly on momentum, slowing to a crawl unless I was actively moving them, but every cell they touched felt healthier, more alive.

I reached for more. I needed so many more. I brought it all into myself, as much as I could reach, gave it momentum, nudged it until it was all moving as one. I made it flow.

The bishop's spell was voracious. It penetrated and dissolved mote after mote when they came into range, but soon I'd gathered so much, the sheer volume of mana flowing through my body overwhelmed the golden light constructs. The motes flooded the cursed area and drowned the invaders in a sea of blue before spreading through the rest of my body like water breaking through a dam.

I lost so much but gained more.

More.

For the first time in seemingly forever, I gasped, sucking in a huge, cold, rattling breath, and my mana rushed into me like a tide, naturally joining the currents I'd already established inside of me and turning the trickling streams into rushing rivers.

My burning limbs twitched as oxygen-starved muscles finally received what they needed.

HP: 30/220

With great effort, I rolled over onto my back, my metal hand coming up to rest on my opposite shoulder.

This was going to hurt.

Devouring Grasp (Magivore) [5 MP/sec]

The metal fingers dug into my flesh. The bones in my shoulder cracked and popped under the pressure. This was physical pain, though—something I was familiar with. The important part was still—

Fuuuuuuuuuuuuuuuuuuck!

Like metal fillings being pulled to an industrial grade magnet, the sharp-edged golden constructs were ripped from my body. Blood vessels burst, and my mana channels blew ragged holes in their sides. The little golden bastards did a lot of damage on the way out, but they *left*.

Create reservoir? Y/N

No way I wanted that stuff inside of me again, even to use as fuel. I chose "Yes."

Reservoir created: Purge Unclean [Total value: 210 MP (light)]

I lay there, weak and hurt but *alive*. The bones in my shoulder were a mess, my insides scrambled. The pain was absolutely overwhelming.

My mana, however, flowed within me, which I consciously encouraged.

There was nothing else I could do. Wherever my mana touched, I felt better. When I searched for more to sweep into myself, there was none to be found.

> Skill unlocked: Mana Manipulation
> Your current Skill Level is 1.
> Skill unlocked: Curse Breaking
> Your current Skill Level is ERROR (invalid_me:core).
> Resolving . . .
> Skill unlocked: Curse Breaking.
> Your current Skill Level is 0.

Slowly, normal feeling returned to my limbs as my HP climbed toward its max. The bones in my shoulder stabbed and sliced my already-tender tissues as they came together again, and I longed for the days of being unconscious for that part. However, I wouldn't let myself slip into sleep. There was too much to do.

I kept my mana moving, healing. I didn't think I needed to anymore, but it felt right. My climbing HP value agreed.

By the time I was near max HP, I was feeling energized. More so, I was feeling pissed. Increasingly pissed as time went on.

Kolash had tried to kill me. Worse, he had tried to kill me in front of my friends. He'd hurt me, and he'd hurt them in turn. What were they all thinking right now? Were they mourning me? They had to be thinking the worst. I heard the pain and fear in their voices when I was dying. Kolash had done that.

I opened my eyes and rose, slowly, from the ground, muscles flexing as they remembered their purpose. I was aware now of how my mana flowed in my channels and how my heart was humming again.

Kolash, we need to talk.

A finger-sized yellow crystal fell to the stone floor with an angry clang.

Oh, yeah. My captured spell.

I didn't want it anywhere near me. I tossed it away, and it made satisfying clattering sounds as it tumbled a good distance.

Finally getting a look around, I realized I was somewhere else now: a different room. This one was dark and dirty. A little damp, too. The ground under me was stone, slightly wet with condensation that pooled in the grouting. Wooden pillars jutted up from the floor and held up thick, cobwebbed joists that supported the flat ceiling. A basement, maybe? The area around me was littered with odds and ends. Leather pouches, bowls, cups, stained cloths, a tiny mortar and pestle. Pungent smoke slithered up from a stick of some kind of incense.

I needed to find my party, get them out, tell them everything, save the world. What about Kolash though? Kolash was—

Someone cleared their throat.

I whirled around to see . . . no one. Wait. *There.*

There among the shadows in the corner of the room, a figure picked his nails with a tiny knife. A quick pulse with Detect Steel revealed lots and lots of otherwise hidden blades like little constellations of stars.

"I know that look, Monk," Bole rasped in the dark. The knife danced across his knuckles before disappearing into his sleeve. "And it warms my black heart to see it there. Who do we kill first?"

CHAPTER SIX

Break the Machine

Bole grinned, showing off those stupidly perfect teeth. "You're part of a big club now, Monk. The Church has decided that you should be ground up to grease their wheels. How does that make you feel?" His words oozed smug satisfaction. He was reveling in the pious monk being brought low.

I decided against punching him. Not because I agreed with him. The fleeting desire to hurt him came from Bole just being Bole. He wanted me to feel betrayed by the Church, maybe spur me on to take revenge. I'd thought about it, angry as I was, but I just couldn't get there. Despite what Bole mistakenly believed, I had never been a part of their faith. I was a big dumb fraud, and that was insulating me from whatever feelings of betrayal a real Rising Sun might have in this situation. Hell, Kolash wasn't even on the top hundred list of things that had tried to kill me on this planet. He did get a prize for coming close, though.

Taking a deep breath in order to allow me to reply with something pithy just resulted in my coughing up some kind of bitter, pasty substance into my hand. Wincing, I rubbed it between my fingers. It looked gray in the half-light of the basement, and I could see little bits of leaves or plant fiber in there. I spent the next minute spitting the rest out onto the floor.

"*Blech.* Guess I was the first to fall asleep at this party," I said, sticking a finger in my mouth to dredge up the rest of the debris. "Waking up with weird things in my mouth is probably the tamest thing I could have hoped for. To answer your question: I'm feeling pretty good, all things considered."

Someone shouted outside. The walls muffled the noise enough to the point where I couldn't pick out individual words, but they sounded insistent.

Bole spared a look for the ceiling above our heads but went right back to playing with his knives. "Don't worry about them. They've been blustering outside since the goblins brought you in here, but they don't have the muscle to break in and defend the walls at the same time. The mighty Church of Light have been reduced to diplomacy. Heh."

With some effort, I got on my feet and stretched myself. My entire body felt like it had been through a blender, especially in the shoulder.

I looked around and tried to get my brain back in gear.

Basement. Pouches, herbs, incense, bandages. People outside that want in. Bole.

Bole didn't fit into this picture.

"I didn't figure you for the healer type, Bole," I probed.

He sneered as he rolled the knife across his knuckles. I wasn't really playing into his revenge fantasy right now, and he didn't seem to like it. "I would like to reiterate that you don't know me, Monk," he replied, then spat on the floor.

I arched a disbelieving eyebrow at him, holding the stare until he gave up. He rolled his eyes contemptuously.

"Alright. Alright. I'm not a healer," he admitted. "The goblin queen brought you back."

He snatched his knife out of the air and gripped it tightly as he pointed its end my way. "I swear, Monk, if I had half the luck you have with women, I'd move to Manse and sire my own army."

The comment hit me like a punch. I blinked, trying to grapple with pretty much every part of that sentence. "Hold on now. What do you mean my luck? Goblin queen? Why would she help me?" I let the whole comment about Manse and armies be. There were some things I really didn't need to know about Ralqir. I was just content with saving it.

Since when did the goblins have royalty, though? They were a tribal people, and the highest station I'd ever encountered was a chief.

"Fuck if I know. She must have just liked your face. Like, really liked it, because they were about to throw you on the pyre when she happened by and lost her mind. Her guards held the Church lackies at spearpoint, wouldn't let 'em touch you."

"And this is all her stuff?" I asked, gesturing to the scattered healer's items. "I assume that the voices outside are the Church guards asking about me."

"Demanding your body, yeah. Everyone gets burned. Amazing just how fast the Church throws away its tenets, eh? No last rites for you."

"So, they're assuming I'm dead."

Bole nodded and licked his lips. "Makes plotting your revenge a bit easier, doesn't it? What would you say is a proportional response to what they did to you, Monk? I was thinking a direct approach, but, then again, we could just leave them to their fates, too. A bit poetic on that one."

I gave him a look that I hoped communicated just how disinterested I was in what he thought was a proportional response. "I'm less worried about revenge than what they've done with our people."

"Fuck 'em," Bole spat a bit more forcefully than I'd expected. The prodding, playful tone in his voice was gone, replaced by something dark and cynical. "They'll get their minds right soon enough, probably quicker when they're convinced you're dead. They'll be taking orders like good little children by sunrise. It'll be like you never existed."

Of all the things the man had said, that got the most response out of me. My anger bubbled up from inside—hot, explosive. The world turned red for a microsecond, but that was enough to loosen my tenuous grip on my mana, and the flowing streams of blue inside of me came apart. I tried to recover, but I just wasn't in the right mind for it. My aura bloomed to full strength again, exploding out from me and announcing my presence to every practitioner in the city.

Bole's knife clattered to the ground, bouncing end over end across the floor. He cursed, producing another within a heartbeat.

Well, damn. So much for doing this quietly. Kolash would know I survived.

The desire I was feeling to go kick in Kolash's door and hash this out right now wasn't a good sign. It meant that, on some level, I found Bole's predictions believable, and I hated that. My fear of being discarded and forgotten wasn't a rational one, but that didn't stop it from hijacking my entire thought process.

It was too plausible, especially to a kid who had spent the last seven years as the clan pariah.

Break the machine.

My cover, despite Jassin's intentions, had become a part of that machine. Time for it to go. It had become a weight that was holding me back more than helping anyone.

Decision made, I turned on my heel and made for the stairs, not sparing another thought for Bole.

"Hey! Monk! Where are you going?" Bole called from behind me. I could hear him scrambling to his feet, knives being slipped into sheaths.

I stomped up the wooden stairs, probing my Spatial Storage to take inventory. I had my sword, some stones, a bunch of turret parts, assorted ammo, scrap wood, a bit of metal, an exploding broken blade, and a bunch of odds and ends that were more useful in a workshop than here. It would have to do.

The door at the top of the stairs was unsurprisingly gone, probably part of the barricade outside now. I came out of the basement and rounded a corner to enter a large, open area, long and narrow with a low ceiling and regularly spaced windows. It gave off the vibe of a barracks, minus the beds and footlockers.

In place of whatever furniture had been here before were goblins. Lots and lots of goblins. Goblins were stacked like folded laundry, some sleeping, some in little circles talking among their immediate neighbors, and still others were . . .

I looked away from those. What an interesting and open society goblins had. Not at all weird. At least they were under blankets.

My heavy, human footsteps trumpeted my presence to the room as effectively as someone announcing me by name, and, one by one, every green face turned my way. Even the goblins under the blankets. At least they had the courtesy of stopping what they were doing. Not sure how I would have handled it otherwise.

I cleared my throat uncomfortably. The wind had really left my sails fast, probably a sign of a weakness of character, but if I didn't go through with this now, I was never going to do it.

"Can anyone tell me where my friends are?" I asked.

The goblins looked at one another, exchanging unsure glances.

"The people I came here with," I clarified. "Two dragonkin, a Leori, and a vulpa."

Recognition blossomed in more than one green face. That sparked a flurry of activity. Goblins jumped up from their sleeping piles to put on clothes. Others grabbed spears from the floor and slipped on weird, hodgepodge armor made out of rope-bound wooden planks. Soon, I had an armed entourage.

Bole came up behind me, using his hand to cover his nose. "You'd think you'd get used to it eventually, but you don't. I'd take musty basement over this," he said.

I shrugged. He'd probably get used to the smell too if he'd lived with goblins as closely as I had.

The leader of my new group—a balding, older goblin with a scar over his eye—stood up as straight as he could, craning his neck to look me in the eyes. "The cells. We're escort," he said, tone flat.

"Thanks. Uh, what is your name?" I asked.

"Paula of the White Beaks," he replied, puffing out his chest.

"Paula?"

"Yes. Paula."

I nodded. Just one more thing for the "I'm far from home" list. "Thanks, Paula of the White Beaks. Are you sure you want to, uh, escort me? I can probably find it on my own, and then you guys wouldn't have to get caught up in my trouble."

"We're sure. You're goblin, and we all stand together."

"I am?" I wanted to add a "You do?" to that, too, but I decided against it. Goblins were contentious little guys, all too ready to screw over their fellow goblins if that meant an advantage for their own clan. At least that's the impression I got from Chief Kuul and then from Jassin when we'd talked about it.

"Yes," was all the answer I got.

"Any Stone Hearts among you?"

"Yes."

"Where?"

"Outside." He really wasn't giving me much to go on. I'd get answers to my questions faster if I just went with it.

"Okay. Uh. Lead the way then, Paula."

Then we were moving to the far end of the building and out into the night. Immediately outside, there was another loose group of five goblins, but they were facing off against a very annoyed-looking Miur and his two buddies. No one had drawn their weapons, though the goblins had no way to sheathe their spears . . . Familiar-looking spears. I did a double take. The armor they wore was familiar, too. Iron, bulky, and loud, an amateur attempt at Shaping that, now that I took it all in, could probably be improved in a bunch of tiny ways.

In the middle of the two armed groups was—

"Holy, shit. Tiba?" The astonished words burst forth from my mouth, loud and clear without consideration for my situation. Everyone within earshot turned my way.

The Church guards reached for their swords, the goblins leveled their spears at the guards, and my gaggle of escorts rushed over to surround everyone involved. Tiba turned into a green streak. She squeaked a sort of girly goblin yowl like a cross between an angry cat and a bird call, and she was hugging me in short order, my bottom half at least. She was short.

"Ryan!" She squealed. "You return to us! You're a goblin now, by the way. Hunty would be proud!"

I tentatively reached down and returned the hug as best I could, mostly making contact with her shoulders.

"Uh. Thanks, Tiba. I—Wow. What is all this?" I asked with a general flourish of my arms that I hoped encompassed everything. What was going on?

Tiba pulled away and stood, back straight, chin raised proudly. She looked different. She wore her hair down now, long enough to flow down her back, her posture was straighter, stronger, and in her hand she held Hunty's spear like it was an old friend. It had acquired a bundle of bright feathers that bristled out from behind the head since I'd last seen it, along with a few notches in the shaft.

I tilted my head.

Was Tiba taller too?

On top of all that, there was something my brain purposefully avoided processing until absolutely necessary. Tiba was what I would describe as "underdressed." Her outfit was all strings and rough, thin strips of recycled linen that had to have had the toughest job in the camp just trying to preserve her modesty.

"He lives, and he speaks their tongue," the leading guard said, immediately earning him the mental label of Captain Obvious. I didn't actually know his rank, but he was a captain now as far as I was concerned. "Send word to His Holiness immediately," Captain Obvious ordered the Miur behind him.

"No need, Captain," I said. "He already knows."

"It's, uh, lieutenant, actually, sir. I have orders, though. We were assigned to dispose of your body, but . . ." He trailed off, not quite sure how to handle the new development. "Would you be willing to come with us, and we'll get this cleared up? You're obviously not infected."

"No, I don't think so," I said flatly. "Tiba, was it you who healed me?"

She beamed up at me. "I keep you alive. You are strong, though. I barely have to help."

"Sir. Rising Sun. I really must insist." Lieutenant Obvious took a step forward, but the Stone Heart warriors put a stop to that quickly with the tips of their spears. They didn't draw any blood, but the Miur was good and stopped with the pokey bits in uncomfortable places.

"Thanks, Tiba. You saved me again. I won't forget it."

"Sir, could you tell the queen we mean no harm to her people or yourself?" Lieutenant Obvious asked. His hands were raised now, his sword held in a loose grip by two fingers, and his underlings were following his example.

I smirked at Tiba. "He's calling you a queen."

"He is?" Tiba's eyes went wide.

"Yeah. Queen Tiba. I'm guessing the linen bikini is part of your royal attire, then."

Tiba blushed slightly but didn't seem all that bothered by it.

"There's a story there, I bet," I added with a raised brow.

Tiba grinned in a way that showed off all her canines. "I don't know what a bikini is, but the title of chief of the Stone Hearts comes to me. Then, when the Baned come, the rest of the tribes look to me for answers, too. The 'chief' title grew big. Way big! Me too! Do you see?" She looked down at herself and reached down to adjust her outfit to make sure it covered as much as possible. "And warriors need help sometimes to remember to fight hard."

She shrugged.

If it worked, it worked, I guessed. Guys really were that simple sometimes.

"Should I tell him?" I asked, gesturing toward the lieutenant with my head.

"No!" she squeaked, holding out a hand to forestall anything else. "No—ah— if he wants to call me a queen, I—Well, he can if he wants to." Another blush.

"Your secret is safe with me," I said, putting my finger up to my lips.

The pair of guards assigned to the cells didn't really know what to make of it.

A boisterous gaggle of goblins boiled around the corner of the barracks and approached the doorway to the building. In their midst, a lone human who had just come back from the dead, walking up to them like they ruled the place.

As far as the goblins were concerned, Tiba really did own the place. When she barked her orders (which was both shrill and intimidating at the same time, even to me) they hopped to it without question. The Stone Hearts with Kotes' brand armor never left her side and never let anything that wasn't a certain shade of green anywhere near their chief, except for me. The other goblins took their jobs seriously as well, mean-mugging the guards, the open windows, and the darkness in general. They didn't seem to believe they were doing their jobs unless they were mean-mugging something.

"I need some privacy," I told Tiba. Then, I turned to try and convince Bole to wait outside, too, but he was nowhere to be found . . . again. Did I leave him back where we detained the other guards?

"Okay, Ryan," Tiba chirped happily. "Boys!" she shrieked. My ears rang at the sheer pitch of her voice, not to mention the volume.

Holy hell.

The goblins fanned out, not-so-gently ushering the Church guards away from the doorway. No one got hurt during the change of the guard, but let's just say they knew they were being changed. The guards seemed unwilling to draw on any of the goblins, which I was thankful for. They'd all been fighting side by side for weeks now, after all. The Church folks just looked confused.

I smiled at them as I passed in a way that I hoped was interpreted as friendly.

The building itself was small, maybe the size of a single-family hab back home. Most of it was taken up by stone cells finished with iron bars and a walkway on the right side that allowed you to patrol down the entire length of the building and check on all the prisoners.

I stepped over a discolored spot on the floor that I bet used to contain a desk. All that was left of that little area was a corkboard inlaid into the wall and an empty rack of key hooks.

The interior was dark, but moonlight streamed in from high-set windows all along the top of the walls. The shadows cast by the windows were deep, however. It was hard to see anything other than the shining pale beams and what they fell upon.

It sure was quiet here. Nothing moved, not even the wind. I'd expected to come in and hear snoring or yelling or fighting, but the place was as silent as a tomb.

Tentatively, I took a heavy step, driving my heel into the dusty floor. The sound it made felt wrong, like my ears were under pressure and had yet to pop.

I narrowed my eyes.

Interesting.

I switched on Detect Iron and scanned the place again, not having to use my eyes. Three cells with iron bars that went three or so feet into the ground. Bars on the windows. Four figures in the last cell of the row. Two were pressed up against the bars: the largest one—Geddon, I assumed—and one of the sisters. Trix was in the corner, trying to scrabble up what had to have been the wall.

Lots of motion from that cell. I couldn't hear anything, but from the way their chests were expanding and how rapidly their blood was rushing through their circulatory systems, they seemed to be shouting.

There was another figure in the cell adjacent to my friends. It was large—round in the middle but thick in the shoulders and arms, as well—and it carried something in its left hand. Meanwhile, the right one was raised just above shoulder height, its three fingers at an unnatural angle (for a human hand, at least).

Kolash.

With the realization that something was wrong here, I felt my perspective change slightly, and I could suddenly observe the scene from the outside. I felt it then, the thickness in the air.

I let my eyes un-focus and focused on the motes of my aura and how they moved. It was all wrong. They were there but being shaken, brushed by something invisible. There was magic in the air.

Well, I guessed I invited something like this when I let my aura do its thing. It was an accident, but I'd hoped Kolash would sense me and either seek me out or make some other kind of move than his current one, which was apparently to wait in ambush next to the rest of my party.

But that told me something, didn't it?

I had been preoccupied at the time trying not to die, but he'd told Sissa that he was purging the infection from my body. *Purging it.*

No one had survived the process so far, but if I was strong, maybe I'd be okay. If he was openly hostile to me now, despite having survived his purge, then I had to assume he did not want me to survive.

He knew what I was.

It was the only explanation. You wouldn't kill an elite fighter like a Rising Sun on a whim. You'd rejoice that he had shaken off the evil plague and welcome him back or maybe examine him again.

Assuming he knew I was a human, his lie about trying to cure my infection made sense. Waiting in ambush made sense too.

Why hadn't I ever researched non-lethal ammunition?

Carefully, I began my slow, methodical walk forward to the end of the room. I kept it casual, a slow stroll in the moonlight, without a care in the world. I forced myself to seem relaxed, look straight ahead. I was just here to rescue my friends. Nothing at all suspicious here. I didn't get any levels in Stealth or Deception, though, which wasn't a great sign.

Man, was I bad at this sort of thing.

Kolash didn't reveal himself as I went past. In my mind's eye I saw him tense when he saw me. I could perceive that much with Detect Iron, but, apparently, he was waiting until I was good and distracted before he made his move. Curious, I let my eyes glance his way, but there was just an empty cell, all bricks and moonlight. The big guy could hide if he put his mind to it, or maybe it was part of his magic.

Then the third cell came into view, and it nearly made me forget about Kolash, despite him being my most immediate concern.

Samila was there at the bars, both hands gripping them tightly, and screaming at the top of her lungs. Again, silently. No sound reached my ears. Geddon was halfway up the bars, arms gripping the top and legs braced against the bottom, flexing to try and dislodge the barrier. Sissa leaned on the wall behind them, eyes scanning the floor in thought.

When they saw me round the corner, they didn't look relieved. They looked horrified.

The air was sludge, so thick it messed with my inner ear, making the room swim.

Samila silently screamed my name and shook the bars. I caught her eye, and she said something that seemed to have been urgent, but it was useless. I held up my good hand in a gesture I hoped was calming, then I gave her a wink.

I jerked my metal hand up to eye level, the fingers curled into claws, and caught the bishop's outstretched hand before it could make contact with my body. My fingers wrapped around the giant frog's wrist and dug into the complex, essential bones in the joint.

Iron Grip [0.1 MP/sec]

turned to look the bishop dead in the eyes, giving my head a tiny shake. His mouth dropped open in shock.

Kolash now firmly in hand, I wrenched my body at the waist, took a step to my right, and flung the hulking frog bishop off his feet and over my outstretched leg to come crashing down to the ground. I felt more than heard the impact of Kolash's mass smacking into the stone floor through my boots.

My other hand snaked out, caught Kolash around the throat, and squeezed. Suddenly, Kolash's vocal cords weren't working like they needed to.

RRRRRRMMMMGGHHGGGPHLMP!

The room brightened significantly. Glowing bulbs I hadn't seen before sputtered to life, bathing the room in white light. The world exhaled, and the air began to move. Suddenly, the tiny building echoed with shouts and cries—muffled struggles.

Below me, Kolash sputtered, struggling to bring his other hand up to my face. He was much bigger than I was, his arms longer, but the 40 Body I was rocking after my drastic jump in Levels more than compensated for that.

Plus, I was heavy. I put a knee to his chest and tried to get my foot around to stomp on the upper part of his arm, but his hand got to me first. Golden light coalesced around the bishop's fingers, and his sticky palm wrapped around my forearm.

"Stop! What are you doing?" Sissa's voice came from the cell. I couldn't tell which one of us was the target of the question.

Kolash croaked something I couldn't understand. The System didn't translate, so maybe it was unintelligible due to the choking or—

A look of victory fell over the bishop's face.

No. Not this time.

With a crack, I broke Kolash's wrist, freeing up my prosthetic. The bishop, had he free use of his vocal cords, would have yelled or screamed, but it came out in a series of choked gurgling sounds instead.

Meanwhile, the golden light seeped from Kolash's hand into my arm, the sensation subtle but all too familiar. This was the more pleasant part of the curse's application, but the fangs would be out soon enough.

I reached over with my now-free prosthetic and made with the curse-breaking.

> Devouring Grasp (Magivore) [5 MP/sec]
> Create reservoir? Y/N
> Reservoir created: Purge Unclean [Total value: 210 MP (light)]
> Previous reservoir destroyed.

Our bones broke together: his hand, my arm. Good thing it was just the spell being consumed, or this would have been a lot more gruesome. This time, Kolash did get to scream.

That was okay, though.

The little yellow crystal that contained Kolash's spell materialized about an inch from my chest, a perfect sphere of yellow at first that then formed sharp edges and shining faces like a gem until it grew to the size of an apple. It hovered there for about half a second, then tumbled down to bounce off the bishop's forehead.

BINK!

My arm felt like it was on fire. Blood rushed to the injury and pooled there. Already, I could feel the tissues swelling around the break in the bones and the Damage the spell had done on its way out.

I looked into Kolash's eyes and put my full weight on his chest through my knee. "Not this time." I ground my teeth around the words.

"You do not belong here. You have killed us all," Kolash croaked, shakily reaching up to rub his throat with his hands, but they were useless wrecks.

"Brother Ryan! You're alive!" Trix yipped. He was up against the bars now, hanging from them like he'd been climbing them.

"He is no brother of yours," Kolash burbled. "He is a thing from beyond, hiding among us." His eyes were wide, darting around the room, manic. There was madness there, along with the pain he was experiencing. "I should have seen it! I should have seen it before!" he cried.

"Bishop, I am not here to hurt anyone," I said as calmly as I could. The pain and adrenaline weren't helping with that.

Kolash didn't hear me. His stare was beyond me, his wide-set eyes focused on something far, far away. "I should have seen it before all of this," he replied very quietly. Aching guilt seeped from his words. "I should have seen it. I should have seen it before. You. The thing inside of them. I should have—"

So, he blamed me for the plague. He blamed me for everything. He blamed himself, too.

I shut my eyes and summoned my calm.

What a mess we'd caused, us humans. Not purposefully, but that didn't matter.

I'd blame us, too, if I were Kolash. Who else was alive to blame? The Dark Lord was long gone, along with the civilization that produced him, his pet human was an ax hanging above the head of every living thing on the planet, and the gods had all gone to sleep.

Now the rotten fruit of that pestilent tree was good and ripe, and there was no villain left to rally against. We were all tiny pieces in a game set up and abandoned a long, long time ago.

Sighing, I reached over and snagged the glowing hand the bishop had just been about to place on my calf.

The curse fizzled harmlessly without my having to Consume it.

Thanks, Detect Iron.

I bottled up my anger and indignation at having been tried and convicted of something out of my control and then sentenced to death on the spot, a sentence the bishop kept trying to carry out.

These emotions weren't going to help me right now.

I opened my eyes and looked down at Kolash to see him renewed, determined. Even though his limbs were broken and he was on his back, he was still trying to kill me.

"You know what I am, yes?" I asked him. "*Precisely* what I am?"

His eyes narrowed, and his lips curled back to bare pink gums, entirely lacking teeth. "Yes," he gurgled.

"Good. You don't need to be awake for this part, then."

I hauled back and punched him in the face. My metal fist *clanged* off his jaw, and his head lolled to the side. His eyes blinked rapidly as he fought unconsciousness.

Ah. Damnit, that would have been much cooler . . . and more humane . . . if it would have worked on the first try.

The bishop was a big dude. Big dudes needed more than one punch, I guessed. The second time worked like a charm.

Slowly, I stood up from Kolash's chest and let his ruined arm fall to the ground.

Bishop Kolash Mro'ahn defeated.

You have been awarded 10 Experience points. [50 capped for non-lethal, -40 non-combat Class]

Out of breath, despite the encounter only lasting about a minute, I had to collect myself for a handful of seconds. Then I turned to my friends, who all had expressions ranging from horrified to . . . whatever one Samila had on. I was terrible with girls.

Rolling my shoulders, I bent down and grabbed Kolash by one of his feet. He was heavy but not terribly so. Honestly, I was still coming to grips with having so many points in Body now. My scale was all out of whack.

"Trix," I grunted, "do you mind? I want to make sure I didn't hurt him too badly."

Trix hesitantly reached out from the gap in the bars and pushed aside Kolash's robe to touch the flesh of his ankle.

"He'll be okay, in time," Trix announced after a handful of seconds. "I don't understand, Brother Ryan. What is going on? Why?"

I just needed to do it. Rip the bandage off. Do it now or it would never get done.

"So, I've been meaning to have this talk with you for a while now," I began.

CHAPTER SEVEN

Show Some Humanity

I'm human."

There it was, out there for all to see. I said the thing I'd been dreading to reveal for the majority of my time on Ralqir. The knowledge was radioactive. It damaged everyone it touched, and they might not even feel the effects of that damage until much later, when I was long gone.

At least that was the situation according to Jassin. I'd been willing to go along with that interpretation too, all the way up to the point of my secrecy becoming an integral part of the trap I was in. How was I going to help these people if I had to hide from them? Those were two very difficult things to have on my plate, made even more impossible by them being opposing forces. I was convinced now, that I couldn't do both. Either my secret was going to indirectly get someone else or me killed, and I had way too much shit to do to entertain the idea of being dead.

My revelation hung in the air like the ringing of a bell that couldn't be unrung.

Everyone in the cell blinked, looked at each other, and turned back to face me, each in their own time.

Geddon gave voice to the collective sentiment.

"Wow. Uh. Is it . . . treatable?" he asked, reaching up to give the top part of his mane a scratch.

I could feel the corners of my mouth turning down, losing their fight with Ralqir's gravity. My disappointment was immeasurable.

Right. The word "human" wasn't known to any but the privileged few, probably people with direct access to the Dark Lord's notes.

"Uh. Okay," I began again. I'd need to do this carefully. "I'm from another world."

I stopped, checking for any signs of understanding from the rest of the group. I didn't get as much as I wanted, especially from Geddon, but they were at least all paying attention. Everyone was up against the bars now, hands resting on the metal. Trix was the hardest to read. He was looking down at the bishop, ears drooped, hair bristling.

"I'm from another world that's not like this one. Another universe, in fact. Where I come from, a very select few people are Exotics—uh, practitioners—and they are either born to other practitioners or chosen at random . . . or at least in a way that we can only guess is random. That's not important, I guess. Sorry. Back home, I was no one. I was a crippled kid from a shitty rock at the ass-end of space. I'd carved out a sort of niche in my community as the guy who could fix things. I was good at that, and they were okay with me doing that, as long as I stayed out of sight. Then, for no reason other than pure, stupid cosmically impossible luck, the System chose me and sent me here. Don't get me wrong. I'm not complaining. I was being impaled at the time, so anywhere would have been better than right there. I'd just seen my only friend in the world murdered, and I was about to join him, and then the cosmos were like, 'Hey, kid, here's a whole new life!'"

I pointed at the back wall of the building that I hoped was to the south.

"My new life started somewhere over that way, in the middle of a forest where the first living being I saw tried to eat me. Since then, I've been hunted, enslaved, eaten, blown up, immolated, disemboweled, and—most recently—cursed. Worse, though, is that I'm pretty sure I played some kind of role in the current apocalyptic conditions we're living through, and I have no idea just how large my share of the blame is."

They were all looking at me now in that way I had feared they would: like I was a stranger. I didn't blame them. I *was* a stranger. It didn't make things easier, though.

I sighed and let my eyes drift down to the floor.

"I've been telling the truth. I really do want to help. I started small, just . . . trying to save who I could, but that was in the short term. I have no idea what to do to keep the rest of the planet from becoming like this place. Deep down, I think I'm still that guy who's good at fixing things, but I'm way out of my depth here."

"You're the Fulcrum," Trix said, awestruck. "The Harbinger of Change."

I did a non-committal wobble of my head. "I'm *a* fulcrum, I guess, though I contend that I am a person, not a thing. I don't want to act as a fulcrum. The last one that came here didn't do you guys any favors, and he's not looking so good nowadays, anyway."

Trix's use of the term sparked recognition in everyone else's eyes. The sisters' demeanors changed the most, from trepid curiosity to stunned realization with a healthy bit of fear. I could see them putting the pieces together in real time.

Sissa spoke first. "Assuming this is all true, you know nothing, do you? About our world."

I shook my head. "Not much. I picked up what I could from the people I met."

"I should have known. I'd say something, and you'd get that look in your eye like I'd just given you a precious gift or asked you to do Miur calculus. The whole time . . . Light and gods of old, we thought you'd just never left the monastery . . . Wait! How did you know to impersonate a Rising Sun?"

"That was kind of foisted upon me," I answered with a shrug. "I was hairless at the time, so I guess it made sense."

"No, it doesn't," Sissa sputtered. "There's a whole—You have to—Ugh. The whole godsdamn time?"

"Yeah," I sighed.

"He did seem very talky, in hindsight," Geddon observed.

"I'm not very good at lying," I replied. I'd been getting by on being vague, the immediacy of our circumstances, and probably a nudge or two from my Gray Man Skill, but I really didn't want to open that can of worms. I'd already lied to these people. Best not to spring knowledge of mind-altering magic shenanigans I had no control of onto them just yet.

"I couldn't just come out with the truth, though. If this . . ." I gestured down to the unconscious bishop on the floor. "If this had happened the first day I'd shown up on Ralqir, I'd simply be dead, and I'm pretty sure, at that point, all of this would have happened anyway, given time."

Sissa put her hand to the side of her head and stared into the middle distance as she thought. "From a strategic perspective, you . . . probably made the right call. I could think of two—no, three—different groups of people who would have wanted to use you. Oh. The dragons. Some of the dragons would definitely be tempted to reverse the Purge. Wait. The wretch down in the tunnels—it knew, didn't it?"

"That's the impression I got," I replied with a nod. "It knew a lot. Too much."

"So you killed it," Trix said. The accusation hit me out of nowhere.

I blinked. "What? No. I killed it because it was going to eat me and then the rest of you."

"Furball, don't," Samila warned the vulpa.

"No!" Trix shouted. The anger in his tone shook the air and left the others silent. "No . . . Brother—No. Just Ryan, I guess. Ryan has been lying to us since the beginning, and I believe that his slaying of the only other being that knew his secret is a valid subject to question. I know not everyone spends all their time in the sanctuary like I have, but you should all have at least some understanding of how dangerous the Fulcrum is. There is a reason they are represented as the tip of the triangle, at the intersection of light and dark. He indulges in both aspects. He hides when he must, kills when he must . . . ." Trix stuck out an accusatory paw to draw everyone's attention to the unconscious bishop. " . . .brutalizes when he must. This I could forgive of an animal attempting to survive far from home, but he is not an animal. Upon first contact with our civilization, his first instinct was to lie. What we see all around us right now, that is the cost of those lies."

"I—" I began but stopped myself. Would defending myself accomplish anything right now?

Yes, I had lied to them all, but it was with sound reasoning at the time, given what I knew. I didn't realize the Scourge-Touched were already in Eclipse nor that they were after me specifically nor that my presence would be such a big damn deal to everyone.

Did my ignorance actually matter, though? What happened happened, whether I intended it to or not. Would someone buried under a landslide care if the person further up the mountain had meant to trigger it or not?

Trix shook his head mournfully and looked down to the floor. "Brother— Dammit. Ryan, the night we met, do you remember?"

I nodded, thinking back to Kolash escorting me through the streets and into their sanctuary. The altars. The glass. Trix and his sandwiches.

"Yeah," I replied.

"Vulpa do not have the best of reputations," Trix lamented. "Did you know that? Of course not. That's obvious now. We, as a people, are known as deceivers and cheats. We lie, we steal. It is our way of life. If you are taken in, it is commonly accepted that you trusted too easily and somehow deserved it. Our magic is the same way. It is mist and shadow. The illusion of power. It has no substance to speak of, nothing that survives a light brush with truth anyway. We are all like this, or, at least, the vast majority."

He was shrinking before my eyes, like a balloon losing air. I wanted to reach out.

He continued. "So, when you came into the sanctuary that night and trusted me to share in your voice . . . it was a minor miracle to me. Instant trust from an accomplished warrior. What a joyful gift, a reward for living my life without guile! The very next day you had me watch your back in *combat*. Me! You trusted *me*! Then you gave me the means to fight. It was horrible, bloody, beautiful stuff, and it . . . was . . . *real*. You made me believe I belonged here, among heroes doing something that mattered."

He took a deep, shuddering breath, finally lifting his head with what looked like monumental effort to look me in the eye.

"And it was all because you didn't know any better."

That was it. He said no more. Neither did I.

Everyone stood silent and watched Trix weep. It was a quiet thing, no theatrics or wailing, just soul-crushing sadness eating someone from the inside.

Eventually Samila reached tentatively down to put a hand on Trix's shoulder, but he shrank away, getting down on all fours and scrabbling into the darker parts of the cell before curling up in the back right corner.

* * *

I shut off Detect Iron out of respect for his privacy. Of all the things I could give him right now, that was probably what he wanted the most.

Then the spell was broken by the bishop letting out a long, wet snore at my feet.

I squeezed my eyes shut and tilted my head back in hopes a new angle could rattle loose the right thing to say. I came up with nothing.

Instead, I figured it was time for action rather than talk.

I patted down Kolash and came up with the keys.

Finally, as the cell door swung open, there was nothing left to separate us. My friends all stood there, though, hesitant to—

Samila surged forward and nearly bowled me over, her arms around my back, her face buried in my chest.

"That all sounded very lonely," she said, looking up at me with those big, golden dragon eyes. They had stars for pupils. I'd never noticed that. "And I'm sorry about your friend. I'm sure he was wonderful."

I made a wordless noise that rushed out of my throat and got stuck somewhere near the back of my tongue. The room blurred until it was just blue and gold.

"Uh—" I turned my head, tried to take a step toward the door, to get away, shield them all from . . . I didn't know.

But Samila was holding on tight.

I reached up to push her away, but I didn't have it in me. The tension and stress I'd been holding for months flooded out of me in a rush, leaving me empty and weak, the muscles in my body no longer having the strength or will to carry on. I eventually stopped struggling. Someone else put a hand on my shoulder. I wasn't sure who.

Then, for the first time since I became an Exotic, I just let myself be human.

CHAPTER EIGHT

Take the Streets

B*RAP! BRAP!*

> *Scourge*-Touched Undead takes 18 Damage. (18 base) (Piercing)
> Scourge-Touched Undead is marked.
> Scourge-Touched Undead is cursed.
> Scourge-Touched Undead is bleeding.
> Scourge-Touched Undead takes 15 Damage. (14 base, + 1 Marked bonus)
> Scourge-Touched Undead defeated.
> You have been awarded 12 Experience points. [10 base (-6 Level, +2 nemesis, +10 group, +4 chain, -8 non-combat Class)]

I loved the smell of Volatility in the morning. It gave off a sort of tingly, ozone scent, with a dash of purple that really blended well with the sunrise.

I also loved the smooth efficiency of a machine that had been well-made and put to use in the right way. This was the good stuff.

The turret I'd just activated tracked and fired, cracking off short bursts of thunder in oddly spaced fits as it dealt with the many separate tracking angles and the complicated field of fire it was tasked with keeping clear. The time between volleys was longer in this iteration, the targeting program taking more time to hone in on things and take them down, but I'd designed them for economy over firepower this time. Gone (hopefully) were the days of a partially obscured monster wasting ten or twenty bullets of my turrets' magazines. Now the turrets dealt with the monsters out of cover first, then worked their way down from least-obscured to the most.

At this moment, the newly activated death machine didn't need to track very wide, the horizontal angle only about thirty degrees or so, but the alleyway it was facing down had lots of cover, such as drainpipes, balconies, gutters, and rubble, not to mention four stories of vertical space to keep clear.

BRRRRAP! BRRT! BRT!

Scourge-Touched, previously allowed to roam and slink around with impunity to pick over the remains of a city they'd decimated, found themselves and their closest friends suddenly very unwelcome in this part of town.

This was my alleyway now, so sayeth my meticulously crafted, magic-powered, automatic, boom stick.

My turrets tended to start high, I'd noticed. This one, like the others, was tracking up to a windowsill high above where a Scourge-Touched goblin was perched like a gargoyle, sniffing the air, quivering, twitching, and generally being creepy like they did when they didn't have a living being to chase down and kill immediately to hand.

A burst of automatic fire—three rounds in under a quarter of a second—took the creature in the temple in a glorious show of precision marksmanship. The monster's head rocked sideways and slammed forcefully into its right shoulder as the rounds drilled neat holes in its skull. The Scourge-Touched's body spasmed just once more before it tipped forward, arms shooting out in front of it like an old-timey pugilist as nonsense nerve signals were sent to its limbs from a brain that had just been forcefully rearranged.

As it fell three stories to the street, the Scourge-Touched's scalp flapped in the rushing wind to expose the collapsed remains of its skull until its body came to a full stop against the cobbles with a wet *slap.*

The turrets' aim was good before, but now it was uncanny. I'd dialed the power on the individual Volatility explosions down slightly with this latest iteration and shrunk the buffer spring, giving this model a sliver less of punch but far, far less recoil with every shot. The result was a marginally quieter, far-more-accurate machine that could put a grouping of three or four rounds in a circle about the size of a coin. I wouldn't trust them at extreme ranges, but that's not what I needed them for today. What I needed was lots of things dead at medium range, and I needed my machines to go the long haul, and leave them cool enough to grab and store when the time was right, as well.

I made a mental note. The slower, less-energetic projectiles didn't have the penetrating power of their previous iterations, but they did their job well on small fries such as this. I dared not go any lower on the power output, though. The last thing I wanted was to reduce lethality.

This was the sweet spot—enough to crack through bone and get to the vitals but not so much that it was overkill. In theory, it would delay the rate at which the action and barrels overheated, but I probably wouldn't get entirely past that problem unless I developed some kind of cooling system.

Yes. I was aware of exactly how my thought process sounded, cooly calculating just the right amount of oomph to put into a machine so that it could kill hundreds of (kind of) living beings with maximum efficiency. I got it. My conscience just couldn't seem to muster up a whole lot of sympathy for the

Scourge. Not anymore. When I did get a flare-up in the conscience department, all I had to do was look at the bloody streets and remember how full
with life they used to be. My sympathy generally sat down and shut up for a
while when I did that.

The Scourge-Touched killed for killing's sake, and I wasn't about to waste
emotional bandwidth on pondering if I was doing the right thing.

As they'd done with every avenue of approach I'd fortified so far, the Scourge-
Touched reacted to the sudden change in their circumstances with aggression.
Every face on the street turned my way, and they surged forward as one. They
howled and bared their teeth, just as they had on the other approaches I'd set up
today, but it wasn't the suicidal-rage mode they entered when they saw me without my disguise. Their special brand of hate was, apparently, for humans only,
and they could only get good and frothy if they *knew* their target was human.

The monsters came on as a coordinated group, the old and the new. Infected
beasts were a more-common sight out here near the outer walls apparently, and I
was just getting acquainted with dealing with them.

Goblins leaped from building outcroppings. Gangly, misshapen Undead
lurched over the filthy puddles and loose stones of the street. Blind, hissing
rodents that looked like they would be at home digging through soft soil and
munching on crops, scrabbled toward me, their metallic claws sparking off stone.

Some kind of gray-skinned, amorphous something tried to pull itself out of
the gutter half a block from my position, but it didn't get far enough into the
open for me to get a good picture of its full form. The turret was on it immediately. A dozen buzzing bullets ripped down the length of the monster's body in a
neat line until its wrinkled skin burst open and spilled black fluid onto the street
like a burst water balloon. After that, the rest of the corpse slipped back into the
sewers below.

That was a new one.

I pulled up the combat log to take a look.

Scourge-Touched Smothering Thrag takes 9 Damage. (16 base, -7 resist) (Piercing)
Scourge-Touched Smothering Thrag is marked.
Scourge-Touched Smothering Thrag is cursed.
Scourge-Touched Smothering Thrag takes 11 Damage. (16 base, -5 resist) (Piercing)
Scourge-Touched Smothering Thrag takes 17 Damage. (16 base, -2 resist, +3
Knife in the Dark) (Piercing)
Scourge-Touched Smothering Thrag takes 16 Damage. (16 base, -1 resist) (Piercing)
Critical Hit!
Scourge-Touched Smothering Thrag takes 32 Damage. (16 base, 16 bonus) (Piercing)
Critical Hit!
Scourge-Touched Smothering Thrag takes 35 Damage. (16 base, 16 bonus, +3
Knife in the Dark) (Piercing)

Critical Hit!
Scourge-Touched Smothering Thrag takes 32 Damage. (16 base, 16 bonus) (Piercing)

Not the first Resist text I'd seen, but despite the animal dying quickly, I didn't like to see it. It meant we were starting to pull wild cards from the deck and things were going to get progressively more interesting as more of Ralqir's wildlife was turned. The Smothering Thrag was emblematic of a shift in threat level. I probably should have seen this coming, since I'd nearly died at the hands of something called a joroba the last time I'd been outside the Spire.

"Sir, they're getting close. Shall I call for a volley?" Lieutenant Obvious asked nervously, mouth right next to my right ear so he wouldn't have to shout over the guns. The archers, guards, and goblins alike were set up behind us down below in the yard, prepped and ready, arrows nocked and awaiting the signal.

I shook my head, hoping the gesture translated well enough through the hood and the mask. This was a pretty narrow approach. The turret didn't have much area to cover—at least not as much as I'd seen them do on the other avenues. It should be fine, barring a legitimate swarm.

"I think they're getting it, Lieutenant! We're good!" I shouted, resisting the urge to give a thumbs-up (*stupid alien culture*) while trying to sound reassuring, but the volume I had to use probably diminished the calm I was trying to convey.

As he and I watched, the turret cut down dozens of monsters as they tried and failed to swarm our position. The narrow alley was near-perfect ground for the gun to dispense death. Any charge of sufficient numbers the Scourge pulled together was quickly decimated, the front rank getting a face full of lead, forcing their friends to jump over their corpses or take the time to dodge around them, but the turret's tracking was quick and exacting. Those that took to the air came down dead, and those that stayed on the ground were picked apart even as they dodged.

The climbing monsters were no better off. Their bodies rained down from above to splatter on the stones and stain them an unnatural black.

Just as they had on the other approaches, the Scourge's charge broke just as suddenly as it formed, and the disparate survivors scattered into the empty doorways and the interiors of the buildings or slipped into the storm drains and gutters.

Bodies of slain monsters littered the open ground—three here, ten there, a straggler or two in odd repose draped over rubble or debris in the middle of the street. The closest they'd gotten was maybe six feet from our barrier.

If they kept to their previous behavior pattern, the Scourge would keep their heads down now, at least for a while. They got way more timid after a showing like this.

As a general strategy, the Scourge seemed to be opportunistic by nature, content to nip at and harass scattered pockets of armed resistance over time as opposed to committing to a big stupid battle where they risked a lot to gain very little. It showed some kind of tactical or strategic thinking that I wasn't comfortable seeing from the murderous assholes.

Then again, maybe the swarm tactics were simply saved for special people such as myself. I resisted the urge to retie the catch on my mask. No need to call attention to it.

The camp was essentially approachable from five avenues, three of which—the ground-level ones—I had pretty much cleared of monsters now. There were two side alleys like the one I'd just taken care of and the main road that led straight away from the gate. Four turrets now stood sentry to cover all that ground.

The main road, blocked off by the big semicircle of piled-up crap—or "junk berm," as the goblins called it—was framed at the corners by two old stone-and-mortar buildings that had once been businesses that had served incoming traffic from the gate. The avenue itself was at least fifty yards wide here and roughly straight with only a few overturned carts and piles of rubble from collapsed buildings to get in the way of my turrets' lines of fire. Its size, though, warranted two separate guns to cover it all.

If it were me, I would have shrunk the junk berm a bit to give my guns a bit more room to fire without big old buildings giving the monsters cover and concealment to aid them in approaching the wall, but the survivors hadn't designed the defenses with me in mind. They were just trying to make it to the next day. I'd just have to make do with what we had and hope for the best.

The other two vulnerabilities in our setup were both due to the city wall. It was higher than any of the other buildings' roofs, and it was nearly impossible to prevent climbing monsters from finding their way up there and getting into the camp by jumping or scaling down. That was my next problem to tackle. Right now, it was being handled by a firing line of crossbows and a detachment of spear goblins who would finish off any living stragglers and retrieve all the bolts, but that wouldn't work during the upcoming evacuation. We'd need all those people down on street level.

Lieutenant Obvious and I slid down from the top of the berm to land in the yard again. Preparations for our escape were happening at a breakneck pace. People ran everywhere, carrying assorted things, piling them into crates, and stuffing them into packs. The mood was generally rushed but hopeful with some smiles even popping out here and there. Everyone was more than ready to get out of here and finally have real walls between them and the monsters, and I didn't blame them.

Tiba and her honor guard marched up as we got to our feet but didn't waste time with pleasantries. "The Tribes are ready soon, but things are uncertain," she announced with a hint of tiredness. Though her words were dutifully stoic for her followers, her expression held a hint of doubt. "Before, when we try to move, the Baned are everywhere. I feel like it happens again if we wait too long *or* move too soon."

I did a quick sweep around the yard, making note of all the angles, trying to picture a gaggle of people waiting to stream out of here and down the alley to safety. Once the barrier came down, there would be a bottleneck at the exit, followed by a run down the narrow street my party and I had used to get here. Then, even if we had someone there with the key to open the door to the tunnels instantaneously, we'd have to contend with an even-narrower bottleneck as every-one streamed into the underground, all while the enemy closed in for the kill.

The last people to get off the street would probably have a hell of a time.

That's why I was going to be one of them.

How the plan would hold up against a nearly instantaneous swarm, I didn't know. That would be the worst-case scenario, and I was increasingly worried that was exactly what we were in for.

If I were the one giving orders to a few hundred thousand ravenous monsters, I wouldn't waste numbers going after fortified positions like this one, especially considering said monsters didn't have to eat or drink like regular folks. No, I'd wait people out, starve them, and end them when they were vulnerable—such as, say, when they were making a desperate dash for safety.

"Yeah, they'll come at us hard. That's the feeling I get, at least," I admitted. I wasn't going to sugarcoat it for her. I respected Tiba too much. "I think they'll pounce when they sense we're vulnerable. The bright side is that we're not going far and we've brought lots of firepower."

"They surround us like hunting dogs," Tiba remembered. "You see it in the caves, and I see it again outside the walls."

"This time, we have a plan and a real place to go, and I'm not stuck in a cell." I tried to smile reassuringly at her. I was doing a lot of that lately: reassuring people.

"Your human magic is not much like the stories say," she said, sparing a glance for the turret over my shoulder. It came off like an apology, like she was sorry she'd gotten it wrong or the stories got it wrong. "That is probably good, because I don't see how sharper spears help us here. The stories speak of great things but nothing like what you do."

"I think my path has deviated somewhat from what it was supposed to be. Maybe that's for the best, though," I posited. I was probably only alive thanks to said deviation, so I wasn't about to complain. "What do the stories say, though?" I asked, curious.

She shrugged, her forehead wrinkling as she tried to remember and boil it down for the tourist. "Mastery over metal. Unbreakable armor. Swords that cut through whole trees. We trade for these things before the Dark Lord finds out, but the best things are lost or broken now."

I fought to pick my jaw up off the floor, blinking once, twice. "Hold on. You— *Goblins* traded with humans? Like . . . before me? Before the Dark Lord, even?"

Tiba's eyebrows knit together in confusion like I'd just made the most obvious observation there ever was. "Yes? The stories say word reaches to the tribes that a human is here, and many of us pick up our best things and come see, the smiths especially. They are always excited to meet new humans. This is before the Dark Lord and the Baned. One of our old ones can tell the stories better than me, though. They hear many times and are better at telling."

"Uh. Yeah. Just—Did the goblins live near the place where humans—" I searched for the right word to describe the insertion point, something that would be understandable from a goblin perspective. "—the *ruins* where humans would appear? Did you guys live near there?"

Tiba shrugged. "Different clans back then, so maybe. Doesn't matter. The Baned live there now. No one goes there anymore, except the very stupid and very brave."

"Yeah, I've been told I ride that line myself," I said absently. Tiba had just thrown me another piece of the puzzle. The Baned territory encompassed the tutorial facility. That was the reason they were the first living things I'd encountered on Ralqir. This meant . . . what? That they were spawn campers? They couldn't even talk. How did they know to stick around and wait for newbies to get tossed into a new universe when they could be out murdering to their dark hearts' desires?

Tiba didn't wait for me to think things through, though. She was concerned with the now. "I am still worried about moving, Ryan. We don't leave goblins behind to become Baned. *I* am not leaving goblins behind." She held her chin high, daring me to contradict her, and her eyes went hard as stone.

I nodded, not about to tell a queen how to take care of her people. "We'll make it happen. Lieutenant, you hear that? Oh. Sorry. Of course not. Uh—Queen Tiba is expressing concern for our dead if the worst is to happen. What can we do for her?"

The man stood up tall, shoulders back, and actually saluted the little goblin chief. The gesture went over her head, of course, short as she was. Hard to stand at attention and salute a woman who only came up to your navel.

"Assure Her Highness that no one will be left behind, dead or alive. Our crossbowmen will get one, maybe two shots off before they will be on crowd-control duty. They will be tasked with taking care of the wounded—goblins and tall folk alike."

I translated for Tiba and saw her visibly relax as I did. Her grip on her spear never loosened, though.

"That gives me some comfort," Tiba said. "Our dead burn or we risk them being taken."

"I've been meaning to ask about that," I said. The goblins knew more about the Baned and, by implication, the Scourge plague, than even all the healers and scholars still alive in the city. We'd have to sit down sometime and talk about what she knew about the Baned . . . About a lot of things, actually.

A short Miur and a team of goblins rushed past us, carrying a half dozen coils of thick rope between them. Together, they started tying the ends of the rope to different points of junk in the wall. The old goblin engineer—whose name was Flog, I'd learned—was among them, directing workers on where to pull and what to anchor to. Together, they'd be bringing the barrier down when it was time for our exodus.

Apparently, it had been designed to fail in this way, according to the ancient green man. Made of junk or not, he'd directed every piece of wood, every length of rope, every hinge that was placed upon the pile to make sure it was fit for this purpose. He knew where the keystones were and what it would take to bring it down.

"Goblins," he said, "always have a way out. We know it, or we make it."

On the other side of the bonfire, I spied Sissa, Samila, and Geddon as they knelt in a loose formation with another company of guards, listening to a briefing by the last remaining captain in the camp. Everyone, including them, would have their place in this operation, and the professional military people would have to pull a lot of weight and be ready to pick up more when things inevitably started to fall apart.

As if she sensed me looking, Samila turned her head slightly and met my eyes, and that little smirk of hers sprouted on her face as she shot me a semi-private wink. I returned the sentiment with a tiny wave, but that was the end of our momentary indulgence. She was right back to listening intently to what the captain had to say, and I had to get back to my part in all this.

I scanned the rest of the camp, running my eyes over all the motion, following the activity, checking down at shin level for what I wanted to find. Nothing.

No Trix.

There was that hollow, chilly feeling in my stomach again.

I hadn't seen him since last night in the cells. Kolash was similarly absent.

We—the Church guards and myself—had made the collective decision to not lock the bishop, up despite some good arguments otherwise. The arguments against restraining the big frog came down to a few inescapable facts. Firstly, we couldn't spare the people to carry him hogtied or unconscious when we evacuated the camp. Second, we needed him. He was the only healer in the city that we knew of, and it would save lives if we made nice. Third, no one was comfortable with keeping him a prisoner just because he was afraid for his people. Yes, he tried to kill me, but the aim of the act was to keep others safe.

I could respect that.

He'd just need to come around or stay out of my way.

Besides, I wasn't overly worried that the bishop would come at me with a curse or get his guards to kill me, either. No, he wanted my existence kept a secret, like Jassin. Why else would he curse me, then tell everyone else that it was an attempt to cure me?

Well, that was about to backfire on him if he was still interested in a fight. The fact that I'd survived the spell and wasn't a member of the shambling monster horde was public knowledge now, and the bishop would have a hard time explaining why he wanted one of his supposed elite fighters and only practitioners dead on the eve of battle.

No, he'd have to come at me in secret if he still wanted me dead, and he'd have to wait in line like everyone else.

Suddenly, the turrets on the main approach simultaneously came to life, letting loose a long, sustained stream of fire, drowning out all other sound. Everyone turned to look, all conversations put on hold. The guns hadn't done this since I'd first set them up, and not nearly for so long. They should at least have paused momentarily as they acquired new targets and reengaged.

It was over in under ten seconds, but the quiet afterward was equally deafening. It had a chilling effect on everyone in the camp. No one went back to what they were doing. They stared in silence at the guns.

Wow. That must have been a big group out there. Maybe the Scourge were massing for a charge after all.

I poked the part of my brain that seemed to keep track of things with Detect and, more recently, Marked things. Nothing.

Then it happened again. The guns spun up, this time in fits and starts, and then a big, grinding crescendo to finish. That was a lot of rounds spent.

Detect, again, showed nothing.

Wait, no. There *was* something out there—distant, indistinct, but getting closer. The shape was strange, angular, winking in and out of my awareness as my Mark struggled to keep whatever it was highlighted for me.

I looked down at Tiba, raising an eyebrow. Maybe I needed to—

Again. The air split with sustained gunfire.

What the hell is going on out there?

I took a breath to excuse myself from the group, simultaneously pulling up my Combat Log to get some kind of clue as to what the turrets were killing, when one of the goat-legged guards did what I was about to do. He shouldered his crossbow and bounded up the junk berm in long sure-footed leaps, until he reached the top. Once his head was above the crest, he froze. Whatever he saw up there, he didn't like it. He staggered backwards in shock, then turned back to us, wide-eyed. He cupped his hand to his face.

"It's a Bra-!"

BRRRRRRRRRRRRRRRRRRRRRRRRRRRRR!

The goat guard's message was cut off as the turrets went full blast on something very, very close.

Then the far edge of our defensive wall of junk exploded.

CHAPTER NINE

Seal the Breach

The left side of the semicircular junk barrier exploded into a cloud of wood splinters, dust, and debris, the force of it so intense it sent individual cracked and broken pieces rocketing through the air to career into the stunned crowd. Clusters of goblins were slapped to the cobblestones. The bonfire caught half of a wagon wheel at its base and toppled over in a shower of sparks that forced the formation of guardsmen to scatter.

Splinters hit the material of my cloak as I spun around to shield Tiba from the storm, wrapping the two of us in at-least-cursory protection. Thankfully, I didn't get any Damage notifications, but it was as far from the origin point as you could get. Others probably weren't so lucky.

The air shook as the turrets on every approach began to lay into targets in their field of fire. Too many. Too constant.

I stood up again, flinging the cloak to the side to scatter the debris that had landed on my back and turned to survey the damage.

The barrier on the far side was now a scattered mess of rubble, obscured by a slowly dissipating cloud of dust. In the middle of the cloud, a dark shape shook itself and stomped one heavy foot into the street. Old pavers shattered under the force of it.

This creature was massive, seven or eight feet tall at the shoulders, nearly as wide, blocky—almost like carved stones stacked on top of one another until they were the general shape of an animal, except exaggerated in every way. Its front half was bulky to the point of absurdity, massively muscular, armored in grayish tan rock with lots of hard corners and straight edges that eventually tapered organically into a back half that wouldn't be out of place on some kind of bovine animal, complete with thick fur and a long, tufted tail. Its four legs ended in wide-based hooves, the front of which had sharp edges like shovels or rounded axes.

I struggled to make sense of what I was looking at. The thing was a mountain in the front, a buffalo in the back, dwarfing everything else around it. I squinted, trying to differentiate the moving parts in the midst of the armor plating in order to spot the creature's triangular head, which was almost comically tiny in the middle of all the bulk. This, too, was armored, including the eyes, leaving only a small, horizontal slit across, almost like a knight's visor.

Everyone stood there for a shocked few seconds, taking a collective breath in dread of what was about to come. Our party had just been crashed by a completely different Class of monster.

The thing shook its head, the armored plates clacking and grating against each other loud enough even to be heard over the remaining guns.

It snorted.

BOOF!

The dust that remained in the air around the creature, along with a good bit that had been lodged between the cobblestones, was blasted away, and I could feel particulates pinging against my cheeks.

A long, mournful lowing escaped the creature's mouth as its body exploded forward, this motion alone creating a miniature shockwave that I could feel in my stomach. Ancient sediment between the old bricks of the structures around us fell down in dusty trickles.

Goblins who had been assigned to stack and pack the food and supplies scattered to make way for the beast, abandoning their goods and trying to evade the oncoming charge. The slippery little green guys juked one way, then another to shake their pursuer, but the creature could corner surprisingly well. It chose one out of the many goblins it had targeted and lowered its head like a battering ram. The goblin ran, trying to dodge, but the creature had him dead to rights.

I watched in horror as the monster closed in, got within inches of the goblin and . . .

The triangular head clicked and spasmed, turning itself clockwise like a tumbler in a lock, then retreated back into the armored plates, ending in a final *CLACK!*

BOOM!

An explosion without sound tore through the area directly in front of the creature. The cobblestones rippled with the force of it before giving way and flying out in a wide arc that slammed into the stone of the city wall and the locked gate. The poor running goblin was nothing more than a cloud of pink mist.

Holy—What the hell is this thing?

I brought up my Combat Log, searching for the messages from the past thirty seconds.

Where? Where? Where? Whe—There!

Scourge-Touched Bray Knight takes 0 Damage. (13 base, -13 Armored) (Piercing)
Scourge-Touched Bray Knight takes 0 Damage. (11 base, -11 Armored) (Piercing)

Scourge-Touched Bray Knight takes 0 Damage. (16 base, -16 Armored) (Piercing)
Scourge-Touched Bray Knight takes 0 Damage. (18 base, -18 Armored) (Piercing)
Scourge-Touched Bray Knight takes 15 Damage. (16 base, -4 Resist, +3 Knife in the Dark) (Piercing)
Scourge-Touched Bray Knight is marked.
Scourge-Touched Bray Knight is cursed.
Scourge-Touched Bray Knight is bleeding.
Scourge-Touched Bray Knight takes 0 Damage. (18 base, -18 Armored) (Piercing)
Scourge-Touched Bray Knight resists Mark.
Scourge-Touched Bray Knight takes 0 Damage. (16 base, -16 Armored) (Piercing)

"Uh—Tiba! Get your people to high ground!" I shouted, not entirely sure what they would be able to do after that, but up the wall was better than nothing. The thing looked too big to be able to climb or to get up the stairs to the battlements. Those stairs were meant for soldiers, not walking tanks.

I already had my sword in my hand as I started forward. I didn't know what I was going to do about this thing, but I knew I had to do something. I had a couple more turrets in my Inventory, but then there was the problem of the armor and—

"Ryan! Stop!" Tiba called. The way she said it pulled me up short before I could get very far. I looked back, sword still up and body still trying to carry me into the fight.

Tiba was pointing with her spear toward the collapsed part of the barrier the Bray Knight had just come through. "There's a hole, Ryan! They come!" she yelled. Even now, pale faces of the Returned were streaming into the breach, capitalizing on our distraction. Everyone was so focused on the armored nightmare buffalo thing, the other Scourge were coming in uncontested.

I looked from the hole to the bray to Tiba to the bray and back to the hole again. Which threat was greater? Where could I—

A shovel-sized hand slapped me hard on the shoulder.

"Go plug up the breach, Ryan," Geddon bellowed, an intense glowing grin on his face as he slipped his helm down onto his head. "Once that's done, maybe you can watch us work."

"Work fast, and maybe we'll save some for you," Samila said from behind the giant Leori. She already had her helmet on and her shield strapped to her arm. Her eyes were locked on the Bray Knight with a hungry intensity that sent a chill through me.

"Ready, Big Guy?" she asked.

"I've been ready my entire life," Geddon replied, not even getting to the end of the sentence before he was running, shield forward, sword in the air.

The armored monster hadn't charged anyone else yet, seemingly content with rubbing its head on the bloody, shattered ground where the goblin had met its end.

It didn't even seem to notice the crossbow bolts that pinged against its plated shoulders or even the lucky ones that sank into its furry hind legs. If the Combat Log hadn't told me it was Scourge-Touched, the lack of pain aversion would have clinched it for me.

I spared a glance for them before I went my own way, wishing I could do something for them . . . *anything*, but no. They knew the situation and had asked me to do this.

Giving my head a brief shake to narrow my focus, I ran toward the breach.

They were right. I was good at this. I could do this part, and I would need to trust them to do theirs.

While in motion, I loosened my shoulder and settled my grip on my sword. The Returned were slowly streaming in, pale grinning faces furtively checking for signs they'd been detected by the defenders. Touched goblins came through as well, climbing over the much-reduced pile of rubble before bounding off to make trouble elsewhere in the camp. There wasn't a flood of them like I'd seen in the past, but I got the impression these were as many of them as were available in the area.

There was that strategic thinking again. They'd sent in a battering ram and had troops ready to head into the breach it had created. Had they noticed we were gearing up to move and decided to do something about it, or was this something else? What level of thinking was I witnessing here?

Somewhere out there, I had a gun down, among the rubble. It hadn't been positioned in the disintegrated part of the berm, but it had certainly caught a part of the blast. Now it was missing. If I could get it back up, that would go a long way toward stemming the tide. The question was: would I be left alone long enough to do that?

I scanned the area, looking for signs of metal or movement, hoping the gun was still trying to track and fire while it was on the ground, but I came up with nothing before my grace period was done. Then I was set upon by the horde.

Two Returned—gangly, pale, emaciated Undead draped in rags—charged me on all fours, springing up to swipe at my face once they got in range. Their dirty nails raked over my cloak, grasped the material before their owners went in for a bite. I stabbed with my sword to take the first one in the midsection, but it dodged back before I could do any real damage.

The other tracked me from my left, slashing at my collarbone. I blocked the strike with my prosthetic, spinning on my leading foot to shift into a punch that landed solidly in the middle of the Undead's face. Its head snapped back, and I heard popping sounds from the vertebrae in its neck.

Willing Edge [10 MP/sec]

My sword's follow-up downward slash nearly bisected the creature, slicing through the top half of the Returned from the shoulder all the way down to the pelvis.

My mouth dropped open in shock, only to get an intense sample of that all-too-familiar Scourge ick.

Right. 40 Body. Need to get used to that.

The other Undead capitalized on my sword being lodged in its friend's insides (now outsides) and lunged. It wrapped itself around me in a tight bear hug from the back. The hold tied up my sword arm while it went to bite the side of my face. I struggled to get my metal hand around to peel the thing off, but I had no leverage or reach to get my fingers around more than its clothes. My eyes widened as the misshapen mouth closed in on my tender face.

It will come as no surprise to anyone that even the *threat* of something biting you on the face can have a tendency to cause mild panic.

"No! Gah! Gahhhh! Get off!"

My mind was a whirling tornado of *No no no no no.* I screeched, fumbling for something to use.

Hardened Defense [9 MP/sec]
Hardened Defense: User may harden one part of their body for 1 second for X MP/sec where X = 5% of total MP, increasing resistance to cuts, abrasions, burns, broken bones, etc.

It wasn't a perfect fit, but it was all I could think to do in the situation to keep my cheek from being ripped off.

I'd gotten this new ability when I'd Leveled Up my Unarmed Combat to Level 5. In my subsequent tests after selecting it from the menu, I'd determined that the part of the body that I could harden was distressingly small, about the size of a fist, but I wasn't thinking about the limitations of the Ability just now. I just wanted my face to stay where faces should be.

I didn't have a hard time concentrating on the area I wanted to harden. I felt the mana leave my Core and coalesce in my right cheek, cold and fortifying.

The Undead's teeth stopped cold, cracked, and shattered as it continued to try to maul me. It didn't seem to care, though. It bit and bit, getting nothing for its efforts but dental destruction until it was just chowing down on me with bleeding gums. It didn't occur to the thing to stop and preserve its only effective weapons.

Breathing hard, I got a shoulder out of the bear hug, then jammed my metal hand into the creature's mouth, slipping around the cheek and getting a good grip on the bottom jaw.

Devouring Grasp [5 MP/sec]

Then it was just a matter of peeling the defanged Undead off me, far enough to run it through with my sword.

The light left the monster's eyes and it dropped to the ground only to be replaced, immediately, by another. I dropped my Hardened Defense to preserve my mana and cut this one down the old-fashioned way.

"Duty and mercy!" Sissa shouted from somewhere behind me. She'd joined the fight sometime during my face-biting fun time. I was out of range for the buff, but it was nice to hear she was alive. Other shouts from afar—wavering, fearful—didn't sound nearly as confident as she did.

Already breathing hard after just a few kills, I advanced upon the breach until I was within about ten feet of the edge of it. Only a few of the monsters seemed interested in me at a time, content to send a few of their number to tie me up while the rest spread around the camp.

I was small potatoes, apparently. What a nice change after the last time we'd met. I counted myself lucky that the face-biter hadn't ripped off my mask.

This position was as good as I was going to get. I needed to plug this if we were going to get this situation under control.

The Scourge-Touched clawed and snapped at me. I deterred them with wide slashes of my sword while I thought about what to do. My downed turret was nowhere to be seen near the wreckage. It wasn't firing, either. And these things clearly weren't going to let me pick through the rubble to find it.

This is a bad idea. A really bad idea.

I had been hoping to avoid this until we were good and ready to leave. Then again, the camp was in danger of falling apart right now. What more damage could I do than had already been done?

A lot, actually, but it was either this or nothing.

I slashed at an Undead face and bounded backward to get some space, flipping my sword into my left hand and using my right to summon the top part of one of my new turrets. The stubby cylindrical action, about the size of my forearm, was already loaded with multiple pressurized bulbs, and the Volatility-charged ignition stick on the end of the turret's barrel glowed menacingly at the tip.

Two more slashes with my sword and another step back, and I had enough room to position the turret in my metal hand. I wasn't stupid enough to do this with my fleshy one. I had had enough of being on fire.

I held the top half of the turret out as far from my body as I could possibly get it, and the corners of my mouth turned down as I reached over and opened the pressure valve.

FWOOSH!

A bright yellow jet of flame spewed from the barrel of the flamethrower, a solid line at first, which then dispersed into a loose, globular spray, producing a solid three-foot-wide cone of hurt. I'd just so happened to be aiming directly at one of the Returned when I activated the targeting card, so the programming just decided to do what it did when it had a lock on something. The yellow stream was so bright and hot I grunted and growled as I held on for dear life, unable to look directly at what I was doing.

I blindly waved the flamer back and forth in a wide arc, covering everything at eye level and below. The turret sputtered and spat as its nozzle passed over valid targets, turning on the juice when it saw something to burn, only to instantly cut off when the nozzle passed over empty space. It wasn't full coverage like I would have wanted, but you couldn't argue with the results.

The monsters went up like flares. The burning pex oil/alcohol mixture stuck to the creatures' skin like syrup, then popped and fizzed as it spread, as fire is wont to do. The Undead were especially susceptible to it for some reason, their skin going up like dry paper, their insides sizzling as whatever they were using for blood boiled away. The flames also blinded them, and they struck out at their comrades in their desperation to kill me even as they met their doom.

It was about as chaotic as chaos could get. My world became a raging inferno.

"Aaaaaahhhhhhhh!" A tortured, panicked scream escaped my mouth, more high-pitched than I would have admitted to anyone back home.

I think I might have developed a minor aversion to fire since I'd last nearly burned to death.

Of course, the metal part of my body felt nothing, just the vague pressure from the recoil as the turret discharged its payload into its targets.

The skin on my leading leg and my neck stung with the heat, and the edges of my cloak smoldered. Meanwhile, everything in front of me was engulfed in sticky, liquid yellow.

Regardless of my misgivings, I advanced, waving my firestick in the general direction of the enemy. The disembodied turret head did the rest.

I was right in front of the breach, feet crunching over splintered wood, by the time the turret stopped activating at all, with no targets in range to engage, but I needn't have bothered going this far. When I finally looked, the breach, the berm, the building next to it, along with a multitude of twitching corpses, were already on fire, and the fire was plugging the hole better than I had any hope of managing with a fixed turret.

And the fire was spreading.

CHAPTER TEN

Make Things Worse

The wall was on fire.

The ground was on fire.

Most pressing, however, was that my cloak was on fire. I tried to put it out, but the liquid flame I'd used in my flamethrower design was sticky stuff. I ended up having to grab the offending edge and trigger Devouring Grasp. Interestingly, my Engine buff flickered on for about a quarter-second when I did that, but it was gone before I could look at the values. I'd check the log later, if I remembered to.

I backed away from the flames. They were already climbing up the facade of the corner building, devouring the wood accents and window shutters and spreading to the interior. The adjacent junk berm . . . well, that was 90 percent wood, and there was a healthy breeze coming from the west, making the spread of my little campfire an inevitability.

The window of time we had to get out of the area was definitely measured in minutes—probably in the single digits.

Behind me, all the shouts, twanging crossbows, hissing monsters, and the hollow roar of the Bray Knight told me that I still had work to do.

Maybe it was best I put the flamer turret away just now, though.

The yard situation wasn't that much better than the raging inferno that had once been my part of the wall. While I'd been fighting the Scourge and plugging the breach, the big Bray had been having a field day with every solid structure in the immediate area. Half of the building that had held the cells was now a collapsed heap along with the gatehouse adjacent to the stairs that had climbed up to the top of the wall. The crates where we'd been gathering equipment and supplies were now a vaguely conical splatter of debris.

Currently, three guards were in front of the Bray, slapping their swords on the edges of their shields and dancing side to side to keep its attention while the monster shook its tiny head and huffed. Tens of crossbow bolts stuck out of the creature's back and out of its sides, but the problem was that the Bray just wasn't feeling it.

It was bleeding from countless wounds, but nothing was even close to slowing it down, much less killing it.

Approaching the monster from the back, Sissa and Samila flanked it, armed with a white bedsheet or tablecloth. While the other guards ran distraction, the sisters crept up on the monster's side and, with a surprising amount of strength and grace, Samila vaulted up and over the Bray's back, letting the sheet billow in the wind to cover a good portion of its head.

Then it was time to scatter.

The Bray went insane. It bucked wildly, trying to remove the sheet from its head. The hard edges that made up its armor were working against it just now, keeping the cloth from slipping down to the ground, and the beast didn't have the wherewithal to stop and remove the blindfold with one of its hooves.

The surrounding guards closed in to capitalize on the situation, chopping with their swords at the tender flesh on the monster's back, but it was dangerous business. One guard got too close and failed to retreat quickly enough, and the back end of the Bray came around to knock him to the ground. His desperate scream was cut off as a heavy hoof came down directly on his chest, silencing him forever.

I briefly considered summoning the flamer again to see what that would do, but I decided against it. We had enough problems dealing with the Bray Knight without making it a Flaming Bray Knight.

The remaining turrets barked as more Scourge-Touched approached the berm.

Level Up!
You are now Level 17.

Well, that was nice at least. What could I do now, though? We had a definitive time limit. Our defenses were about to cook us, and if they didn't, we couldn't hide behind a pile of ash afterwards.

I sprinted forward, getting my sword out again and casting Willing Edge. After all, 40 Body and a sharp sword had worked so far. Maybe I could do damage where the others couldn't. I took a curving route to keep behind the Bray, twisted at the waist like a coiled spring, and let loose with a high vertical chop as it kicked out. My sword's edge cut through the meat of the monster's thigh and sank deep.

Scourge-Touched Bray Knight takes 4 Damage. (26 base, -22 Resist) (Slashing)

My sword stopped cold, my arm vibrating in its socket like I'd just hit a steel beam.

BONG!

Scourge-Touched Bray Knight attacks you for 40 Damage. (-50 mitigated)

Then I was flying.

It was a brief flight—less than a second. I barely had a chance to register what was happening.

You take 1 Impact Damage.
You take 2 Impact Damage.
You take 1 Impact Damage.
Status gained: Stunned [10 seconds]
You take 6 Impact Damage.

Then I was rolling. My world alternated between gray and blue and back to gray a half-dozen times before I finally came to a stop against the collapsed structure of the cells, staring up at the sky.

"Umph," I grunted as the sky wobbled in my vision. My thoughts spun with it, whirling drunkenly, refusing to coalesce into something coherent.

Sluggishly, I got my arm moving and ran a hand over my body, checking for missing or broken parts. Everything was sore, my clothes were ripped, and the inside of my hood felt sticky, but I was otherwise intact. The flesh surrounding my prosthetic side did seem tender, though. Had I taken that blow in the spooky metal parts? That would explain a lot.

A hand reached down and pulled me to my feet. My still-recovering equilibrium didn't like that.

"A good try, Monk, but a bull like that is not a job for swords," Bole's voice said.

I closed my eyes and shook my head, trying to get the world to stand still again, and it seemed to do the trick. The corporal's face materialized nearby.

I focused on it, fighting to keep my stomach from expelling my breakfast.

"Umph," I said again. Real speech was still an aspirational thing right now.

"Around. These Church zealots make me want some alone time," Bole answered a question I hadn't thought to ask. He squinted, scanning the remains of the camp, not lingering on any particular thing while rolling one of those knives on his knuckles.

"Well, that's us fucked, then, isn't it?" Bole said. I assumed the question was rhetorical.

I worked my tongue around the inside my mouth and spit out a mouthful of blood and a bit of something soft and chewy.

"Not if we kill thissh thing firssht," I said. Damnit. Had I bitten my tongue?

Bole's assessment did have merit, though. I didn't know how to kill this thing without time we didn't have. We couldn't move, either—not with the Bray at our backs. If we tried to bring everyone down the alley while the hulking cow was still alive, we'd just be lining up bowling pins. Squishy bowling pins.

Another guard died as the Bray suddenly stopped bucking and charged forward blindly. The guard tried to dodge, but the edge of the creature's armored shoulder clipped her trailing arm and its weird shockwave attack ripped the woman in half, along with the tablecloth blinder.

I reached around for my sword, finding it only a few feet away, my mind whirling for a solution.

Bole put a hand on my arm, stopping me.

"Don't. Let them distract it."

"We're losing people," I growled. "Sissa, Samila, and Geddon are still—"

Bole pulled on my arm, but I was heavy. He couldn't budge me. Instead, he ended up just pulling himself forward until he was in my way. "Stop. Let them do their job," he said, pointing to my right with his chin.

The stairs. The stairs that led to the top of the battlements were a popular place right now. A circle of goblin warriors were gathered around their base as people rushed upward to flee to high ground, two at a time. A few of the Scourge lay dead around there, ragged holes in their bodies from sharp goblin spears. The Church guards were getting personnel up there, too—mainly those with visible injuries, I noticed.

I had told Tiba to get her people to high ground, didn't I? She worked fast.

There had to be a way I could help.

"Brays are tough bastards," Bole said in my ear. "This one's just under a Prince—only three or four of 'em in a herd. Culling one of them usually means digging a spike pit or burying a blade trap, then running like hell. Unless you've got any of those in your magical mystery pockets, you're just going to get in the way."

"Brother Ryan, Brother Fidus, do you require healing?"

Suddenly, a hand clamped down on my shoulder. Three thick, black fingers stuck to my cloak. I gritted my teeth, preparing myself for anything, then spun to find Bishop Kolash there, his robes dirty, his face lined and wrinkled with exhaustion. His still-broken hand held his staff loosely while the one on my shoulder seemed whole. I glanced at the appendage twice to make sure there was no glow from a curse or some other attack. Nothing. Kolash saw me look, let me look, but kept staring at me and not letting go.

Bole had another knife out in a flash and held it between himself and the bishop like a crucifix warning away a vampire. "Don't you call me that. You don't get to fucking call me that," he spat.

Kolash only had eyes for me, though. "We have no time for this. Am I required here, or shall I move on to assist others?" he asked. That was a strange way to phrase the question. Additionally, he wasn't trying to kill me, despite having a free shot while my back was turned. He'd called me "Brother" just now.

Kolash, without saying as much, was proposing a truce.

"We're fine for now, Your Holiness," I replied tentatively.

Bole just spat at the bishop's feet.

Nodding slowly to me, the bishop turned and began to limp away, working his way around the edge of the yard toward the next clump of soldiers.

Well, if Kolash was a problem I could put off until later, I was okay with that.

I looked up to the top of the city wall, fifty or so feet above our heads, at the line of people filing upward and disappearing onto the battlements.

"Corporal Bole?"

I had a plan formulating, something that would work with our current situation.

"What?!" he snapped. He spun to face me, only just now tearing his burning glare from the bishop's back. His expression was one of white, hot rage.

"The stairs," I began, picking up my sword and pointing toward the wall. "These can't be the only stairs that lead up to the top of the wall, right?"

Bole's face went slack as his brain switched gears. He blinked a couple of times, his mouth screwing up into an absent sneer. I was beginning to think that was his default look. "A—eh—a half-mile or . . . No. Every quarter of a mile or so," he amended.

"How close is the next one to our basement door?"

Bole caught on quickly, but he didn't like what I was proposing. "No way. The wall isn't the road to your gran's house. It's even narrower than the side street, and it's exposed."

THOOM!

The Bray Knight laid waste to the entire bottom floor of the barracks. The structure sagged on its mutilated supports and collapsed, the first floor simply disappearing like it was never there.

"Better there than trapped in an oven with that," I countered.

"Fuck," was all Bole had to say.

"Make sure everyone gets up there!" I shouted over my shoulder as I took off at a jog, not waiting for more input from Bole. I circled wide around the Bray fight and bounded up the alley-side junk berm with more grace than I thought I had but not quite as much as one of the goat-legged folks. I'd need to find out what they were called.

I only fell once, the janky construction giving way under my weight and causing a minor avalanche of cabinet drawers and chairs.

The turret I'd been aiming for was still dispensing lead. The Scourge-Touched were bolder now that they had monsters on the inside of our defenses, streaming out from doorways and slinking behind cover to get closer to the gun's position. A couple of bodies lay splayed just below the turret's leading leg, a close call. Subsequent ones would get closer and closer as the enemy became more numerous. I wasn't going to allow that to happen, though.

I disengaged the activation lever and detached the magazine, working quickly to disassemble the gun and get it stowed. The Scourge didn't catch on right away that the gun wasn't firing anymore, but once they did, they came in greater numbers, scrabbling from hidey holes and jumping from windows to go in for the kill.

The legs were the last to go, disappearing in a flash into my Spatial Storage, then I leaped down to the yard, the flamer already appearing in my hands again. The bravest of the Scourge was just poking its head above the berm when I triggered the activation sequence, dousing its face in fire.

I winced. Even though the Scourge wanted me dead, it looked like an awful way to go. The berm immediately around the dying monster went up like a tinderbox.

A good start.

I waved the decapitated turret around, catching the Scourge-Touched as they tried to climb over, and the berm's fire problems soon got much, much worse. In no time, the entire mouth of the alley was ablaze.

Stowing the flamer again, I moved on to the next turret, running across the yard, through our beleaguered guardsmen. Every turret I could save from the oncoming fire was another I'd be able to use up on the wall.

"Sir, what are you doing?" Lieutenant Obvious called after me as I sprinted to the other alley approach.

"Get everyone onto the wall, Obvious! Do it quickly!" I didn't have time to look at him. I just hoped he understood how urgent this was going to be.

"It's Begdel, actually, sir!"

"Get them out now, Lieutenant!"

"Yes, sir! Very good, sir!"

The other alley approach worked the same way. Pack up the turret, wait for the Scourge, set the berm on fire. The temperature in our general area was sweltering now. The fire was closing in. Sweat beaded on my face and ran down the sleeves of my jacket and shirt.

One more.

Up onto the main approach. The fire was close to this one. I had to dance in and out of the heat while I worked, unable to stay more than a couple of seconds, and the gun was extremely hot to handle. I did the dismantling mostly with my prosthetic, slapping the component pieces in my fleshy hand and stowing them away before they could do real damage to me, but I still ended up with burns. Exotic Healing would have to carry me through.

I stowed the legs and leaped down into the yard again, not bothering to slide down the side. The flamer was already in my hand by the time I got back to my feet. I peered up through the smoke, waving my fire-spitting pain machine back and forth frantically to sweep over the much-more-extreme angle I was having to cover.

"Come on. Come on," I whispered. I needed one to show its face so I could start the fire. Dammit, why didn't I create a manual firing mechanism for one of these? Oh, yeah, because it would be super dangerous and stupid to hold one while operating it . . . like I was doing now.

"Look out!"

My cloak wrenched itself to the side, pulling the catch across my neck, choking me and making me stumble. A good thing, too, because something huge blew past me on my left, so fast and powerful it didn't even register before it clipped the wrist of my prosthetic and—

BOOM! BOOM!

My world went white.

A few things probably happened at once. The Bray Knight, having just made contact with something it wanted dead (me . . . or, more specifically, my metal arm), unleashed its shockwave attack, disintegrating the junk berm, the cobblestones, and—most distressingly—my flamer turret.

Said magical shockwave tore through the payload of my flamer, making it go up in an angry, demonic fireball that blasted out from ground zero, propelled by the Bray's magical force attack directly into an already-very-flammable pile of wood.

The shockwave turned said pile of wood into an aerosolized cloud of splinters and sawdust that mixed with the air and kicked off a secondary explosion, maybe a millisecond after the first, that washed over me and sent flaming wreckage hurtling in all directions, including mine.

A wave of burning junk blasted my front side. Something slammed into my stomach, punching the air out of my lungs.

Nope. Nope. Nope. Nope. We are not catching fire today.

Whether it was the adrenaline or being more accustomed to life-threatening situations as my Exotic life went on, I was up on my feet before I had even gotten my breath back. My legs carried me, stumbling, away from the flaming wreckage and in the general direction of the gates.

Something clawed at my back, scrabbling through my cloak and wriggling its way up and out until we were sharing the same hood. A fuzzy brown head suddenly took up half of my field of view.

"Run, Ryan! Don't stop!"

I let out a hollow moan as my diaphragm finally decided to work again, allowing oxygen back into my lungs. "Guh—Trix?" I gasped.

I spared a look over my shoulder, but I wished I hadn't.

My theory about a Flaming Bray Knight being much worse than the vanilla kind was, sadly, correct. The Bray Knight was a lava-powered freight train. Its hooves pounded on the cobblestones, cracking them underfoot. Liquid fire dripped from the creature's armored shoulders, head, and back, leaving a wake of nightmare fuel behind, and it was gaining on us. I could feel the heat on my back.

Trix clawed my face, forcing my gaze to lock onto the battlement stairs.

"Don't look back! Run!" he shouted. He didn't take his own advice, though. He wriggled until he was halfway out of the hood and contorting to look on, horrified, at the monster giving chase. The barrel of his slung carbine jammed itself into my eye.

"Trix! What the—Ow!" I sputtered.

"I'm sorry, Ryan. I would ride on your shoulder, but it's on fire!"

"I promised myself I wasn't going to be on fire today!"

I pumped my legs as fast as they would go. Breaths came to me in short, desperate puffs. My heart was humming, chugging, trying to keep my body from flagging. Being blown up did something to my nerves, though. My body felt loose, like I'd replaced key muscle tissues with gelatine.

The base of the stairs loomed in front of us. Guards and goblin spears, upon seeing what was coming, scrambled upward as we came on, their eyes wide, as they pushed each other to get the hell out of the way before impact.

We couldn't go that way. If the Bray hit the staircase when we did, we'd all turn into bloody chunks.

I cornered to the right, making for the piled wreckage of the gatehouse instead, the Bray right on our heels.

CLACK! CLACK! CLICK!

Oh, no. Here it was. We were about to die.

I managed a burst of speed. My legs felt like they would give out any time.

"Hold on, Trix!" I puffed.

I shot forward at a full sprint, up the broken wreckage of the gatehouse, praying the footholds I chose were stable enough to support our weight.

Up. Away. Over. To the apex of the rubble.

I gathered all the strength I had, willing it all into my burning legs, and jumped.

I skipped the bottom of the battlement stairs, choosing, instead, to fly right up to the first landing where the stairs folded back upon themselves. It was a bold move—a fair distance to cross even if I had been fresh and not stupidly heavy thanks to being made partially of metal. Unfortunately, it wasn't going to work.

Too soon in my arc, the lip of the landing started to fall upward, away from us. *No. No. No. No!*

My arms flailed in midair; my legs, too. I needed distance. Height.

Tension Step [4,000 MP/sec]

Leveling the Running Skill to 5 had given me this one. It was a choice between this and reduced energy usage while running, or increased inertia while sprinting. Of course I was going to choose a double jump. Every platformer I'd ever played taught me that it was awesome. For me, though, it was . . . not awesome.

Tension Step: User may treat any fluid as solid matter for the purpose of running. Limit: 1 step. MP/sec based on weight, fluid composition, and surface area used.

My mana bottomed out immediately. It hadn't been full to begin with, but this . . . this was an instant descent into migraine hell. The light became too much for my eyes. Everything blurred, sound buzzed, and my head felt like it was about to explode.

Yeah, this was not how this Ability should have been used. Hell, of all the Abilities I'd picked since I Leveled Up in the past, this one was probably my only true dud. I was just too damned heavy, and the air was just too damned squishy.

The Ability failed almost immediately. My leading foot caught something not exactly solid—more like an ephemeral, feathery puddle that didn't support more than a tiny fraction of my weight. I pushed down, sinking my leg into it, getting as much force under me as possible.

This wasn't a jump, per se. More of a slight delay of falling, a change in our arc to something wider—wide enough to slam us into the wall just under the lip of the stairs. My fingers scraped over the stones, trying to get a grip, but I was, again, too heavy, and the ancient stone was too weathered and smooth.

Trix's hands shot out to claw at the surface of the stone, as well, his back legs wrapping around my neck to help me. Good on him, trying to pull me up, but never in a million years would it actually work.

I felt the two of us slipping and beginning to fall. I had the fleeting thought of attempting to grab Trix and throw him up onto the landing, but I didn't get a chance.

Strong, iron hands caught me around the wrists, arresting my fall.

BOOM!

A plume of dust shot up from underneath us, catching my cloak and making it billow up in front of my face. My mana migraine chose that moment to reassert itself, and I threw up a little in my mouth.

We were alive, though. The Bray had hit somewhere down beneath us, but the wall still stood. The Dark Lord had made it to last.

Trix shuddered, letting go of my neck, slumping down next to me in the hood of my cloak as we hung there. We looked down at the monster's silhouette in the dust cloud as one and let out sighs of relief.

"Sorry I lied to you," I said. I had meant to say something clever, but somehow, this was what came out.

"And I . . . am sorry for not . . . seeing things from your perspective," Trix replied breathlessly. "It was selfish of me."

"You really are a warrior, you know," I said after swallowing to keep from throwing up again. Constance, my head hurt, and the world was too damned bright.

"You don't need to do that. It's—"

I couldn't keep doing this. I needed to lie down. "Shut up, Trix. You killed so many monsters. More than anyone else. Saved people. That's real."

"That's—" Trix paused to think. I could feel him do one of those vulpa shudders again. "That's not inaccurate."

"No one else I'd rather have watching my back." There, that was it. I was done talking.

Trix reached up and gave the top of my head a tired scratch. "Thank you, Ryan," he said, shakily.

"That is so beautiful! Finally!" Geddon sobbed from above us. I looked up, squinting, to find the giant Leori's two massive shovel-hands gripping my wrists. Tears streamed down his face, and his bared teeth formed the tortured shape of an overwhelmed smile, the kind a mother would wear on her beloved child's wedding day. "Now kiss already. Then maybe start climbing."

CHAPTER ELEVEN

Jump in Front

BOOM!

I watched the smoky silhouette of another building crumble and fall in the distance as I leaned on my vomit-covered crenelation. I'd Consumed some of the fuel in my Spatial Storage to top myself off again mana-wise, but this migraine was a stubborn one. I would have given anything to just be able to sleep it off, but that wasn't in the cards today. Thankfully the nausea had gone down to a manageable level, at least.

Needless to say, sucking out my entire mana pool in less than a second was not something I'd be doing in the future if I could help it.

The Scourge-Touched Bray Knight, after a fruitless five minutes of pounding blindly at the base of the wall, had moved on to greener pastures. Right now, it was having a grand old time charging at and through every building in the vicinity, just in case we'd left someone behind. At least the stubborn monster wasn't burning anymore. It was already scary enough without the dripping flamer fuel. The rest of the immediate area, however, was fully alight.

What a mess. The only upside here was that the Scourge-Touched couldn't swarm us just yet, having to go around the fire to get to us, and even then, they would be limited to those in their number that could climb up the perfectly fitted stone of the wall or . . .

I looked up to the sky to make sure it was clear. I hadn't seen any flying Scourge yet, but I wasn't about to make assumptions anymore. Right now, though, we only had the climbers to worry about. Even as I watched, I could see silent figures scaling the rooftops and jumping up to mount the walls, as we had. Our crossbowmen would have a lot to shoot at soon.

Head counts told us we were missing people, only coming up with just over two hundred, but there wasn't much we could do about it. Ground level was a no-go, so any chance of recovering our dead was gone. The only consolation was that the fire would keep their remains from being turned against us.

"Well, this isn't going to be as safe and orderly as we'd hoped. You okay, Ryan?" Sissa asked from behind me. Her voice was subtly tinged with anxiety.

I turned my back on the blazing city. Slowly. Moving still triggered my gag reflex. I wanted to shake my head, but that was not in the cards for now, either. So, I settled for a short "No" to answer both.

Sissa looked like she was going to be sick, too, the way she folded her arms as she blinked the smoke out of her eyes. A line of guardsmen pushed between us and jostled the crowd to get to the edge of the gaggle we'd formed. I did my best to give them space, but there was only so much to give.

We had room up here on the wall, but we weren't using it. The battlements stretched on forever in either direction, a long band of stone with crenulations on either side, widening only briefly on rounded structures that I assumed would be mounting points for trebuchets or the Ralqir equivalent of them.

The problem was that people were frightened and disorganized. Folks were wounded and worn out, and most had lost someone in the mad scramble up here whom they were now doing their best to track amidst the gathered bodies below.

Meanwhile, Scourge-Touched—though few and far between—lunged at us, howling, from either side of the battlements. They never made it within striking distance; each was shot down before they could get close, but they certainly reminded us that they were there and more were coming. Other, more nimble monsters climbed up from the outside of the city, having to be put down only after they took a swipe at someone who'd strayed too close to the edge.

It all added up to a situation where the goblins and tall folk were gradually squished together, spears having to be held high so as not to stab one another. With every howl we heard in the distance, people huddled closer together until we were effectively one big mass. I heard someone out there crying, but I couldn't see who it was. Everyone was feeling tired, hurt, and scared, and no one was taking charge. Nervous susurrations rippled through the crowd constantly.

Again, I questioned how intelligent the force that directed these monsters was. It was smart enough to hold its troops in reserve for when we were vulnerable. Even now, when it didn't have overwhelming numbers to send at us, it pushed a trickle of enemies our way to harass us and never let us truly rest.

Was I witnessing effective psychological warfare, or was I giving the hive mind too much credit?

Geddon shoved his way through the press of the crowd to get to us, as gently as he could, large as he was.

"We've got our fighters generally on the outside of the formation now, civilians in the middle. Folded some enlisted in with other units, too. Mostly crossbows. We can't stay here much longer though," he said in a low growl. The big man wore the same worried expression Sissa did.

"No other officers?" Sissa asked.

Geddon shook his head. "Best we have is the lieutenant."

"Anyone else?"

"No. There's even stupid talk of splitting the group and making for different strong points. Just a good way to hasten the end, if you ask me." Geddon was practically whispering now, as if the words were dangerous for others to hear.

Sissa looked up to the sky and closed her eyes for a second to collect herself.

"Ryan," she said quietly.

"Yeah?" I croaked after clearing my raw throat.

"Geddon's right. We have to get moving, and soon. The fire is going to spread quickly, and the wind isn't in our favor." Her tone was pained, as if she had to dredge these words up from the deepest, most private part of her soul and expose them to the world, and it was killing her.

I nodded slightly. I knew that we had to get moving soon. This was part of the . . . Well, it had never been part of the plan to do it up here, but I knew this would happen as soon as I started the fire. We needed to get moving now before the fire spread to engulf our exfil.

She looked at me pleadingly, like I was supposed to say something at this point. I, however, had no clue what she expected of me here. She stared. I stared. We stared at each other. The edges of her mouth twitched, her face contorted with frustration until, after a handful of silent moments, she finally broke. She leaned in to put her face right next to mine.

"You need to take charge of this group, Ryan," she whispered in my ear. "I need you to take control."

I nearly tripped over the railing and went tumbling down to ground level.

"What? Why?" I sputtered.

Seriously, why? Pretty much every single person in uniform was more qualified than I was to order people around. I wasn't a military man or a warrior or even a full adult by the standards of my . . .

But wait . . . Does time in another universe count toward your birthday? If so, maybe I was a full adult now.

"I know. I know," Sissa rasped. "I don't like it either, especially now that I know . . . uh . . . your situation, but this is our best play."

"Sissa, I'm a backwater mechanic at best. I fixed farm equipment before this. What am I supposed to do?" I was having a hard time keeping my voice down. Panic was short-circuiting my subtlety array.

"Hush!" Sissa put a hand over my mouth and fervently glanced around to make sure no one was listening. Geddon inched closer and blocked us from view of most of the crowd.

"Listen, Ryan. I know how you feel. Trust me, I do. And, no, I already know the question you're about to ask. It can't be me."

"Mmmph," I said. What did she mean she couldn't do it? She'd been our group's leader the entire time I'd known her. She practically lived with the entire weight of the world on her shoulders. Now she wanted to take a step back and let the crippled boy from the Outers jump in front of this parade?

"Because I'm just one of five sergeants left alive," she countered. "The captain and his executive officers died to get us up here, and we have no other leadership. The sergeants are all the same rank as I am, but they argue over what we need to do now. We need someone to take charge before the group splits, and if I try to do it, they'll question everything I say and get people killed. You're an elite. They'll listen to you."

I reached up and tore her hand away from my mouth. "Have you hit your head on something?! I told you—"

The hand was back over my mouth quickly. I didn't resist, but I gave her the angry stare to end all angry stares—or maybe it was more of a wild-eyed, spooked-deer panic I was giving off. Hard to know from where I was sitting.

"Shut up. Shut up!" Sissa checked behind her again to make sure no one was close enough to hear. "You *are* an elite, Brother Ryan. Today, you are who you say you are. These people need the Rising Sun of Eclipse, and you need to give them that right the hell now, or we are going to die."

This was a horrible idea, and she . . . no, *I* was going to get people killed if I took on this responsibility. There was so much. So many moving parts to this machine. The fire, the spears, crossbows, Kolash, Tiba and her goblins, the sight-lines, the bottlenecks, and that was just the beginning. It wasn't even counting what I would need to do on top of all of that.

"I see it in your eyes: the pressure, the concern for everyone's lives. You feel it," she whispered, slowly allowing her hand to slide down my face, trusting me (wrongly) to have my shit together.

"But," she continued, "I think, if you're honest, you've been secretly holding yourself responsible for everyone in the city for the entirety of your stay, haven't you? Otherwise, you wouldn't be so ready to kill yourself for even the slight-est chance of saving another of them. Compared to burning yourself alive, the mantle of leadership should be a reprieve."

She paused, tilting her head slightly to see if I had anything to say, but I didn't.

"You're not going to do it alone," she assured me, pinning me in place with those golden-dragon eyes. "Whatever orders you give right now will be better than the zero orders we currently have. Get us moving, and I will back whatever play you make."

I shook my head, staring daggers down at her but unable to look away. I bit my tongue, my breaths quick and shallow, the arguments I wanted to make dying before they ever surfaced in my mind. Then my eyes slid over to the peo-ple, their tired, scared faces, the long ribbon of wall we needed to cover . . .

Something gave. It felt like an implosion, my mind giving way to all the external pressure. Then all was calm in the aftermath.

"I hate you right now," I muttered.

Sissa nodded, understanding, but there was a tiny, knowing smile on her face that reminded me of her sister.

"Where's Bole?" I asked.

Her expression soured instantly at the mention of his name. I tried not to enjoy that, but I wasn't above being a little petty. Not now.

"Why?" she asked.

"He's going to get us underground. Get him in the front of the group. We're going that way, taking the next set of stairs down and to our exit," I pointed to my left where the next stairwell would be.

Sissa considered the idea briefly, biting her lip as she ran my words through her mind. "Okay." She sighed, resigned. "I trust you. Now tell *them*."

I looked around at all the worried faces—goblins, tall folks, military and civilian. Then I balled up my insecurities and threw them in the metaphorical furnace. If I could have Consumed them, I would have, and Engine would have burned long and hot. Maybe when I had time later, I'd be able to explore my feelings and have my little crisis of identity when we were good and safe . . . or we'd just be dead and I wouldn't have to worry about them after all.

Pushing forward through the crowd, I made my way to the outer edge of the wall where I climbed up on a crenelation, the grassy glade beyond the city at my back.

"Listen up!" I shouted, propelling the words forward with lots of air, lots of diaphragm. For the second time in my life, I was taken aback at how much I sounded like my dad. Everyone froze, blinking as they turned toward me.

"Hello. Uh. You all know who I am, yes?" I asked. A shaky start, but at least I'd started.

Nods from the crowd—from the tall folks, at least. The goblins just tilted their heads and stared, since they couldn't understand what I was saying.

I cleared my throat and swallowed, my mouth suddenly dry. "Alright. Great. The plan we had earlier today is still good," I said, hoping saying the thing would help it manifest in the world. "The only thing that has changed now is the route we're taking. This—" I swept my arm to my right to indicate the battlements of the wall. "—is our new road. It's narrow. It's exposed. It's dangerous. The enemy is closing in on us, and we will need to face them if we want to make it to safety."

I paused, thinking ahead. What I'd said so far was true. Utilitarian. Probably too much so. They all probably knew the score and needed something else to get them going.

What would Dad do? Something provocative but attainable. Solidify the group and give them a goal.

"The enemy is coming for us," I continued. "But our road, this wall, is high ground. It's defensible. Hell, it was made by the Dark Lord to *be* defended, right? Taking this wall was no easy feat. Just ask your crusader ancestors."

More nods.

"And you!" I pointed to the nearest Church guard. "This is your home. You've drilled on this very wall, haven't you? You've been taught by the best on just how to make the enemy pay dearly for even daring to take a step up here."

I was just guessing at this point, but it made sense that guards who lived in the city would have places on the wall they were trained to man when the time came. I was rewarded for my presumption with more vigorous nods.

The cold ember of my confidence gained a small puff of oxygen at that. "These monsters are strangers. Invaders. They invaded your home, but as long as you are alive, this place is still yours. This is still your wall."

Bishop Kolash stood out amongst the crowd as one of the tallest, his black eyes hard, his mouth turned down in a displeased frown. What did it look like to him, I wondered, to have his worst-nightmare-made-flesh taking charge of a small army? I needed to address Kolash—give him something to hold onto. Include him, if only to keep him onboard.

"This will be a moving fight, a bit slower-paced than we previously anticipated. We need fresh arms at the edges of the formation. If you're wounded, make your way to the center where His Holiness can take care of you. As he's done tirelessly for so long, he will be the heart of our group."

The bishop seemed loath to pull his eyes away from mine, maybe afraid I'd do something terrible and world-ending if he didn't keep me in sight at all times, but his love for his people conflicted with his fear of me just now. The nods and quiet thanks from the guards and civilians eventually warranted his attention, if only to return their sentiments. He, begrudgingly, gave everyone a quiet, toothless smile and bowed graciously.

Good.

"We won't get out of this without a good bit of blood," I continued, "but you are on your home turf. Fight like it. Talk to your sergeants about specifics. Keep the civilians in the middle of the group, away from the fighting—especially the children, unless you want your pockets picked."

There was a collective, nervous, chuckle from the guards, and knowing looks passed between them all. They'd lived together with the goblins for a while now, and there was no shortage of missing coin purses among them, I was sure. Not that there was anywhere to spend money around here anymore.

"As for the rest . . ." I hesitated, wondering if there was more I could say. No, probably not. Better to be brief. "Well, you know how to defend your own wall better than I ever could. You do your duty, and we'll all get out of here, one way or another. No one's getting left behind."

Now I was getting raised fists. Guards were slapping each other on the helmets and making little side comments. There were no psyched-up roars nor any cheering. That was fine. It didn't matter if they thought I was inspiring. What mattered was that they now had direction.

I channeled my dad once more: "Form up. We leave in five minutes."

That was all it took. The military units were off like bullets from a gun. The leaders took charge of their specific people. Meanwhile, Sissa, Samila, and Geddon quietly made their way toward the front of the group.

Skill unlocked: Leadership.
Your current Skill Level is 1.

On her way past, Samila shot me a look that was borderline lecherous. The woman looked hungry—greedy, even—in a way that only her complete and total ownership of the object of her desire could satisfy, and I found myself unable to move until her attention was elsewhere.

Dragons. Constance, save me from dragon women.

I climbed down from the crenelation only to find Tiba there with her two ironclad honor guards.

"We're moving now?" Tiba asked, grasping the gist of my speech already.

"Yes, Chief Tiba," I answered, followed by the slow release of the tense breath I'd been holding. "It's going to get bloody, but we're going to live or die trying."

It was Tiba's turn to look hungry, though it was nothing like Samila. She flashed one of the goblins' trademark wide, sharklike grins, but hers looked especially disturbing on a face that was otherwise so . . . adorable. "It's 'Queen Tiba,' actually. We all like the sound of it."

She turned to address her people. They were like another, separate crowd down there at leg level.

"Bows!" Tiba shouted. The goblins cheered—a screeching, animalistic sound. "Spears!" Another cheer. "Tooth and claw!"

Whatever that meant, it was far more inspiring than whatever I'd said. It lit a fire under the little army of green people. They scattered out amongst the tall folk and attached themselves to various groups, intuitively lining up on the soldiers' left sides.

Tiba pulled her fingers out of a pouch on her belt and smeared a crooked line of black grease diagonally over her face.

"I go to the front," she declared. It didn't sound like a request. I didn't take it as one.

As for me, my Abilities would be wasted in a running battle. As a bonus, that would get me out there on my own. There was no way I was going to keep up this leadership thing for an extended period of time, and it was probably best I made myself scarce before that useful illusion was dispelled.

I pushed through the middle of the crowd to the inside edge of the wall and peered over the side at the rooftops of the buildings down below.

"Trix!" I called. "Trix!"

The vulpa appeared on a passing guard's shoulder, which he used as a springboard to jump gracefully over to join me on top of my crenelation. Once he was on solid ground, he stood up straight, his deft hands playing over the trigger and bolt-carrier of his carbine.

"You have need of me, Ryan?" he asked.

"Oh, yes," I replied, bending down to let him climb up my arm. "We have a different role in this fight. Ready?"

Trix nodded as he dug his claws into my cloak and crouched low.

Then we took off in a run, hopping from crenulation to crenulation to rush ahead of the group. Our contribution to the battle was going to require a little setup.

CHAPTER TWELVE

Control the Field

I slapped a magazine in the final turret and secured the release lever. With a gentle whir from the aiming arms, it came to life, tracking back and forth in a roughly 60-degree angle that covered a block's worth of buildings and a long stretch of the city wall.

In front of us was a sprawling garden of rooftops, none of them the same height but uniformly rimmed with ornately carved railings braided with some kind of ivy or flowering vines. As with other parts of the city, most structures were less than a couple of feet apart, but that didn't mean you could traverse the rooftops easily, given how varied their heights were.

Smoke blew in from the west, giving everything a hazy, dreamlike sort of softness that belied the amount of violence that was happening in spurts and the rare gush.

The turrets were doing a good job of keeping the climbers from mounting the wall so far, but the Scourge-Touched were still systematically testing the defenses.

A cluster of monsters boiled up from the interior of a building adjacent to the wall, crouching low in one of the rare blind spots of the other emplacements, but our newly deployed turret was on the job, filling the clever creatures with holes before they could even get a good look around.

Trix's rifle barked twice behind me—two short, quiet reports followed a second later by the distinct sound of flesh hitting pavers at high velocity. That sounded close. Leaning over to my left, I looked down to street level four stories below, where two gangly figures lay broken and bloody.

Slowly, I turned and caught the little vulpa's eye, raising a questioning eyebrow. Trix's ears flattened in an expression I took as sheepish.

"More of the sneaky ones," he squeaked.

I shrugged. I couldn't fault him for letting them get so close. I hadn't heard them, either. The Returned could be very ninja-like in how little noise they made when they were "built" correctly. Lucky for us that the Dark Lord didn't tend to bother with maintaining good proportions for most.

"This was the last one. Third of the triangle," I informed him, putting a hand up to shade my eyes in order to better survey the battlefield. As I watched, four small, black shapes slipped onto a rooftop adjacent to the wall, prompting a double volley of fire from our main emplacement a block over. The fully automatic fire tore into the monster nearest the turrets and threw the thing's body back into its friends, where they all went down in a tangled heap. My programming was, in a word, merciless. The monsters were down but not dead, so the turret hosed the area with a long, sustained stream of lead until everything was still.

Knife in the Dark is now Level 23.

Another monster, this one cleverer than his dead comrades, came up on the other side of the emplacement, attempting to sneak onto the fortified roof and maybe flip one of the turrets. However, we'd put these turrets back-to-back, and before the Undead could get a hand on a support leg, one of the barrels tracked down and gave it a full three seconds of sustained fire directly in the chest. It fell away from the building's roof in pieces.

"This position's also the one I'm most concerned about getting overrun. Do you feel like you can defend this turret and make sure it stays up?" I asked Trix.

He stood tall and looked around much like I was, with a hand up to shade his eyes. "Not from here. But put me on that roof over there, and I think I can provide support," he replied, indicating a rooftop slightly farther into the city, across the street from our current spot.

I shook my head. "No, I don't like it. I wouldn't want something to sneak up on you while you're scratching the turrets' backs. The cool thing about machines is how expendable they are. How about that one?" I asked, pointing at a roof almost right next to the city wall, slightly taller than the one where we stood.

Trix let out a long breath. "It's very far away from here. I will not be able to aim as I'd like."

I looked at him with more than a little incredulity. "Really? You're, like, a prodigy when it comes to guns. It's—what? A block and a half, maybe two blocks away? You could make that."

"It's not that I can't hit at that range, but I am running low on ammunition. I need to kill with every shot if you want me to 'scratch their backs,' as you say. I don't like having to aim at that distance."

"I'm confused."

"I would need to—Alright, just hold on," Trix replied, bowing his head, bringing his claws up to rub at his face. He looked like he was crying or maybe rubbing dust out of his eyes or something. I was about to ask if he was okay, but he finished whatever he was doing before I could interject.

Then he raised his head, looking up at me with big, black, foxy eyes. They shone in the muted light of the morning, the picture of innocence and purity, like someone had crossed a kitten and a baby seal.

What the actual hell?!

I nearly fell off the roof. His eyes, while sizable before, had become massive, dominating the surface area of his head to a ridiculous degree. They were huge, deep-black, shiny, and just . . . so damned cute.

"Not one word!" Trix commanded, his tiny fox eyebrows angling down to give me the most adorable frown there ever was.

My fingers twitched. I longed to brush the little guy's fur, but my body tensed like an animal about to bolt. This felt so . . . unnatural. It was uncanny.

I froze, my brain becoming a metronome beat, wobbling back and forth between the opposing impulses of "run away screaming" and "run forward hugging." I'd seen cartoons with something like his current facial proportions, but seeing them in real life was both better and worse in every way.

My mouth engaged before the rest of me could.

"Trix, what is happening? Why do I want to dress you in overalls and call you Mr. Cuddlebums?"

"I know," Trix lamented with a sigh. He passed a clawed hand over his face, and suddenly his eyes were back to normal and my cuteness reflex went back to a manageable state—mid-combat levels, at least. Trix's pointy vulpa ears drooped down until they were lying on the top of his head, as if in shame. "I told you my species' nature is based on deception. Part of that is distorting perception."

Still confused, I took a second to consider. "So, you magnified your eyes. Like you magicked up some thick glasses? Then why did I—uh—want to . . . you know . . ."

The diminutive vulpa could no longer meet my gaze. Instead he focused hard on the roof directly across the street from us. "It is a glamour," he explained. "An old one that enhances my perception and beguiles others. Easier to see danger, harder for said danger to hurt us. It is the first one we learn when we are kits."

I shrugged. "That sounds pretty awesome, actually. Telescopic vision with an . . . adorability shield? What's the problem, then?"

"If you could have seen your face when I used it, you would understand. I don't just bend the light. I affect the mind. You were not yourself, and I had no right to influence you in such a way."

"That's fair, I guess," I admitted tentatively. Just as his glamour had overloaded the affection section of my brain, his healing magic was much the same, tricking the subject's body into healing itself using whatever reserves it had to hand. That probably wasn't healthy in the long run despite the short-term benefits. I still couldn't get past seeing these things as tools as opposed to grave offenses like Trix did, though. Then again, I was the guy with Level 5 Deception, and I'd hated every time it Leveled Up. If I tried to convince Trix to use his magic, I'd be a pretty big hypocrite.

"Okay," I began, thinking of how to get around this. "We can find a different rooftop or—"

Trix tilted his head slightly, distracted. Then he snapped his rifle's muzzle up to blast another Returned in the face. This one had climbed up the gutter nearly right next to me.

"Sneaky," Trix pronounced, finally looking me in the eye again.

"Yeah," I replied, drawing the word out as I thought.

BRRRAP! BRAP!

Two more short volleys of turret fire cut through the late morning air, and I got another triple grouping of Experience messages.

There was a shout in the distance. The long formation of refugees was finally getting into range of our defenses.

"Well, that's it," I said. "I guess the setup phase is over."

Trix knew as well as I did we were out of time. That's why he was already shouldering his rifle and skittering toward the edge of the roof. Before he had a chance to leap off, I crouched down and put a hand on his shoulder.

"Hey, you don't have to use it. Find another roof, and we'll deal."

"No, it is fine," Trix replied, shaking his head. "Perhaps it is time I used all the tools at my disposal." His voice was full of trepidation. There was a fragility in its tone that hurt to listen to.

"You know, Trix," I began, hoping I was doing the right thing here, "there was a famous general once, a human, probably the most famous general our planet ever produced. He was a military genius who literally wrote the book on the art of war. One of his most famous quotes, probably the only one I can remember offhand, was something along the lines of 'All warfare is based on deception.' I know you have your reasons, but the way I see it, if your cause is just, it's probably worth giving it everything. Maybe there's a very real, tangible use for tricks in times like this."

The little vulpa turned back to give me a quizzical look, one ear up, head tilted.

I gave him my best, most confident grin. "I don't know. It's worth considering, at least. With everything that's at stake, I, for one, plan to fight dirty."

Any man worth killing is worth killing in his sleep.

Barrow's words he'd intoned just before killing my only friend in the world echoed in my mind. Where had that come from?

I suppressed a shudder. Yes, I would probably go down as the first person in Ralqir's history to kill monsters on an industrial scale, but I wasn't anything like Barrow. I would never be that far gone, even with the corrupting influence of the System.

"Thank you, Ryan. I will think about what you said, maybe after this is over." Trix said, leaning in conspiratorially. "Can we keep my methods a secret, though? If it gets out that I can—Well, I get enough unsolicited hugs as it is. While it is more than fine coming from wayward children, the adults make me uncomfortable."

"Not one word," I promised. I held a finger to my lips for emphasis.

The air was thick with the sound of gunfire.

So far, the plan was working, though not without some problems. Some I'd foreseen, others not so much.

The plan, on paper, was simple: A triangular formation of overlapping fire.

In practice, though, things were getting increasingly dicey.

Trix and I had set up turrets in three separate places along the route the refugees would take. We'd placed two of them on the tallest roof we could find as close to the wall as we could feasibly get. These were our scraper turrets. They stood back-to-back, angled in such a way that their fields of fire traversed along the wall's face and the rooftops that the Scourge would theoretically be using to jump onto the wall.

A block away, deeper into the city, was the overwatch turret that kept monsters that actually made it onto the wall in check, as well as covering the other emplacements and keeping them from being attacked en masse.

Then there was the turret that covered our exfil stairs. That one, while initially our hottest attraction, had quieted down in the last few minutes. That concerned me.

Right now, the gun that was engaged the most was the far overwatch turret, taking care of the Scourge-Touched that the others had missed and felling foes that had been lucky enough to make it onto the battlements.

I'd not designed this model for long-distance engagements, but it was doing a fair job. It might not hit the tiny monsters like the Touched goblins on the first shot, but it almost always got them in three— no more than five. It also picked off curious Scourge-Touched that decided to make the rooftops their road like Trix and I did.

The number of climbers was steadily increasing, meaning the general saturation of Scourge-Touched was probably getting worrisome as well. The question was: *where were they?* Occasionally, a Returned would stick its head out onto the rooftops that Trix and I had made our area, but it wasn't nearly as often as it should have been.

If the Scourge weren't funneling over to the stairs, what were they doing?

The overwatch turret would run out of ammo first, I was sure of it, but until then I was staying close to the wall with Trix.

BRRRRRRRRRRR!

Suddenly the overwatch turret went full auto. I put my hand up to shield my eyes and squinted through the ever-thickening smoke to see where it was aiming.

Something dark and heavy slammed onto the rooftop a couple of buildings away, crashing through ivied latticework and sending sticks of splintered wood flying. Another something slapped wetly down on the edge of the wall behind me, and when I turned to see what it was, I got a face full of feathers as the body rebounded off the railing to come to rest at my feet.

At first I didn't know what I was looking at, as twisted as the thing was from its fall, but I quickly recognized it as a bird. It was a strangely built one, too, with a solid-looking daggerlike beak, dark green, almost-black feathers, and a compact body attached to long, reedy legs and claw-tipped feet. The smell of it flooded my nostrils—wet fur mixed with something spicy like cinnamon.

I knew it. Flying Scourge. It was bound to happen eventually.

We didn't have birds on Proxis 3—not like this, at least. The closest we came were kite lizards, but those tiny nomads rarely came down from the upper atmosphere except to mate. My home sky was dominated by Proxis 2 but empty of living things. The thought of flocks of birds flapping and swooping everywhere had always held a sort of magic for me, an element of myth and legend from a home I'd never set foot upon. A sort of instinctual nostalgia for a place I'd never been.

The creature at my feet was alien yet familiar. Beautiful too.

And I'd killed it instantly.

Was there any wildlife on this planet I hadn't killed the moment I met it?

I took a moment to check my Combat Log.

Scourge-Touched Pickur defeated.
You have been awarded 16 Experience points. [10 base (-8 Level, +2 nemesis, +10 group, +10 chain, -8 non-combat Class)]
Scourge-Touched Pickur defeated.
You have been awarded 16 Experience points. [10 base (-8 Level, +2 nemesis, +10 group, +10 chain, -8 non-combat Class)]
Scourge-Touched Pickur defeated.
You have been awarded 16 Experience points. [10 base (-8 Level, +2 nemesis, +10 group, +10 chain, -8 non-combat Class)]
Scourge-Touched Morblin defeated.
You have been awarded 34 Experience points. [40 base (-2 Level, +8 nemesis, +10 group, +10 chain, -32 non-combat Class)]

Oh, thank Constance it was Scourge-Touched.

Still, I suddenly felt the need to share.

"Hey, Trix! Birds!" I shouted over my shoulder in the general direction of where I knew the little vulpa had found his perch, somewhere up on the lattice. I would have joined him up there, but I'd already broken a section of it earlier. Oh, the curse of being heavy.

"Yes, I see!" Trix replied, taking time to put two rounds into something far away only he could see. "Very worrisome!"

"We don't have those back home! I always wanted to see one!"

"That is unfortunate!" Trix shouted back to me over the sound of the guns. "These are diving pickurs! Very dangerous! Do not let them hit you!"

"I hadn't planned on it! They're infected! Just saying, this is a first for me!" I wanted to share the moment with someone, but, apparently, being a local took some of the magic out of birdwatching.

"Our planet has not sent its best ambassadors, I am afraid! Keep your eyes on the sky and watch for divers! They kill by burying their beaks into your skull!"

Another rooftop exploded in shattering wood and loose feathers further down the wall.

"Noted," I said, sparing a glance upward. The smoke and the chaotic light from the aurora around the moon were making spotting anything moving up there challenging, however. At least the turrets weren't having a problem.

Behind me, the refugees made their way forward slowly—more slowly than I'd anticipated. I'd hoped for a sort of jog to the stairwell and then a shuffle down the stairs to the street level, but that wasn't happening. The long line of people was shuffling forward in a strange sort of inchworm fashion, the front of the formation surging ahead, then stopping while the rest of the line hurried to catch up. Meanwhile the back of the formation lagged behind everyone, having to shuffle backwards as they kept their crossbows aimed at the monsters coming up from behind to chase.

Geddon and the heavies were in front, as we'd planned, Sissa and Samila with him, along with Tiba and her honor guard. Bole was there, too, floating between the lot of them. However, most of their time and effort were being put into finishing downed monsters and throwing perforated corpses over the sides of the walls.

While the tall folk were in an orderly wedge, Tiba was going about her duties with an enthusiasm that was downright disturbing. She screamed at the top of her lungs and dove upon any living Scourge in range, laying into them with Hunty's spear, stabbing them over and over until they stopped moving. Then she was onto the next one. No hesitation. No mercy.

Once they were in earshot, I cupped my hands over my mouth and asked them what they needed.

"Less smoke, if you can manage it!" Sissa yelled. Her sword was black with Scourge blood, and her armor was stained with more of the same. "Hard to spot the clever ones until they are right upon us!"

I looked over at the former refugee camp where the fires were still raging, along with a good portion of the adjacent neighborhoods. That problem was just going to get worse, and I hadn't bothered developing a giant fan-turret.

Our Scourge problem was, concurrently, going to get worse as well.

"Any way to pick up the pace?!" I asked.

"Unless you can guarantee nothing will approach us from behind, no! We can't afford for the rear guard to turn around! Too much risk!"

Now that they were well within the overwatch turret's field of fire, that should take care of most monsters before they could approach the back rank, but it wasn't a 100 percent success rate. We could be stuck for the long haul unless something changed.

"Okay, just keep coming. I'll think of something!" I replied.

"Ryan!"

Trix noticed it before I did. I was just reengaging the lever on one of the two wall scraper turrets when an entire barn-sized piece of the city wall ceased to be a piece of the city wall. What was once grayish black stone, wobbled and distorted, peeling away from the whole. Gray, wrinkled flesh replaced the stone camouflage, and the bumpy, pimpled skin of whatever-this-thing-was stretched itself so thin, I could almost see the wall through the thin membrane of flesh as it reached up toward the top of the battlements.

BRRRRRAP!

The turret's attacks covered the length of the creature with withering fire now that the monster had revealed itself. The monster let out a high-pitched keening sound as it shuddered—a disturbing ululation as the stone color returned to its skin, but it didn't seem to be a pain or fear response. The massive creature was still drawing itself fluidly upward toward the lip of the battlements.

Heedless of the Damage it was taking, the monster flexed, reaching up to skewer a guardsman with a sharp, protruding bone appendage that poked out of the top of its body. The guard screamed as he was plucked from between the crenulations and over the side. Displaced air whooshed past me as the monster proceeded to repeatedly slam the guard's body into the wall with near-supernatural speed, pulping the man against the stone. Mercifully, he was probably already dead after the first blow.

Constance save me. We're drawing wild cards again, aren't we?

Ralqir's wildlife, as strange and alien as it was, continued to surprise me with how dangerous it could be when turned to murderous purpose. Scourged undead and goblins I could wrap my head around just fine, but these things . . .

The creature's skin rippled again and changed color to blend better into its new position on the wall, but I had its number now and so did the turrets.

Maybe it had something to do with its size or mojo, but despite knowing it was there, I almost lost it again instantaneously, like my brain couldn't handle something so large changing color and texture right in front of my eyes.

The turret wasn't fooled, however. It raked the monster with Damage, but the bullets weren't finding anything vital. What holes they were making, dripped black, giving the false wall the appearance of weeping.

If gunfire was ineffectual, I'd need to implement Plan B. I bounded forward, jumping from my roof to the next one over, sailing down one floor to crash onto the wooden surface. My foot sank into the roof slats with a crunch, but luckily that was as far down as I went. My flamer turret was in my hand before I'd even dislodged myself.

FWOOSH!

The "wall" wailed and separated itself from its perch. Like the Returned, this thing seemed particularly flammable, the crackling yellow crawling up the thing's skin and overloading whatever process it was using to blend its color with the wall's. The full mass of the creature rippled with yellow and red waves as it keened, flapping its skin to attempt to shake off the homemade napalm with little success. After a couple of heartbeats, whatever-it-was lost its hold on the stone, the top of the monster letting go first and peeling away, a slow-motion falling from . . .

Oh, shiiiiiiit!

I'd turned the flaming monster into a giant, crushing wave of cooking meat, and I was about to get a face full of it.

Cursing, I dropped the flamer, ripped my leg out of the floor, and dove from the roof, barely ahead of the sound of snapping wood and crackling fire. Superheated air blew my cloak up and over my head, obscuring all but what was directly below me: mostly just hard, unforgiving cobblestone.

The street rushed up to meet me, but, for better or worse, I had lots of horizontal momentum.

It was worse, actually.

I slammed face-first into a planter someone had set on their windowsill, smashing through the soil and terracotta pottery while shards of it sank into the flesh under my chin. The impact blinded me and flipped me over until I was falling backward.

I didn't see the cobblestone before I hit it. On the bright side, I didn't hit it head-first.

Jumping is now Level 3.

Groaning, I gasped for breath as my eyes struggled to focus.

My back felt like I'd landed on it wrong, cracking and popping as I rolled over onto my side. The sky above me was occluded by something semi-solid, draped over the rooftops of a few of the nearest buildings while sagging in the middle like a wet tent. Smoke billowed from the crisping creature as pieces of thin, shrinking flesh flopped onto the street like melted plastic.

"Ryan! Run! Now!"

I shook my head and panted as I got my feet under me.

Another series of pops from my spine. Oh, that felt better. Not all the way better, but . . . I would definitely be sore later.

I cast about looking for the best direction to run, as Trix had ordered, but then the facade of one of the buildings a short way down the street exploded as an armored train plowed through its ground floor. Dust, various bits of cloth, upholstery, and shattered wood vomited out onto the cobblestones as the Bray Knight tumbled blindly over and through the ruin it had made, thumping to a stop against the corner of a building across the street.

It had looked better. Its body was now a charred and cracked mass of rage, the once-straight, functional edges of its massive, armored plates warped and soot-covered. Its visored eyes wept black sludge, and its hooves were just ragged sticks of exposed bone and sinew. It wobbled on its feet, shaking its head and chuffing, sending loose dirt flying in all directions.

Its head clicked as it rotated nearly all the way around, winding itself up for what was about to come.

I couldn't be sure, but I could have sworn the thing's visored gaze was affixed directly upon me.

Now I really had to run.

CHAPTER THIRTEEN

Be the Bait

R un!" Trix shouted at me, as if I needed to be told twice. The last place I
wanted to be was on ground level. None of our turrets' lines of sight covered
it, with the exception of the one by the stairs, and I was nowhere near those. Oh,
and I was also about to be turned into jelly by an angry cow.

I ran.

"Not that way!"

A wave of pale and dark bodies slammed into me from the side, out of the
thin gap between two shops I'd already written off as too narrow to contain any
danger. The Scourge broadsided me, nearly forcing me to the ground before
I even knew what was happening, but my enhanced reflexes and greater mass
helped me convert the hit into a staggering blow instead of an overwhelming
dogpile.

Hands reached for me and teeth snapped at my legs as I angled away and
sprinted in the only direction I could see was clear. Most of my attackers fell
away, unable to cling to a fast-moving target, but I felt the claws of the shorter
Scourge-Touched tear holes in my pants and rip the edges of my cloak. Only
two of the particularly ambitious among them managed to hang onto me—one
onto my leg, the other on my back. They didn't slow me down, however. I had
inertia on my side. Where I was going, they came with me, all the way across the
miniature intersection to blast our way through the double-doorway of an inn.

I used my prosthetic to take the initial impact against the well-crafted wooden
doors, while my weight did the rest, blowing them off their hinges. As my new
friends and I barreled through, I leaned sideways to clip the solid-looking door-
jamb on my left, hearing a slightly different type of crunch as bone gave way and
one of the monsters lost its grip.

The Scourge on my back gibbered and slobbered on the base of my neck,
tearing through the thick cloth of my cloak with its sharp teeth to get at the
tender flesh beneath.

Reaching back, I grabbed onto its face, trying to trigger Devouring Grasp, but it wriggled out of my grip before I could clamp down.

I knew the rest of them were right behind me along with the Bray, so I didn't stop or even break stride. Instead I kept moving, weaving between round tables in the middle of the communal dining room, which seemed to have been set up for the express purpose of slowing you down if you were on your way to the stairs at the back of the building.

I needed to get higher. Street level was absolutely a no-go considering I'd been down here for all of ten seconds, and I was already fighting for my life.

FOOM!

Sure, I'd made a bit of a dramatic entrance by smashing through the door, but I had to admit the Bray Knight's was better.

The doorway, tables, lacquered wooden floor, and half of the bar became a hurricane of aerosolized wood. I wasn't in the magical cone of destruction, but I was close enough to be blasted forward with the rest of the displaced air, stumbling to my knees before rolling into, then *onto* the stairs. My passenger and I flipped end over end to crash against the far railing. The creature let out a choked sort of gurgle as I landed on it hard.

With a snap, one of the thick logs that made up the inn's series of support pillars partially gave way, its tree-trunk-thick wood bending while fibrous bits exploded out from its side.

I didn't have time to get to my feet. Coughing, I rolled over and bear-crawled up those stairs, hands and feet frantically taking whatever hold I could find, getting more distance between myself and death. The Scourge on my back was stunned but still there. Its hands clutched at my cloak as if I were a life preserver.

The second-floor landing had a lean to it—understandable given a good chunk of the building was now gone. Sawdust clumped in my mouth and irritated my throat as I panted and looked for a way out.

Where was the access to the roof? Every stupid building in Eclipse had roof access. I couldn't find any here, though.

I turned and sprinted the only way I could go, down the hallway, passing a line of doors that I assumed led to sleeping accommodations.

CRACK!

The entire structure groaned as it leaned further out of whack. I cursed whoever it was had designed this building. They must have thought themselves so clever, bucking tradition and putting the stairs far away from the entrance.

Scourge-Touched Goblin hits you for 8 Damage. (slashing)

"Grplgblaaagh!" the asshole on my back said as it ripped into me anew.

"I know! I know!" I shrieked. My panicked mind could only deal with one life-ending threat at a time, and the thing on my back wasn't even in the top five on my priorities list at the moment, paling in comparison to the Bray Knight and the collapsing building. But if we stayed here much longer, we would both end up in pieces.

Stairs. Stairs. Where are the stairs?

Around a corner and down another hallway, I found my answer. There was a ladder that went up and through a hatch to get to the roof. Wonderful.

Heavy hoofbeats followed me all the while. Ever since I'd burned a large part of its throat away, the Bray's tone was a mournful, multi-toned thing, making it sound like an old train whistle.

BOOMF!

The shutters at the end of the hall blasted open, and the world tilted on its axis as the Bray Knight reminded us we weren't safe even up here.

Status gained: Concussed [3 seconds]

My ears rang as I stumbled to the side, vaguely feeling my Scourge-Touched passenger sliding off my back to finally land on the floor.

Weaving drunkenly, I rebounded off the far wall and got a hand on the ladder to start pulling myself up, when half of the hallway disappeared, crashing down to the lower floor and bringing a significant part of the roof down to my level. The wood underneath me splintered and buckled, a floor slat at my feet snapping under the pressure and shooting sharp shards of wood into my calf.

Status Gained: Bleeding [1 HP/sec]

"Gaaaaah!" I shouted in pain, hopping onto the first rung of the ladder and using my upper body to get extra height. Up the ladder to the roof.

I reached daylight. Then I saw the rooftops of the buildings across my street, except everything was at an angle, tipping.

No. No. No. No. No! No!

I had to focus all of my attention on steadying myself with my hands and feet to try to not slide off into the street, while down below, the Bray kicked and stomped through those precious supports that had previously been keeping the building upright.

Meanwhile, the Scourge—maybe a hundred of them—poured into the street, pooling at the base of my perch's closest wall, waiting for me to come down and join them.

Wincing in pain, I limped up the slope to the roof's railing and leapt for the closest adjacent structure on my side of the street. I aimed for an open shutter about five feet above my current altitude, but unfortunately, the inn chose that moment to collapse entirely.

I had a moment at the apex of my short flight where my target window was almost within reach—where I considered trying to activate Tension Step again—but the memory of just how badly it had debilitated me last time warned me away.

Then the moment was gone.

I landed in a heap amid the still-settling rubble, back on street level but not swarmed with monsters as of yet. The inn's roof came all the way down with a *woomph!* and sprayed the area with a cloud of dust.

Adrenaline had me up on my feet again within a second, and I turned to discern some kind of direction where I might be able to run, but all I could see was the looming shadow of the wall. With no other landmarks, I coughed up something akin to mud or paste, then limped in the general direction of the sound of my turrets.

My eyes stung with all the irritants in the air. Hopefully, it would be as debilitating to the Scourge-Touched.

I summoned my sword and turned on Detect Iron as a precaution, reeling slightly at all the new sensory data. Running with it on would probably have been a bad idea even on a good day. Right now, all it was showing me was my body, my sword, and the trail of blood I was leaving as I limped on.

"Ryan!" Trix called from above me. I looked up but couldn't see where his voice was coming from.

"What?" I asked, staggering to a stop but bending at the knees to be ready to strike at the next monster I saw.

"They're at the stairs! Keep doing what you're doing!" Trix shouted.

"I've got a mad cow chasing me!" I replied. My voice echoed eerily off the hard surfaces of the empty alley, and my eyes darted nervously from window to window.

"Yes, I know! We cannot let it go near the main group! Keep it busy and off the route until they get to the exit!"

I did a full 360-degree turn, blinking the dust out of my eyes while I tried to get my bearings. "Which direction is the exit?!" I asked.

There was a pause as I assumed Trix did some checking. "One street over and that way!"

I spun in a circle, looking for where Trix was, but for the life of me I couldn't see him. "Which way?" I asked. I had to move right now, or I was in danger of being swarmed.

"Toward the wall and to the left!"

"Any chance you could toss a turret down here?" I asked, already not optimistic for the answer. A short, muffled howl came from one of the buildings behind me. "And soon?"

"Too heavy," Trix lamented. "And those metal claws really hold on tight. Maybe if I had a saw or an ax. You should really consider making a release for those."

I cursed. My own shortsightedness was coming back to bite me. Again.

The gears in my head ground together as I searched for a plan, then found one I didn't like.

I summoned a vibrating purple fuel rod and cradled it in my hand as I made ready to throw it. "Trix, whatever you do, do not drop this!"

I gasped for breath, coughing and gagging. The smoke choked me and stung my eyes as I stumbled through the burning alleyway. With every step, my left boot squished and popped as tiny bubbles of my blood were forced out through the seams. My cloak was mostly gone now, ripped away in a half-a-dozen close calls.

Honestly, with how badly the rest of my clothes were faring, I felt lucky I still had part of my mask. It had a few ragged holes now, so it no longer covered the entirety of my face, but it must have been enough, because I hadn't been swarmed yet. I hadn't heard that world-shaking howl yet, as I had the first time I ran distraction for others.

The wall loomed up in front of me through the smoke. It was thick here—black and suffocating. Many of the buildings in this part of the neighborhood had been on fire since this morning, and they were all well and truly unsalvageable by now, their insides burning, their outsides pouring obscuring smoke into the air. Some of the roofs had already collapsed and become fuel to hasten the rest of their demise.

Everything in my immediate vicinity was on fire. That was bad. The upside was that it protected me from a lot of the small fries that were tracking me too. While I'd made my way through the burning neighborhood at great cost to myself and a significant loss of HP, my pursuers weren't nearly so durable. They had to go the long way around or risk falling to the blaze as I nearly did. It was sad that I didn't get the XP for those kills, though.

HP 102/230

The trick with this little maneuver was keeping the Bray Knight's attention while staying just enough ahead of it to not be blasted to pieces. It was an art more than a science, one I hadn't really gotten the hang of. I had never been good at art.

The Bray was plenty pissed at me from when I set it on fire—even more so for my having managed to avoid its overwhelming strength for so long. Honestly, it was strange that the plan was working as well as it was. If I were the collective mind of the Scourge-Touched, I'd have most definitely pulled my heavy hitter off the slippery guy and gone for the more vulnerable folks after the third or fourth near-miss. That hadn't happened yet, though.

Could it only control its monsters to a certain degree? Was there a limit? Was it more like a nudge than full control? Maybe compelling its troops to do things took more energy than letting them operate on their own wherewithal until they were needed. That made sense.

This was all speculation, though. Maybe when I became a Scourge monster myself, I could put that mystery to bed. Hooray.

I shook my head. Whatever the answer was, I still needed to stay one step ahead of the Scourge—as long as it took to get people to safety. If my internal sense of direction was accurate, I was now close to where I needed to be. The wall was right here on my left, near enough to touch. The burning husks of the buildings looked vaguely familiar, and I could just barely make out a thick concentration of flames in front of me that just might be the junk berm I'd set ablaze not too long ago.

If this was my alley, which I was inclined to believe it was, then this was as good a position as I might get. I stumbled forward, coughing, my sword slippery in my hand from sweat and a little blood from the multitude of cuts on my arm. I'd need to be in position by the time the Scourge found me, then I'd just need to hope Trix had done his part of the "plan"—if you could call it that.

I listened for the right sounds. There was at least one turret out there that was still operating. I wasn't sure which one. Its *brap! brap!* cover fire confirmed we were still in a fight.

Something big snapped behind me—a wall or a pillar that finally gave up after enough of it had been consumed by the flames.

The Bray should have gotten here by now. Had I lost it?

How long had it been? Twenty minutes? Thirty? Had to have been. They had to have made it to the smugglers' tunnels by now.

Just one more thing to do.

I knew my opponent was out there. It just needed a little encouragement. The Bray itself couldn't actually see. I'd figured that out. Probably a side effect of taking a face full of homemade napalm. Instead, it relied on its comrades to see for it, having the collective consciousness feed it my position continuously.

So, I surmised that I needed a volunteer.

I hobbled forward, drawing upon the supernatural awareness of Detect Iron. My timing would need to be right.

The muscles in my shoulder and torso tensed in preparation. Then I lunged, grabbing a Scourge-Touched goblin by the throat. He'd been waiting there on the surface of the city wall and probably hadn't seen me yet, but I'd certainly seen him and his iron-rich blood. Thank Constance the Baned had at least some real blood in them.

The creature gurgled as I gripped its throat and held it out at arm's length, giving it a nice, clear picture of my masked face, making sure it knew I was the guy.

I got what I wanted.

With a roar, the Bray crashed through one of the burning buildings, sending a shower of sparks into the alley and stumbling as it caught itself. Like me, it looked rundown, burned, and bleeding.

It was slow to get up, as damaged as its underside was, but it was hanging in there just for me.

This was the place, I was sure. I just had to hope it was also the time.

I reached up with my sword hand and pulled off my mask. My lips were too dry to whistle, so I settled for words.

"Come on, you little shits," I said directly into my captured Baned's face, making sure it got a good look.

With that, the world around me shook with the rage of the Scourges' howls. The city was alive again with the fury of the horde. Good luck getting to me in time, though.

Now that I had their full attention, I skewered the corrupted goblin and let it fall to the ground. Then I started backing up, feeling the heat intensify on my back as I approached the remains of the junk berm.

The Bray fumed, its lungs letting loose a long, angry roar as it charged forward.

The cobblestones under its feet split, the drunken line it ran slamming it hard into the stones of the wall, rebounding to clip the charred corner of one of the buildings and sending a storm of sparks flying.

With a fortifying breath and a silent prayer, I finally triggered the rod I'd given Trix.

Near-instantaneously, the alleyway became an epileptic's worst nightmare. Hundreds—no, *thousands*—of flashing, pulsing, purple lasers poured out of the far end of the alley, where the laser turret I'd set up upon our arrival yesterday was still functioning—the one Trix had reloaded for me.

The lasers split wood, panged off stone, splatted and sizzled when they struck water. Their accuracy hadn't improved since yesterday, but they still did the job. They collectively ripped into the back of the Bray Knight, thousands of tiny attacks chewing up the monster's flesh, dissolving it like acid.

You hit Scourge-touched Bray Knight for 3 Damage. (0 base, +3 Knife in the Dark bonus)

Scourge-Touched Bray Knight is marked.

Scourge-Touched Bray Knight is cursed.

Scourge-Touched Bray Knight takes 3 Damage. (0 base, +3 Knife in the Dark bonus)

Scourge-Touched Bray Knight takes 1 Damage. (0 base, +1 Marked bonus)

Scourge-Touched Bray Knight takes 1 Damage. (0 base, +1 Marked bonus)

Scourge-Touched Bray Knight resists mark.

Scourge-Touched Bray Knight takes 3 Damage. (0 base, +3 Knife in the Dark bonus)

Scourge-Touched Bray Knight is marked.

Scourge-Touched Bray Knight is cursed.

Scourge-Touched Bray Knight resists mark.
You hit Scourge-Touched Bray Knight for 3 Damage. (0 base, +3 Knife in the Dark bonus)
Scourge-Touched Bray Knight is marked.
Scourge-Touched Bray Knight is cursed.
Scourge-Touched Bray Knight takes 1 Damage. (0 base, +1 Marked bonus)
Scourge-Touched Bray Knight takes 1 Damage. (0 base, +1 Marked bonus)
Scourge-Touched Bray Knight resists mark.
Scourge-Touched Bray Knight takes 3 Damage. (0 base, +3 Knife in the Dark bonus)

Not every laser hit, but they didn't need to. This was a hurricane of purple light. The particulates in the air contrasted with their brightness, widening and diluting the intensity of the beams, but every one retained its lethality.

The Bray charged, but the back half of the monster simply fell apart, collapsing in upon itself, the skin, muscle, and tissue flaking away to expose raw bone, rainbow-colored with the greasy, vaguely organic byproduct of the weird bonus damage from Knife in the Dark.

With no muscles to support its weight anymore, the knight sagged in the middle and tumbled forward, mid-stride, as the laser-light show concluded. The juggernaut's prodigious size and weight gave it substantial inertia, however. It slid inexorably toward me, the cobblestones and packed dirt beneath cracking and piling up in a wave of earth until the dying monster came to a stop just feet away from me.

The Bray Knight's head flicked, spasmed. Its breaths were weak.

click clack CLACK!

The head turned in the Bray's pitted and cracked armor. I couldn't see its eyes, but the black-stained visor stared into me as it prepared to strike one last time at me as its final act in this universe.

CLICK!

Lunging forward, I snagged the Bray's head in my Iron Grip, the metal fingers of my hand curling behind the outer edge and clamping down. The armor bent under my fingers, and tiny cracks formed in its surface.

Devouring Grasp (Magivore) [5 MP/sec]

The strange metallic bone that made up the Bray's shell suddenly crumpled like a beer can, and black liquid shot out of the monster's visor and onto my pants.

Down at my feet, a smoky, gray crystal clinked off the cobblestones.

"Better luck next time, asshole," I said. I hoped the Scourge heard me.

Scourge-Touched Bray Knight defeated.
You have been awarded 8,082 Experience points. [14,300 base (+1,222 Level, +2,000 group, +2,000 chain, -11,440 non-combat Class)]
Level Up!
You are now Level 18.
Loot Scourge-Touched Bray Knight? Y/N

Yes.

I queried the System and let the rest of the messages scroll by, two levels worth of achievements.

Summary - Levels 17 and 18:

1x All Natural: You have spent 80% of this Level with full mana. [+1 Body]
2x Spirit of the Warrior: You gained 51% of your Experience this Level from defeated foes as a non-combat Class. [+3 spirit]
1x Near Death Experience: You fell below 10% of your HP this Level. [50% bonus Experience gain for next Level]
2x Doing Your Part: Some of your creations have been used against agents of the Scourge. [+200% Experience awarded for new designs next Level]
2x Big Spender: You have spent 5,000% of your total mana pool this Level. [+1% mana regeneration per second]
1x Rift Hunter: You gained 51% of your Experience this Level from Nemesis-tagged foes. [+1 to all Attributes]
1x Inventor: You have created at least five new designs this Level. [+1 Mind]
1x Boss Killer: You have defeated a foe far above you in Level. [+2 to all Attributes]
1x Ambitious: You have defeated a foe above your Level. [+1 to lowest Level Ability]
1x Reversal: You gained 100% of your Experience this Level from Nemesis-tagged foes. [+3 to highest Attribute]

Shakily, I bent down as I hurriedly stored the gray crystal that held the Bray Knight's spell. As for the loot from the monster, that was a mystery. It was a shiny silver glob of . . . something that felt smooth and pliable when I touched it—so pliable that it slipped through my fingers like liquid every time I tried to pick it up.

So I made it vanish into my Spatial Storage where I could examine it later.

Now it was time to go.

The Southern Gate burned behind me as I flew down the alley to finally join the others.

CHAPTER FOURTEEN

Learn to Breathe

I sat on the floor with my legs crossed, both of my arms relaxed and resting on my lap. The white, stone floor underneath me felt cold and uncomfortable after so much time, and I knew that when I got up, I'd be sore from being in this position for too long.

Click click click . . . The delicate rhythm of the automatic magazine loader's rubber-tipped plunger kept time for me, since my heart could not. The hopper that fed the machine shifted slightly as some cavity the drain had created over the course of minutes finally collapsed, and the whole device squeaked, wobbling in place as fifty-or-so pounds of ammunition found a new comfortable position.

Far across the workshop, another newly shaped conical bullet slapped onto the corrugated tin with a *POCK!* and gently rolled down the surface to join the rest of its kin in the rain barrel. Judging by the sound, the barrel was almost full, and the automated turnstile would be moving soon to put a new empty barrel in its place. That meant I'd been at this for multiple hours with very little to show for it.

The blue motes floated out there in the ether, tantalizingly close yet stubbornly independent in their behavior. No matter how many times I gathered them and ran them through my mana channels, the moment I took my attention away from them, they seemed to grow a mind of their own and fly off into the wild blue yonder to do whatever me-mana liked to do. Herding cats is how others might have put it but not I. Cats were at least intelligent animals.

Just get in here, so I can be done, you little jerks.

I didn't open my eyes. If I did that, I knew I'd find Jassin there doing that squinty-eyed stare of his that made me feel like a bug under a microscope. There had to be something more important that he could be doing right now. Why was he still here watching me trying and failing to do the thing?

Don't think about Jassin. Think about how you did it before. Focus.

I longingly fantasized about a scenario where a harried guard would burst into the room and yell, "My Lord Headmaster! The goblins have gotten into the tea, and they've begun constructing a giant war barge made of scones!" and we'd all have to rush off and deal with the crisis and forget we were ever going to sit down and do *nothing* over the course of several hours.

We'd been back in the Spire for a day and a half now, and I'd accomplished precious little other than getting the factory humming again. Oh, and getting the magazine loader up and running. The interns had been glad for that. More than a few of them were sporting bandaged fingers and tired eyes now after having been at the job for so long.

We'd lost surprisingly few people getting everyone from the wall to the underground. Given the circumstances, I thought we'd take heavy casualties once everyone got to ground level as they bottlenecked at the entrance to the smugglers' tunnels. However, most of our losses came from surprise attacks like the big camouflage monster that had almost killed me after I set it on fire. Another two fell to the dive-bombing pikurs after my overwatch turret ran dry on ammo, but that was near the tail end of the evacuation. The Church guards took the brunt of it all, doing their duty to the last to protect the goblins and other civilians in the group.

Once we'd made our way through the tunnels and spilled out into the Spire, everything seemed to slow down to a crawl. Maybe it was the adrenaline finally dying down for everyone, but most of the guards and a good portion of the goblins just flopped down on the floor and fell asleep once they got a look at real walls and friendly faces. They must have been running on empty for a long time before we'd even met.

I wasn't one of those lucky enough to pass out. If anything, being back in the Spire was more stressful than being out there and fighting for my life. There were all these people that had come here after I'd more-or-less spurred them on, and I couldn't help but worry for all of them. The problem was that I didn't know *how* to take care of them. The wounded were being tended to by the med students and the bishop, the hungry were being fed, and the tired were being given beds. What was a guy who built autonomous death machines to do at a time like that?

Jassin, with the help of Angol, found everyone a place to stay, mostly in the dormitories, and I hung around the two of them, just in case they needed me in some way. They didn't, though. Angol knew where the empty rooms were, and Jassin had the sway to make things happen. The hardest people to accommodate were the goblins, because they just wouldn't stand still long enough to be assigned anything. I translated for Tiba and Jassin as best I could, but, though the scholar was interested in the goblins, he was also coordinating the care for the tall folk at the same time. Other than telling them they could get together and talk later, there wasn't much for me to do other than translate pleasantries.

Then the bodies of the fallen were lined up and given last rites by the bishop. I hung around there too, much to the displeasure of the bishop, but he didn't say anything directly. His barely functional broken hand did the speaking for him.

I had done that. It had been a for good reason, but I still felt a little guilty about it.

I couldn't pull myself away, though—not until I was chased away by the grateful. It started with one, just a guard, one of the goat-legged ones with furry sideburns and flat teeth. He came up and shook my hand, nodding and saying a very quiet and earnest "Thank you." I did my best to tell him he had done it all himself, and all I'd helped with was killing a few things. He was insistent, though.

Then came the rest of them—the more-lively ones, at least. They would salute or slap me on the back or thank the Light for me or something similar. I found myself in the middle of a swirling vortex of gratitude, but it felt like hail pelting me from above or as if I'd been placed in a pressure cooker. The attention and the earnest affection were a force bearing down on my psyche, crushing me slowly—so slowly I couldn't really perceive it until it was almost unbearable.

Finally, I said my goodbyes and retreated to my lab. I'd tried to sleep, but there was always something on the periphery of my mind I thought I should be doing for them. So, the work began. I tucked myself away and began to prepare for next time.

Next time, we'd lose no one.

Stop it. We're manipulating mana now. What did you do before, other than almost dying?

That was the problem, though. What had I done before to make the mana flow through my body like that? I remember there being this hollow sensation that I needed to fill, a byproduct of my mana having been ripped to shreds by the bishop's curse. I remembered grabbing singular motes, putting them in the hollow, and telling them to flow. It had just worked. So far, however, any attempt I made to recreate the feeling ended in failure. My mana would do what I asked but only as long as I was focusing on it, and I couldn't focus on it all at once.

Split Mind is now Level 10.
Upgrade Paths available:
Efficiency Upgrade (Imbue)
Cognitive Offloading
Alert

Well, if anything, it was a good way to level up Split Mind.

Efficiency Upgrade (Imbue): Your Ability: Imbue now uses 10% less mana and can be used 5% more quickly.
Cognitive Offloading: You may now designate a part of your total MP to facilitate any number of cognitive tasks. Ease and speed of cognitive tasks are proportional to the amount of MP used this way.
Alert: Your mana is now a more-conscious extension of yourself and may alert you to certain objects that come into contact with it.

More toys. Very nice. Cognitive Offloading and Alert were the sexier options, obviously. Only Cognitive Offloading cost mana, and I wasn't exactly hurting for that stuff. On the other hand, it looked like it would decrease my maximum MP, making me more vulnerable to debilitating mana migraines in the future if I didn't use it properly. What's more, I didn't exactly like the idea of the System having even more influence over my mind, even if it was supposedly to help. If the Scourge was a part of the power I was being fed, would letting them into my gray matter really be the best course of action? I didn't think so.

Alert was, in a word, vague. At a glance, it looked like a sixth-sense sort of thing that would let me know if something entered my aura and bumped into one of my blue motes. Spidey sense. Given how my machines could already do that, and all I would have to do is build a machine that did something similar, it made the Ability less appealing to me.

I sighed sadly and chose the Efficiency Upgrade. I knew I was passing up on fun things to play with, but it couldn't be denied that I was building things as my primary means of . . . well, *everything*. Imbue was one of those Abilities that made up the synthesis of Automate—one of the more expensive components, actually. Any way I could make the process cheaper and faster, I felt the need to prioritize.

Jassin cleared his throat quietly.

Oh, right.

I felt like I'd been asked to pee in a cup, but the cup was across the room and there was a guy with a clipboard taking notes on my technique. Very awkward. Very messy.

All right, so the hollow feeling. I couldn't seem to create it on my own, but maybe I could . . .

I summoned a metal hinge from my Spatial Storage, instantly spending 20 mana to saturate it. I watched the mana inside my body flowing into the object easily through my channels and into the metal, and how the metal resisted and ate a portion of the mana I sent its way, my imperfect Affinity doing what it did. All the while, I focused on the feeling of the vacuum left behind by the mana I had lost in the process.

The empty space inside of me—I felt it. It was hollow, and it shouldn't have been.

Taking a deep breath and letting it out slowly, I set about gathering up my motes again. More eagerly this time, they rushed to fill the gap. That was good, but I needed them to do more. I kept them moving past the hollow, even after they had filled it. Their momentum helped me usher them through my body, even those that were already in there. A current formed within me, and soon I had a rushing stream of gray-blue circulating. Victory.

I allowed myself a quiet, triumphant laugh.

"You have it, then?" Jassin asked, his tone purposefully neutral.

"Yes," I ground out between my teeth. Just thinking about conversing while having to do this almost made me lose control.

"Good. Now stay still."

Mana Manipulation is now Level 2.

Jassin's hand passed over my chest, working its way from the metal part to the fleshy part, and a cool, tingly sensation suffused my body.

"Bother." The headmaster harrumphed. "It is as I suspected. Garret, we will need your expertise, I believe."

"What? What does that mean?" I asked, opening my eyes and finally looking at Jassin again. He seemed disappointed, as well as a bit frazzled. Maybe he wasn't a big fan of sitting on the floor, either.

"You—"

FOOM!

Behind the explosion barrier, State Shift Experiment No. Three went off for the . . . fourth time, I believe it was? I'd know the exact number once I counted how many balls I had left over there. I didn't bother looking over to check on it now. Instead, I focused on how Jassin's eye was currently twitching.

"Uh, you okay?" I asked him.

"It's a wonder you're able to sleep in this room, much less concentrate on manipulating the primal forces of the universe."

I shrugged slightly. "Oh, sure, it's busy, but—I don't know. It's kind of comforting to me. Chaotic, but it's my chaos, you know?"

It was true. My machines were a little odd and loud, and they exploded sometimes (on purpose mostly), but I'd made them. They were mine, and they were working while I couldn't. In a way, they were helping people even while I was wasting time playing with my aura. That was a comforting thought.

"You were saying?" I urged him to continue as another two bullets *POCK!*ed onto the chute.

Jassin cleared his throat and squeezed his eyes shut for a long moment before finally continuing, obvious stress in his voice. "As I was saying, you aren't controlling your aura so much as feeding upon it."

I could feel my control slipping even as the man talked. That was okay. Jassin had done his scan thingy.

"I thought about that," I said. "All of the mana I see in the air . . . it's mine, so I thought it was part of my mana pool, but sometimes I'm not so sure. It seems to help, though. Like it helped keep me alive when I was cursed."

"I imagine it did. Your aura isn't necessarily part of the mana you can tap into to cast spells. In a way, it's a spell that you're constantly casting just by being alive. However, you are feeding upon it much as a Warden does. Like Garret here. It's not Dominion magic, but it makes use of what scraps of power you have on hand."

Garret—Jassin's master-at-arms, the Miur with the bushy white mustache and easy smile who had almost shot me the day we met—sat up on my cot and stretched his thick neck. The man must have been sleeping while Jassin and I were sitting here staring into the microcosmos. Lucky guy.

"So you're a practitioner too?" I asked him.

"No, nothing so fancy or accomplished as that." Garret yawned, wriggling his mustache like it was another muscle to be stretched. "My master is one, therefore I am afforded some basic control, but I'm simply a jumped-up warrior."

Jassin flashed Garret a look of frustration. "That is not necessarily true, Ryan. Despite Garret's propensity for understatement, he is an accomplished Warden, one I trust with my life."

I was still stuck on what Garret said, though. "Wait. So because you work for him," I said, pointing at Jassin, "you can use Mana Manipulation?"

"He doesn't just work for me, Ryan. Garret has sworn himself to my family, essentially becoming a part of it. In return for his loyalty, he gains access to the power of my Dominion, which he uses as best he can. Wardens like Garret didn't grow up with their Dominion as I did, so his control over it is different from mine. While unlocking new functions of my Dominion requires study and practice, it is as easy as breathing for me, because I have been under its influence since birth. Garret, on the other hand, has to be very deliberate when even using it for the most basic tasks."

"I simply dabble, young man," Garret said, rising from the cot to stretch his legs.

Jassin explained further. "In theory, he could do everything I do if he went through the work of unlocking all the functions, but in practice it doesn't work like that."

"Is this something everyone with a Dominion can do? Just bring other people into the fold like that?" I asked.

"Many of the noble houses have developed the capability of doing so, yes. Mine was one of the first," Jassin said with some pride. "It isn't a perfect process, but we have come a long way since the early days."

I began to wonder, if people like Jassin could do that, could I do it, too? It seemed unlikely, given that I'd never heard of any Exotics managing it. A lot of them had retinues of people following them around, but I'd always thought it was due to Exotics essentially being celebrities wherever they went. If inducting people into your service gave them access to the System, it most definitely would have come out by now.

Garret seemed to sense what I was thinking. "I am not like my lord, Ryan. What I get from the arrangement isn't anything so grand as what he inherited. It's more that our connection gives me the ability to see what I couldn't before. I'm aware of the magic around me—mostly that of my master and other types I'm familiar with—and I'm able to use it, to an extent. It's hard—painful sometimes, too—but it gets easier as the years pass."

"Will Garret ever be able to match you in the magic department?" I asked Jassin.

"Theoretically, yes, though he would need to create his own Dominion and cultivate it if he wished to bring his capabilities up to the level of my own. The amount of concentration and will that it would take to do what I am capable of without offloading some of the work would be taxing for both the body and mind. If Garret were a genius with perfect Affinity for a certain mana type, he might be able to do it all on his own, but even then, he would still benefit from creating his own Dominion."

I turned the idea over in my head. Dominions seemed to work a lot like magical computers, connected to their practitioners through some kind of metaphysical link. People like Jassin built his own computer back in the day and had been adding onto it and expanding its capabilities for a long time. *Generations.* New generations inherit the link to the computer when they are born. Garret didn't have anything like that, but he was granted some access to Jassin's computational power when he was inducted into the man's family. He doesn't know how to use it as well as the family proper, but he could, theoretically, do it on his own by writing his own code on the fly.

Or something.

The comparisons weren't one-to-one, though, especially when it came to my situation. I turned to Garret. "But I'm more like Jassin than you, right? Should I be able to control it like he does?"

"I have a theory about that," Jassin interjected. "I believe it is a by-product of your explosive growth and your relative newness in your Dominion . . . your System."

"I'm not sure if the System works the same way your magic does, though. Your Dominions may be derivative of the System, but there's too much that doesn't line up."

"Yes, your System is different in many ways, but I am unsure as to why. It is far more advanced than anything we have here, but there is also something wrong with it. It is plain to see if you know how to look. It . . . *forces* itself upon you, flooding you with power but also restricting you and making you reliant upon it, writing itself upon you in a way our magic does not. It is like a medicine that, once taken, your body increasingly depends upon. As you use it, you are becoming, at once, more powerful, yet less able to use that power freely."

With that, the dam finally broke. My control of my aura snapped, and the little mana motes exploded out from my body. With a frustrated sigh, I leaned my head back and finally relaxed my stiff muscles.

"The more I Level, the less freedom I have, then," I said with some trepidation.

Jassin scoffed. "Oh, I'm sure you receive many new boons along the way to give you the illusion of freedom, but, in reality, you are being conditioned to accept less. It is an insidious sort of enslavement, one that you readily volunteer for after being offered a short path to some power. The Dark Lord made note of this change before the Purge. He thought he'd broken his toy, but, in the end, he concluded that the nature of the humans' Dominion had changed. The corrosive influence was coming from without."

I thought back to the error messages I'd been getting since the day I'd awakened as an Exotic. "So it wasn't always like this, then."

"That is the theory."

"Lucky me, inheriting a broken System. So what about my aura? Am I doing it right, then? I feel like I'm sort of containing it. You said Wardens do it like this, too?"

"What you are doing is . . . different. Garret is able to gather mana external to him and use it to fuel himself, but you are doing so with your own aura. You are creating a loop. A system that feeds into itself in a circular way. You take mana from your aura and put it to use elsewhere in your body. Like any closed system, this cannot be done in perpetuity. Stagnation and death should be inevitable. Strangely, however, that is not happening with you. If anything, it is repairing you."

"I've been calling the stuff 'me-mana,' like it's my own personal flavor of mana. I'm good with me-mana. If the System works how you say it does, maybe I've been working with my own mana more than I have the System's. Like, I've been putting all of my input through the engine, and it's been acting as a filter?"

Jassin put a hand on his chin and tilted his head, staring right through me in that unnerving way of his.

"Hmmm. Perhaps. If most of, if not entirely all, of your pool is 'your' mana, then your System may be having a difficult time reshaping you to fit your new Abilities. This may have mitigated some of the corrupting influence of your System but has also made you heavily reliant on your own mana type. Your meteoric rise in power was fueled primarily by your own type of magic as opposed to that which is given to you. In a way, your unconventional use of your System has saved you from its machinations. It has also crippled you in some of the basic areas of control and left large gaps in your capabilities. Unbelievable."

"So, controlling my aura shouldn't feel like pushing boulders uphill using just my breath?" I asked, not sure if I wanted to hear the answer.

"At first," Garret replied in a consoling tone. "You're trying to move something too heavy and complicated for you right now, but at the same time, it's the only thing you can do. I've seen it before in new people with an Affinity for more-complex types of mana."

Jassin spoke up again, this time seeming more energized. He leaned forward, looking bright and engaged. "This may actually be a boon, Ryan. Though it feels difficult now, I believe you may benefit from this deviation to the norm. Your body and spirit have not yet had a chance to acclimate to the power you've gathered, so you have not acquired the instincts to control your magic intuitively."

The thought of my life being significantly harder because I was power-Leveling instead of taking the road more traveled didn't seem like a great boon to me. "That doesn't sound great. I mean, it would be nice to be able to control myself and not blast other practitioners with my special mana juice."

"Yes. That part is obnoxious, to say the least. However, I think, despite the inconvenience, this may be an opportunity."

"How so?"

Jassin's new energy couldn't seem to be contained. He shifted forward slightly, repositioning himself closer to me as if he wanted to be able to reach out and hold me down if I didn't like what he was about to say. "Imagine something complicated like your circulatory system. It works the way it does because that is how you were designed. You are also at the whims of your body's involuntary processes. See?"

I shrugged.

"What if you had the opportunity to learn how to use it from scratch—be able to control it like a muscle. What then?"

I furrowed my brows, trying to imagine. "I guess . . . I could tell my body how fast to pump my blood." I stopped to think about it some more. "I could tell it to bring extra oxygen and nutrients to my muscles, to my brain. Assuming I got better at using it, I could use it to flush out toxins, stop feeding blood to open wounds . . . If I got *really* good at it, I could probably get it to do lots of extra stuff."

"Yes, yes! Exactly. Think of yourself as a blank sheet of paper and your System, an artist. He is currently working on your portrait, but he is only now in the sketching phase. He is working with broad strokes and vague outlines. But you have the opportunity to reach out and guide his hand."

Garret spoke up again. "Think of it like water carving out a river over time. Your Dominion's power is the water. There might be some places where it naturally flows, and those places will one day become the river. Right now, you have some say on where the water flows, while you're flat."

"It is a theory," Jassin said, finally leaning back and stretching as I had. "If you want my advice, attempt to stretch your Abilities in the next few days. Experiment and go beyond what you think you should, and, with your permission, I would like to examine you again once you have done so."

With that, Jassin, without saying another word, got up to leave. He seemed stiff but otherwise fine and almost in a hurry to get out of my workshop. Once the door opened and closed again, Garret sat down in front of me in the spot where Jassin had just vacated.

"Alright, young man, if you're going to cycle your magic like a Warden, let's make sure you do it right."

I stopped, already almost all the way upright again, one knee under me and about to be on my feet. "Uh, right," I said.

"Wrong. That was all wrong. First, you need to learn how to breathe. Have a seat."

CHAPTER FIFTEEN

Dodge a Bullet

Y ou shine up pretty well, Monk. Good thing, too. You have no idea what I had to go through to get a hold of that outfit," Samila said, reaching up to brush something off my shoulder. She'd done that a lot since we'd left the workshop. There was always something I'd done wrong or left undone. At least now she was down to just minor things.

The doublet I wore—a black vest with sleeves, leather trim, shiny buttons, and a fake pocket on the front—was a tight fit around the shoulders and chest and tended to shed from the seams. My shirt's white collar liked to collect all the black fibers, too, like a magnet with iron filings. The worst part, though, was that the pants "fit" the way an ostrich egg might fit inside a python. It made going down stairs, walking, or standing in general more than a little uncomfortable.

Samila herself had changed out of her armor while I'd been busy bathing and figuring out how all the pieces of the outfit went together. Now the dragonkin warrior woman wore a yellow-and-white dress that had no shoulders but seemed to have transferred all of that material to the wrists and a gossamer-like fold of white that connected the arms of the dress to the torso, giving her the appearance of having wings.

Her blue, scaled skin contrasted with the bright yellows and whites like the fabric had been chosen specifically for her, bringing out the otherworldly brightness of her eyes. The dress definitely wasn't made to fit her, though. Her muscular arms and back strained at the loops and ties that held the rest of it in place, and the fabric hugged her hips and thighs while being roomy everywhere else, as if she'd been poured into an odd-shaped glass.

With every step we descended, the quellstones stung my toes until they felt like they were going to fall off, and I had to remind myself that I wasn't actually cold so much as suppressed.

Progress on controlling my aura was slow-going, if you could really call what I was doing "going" at all. Once I mastered the technique, though, I was going to find a way to shoot these stupid death pebbles into the sun. I bet with the right Shapes and enough Volatility, I could find a way to make them break orbit at least.

"So, are you going to fill me in on why we're all dressed up?" I asked as I reached up and re-tousled my hair. When it came to the outfit, I would comply, but I'd just gotten this hair. I wasn't about to let someone else tell me how to wear it, and I liked it just this side of messy—probably a holdover from home.

Samila held on tight to my arm, leading me down the stairs as if she were worried I'd bolt, but the smile on her face told me she was enjoying my discomfort, somewhat.

"Word's gotten out that we're doing something big soon—probably evacuate. Everyone's on edge, so, naturally, it's time for some spur-of-the-moment life-stuff."

"Naturally," I parroted sarcastically. "Wouldn't want to make things too routine in the middle of an apocalypse."

"Stop it." She slapped my arm, but I didn't feel it. Score one for being a cyborg. "Our world has already had its apocalypse, and we're doing fine. Besides, you shouldn't be a downer on someone's wedding day."

I stopped, mid-stride. Samila, with her arm in mine as it was, jerked to a halt as well.

"Wait. We're going . . . to a wedding?" I asked, almost not believing it.

She grinned mischievously as she pulled on my arm to get me moving again. "Calm down. It's not ours."

Her choice of words didn't help matters at all. If I'd have been feeding my Engine back at the workshop, it would have backfired at this very moment, belching a cloud of black smoke and despair. The woman really knew how to throw me off my game. I swallowed hard but tried to keep my discomfort from otherwise showing.

"Uh . . . Here? Now?" I asked.

"What other time do we have?" was all the answer she gave.

My stomach twisted up in a painful knot of confusion and worry, and my mind whirled at the thought of doing something so . . . normal at a time like this. We were in the middle of a dead city with monsters battering our doors.

Plus, I didn't do normal. I hadn't done normal in years, and I wasn't good at it.

"Why?!"

She shrugged slightly, leaning in to give me a playful nudge with her bare shoulder. "The usual reasons, I'd think. Boy meets girl, boy and girl fight monsters for a week straight right next to each other. She likes his thrust; he likes how she receives a charge."

"You're serious." My mind still wasn't ready to accept it. *A wedding?*

"What's so hard to believe? Not everyone is content to sleep on a hoard of shiny metal things like some people I know. Very dragon-like by the way. I approve. These people went through something together and survived. Now they're set to do it again soon, and they don't want to do it single."

"And we're invited?" I asked.

She shrugged and wobbled a hand back and forth noncommittally. "Sure. In a way."

"What does that mean?" I asked, raising a skeptical eyebrow.

Samila kept the pressure up, pulling me downward. I noted how she really had to put her weight into it to keep me moving. "Relax, Monk, we're invited. I believe most people not on wall-duty are. In our cases, I think it's one of those things where you invite someone, not really because you think they'll actually show up but because it was worth a try, because it would be something to talk about on your anniversary twenty years from now if they did."

I groaned. "Wow. My celebrity is really taking off if I'm doing parties now. If only they knew, right?"

"Shut up. Whether you think you deserve the title or not, you're the Rising Sun of Eclipse. Whatever you think of yourself or what history thinks of—" She hesitated slightly and looked around to make sure we were alone. "—your people, you've more than earned a little acceptance. People want to see you and, Light forbid, talk to you." She hit me with another playful shoulder-check, this time lingering next to me a fraction of a second longer as she pulled me back upright. I let myself be moved, but I wasn't done arguing about it.

"Still not convinced. Do they really—"

Samila rolled her eyes and blew a rather-unladylike raspberry through her lips. "Do they really want you there? The answer is 'yes,' but you can't just accept that, can you? You don't have it in you. For someone as capable as you are, you have an overdeveloped sense of . . ." She trailed off, trying to come up with the right word.

"Humility?" I finished for her.

"Shame," she declared with a satisfied nod, as if she had nailed the word choice.

"I do not!" I protested. What did I have to be ashamed of? Maybe I spent a fair amount of time naked among the locals, since I'd not yet encountered fire-proof or acid-proof clothes yet, but I had been barely conscious for a lot of that. It certainly wasn't being human. I was born that way, and, as far as I knew, there was no way to change my species.

"You do, though. Shame just rolls off you like stink from a bog," she countered with a shrug.

I found myself spluttering, shaking my head, and gesticulating as I mounted my defense. "You just essentially used the 'yuh-huh' style of counterargument. What would I have to be ashamed of?"

Samila shrugged again. "I don't know, but you are riddled with it and I've spent far too much time trying to puzzle out why. I figured it was a 'thing.'"

"What sort of 'thing?'" I asked incredulously.

"Whatever thing was done to you to make you like this." She said it so matter-of-factly, as if it didn't carry all sorts of implications and connotations and other -ations I didn't want to address.

I leaned in close to speak to her softly. "Maybe it's because I'm not what I say I am, and I don't like lying to everyone about who I really am?"

"That's different, and you're using your status as a world-ending visitor from the stars to deflect," she countered. "You don't like lying, but this is something else. I can smell it."

We continued in silence for another flight of stairs before I could think of anything to say.

Shame. *No*, that wasn't it. Sure, I had been a pariah back home, cast out and ignored on a good day. Hadn't I moved past that, though? A kid with access to the Colonial network was never really alone, was he? While everyone else, including my father, tried to pretend I didn't exist, there was the vast repository of human knowledge that was the Net, right there at my fingertips. While everyone else was out learning to be the perfect warrior, I made myself something else.

Isolation suited me like it didn't suit others. I was practically made for it.

Once I discovered my love for machines, I found a dark, comfortable hole to bury myself in, and I went about making it my own. Where others might have left the clan in shame, I'd carved my own niche that let me be part of the clan without the need to *be* accepted.

And without Mom, there was no one there to push me into the light anymore. Whose fault is that?

I forcefully derailed that particular train of thought before it could go any further than it did. I was past that. I'd worked hard to get to that point. I became the clan mechanic, their heretic, and then their Exotic.

And now I was on my way to a wedding with a dragon girl. What a fantastical life this had turned out to be.

"I still protest the use of that word," I said quietly.

"Protest all you want." Samila snorted. "I'm a dragon. I can sense these things."

"Imagined motivations?"

"Weakness," she said flatly. "It's your least-attractive quality but also strangely endearing."

"Wow. Thanks," I muttered.

My dragon captor led us away from the stairwell and through a hallway that went toward the center of the Spire. "This is our door," she said, flashing me another smile with a few too many canines.

Once through the double doors, we emerged in a neighborhood.

That was the best way I could describe it. The student accommodations in the Spire that I'd seen before were spartan—just a place to sleep and maybe stow your books. This place was different. Where the dormitories down below were plain and white, these rooms were set in a sort of large spiral that went up and down in a corkscrew with rounded clusters of what looked like landings or porches of elaborate suites at regular intervals along the way.

The floor, composed of shiny gray tiling with green metallic accents, hugged the outer wall and ramped up the spiral, but toward the center was a giant wall of lush, green ivy with blooming white flowers bathed in filtered sunlight, presumably piped in from somewhere outside—maybe even from the same lenses that kept the monstrous human downstairs in check.

Mist fell in little puffs from strategically placed spray nozzles that kept the ivy nice and damp while trickles of water cascaded down a series of inlaid steps and into shallow pools that drained into the ones down below them, until they finally dripped into a grate on the bottom floor.

I'd never seen something so open and green indoors. It was like I'd been shrunk down to live inside a hydroponic grow tube.

Samila caught me gawking and leaned in to speak privately. "What?"

"Just hard for me to think of it as anything other than an evil wizard's tower," I admitted with a shake of my head.

"Well, he hasn't been around for a long time," Samila replied in a whisper, "and his death wasn't exactly the end of history."

I nodded slowly, trying to accept the situation. "Can't let a dark moment from the past define you, I guess."

Of course you can. I've been doing it for years.

Again, I derailed that train. That track led to nothing good.

This place may have been built for some amount of privacy on a regular day, but today every door was wide open. Everywhere I looked there were people of every race, congregating outside their rooms and mingling with one another in that quiet sort of rumble crowds tended to generate. Some wore bandages on fresh wounds, favored a particular side, or limped when they had occasion to walk, but no one let any of that hardship show on their faces.

Many were more modestly dressed, but Samila and I certainly didn't stand out. A lot of the well-dressed attendees had a military bearing that I'd come to associate with the warriors of this culture, but there were an equal number of others here—young and old. I scanned the faces of the crowd, taking in how they stood together and the warmth of their expressions.

Something else of note: despite lots of people being part of the guard, no one wore arms or armor, and I saw more than one uncomfortable hand on a hip where a sword might be.

Still, the atmosphere managed to be strangely . . . inviting.

"You're tense," Samila whispered out of the side of her mouth. "Would it make you feel better if there was a monster to slay?"

I shook my head. "Probably not. It's just that everyone seems so . . . normal, like they've just chosen to forget where we are."

"You and my sister are so alike, it's disgusting." Samila sighed. "Of course everyone knows the situation outside. Not everyone deals with it like you, though, slowly killing yourselves with worry. It's healthy to put those feelings aside for a moment and let yourself be."

"I—" I closed my mouth and thought about it. The way I handled problems, generally, was that I saw a problem, and I worked it. I worked that problem good and hard until it wasn't a problem anymore.

It worked with engines, it worked with games, and, theoretically, it worked with people. Did the attack-it-until-it-goes-away method work with something as big as a world-ending infestation of Scourge, though? Did it work on anything on a grander scale than what a clan mechanic might face? If not, was it useful to me anymore? Was my clinging to it limiting me to only being able to handle clan-mechanic-scale issues?

Samila wasn't thinking about the Scourge like a problem to solve. For her, they were a force to oppose, too big to understand. They were something out of her control, a thing that would be tackled one way or another today or tomorrow. The trick, though, was that she had faith that either she or someone else would handle the problem eventually—just not today.

"I'm not sure if I *can* just let myself be," I said.

"I know, but you need to try while you're here. It'll be good for you. And I need a date."

I felt my eye twitch slightly at that. That was alarming. I had been on a *date* this entire time?!

"Okay, just tell me what to do" I said, bringing my eyes back from wherever I'd been staring and finally looking at her. Really looking at her. She stared up at me, her characteristic smirk gone, replaced by worry and a tinge of sadness. I wasn't being good company.

"Seriously," I continued, forcing a smile onto my face in hopes she'd reciprocate. "I'm clueless on how to proceed unless you need me to make something explode."

I must have said something right, because her smile came back with a vengeance. "Just follow my lead," she replied, reaching up to smooth my hair back, letting her hand linger on my cheek on the way back down. "You can start by unclenching your . . . *All* of it."

I looked around at the people around me. More than one pair of eyes were turned my way. Most of them looked curious; others had a sort-of timid respect usually reserved for people like my father. I put on a little smile and purposefully relaxed, one muscle at a time—the same deliberate method I used to get my mana under control.

Then the bride and groom walked into the room. A young couple, him in a fancy, bright-colored coat and her in the poofiest red dress I'd ever seen in my life. The bottom half of it took up so much space, it might have pushed others off the side of the railing and into the waterfall if they hadn't moved out of the way to give her room.

"Did we raid the prom closet or something?" I asked Samila after they'd passed.

Samila quirked an eyebrow at me. "What?"

"Where did we get all the clothes?"

Understanding came over her face, and she brightened slightly. "Everyone opens their doors and homes for a wedding. People lend and borrow freely—it's considered good luck. We don't have something for everyone, but no one is refused. The women got together last night and found what we could."

The happy couple took up positions in front of the wall of ivy on a semicircular patio that jutted out over the empty space, turned toward each other, and held each other's hands. The two of them were youngish, probably slightly older than me, but they had the look of soldiers to them: well-muscled, good posture, rough hands. That kind of stuff.

Then Bishop Kolash flowed in, in a set of white robes with a big smile on his face.

I willed Stealth to activate, but, as usual, it gave me no hint as to whether it was working or not. But Kolash didn't seem to have noticed me. He only had eyes for the two people in front of him.

The bishop raised his hands to quiet everyone down and began the proceedings. "Friends. Comrades. Brothers. Sisters. We are here today to celebrate the beauty of life . . ."

As weddings tended to do, the party afterwards was a bit livelier than the ceremony had been.

I wouldn't say they had a full band at their disposal, but a surprising amount of people knew how to play.

All tables and chairs had been cleared away and every porch turned into a dance floor. Children ran to and fro between dancing groups of adults, sometimes even stopping to join the dances, making silly spins on the steps.

Additionally, now that the fun part of the ceremony was underway, the goblins had appeared out of nowhere. None of them spoke the language, but they certainly were enjoying the alcohol—their own as well as others'—sometimes straight from the barrel. They seemed to not know the meaning of the word, "moderation."

The children, as children tended to do, were the first to really merge as one group, between tall folks and short. All it took was one group of children playing a game the others wanted to join, and that was it. They were suddenly running around in one big blob, making trouble. No words necessary.

When I asked where the tall-folk kids had come from, Samila told me the guard weren't the only people at the gate they'd rescued in our initial operation. The reason the group had been bogged down for so long wasn't because they couldn't move to a more-advantageous place. After the walls had been overrun, they had also become a collection point for civilians fleeing the horde, and the guard fought hard to keep them all safe for an entire week. When Sissa, Samila, and Geddon arrived to break the mini-siege, it was the first time these people had moved out of their defensible square in a long time. The children were part of that group.

The motion and the general good vibes of the crowd were intoxicating. The majority of the attendees were Miur, wearing decorative garlands and ornate wraps on their horns, but our regular group weren't the only standouts.

Geddon appeared sometime in the night in full armor and was popular on the main dance floor, picking up willing women and carrying them on his shoulders like children. A stubby mushroom person bobbed up and down next to a group of students as a particularly boisterous song started up, and he seemed to comically morph and wobble in time with the music, making them the group to watch.

Samila and I sat on the side, watching the party go on without us, but she couldn't seem to keep herself still. After a handful of songs, she'd clearly had enough standing around, and she snatched my arm and pulled me forward so suddenly I practically felt my shoulder joint pop.

Then we were on the dance floor. Despite being petite and head and shoulders shorter than me, Samila led, since I didn't know the steps. She laughed at my ineptitude, quick to point out where I went wrong, but she seemed to be enjoying herself. She even went so far as to put my hand in the right place on her lower back. That was interesting, as I had to bend over to get it in the right place.

Eventually, though, we found our rhythm. I slowly began to find my way and get more comfortable with the process. My higher Body Stat was probably doing a lot of the heavy-lifting when it came to coordinating my various parts. I even started having fun, as I grew less worried about my feet and more focused on how *good* it felt to have her in my arms.

Then, like a damned magician, Samila was suddenly gone, and I bumped into another blue woman, this one in a gray dress.

Sissa jumped as if something had just pinched her, and she put up her hands to politely pull away . . . until she recognized me.

Her eyes widened and her mouth opened to . . . protest? Say hello? I didn't know. Nothing came out. She didn't punch me in the face, however, so our post-evacuation interactions were trending better, I guessed.

"Uh—Hi." I said.

"Hi," Sissa said back. She smoothed the front of her dress and seemed to fidget like someone caught in the act of doing something wrong. Unlike my clothes, Sissa's dress seemed to be made for her—a gray, flowing thing that hugged her all in the right places before flowing out like a waterfall of mist to pool on the floor.

I looked around one last time for Samila. "I'm just guessing here," I ventured, "but I think we're supposed to dance."

"Is that why you grabbed my—Ah, dammit, Samila!" Sissa fumed, looking around the crowd much like I'd done, a look of embarrassed disapproval on her face. "She takes her role as Second too far."

I raised an eyebrow at that. "Second?"

"Second in our clutch. The youngest." Sissa stood up on her tiptoes. Unfortunately she was shorter than most of the tall folks here, and even if she were as tall as I, she wouldn't have been able to spot her sister. She'd vanished in a proverbial cloud of smoke.

"Do you want to dance?" I asked awkwardly. The question seemed to surprise her. She turned back around so quickly, her hand swept across my face, and I had to duck to avoid getting another Sissa-specialty black eye.

Her mouth opened again, her cheeks flushing a dark navy that seemed to change the shape of her face, accenting her cheekbones.

She nodded. "I guess I wouldn't mind a dance. Seems like it's what we're meant to do."

With a self-effacing smile, I put my hands in the right places and brought my body into line with hers. She was so small—tiny, even—willow-thin and soft. I couldn't shake the feeling that a wrong move on my part might hurt her, but I knew better. She was strong. Stronger than me, probably.

It took a full verse of the song before I got up the courage to speak. "I don't get you and your sister," I said.

"No?" she asked, stumbling slightly before resetting her feet.

Wow. She was just as good a dancer as I was.

"No, I really don't," I insisted. "I'm pretty sure your sister is—uh—interested in me."

"No kidding? What gave you that impression?" Sissa asked a bit too sarcastically. "Was it the long, mournful stares? The intense interest in your backside?"

It was my turn to trip. She caught me before I could fall all the way to the floor, though. I swallowed, suddenly feeling a bit more self-conscious. "Uh, yeah . . . The clues were there, I guess."

"Okay, so you get that. What don't you get about us, then?"

"If she—uh—Constance, I feel like I'm in middle school . . . If she likes me, why did she set us up like this?"

Sissa's gaze slid down, and she seemed to gain a new appreciation for the floor as we went through the motions of dancing. When she spoke again, her voice had a sad note to it—regret, maybe. "She's second-born in our clutch. Dragonkin are invariably born in pairs. It has something to do with how the divine power of the dragon cannot be contained in a single mortal vessel, but I don't know exactly how it works."

She took a deep breath as if preparing herself to explain something she didn't really enjoy talking about. "The eldest is meant to be first in everything. From how tall we are to who gets the first roll at dinner. We're meant to be the picture of excellence, as a representative of our sire. The second is meant to help the first accomplish that. It's a dragon rule, a sort of natural law, one that we follow instinctually."

My stomach soured after hearing that. Samila was *born* to play second fiddle to Sissa? That sounded like something archaic. Out of myth and legend. Who would do that to one of their own children? Why condemn a child to second place from birth? It went against everything I was ever taught. We were all created equal, and no one deserved deference based on the circumstances of their birth. You were not made to kneel to anyone.

"I see you aren't pleased," Sissa observed.

I shook my head. "Sorry, I just can't wrap my head around it. You have free will, don't you? How can firsts and seconds even exist?"

It was Sissa's turn to frown. "Well, I'm not exactly a big proponent of the concept, either, Ryan. I have tried to fight against it—even gone so far as to try and make her stop treating me as her better, but whenever I try, it just comes across as another order I'm giving her. I hate how she's been forced into the background, but, at the same time, she considers it a privilege. We *naturally* slip into these roles. So naturally, you might even think we were made this way on purpose. I am the leader. I make the decisions for the both of us, and she's always there to back me up."

Her eyes hardened as she stared at something in the middle distance, lost in some distant memory.

"No matter how much we want to run from it, that's how it always shakes out. Do you have any idea how infuriating it is to not know if your personality is truly yours or if it is simply a manifestation of natural law?"

I didn't know what to say to that. Of course, I had the System slowly pushing me toward becoming a monster, and I couldn't trust if my thoughts were my own anymore, either. This conversation wasn't about me, though.

I looked around once more to try to find Samila somewhere out there. *Nothing.* The song was starting to wrap up, too.

"This is her asking for your permission, isn't it?" I asked.

Sissa nodded, not meeting my eyes. "Not just mine, either."

Oh, so it was that kind of moment, then.

"So, what's your answer?" I asked, fighting to keep my tone neutral.

The dragonkin shuddered slightly, then raised her gaze in line with mine. I could tell she was fighting to not look away, but she got herself under control and gave me the same stare she did every other challenge she met.

"For her, I'd give up everything," Sissa declared, her determination slightly belied by how she had to wipe a tear from her cheek. The wetness traced a dark line down her scales like an unhealed scar.

She sniffed and let out a little, bitter laugh. "I think you and I are too much alike to work, anyway."

Muscles I hadn't realized I'd been clenching chose that moment to relax. Was I feeling . . . *relieved*? No, that wasn't quite it. It was a *type* of relief, though, I was sure.

"Too alike, huh? Samila said something like that, too. So, what does punching me in the face earlier this week say about your sense of self-worth?" I teased.

"Too much." Sissa laughed nervously, again reaching up to swipe at a tear before it could get anywhere. "In some ways, you're who I want to be, actually. Taking the hard road. Sacrificing for others even if it means denying yourself. To be so empty of want is something I consider noble."

Empty of want? What the hell did that mean? I wanted things. There were things I had to—

I stood there in contemplative silence as I took mental inventory. What did I want? I was an Exotic now. My life had changed. I wasn't the outcast clan mechanic anymore. But now that I wasn't my past self, what did I want in the future? It couldn't all be running for my life and trying to get home. I wanted people to be safe. To not have to pay for consequences I'd caused. I wanted to see them all happy and alive, and—

"See? Empty," Sissa said as the music finished. "Maybe in another life, I'd have claimed you, but not this one." Everyone around us clapped as the band took a bow.

That interrupted my little crisis. I felt my eyebrows climb far up my forehead. "You'd have claimed me?"

"I'm a dragon, Ryan," Sissa replied with a knowing smile. "I'd have claimed you."

We parted without another word, awkwardly. She muttered something about getting a drink, and I just stood there like an idiot. I didn't follow her.

It wasn't more than a couple of breaths before a familiar voice spoke from behind me.

"I told you. Shame."

And Samila was back. Funny how that worked. I gave her my best angry scowl and tilted my head to ask for an explanation. She didn't provide one, though, unmoved by my silent tantrum.

"Come on." She sighed with exasperation. "There's a lot of people that want to shake your hand."

"Just like that?" I asked.

"Well, if you're not going to do the smart thing, you can at least do the gracious thing. People want to thank you for what you did."

"Oh," I said, already wishing for the comfort of whirring machinery and volatile chemicals already. "Oh, no."

"Nope. No getting away now. You're committed. I told them the Rising Sun of Eclipse would sign their naughty bits."

"No way. You better be—"

"Of course I'm kidding. I have an alternative plan, if you want to hear it," she purred, grabbing my collar and pulling herself up on her tiptoes to whisper in my ear.

My breath caught in my throat, but I had the wherewithal to keep talking. "Uh, what plan?"

"How about we get out of here and do something . . . spontaneous?"

"Uh—" That was it. My brain collapsed like a dying star. No more thoughts. Sound was muffled, and the entire world narrowed down to a singular point of blue and gold.

"You spook like a deer, I swear." She giggled up at me. "Seriously, though, I'm barely holding back your admirers. I had to growl at them to keep them away for so long. If we stay any longer, the party might become more about you than the newlyweds."

We stay too long. We can't stay too long. We've—

With a rushing sound, my world came back into focus, so hard it was like a physical blow. I blinked.

"What did you say?" I asked.

She frowned up at me, tilting her head slightly. "What? I said let's get out of here. Sex is still on the table, but if you make me repeat my lines, things might change."

"No. No," I insisted, breaking away a little less gently than I wanted to. My mind was racing, whirling around a central point, a nexus that I couldn't see. "The thing about staying . . . Say that again."

Samila's frown deepened into a confused scowl, but she did as I asked. "Hmm. If we stay too long, the party might become more about you than—"

"That's it!" I shouted.

"What is?"

"Samila, it's the tutorial. I—The other guy . . . he's stayed too long. There's— Oh, Constance. The insertion point! They stay active. His insertion point has been active for over a thousand years, and now there's—Oh, shit!"

"Slow down, Ryan," Samila pleaded. "What do you mean?"

It all fit. Everything from the moment I was chosen up until now, the goblins, the tutorial, the stories, the city, the Dark Lord, the Spire, the Undead, the other Animator. It all fit perfectly. I'd found the failure point.

I clenched my metal fist as the heat of conviction washed over me, and a thousand connections sparked to life in my brain. "I know how to stop this."

CHAPTER SIXTEEN

Put It Together

A chill wind whipped at my face as I leaned against the railing of the Spire's open-air observatory, while the dead city of Eclipse sprawled in gray patchwork down below.

I was at an altitude that seemed to turn all but the largest of the manmade structures into a flat sort of abstract shape, more discernible as a group than as individuals, and it was easy to tell how well different parts of the city fared before and after the Scourge. The decaying grays and creaking, moldy skeletal structures of Riverside and Bogtown, funnily enough, seemed to have fared the best through the apocalypse. Hardly any of them were smoking ruins, maybe because of their proximity to the water. Maybe because I hadn't gone to that part of the city yet.

Meanwhile the well-to-do browns and greens of the richer parts of the city still smoldered in places. I hadn't started those, or at least I didn't think I did. The fire I had started at the south gate was mostly out after the wind changed directions, but that part of the city was still partially obscured behind a hazy cloud of smoke.

Through that haze, I could just make out the dark greens of the glade, the crooked border to the swampland beyond and, above that, the mountains, where I'd first arrived in Ralqir.

Below, the faint popcorn sound of automatic turret fire came in little spurts of violence, though from this height, I couldn't pick out which tiny black dot the guns were trained upon. My log told me it was mostly the small stuff, Undead and goblins with a few mystery beasts. The Experience notifications were trickling in steadily, but I wasn't getting much base XP from any of them. The bonuses weren't great, either, not with the crowd as thin as it was now. The targets were too sparse to keep the chain bonus going, and the System was counting them as small groups as opposed to a horde. The Scourge-Touched were in roam-and-scavenge mode now, so big pileups of bodies were rare.

I wasn't out for Experience tonight, though. Tonight was about preparation. Not mine. My modest little factory was handling that for now. No, tonight, I needed to prepare everyone else for what I was about to do.

Finally, someone cleared their throat from somewhere near the stairwell. I turned, finding most of the people I'd invited to join me up here tonight: Samila, Sissa, Geddon, Trix, Tiba, and her guards, along with Jassin and Garret bringing up the rear. The Church guards were all armed and armored again, Geddon's and Samila's kit still stained with black blood all the way up the sword arms. Either they hadn't had a chance to clean them yet, or they'd been called to put down a breach somewhere.

Tiba carried her spear, and Trix wore his carbine across his back. Garret only had a sword and some kind of loose, padded underclothes but somehow managed to look more ready for a fight than anyone else. Jassin simply looked as he always did, his gaunt face pinched in a mask of calculated neutrality as he took in everything.

I leaned over slightly to see if anyone else was behind them but saw no one. I shot Samila a questioning look, but she only gave a tiny shrug in response.

Well, this was as good as I was going to get, then.

They all filed in and found a place to sit or stand. There wasn't a whole lot of room other than along the scaffold-type railings where I'd been looking out over the city, since the middle of the observatory was taken up by a giant overdesigned telescope.

I say "overdesigned," because it certainly didn't look like a telescope in the way I understood them. The main housing was a cylinder, as I would have expected, ten feet across, pointed straight up at the moon. The material was tarnished gold in color with violet streaks folded into the alloy, and no part of it was visible under any sort of Detect Ability I tried. Where it got weird, however, were the rings that rotated in inconsistent, uneven orbits around the whole thing, wobbling up and down slowly, eerily silent, while some kind of shimmering, translucent liquid stretched in sheets between them. I would have felt better if the thing squeaked or creaked, but the only sound was from the displaced air the rings caused when they wobbled on their different tracks.

Once everyone was in place and as comfortable as they were going to get— Garret clearly the most comfortable, lying down on a bench with his hands behind his head (the man could be at ease anywhere)—I began.

"Well, I guess that's everyone." I sighed. "Thank you all for coming."

Jassin was the first to speak, as I knew he would be. "Your message said it was urgent, so we came right away. It did take some time to give my practitioners the night off, however. I am sure they're not complaining, but I, for one, am quite curious as to why I was asked to do so."

It took a level of trust to do something like that, I knew. Jassin had this place running on a set schedule so that people didn't work too long and burn themselves out, while no one ate too much or slept too much or spent too much time alone. I'd probably thrown that careful schedule off by just plopping my turrets down at the gates and handing the guards spare magazines, but it needed to be done this way.

"I appreciate what this means, Lord Jassin. I just need a few minutes of everyone's time, and then what happens after will be up to all of us," I replied.

Then, the distinct *bap! bap!* of wood on stone echoed up from the stairwell, and my gut clenched slightly. I'd invited our final guest, of course. He needed to be here. I couldn't leave him out, given how much pull he had, but I wasn't fully comfortable with him being here, either. Attempted murder, understandably, did that to a guy.

Slowly, Bishop Kolash dragged himself up the stairs and into the room, leaning heavily on his staff. He paused at the very top of the stairs, winded and sweaty, but his eyes bore fierce determination as he surveyed the room, noting every face with his wide-set eyes. I noticed his broken hand was bandaged but not healed. He had to have had the chance to heal it by now with his magic. Why leave it?

Everyone went still.

"Bishop Kolash," I announced, gesturing to a seat that was in our general area. "Please, sit. Thanks for coming."

"Your message mentioned cleansing our world of the foul presence of the enemy. I would be neglecting my duties were I to not attend such a meeting."

The fact that he considered me one of "the enemy" was not lost upon me. I wasn't going to let him rattle me, though. I gave him a nod and a smile. "That's the gist of it. Please, come sit," I offered.

There was a long pause where he seemed to consider, his eyes not leaving mine while he lingered there, but, eventually, he stepped further into the room, choosing a seat to my right and a bit further distant than the one I offered him.

I fought not to let my smile slip. This situation required confidence. I'd need to channel my dad again, as unnatural as it felt.

"Samila says you think you have a way to end the plague," Sissa said, helpfully prodding me to get on with it.

"Right," I said, clearing my throat. "I know how to end this. The infection, I mean. By that, I mean that I know where the infection is coming from, and I'm hoping that, in knowing where it comes from, we can fix it."

"It comes from you, does it not?" Kolash asked. "Your presence here brings with it the evil with which we are afflicted."

Trix came to my defense first, bless him. "Your Holiness, with all due respect, that is not helping. Ryan did not ask—"

"It doesn't matter what he intended, Brother Yik'i'Trix. If only it did," Kolash cut across Trix's words. "The results speak for themselves. The beginning of this plague coincides perfectly with his arrival on our shores. Furthermore, it has historical precedent. Whether Ryan intended to or not, he has set in motion what will inevitably end in a second Purge."

The others jumped in, speaking over one another to argue, but I raised my hand to cut off any more rejoinders. "Stop. The good bishop is right," I admitted, tamping the guilt down at giving voice to the sentiment. They all fell silent and looked over at me again. *Good.*

"He's right but not entirely. Yes, my presence is causing this, to a point," I stated with a little deferential nod in his direction. "But I don't think there will be another Purge."

"Explain," Jassin said, shooting a harsh look over at the bishop, as if to say, "Wait till the end of the lecture, or you're getting detention."

"Gladly," I agreed. "I believed that was the case, too—that I was the cause of all of this. I'd suspected as much, at the very least. And once you showed me the human you have captive in the basement, it helped confirm some of my preconceptions and form new hypotheses. I began to suspect we were carriers, and we were bringing the infection wherever we went."

Jassin nodded, gesturing with his hand for me to go on.

"Wait. There is another human here on Ralqir?" Sissa gaped. "Now? Since when?"

Kolash made a burping sound. "You spread secrets too freely, Human. We compartmentalize this information as a mercy to the world. The consequences of it spreading would mean untold strife."

"On that, we are in agreement," Jassin muttered, shooting me an annoyed look.

The bishop's sour frown deepened considerably. "It would appear that I will need to have 'the talk' with the lot of you once this is done."

I felt the tendons in my neck tighten. My frustration at all the secret-keeping was threatening to creep back in. I kept my tone mostly conciliatory, though. "For one, if I didn't trust my friends implicitly, I would never have told them. Second, Lord Jassin, you look like you're familiar with the carrier theory."

"Yes," Jassin affirmed, slipping easily back into academic-mode. "The pathogen theory is an old one, but it fits. Ralqir has not seen one of your kind in many centuries, and as soon as you grace our environs once again, we are beset by another . . . uprising. An outbreak, you may call it. If your story is accurate, you are the epicenter for this outbreak."

"Hold on," I said, turning to Tiba and bringing her up to speed on the conversation in Goblin before asking: "The Baned have been around for a long time, right? Before I came around?"

Tiba nodded gravely. "The stories say they come many years after the last human. A lost tribe who lose their minds and deal with demons." I translated as she spoke.

"Perhaps they are carriers like you then, Ryan," Jassin suggested. "A mutation of the pathogen where it may lie dormant until the time is right to spread."

"Except whatever is wrong with them is far from dormant," I countered. "I was in your universe all of twenty minutes before one of them showed up, and it was good and infected. The Baned were the first things I encountered after I awoke, and they were the first things that tried to kill me, almost like they had been waiting for me. The spiders I fought, the Stone Hearts, the mockvine—none of them were similarly infected, even when I spent a lot of time among them. That's a point against the pathogen theory, I think."

"And what of the Returned? The plague spread through them like a wildfire," Jassin asked.

I nodded, yielding that point to him. "True, but I don't think it's because of plague. While it might act like a plague in that case, it can't be cured like one. The bishop can attest to that. That's because it's not a virus or bacteria. It's something my tutorial intelligence called 'void corruption.' I didn't know what to make of the term at the time when she said it to me, but I think I know now."

"I know plague, Young Human, and this one acts very much as one would expect," Kolash argued. "If it is corruption, as you say, why do we not feel the effects as we stand here with you? Surely this corruption can get into living things other than the goblins. They are not fundamentally different than other sapient life in our world. This is why we must be vigilant, lest the sickness worm its way into other vulnerable populations."

"Yes! Exactly!" I shouted, glad to finally get to this point. "Why just goblins but not the Stone Hearts? Why has no one else contracted a case of void corruption? That's the big question. The Baned and their peculiarities were a piece of the puzzle that didn't fit. It has been bothering me for a long time. Then, Tiba informed me that the Baned make their home right next to my tutorial facility."

Samila spoke up for the first time, arms crossed but paying rapt attention. "You believe that this tutorial place is the epicenter of the infection?"

I pointed at her and gave a thumbs-up. I didn't care if that wasn't a thing on Ralqir, silly place that it was. "I do. Theoretically, the tutorial goes like this: When a new Animator is inducted into the System, our hypothetical new Exotic is whisked away and sent to Ralqir, gets some advice from Nali, Shapes a couple things, asks some questions, and Levels Up to one. Then they go back to where they came from the same way they entered this universe. They go back home with an understanding of their class, and Ralqir goes on none the wiser."

"Obviously this didn't happen for you," Samila said with a grin. "Lucky you."

"Yeah," I agreed. "My tutorial went off the rails. I was attacked, and I had to run. It was only after I was a . . . 'guest' of the Stone Hearts that I Leveled Up and the System updated my quest to return to my insertion point." I fought not to look directly at Samila as I said the last bit.

"That still doesn't explain these Baned and our supposed immunity from the plague," Trix observed thoughtfully. Again I asked Constance to bless the little guy. He kept my last statement from hanging in the air for too long.

"Sorry. I'm getting there. Assuming my tutorial quest is fully typical—insert, Shape, Level, go home—then it stands to reason that our friend downstairs went through the same thing."

Realization sparked in Jassin's eyes, and he leaned forward excitedly with fingers steepled in front of his chin. "Except he didn't. The Dark Lord captured him, leading to the first uprising and the Purge."

"Correct!" I exclaimed, glad I was gaining traction. "The Dark Lord got a hold of Ephelir and brought him home to run his experiments. Exotics pretty much can live forever as long as you feed and water us, so the Dark Lord got to torture him for years and years, learning."

"Indeed. This was before he realized the knowledge he gleaned from his pet was tainted and nearly ended the world," Kolash said, bitterly. "The goblins, though. Us. If your new theory is to be believed, why are we immune? It does not make sense."

"Ephelir's insertion point—" I said, cutting him off before coming up with a better way of putting it. "The System's tunnel between universes has been open and waiting for him to return for thousands of years. It was probably a clean process before the corruption took hold, but after . . . Everything the System touches now is tainted. Anything the System is currently spending power on is slowly being poisoned, like dumping radioactive material in a well. That particular well basically glows now, given how long it's been poisoned."

Jassin, grasping the concept quickly, continued for me. "I believe I follow. Your theory would go a long way toward explaining how the plague can affect the dead. The energy has to come from somewhere, and it is not a spell the enemy is casting. I would know. You believe it's coming from the System bleeding corruption into our world. The captive human was probably a similarly bothersome source of corruption before the Dark Lord built his unique prison, but now his corruption is essentially contained or at least burned away by the maelstrom whose light this Scourge can't withstand."

"But the insertion point is not similarly contained," Sissa observed with an uncomfortable scowl. "The insertion point—where these Baned call their home—it could very well have slowly warped and mutated them for hundreds of years, generation after generation, until they became as they are now. Other living things—the animals and beasts—have the sense to avoid the area or haven't been exposed for long enough to have that level of corruption."

"But what about now?" Trix asked. "Why are we suddenly getting a new wave of corruption or infection? It isn't just goblins and Returned, either. There are animals, probably even plants."

"The beasts are susceptible to it, but, very likely, only after being overwhelmed by other corrupted beings," Jassin said. "If we assume Ryan's theory is true, then it is a corruption of the spirit. A subversion of the will that drives the mind. Beasts do not have the required sense of self or 'will' to withstand its effects for long, and anyone who has met a Returned can see that they are a pliable, suggestible people. The Dark Lord made them so for his purposes, and it made them particularly easy prey for what Ryan is describing."

I nodded. This was largely in line with my own thinking. "I think my tutorial intelligence was also susceptible. She was progressively going further and further afield as I spoke to her, even though she had fail-safes that reset her memories every time she detected even a hint of void corruption. Back home, we've had laws against artificial intelligence for a long time. It's illegal to code your own, and governments like the Colony only use it sparingly, then destroy it after its task is done. I think this may be why."

Jassin shared a meaningful look with Kolash. "We, too, do not dabble in autonomous constructs such as golems. It is a lost art, illegal now," he intoned ominously.

"Because they inevitably go insane. More than once, the Church has had to put down some mad practitioner's attempt at creating artificial life," the bishop finished for the headmaster.

That confirmed it. You needed a healthy spirit, an intact soul, to resist the Scourge. AI and things like it were beings of pure intellect but nothing more. They had no will other than to do what was set before them. People, however, were something more—something the Scourge couldn't readily subvert, at least not quickly.

That took time, and, in my case, probably Levels.

"It's a fine theory, Ryan, but how do you think we can end this?" Trix asked.

This was the part I'd been dreading. I took in a long, slow breath and prepared myself.

"Close the insertion points," I answered.

Jassin looked like he'd just been struck. "You aren't suggesting we let that creature in the basement free? Even if we had guarantees that it would go home as you suggest, I'm unsure if I'm willing to let a being of its level of power loose, even in another universe."

"No," I said. "We're not going to let Ephelir free."

"If you are about to suggest we kill it, believe me, we have tried. We cannot do enough damage to kill it, and it heals quickly. What's more, if we do too much damage to its prison, it may free itself, anyway. Even with your inventions, you will not be able to do more than what the top minds of our people have already tried. He nearly killed you with a look last time you saw him," Jassin argued, becoming increasingly more irritated.

Aw. He really did care.

I smiled with as much confidence as I could muster. "That's the thing. That wasn't just a look. It was a challenge. A System-regulated challenge. A duel with stakes. I'd heard about them back home. What I plan to do is to use the System to do what we, as mortals, can't."

"You're going to cheat. You're going to challenge a godlike being to a duel and win on a technicality, and your System is going to do the killing for you." It was Samila's voice. I'd been avoiding her gaze up until now, but that time was up. When I turned to address her, her expression was neutral, but her eyes were blazing furnaces. I suspected that she'd put the rest of it together, and the hardest part of the night was about to take place.

"Essentially, yes," I admitted quietly. I did not let my gaze waver or wander over to the rest of my friends, who I knew were giving me worried looks. "This world needs those insertion points closed, one way or another. One is getting closed tomorrow."

"And in the unlikely scenario that you live, you're going to go home," Samila half-whispered, her voice catching slightly, wavering on the final word.

There it was. To save Ralqir, I had to leave it. I'd realized it back at the wedding, kept it to myself, held it close, even though it pained me. I swallowed, seeing the hurt in Samila's eyes.

"Yeah," I croaked. "I have to leave."

CHAPTER SEVENTEEN

Do for Others

The heavy stone door slammed shut behind me, plunging the cylindrical prison of eternal torture into strange, high-contrast black and white, where the majority of the room was pitch black, shadow on glossy stone. Meanwhile, the pale beam of pure, terrible maelstrom light, even as thin as it was, dominated the room just by being there, so bright to my human eyes that I could see almost nothing within it other than the faint hint of Ephelir's slab.

Finally I was here. No turning back now. I did feel the urge to do so, however. Despite the door being closed and sealed, I could almost feel them all waiting for me on the other side. Jassin, Garret, and Kolash would be in the front—stoic, ready to . . . well, they'd be ready to end me if I came out of the room corrupted. Kolash had insisted upon that.

My friends would be behind them, Sissa and Samila standing side-by-side, hands together. Sissa had "Duty and mercy"-ed me before I stepped into the prison. That was nice. I could feel its golden warmth in my limbs, keeping them fresh and limber. Samila, on the other hand, just sent me in with a promise.

"Live through this, and we'll talk," she'd whispered. Strangely, that seemed to energize me as much as Sissa's magic had.

Meanwhile, Geddon would have Trix on his shoulder as he busied himself, looking over the phylacteries. The big man would keep Trix's mind off the tension they all probably felt.

As for me, I was a wreck on the inside, getting progressively worse as time wore on.

I swallowed nervously, suddenly finding the room to be quite chilly and entirely too still. My shaky breaths echoed off the bare stone and bounced around the room, so loud in the silence, it was impossible to believe Ephelir couldn't hear me. If he did, however, he made no indication. As always, he was still on his plinth bed, restrained and tortured for eternity. I waited cautiously, watching and listening.

Nothing.

Eventually, I got up the courage to move. The soles of my boots *clopped* on the hard stone, loud enough to be mistaken for gunshots.

I didn't walk toward my opponent. Instead, I slid left, skirting the outer edge of the room, a good fifty feet away from the rim of the light.

One. Two. Three long steps.

First position.

I summoned the pieces of my first turret, a traditional slug-thrower with the power dialed up for maximum penetration. No telling how thick this Exotic's skin was, at whatever high Level he was.

My trembling hands fought against me as I tried to fit all the little pieces together. The metal clanked like alarm bells in the still air.

Don't think about it. Just do it. Be in the moment, get it done, and then we can have a good meltdown later.

I couldn't stop thinking about it, though. Where I was right now, what I was doing . . . was it right? I was increasingly unsure. The stakes were so high but not just for me. *That* I could handle. I'd gone into situations before where I was ready to trade my life for someone else's. Hell, I did it so often nowadays that, from the outside looking in, I probably looked like I had a death wish.

Except before, when I'd nearly thrown my life away on a half-cooked plan, I at least had some fathomable goal—an immediate tangible result of my actions. I would risk myself freely so that others could live just a little longer. It was an easy trade: me for them. I was okay with that.

So what made this different? What made my duel with an unkillable creature of vast power so terrifying?

Scale.

I was doing this to save an entire planet. Countless living things: families, merchants, kings, queens, dragons, animals—hell, even trees and carnivorous plants—were all counting on me. If I did the math, which I tried very hard not to do, it would likely come out to be in the ballpark of billions of living things counting on a positive outcome in the next few moments.

The human mind wasn't made to grapple with those kinds of numbers. They were more abstract than real to most. Except I was beginning to understand, and that terrified me.

Until now, I'd been doing little things that I hoped would make a big impact. Save a life here, build a little something there, hope it worked out for the best. Do enough little things, and the big, unmanageable thing doesn't seem so big and unmanageable anymore.

But the scale of this was far beyond that. It had always been so, but I'd made it a point to never think about just how huge it actually was. It would have broken me.

Worse, I couldn't quite place my life on the other end of that scale. I saw the equation: Ralqir's entire population on one side, me on the other, and I reflexively rejected it. It didn't feel right. There was no possible way Ryan Kotes could have the power to do something so massive. Not the crippled kid from the Outers. He could never be worthy of having that kind of impact on anything. Not possible. There had to have been some mistake.

From there, of course, it was all too easy to start doubting my theory and my plan. No one had handed it to me. I hadn't read it in a book. No divine being had descended from the heavens and told me this was the way things were.

This was just me, fumbling in the dark. If I was wrong, I'd be throwing my life away for nothing, or, worse, murdering a fellow human.

But here I was.

The doubt started to become physically crippling.

Just then the turret's magazine jiggled into place, and the release lever was forced down with a *clack!*

I let my eyes un-focus and I drifted into that state of mind where I saw my aura. It was thick in here, all packed into one room like it was. I wasn't sure what the walls were made of, but my aura wasn't able to get anywhere outside of them. My aura also couldn't get into the pillar of light, I observed. As soon as my little, smoky-blue motes wafting through the room touched the blazing light of the maelstrom, they instantly disintegrated.

That was okay. I had already accounted for that. I got on my tiptoes and set about aiming the turret manually. I looked down the barrel and aligned it just so, only to notice that all of Ephelir's numerous eyes were open and focused on me.

My stomach lurched.

How long had he been watching?

I slowly backed away from the turret and took three more steps around the rim of the room where I summoned the pieces for my next emplacement—another ballistic one. Again, I started to put them all together, but at this point I could *feel* him watching me.

I hunched over my work, trembling fingers working over the mechanisms I'd Shaped and fiddled with a hundred times. Ephelir's gaze was a constant pressure weighing me down.

Finally the tension got to me.

"So, Ralqir, huh? What a place," I remarked lamely, the volume of my voice squelched by the tightness of my throat.

Ephelir did not answer. I couldn't even hear him breathing, which was funny, because I could even hear my own breaths echoing around the room. I imagined him lying there, pale-skinned, oddly proportioned, with asymmetrical musculature and a horrifically mutated mouth.

The words seemed to help me in the nerves department, though. Somehow, breaking the silence made things a bit more bearable. This turret was already coming together much more smoothly than the last.

I cleared my throat and started again. "It's got all this history, Ralqir, and I can't really wrap my brain around it. Just years and years of people doing people-things. Strange stuff. You know what I mean?" I contemplated.

I checked over my shoulder to see if there was any change. Nothing. He was still staring at me, though.

"Maybe not." I shrugged. "I don't really know where you're from. Earth? Post-Exodus? The timeline seems right. Well, you'll be happy to know that Exodus worked. I come from a little ball of rock called Proxis 3. Pretty young as far as human colonies go. We don't have the kind of history I'm talking about. Not like this place. Proxis isn't exactly the outermost system mankind saw fit to seed, but we're contenders for the top ten. That means we only thawed and settled in our particular corner of the galaxy about ten or fifteen generations ago. It might sound like a lot, but it's not. Our world is brand-new, empty in a lot of ways. We have to sort of borrow history and culture from Earth to really feel connected to each other."

The next turret was a laser variant. Easier to put together, at least. My hands were steadier now, without having the oppressive silence bearing down on me.

"Ralqir, though—it's got this unbroken chain of stories that goes all the way back to . . . I have no idea, but it's *long*. The place feels old, lived-in, unlike anything I've ever known. It's weird. I feel like I should have a history, something to connect to my home, but I don't have that. I have Earth's. *Yours.*"

Turret set, I retraced my steps back to the stone door, then began to set up that side of the room. Ballistic, ballistic, laser. Symmetrical. Symmetry was nice. The way they were all facing would keep them from shooting each other and myself.

The ballistic turrets would be calibrated to fire upon the center plinth, away from me where ricochets wouldn't be a problem, and the laser turrets would be on mirror angles spraying from the sides, since their attacks didn't hurt non-organic material and didn't ricochet. Fire was out of the question. The last thing I wanted right now was to fight a fire for oxygen, especially if things got weird.

"Makes you wonder why the System sent us here in the first place. I mean, why here of all places? It's not like we have a connection to this place. Why not an asteroid composed of ferrous metals or something?" I considered, turning toward him, the only person in the world who probably knew what I was going through . . . if his mind was still intact. He gave no indication that it was.

Two more emplacements completed in silence. Finally, when the last turret was up and running and pointed in the right direction, I retraced my steps once more to approach the column of light from the side that had the stone door.

I closed in slowly, step by step. The air around me thickened, and the echoes died unnaturally quickly. Then the smell hit me again—that sweet, bitter, tar rot that filled my nose and forced its way down into my mouth. Disgusting. Horrible. *Familiar.*

It was definitely the smell I'd experienced on my first day as an Exotic. The smell of corruption. My own corruption. The System's.

My confidence got a boost from that. I was doing the right thing. My theory was sound, or at least better than anything else we had.

Ephelir's many eyes saw through me. Into me. There was no malice that I could detect, but there was intensity. So much intensity. Ephelir wanted something. He wanted, but he said nothing. Did nothing.

Perhaps he couldn't, not while he was in his prison.

The black tendrils of goo squirmed out of Ephelir's body, bursting from the translucent skin to evaporate into mist, and I found that the most disturbing aspect of all: the back-and-forth of corruption and it being cleansed.

I coughed, fighting the urge to vomit.

"If we were to assume the System is benign, maybe it sent us here *because* of the people—as sort of ambassadors," I continued. "I wouldn't have minded that, coming here and getting to know people. Making friends. Showing them how humanity does things."

Summoning a piece of Mendau Wood and Consuming it, I made sure my mana was topped off and then some.

"Except that didn't happen for us, did it?" I asked my fellow human. "We came here and . . . changed everything. Not for the better, either. We made a mess of things, didn't we? It's not necessarily our fault, I get that. But what if the System sent us here to—I don't know . . . What if it's not benign? I don't just mean the void corruption. That's obviously something new. I mean the System itself. Who made it? No one knows. What is its purpose? No one knows that, either. Why is it so damned determined to inflict us upon other universes?"

No answer. Not that I was expecting one. He just lay there, burning, healing, and burning again.

"If there's anything human left of you, Ephelir . . ." I whispered, having a hard time with this part. "If there's anything left, and you've just been biding your time, waiting for a sympathetic ear to talk to, say something now."

Nothing.

I sniffed, simultaneously mourning what had once been a sentient being like myself and steeling myself to take the next step. "That's what I thought. If there's any part of you that remembers you're human, I just want you to know that I'm going to fix this. You and I are not going to be the end of this world. It sucks. It's not like I want to take on this burden, but . . ." I sighed. " . . . there's no one else. So, I guess it has to be me."

Finally, a breath rattled in the former-human's throat, and its vertically oriented lips flowered open to expose crooked fangs—too many to count. Disturbing, to say the least.

"So, here's my theory," I went on. "You want to kill me. You're Scourge now, and you want me dead like the rest of them. But if that's the case, why the challenge?

That doesn't make any sense to me. Why not just do the thing? Why not just kill me with your mind or your aura or whatever you've got?"

I turned my back on him then, pacing back toward my semicircle of turrets. He didn't strike. No mind blasts or serrated tentacles or anything.

Turning, I narrowed my eyes at him and came back to look him in the eyes. "I think . . . that's all you've got. When it comes down to it, you're an Animator, a non-combat Class. The challenge—it's the only way for you to strike out at me. It almost worked, too, just because of the power difference between the two of us. I nearly died. You're so far above me on the power scale, you could kill me with a simple challenge. Terrible idea to fight you."

I leaned in, just far enough that I could almost feel the maelstrom tickling the ends of my hair.

"I think you showed me too much of your hand, though. What I realized is this: the System is a machine. One thing you have to know about machines is that well-designed ones don't have useless parts. Who would put the time into crafting something like that? I'm new to this Exotic thing, but challenging someone has to have a function outside of a formal fight. It can't be pointless. That got me wondering if challenges are a way to settle differences or train outside of killing each other. You challenge someone, set the stakes, and get something out of it—a System-enforced bet."

With a thought, a menu popped up in my vision.

Issue Challenge to Ephelir. Stakes: ?
Choose:
Currency
Item
Territory
Oath
Experience
Death

I chose Death as the only stake. That's what we were both after, right?

Challenge issued to Ephelir. Stakes: Death
Declined.

Then that budding pressure in the air increased tenfold, and the world around me started to blur as—

Ephelir (Level ???) has amended the challenge.
Stakes: Experience, Death.
Do you accept? Y/N

The exact same stakes as his last challenge, but this time I didn't pass out. Why? My higher Level? Maybe.

What did he have to gain by betting Experience, though? Why was Experience so important to him? My Level wasn't anything special, not to something like Ephelir. It would be a drop in the bucket. What was it—

Oh, you clever son of a bitch.

I tried amending the challenge myself back to just Death, but it was instantly rejected. Again. Then again. All the while, Ephelir stared at me.

He wasn't budging. He also had me over a barrel. I needed this. I needed to close the insertion points to save this place, and Ephelir had literally no other aims than to try to hurt me.

"I know what you're doing," I murmured, trying and failing to keep the anger out of my tone.

Ephelir's eyes vibrated, pupils pulsing in what I assumed was excitement. I was spending too much time talking to this thing. Did it look . . . pleased?

"Fine," I relented, preparing myself for anything. "Give me all the Experience you like. I'm going to use it to make sure the Scourge never troubles this place again, and I'm going to do it as a human being, Ephelir. If you are still in there, I'm doing this for you, too."

With that, I stepped away, retreating to my firing line as I accepted the challenge.

Challenge begins in 5 seconds.
Begin.

I was well away from the plinth by the time the challenge began. After a slow exhalation, I mentally triggered the activation of all the turrets at once.

The room exploded into light and sound.

Over the course of a minute, give or take, 3,700 rounds of supersonic lead combined with unknown hundreds of thousands of laser hits scoured the Scourge-Touched human on the plinth. Purple laser light blinded me while the sound boomed off the walls and shook the air.

My turrets spewed their payloads into the light, piercing the Scourge's body. The lasers chewed its flesh. At this range, not many of them missed, and they ground through it like chainsaws. The plinth glowed and smoked as Ephelir's insides were turned to outsides and his mutated flesh splashed onto the floor before charring to ash. The entire Bera Maelstrom, focused and refined by years of research and development by the Dark Lord, blasted the monster's now-exposed internals.

Then it was over. The ballistic turret's barrels glowed red-hot in the relative dark where they stood. Acrid smoke slithered up from ventilation holes in the laser turrets' flash housing.

Yet Ephelir lay there on his plinth—more or less. Pieces of him. Pieces that still twitched and writhed.

Before my very eyes, I saw it regenerating, putting itself back together, much as I did when I was hurt, only this was much more thorough. Its disparate pieces practically crawled toward one another, knit themselves anew, sinew by sinew, after having been shredded like pulled pork. Its tendons grew, snapped together, and its muscles bubbled and seethed up from its bones. The last to reform were its eyes, wet and energetic as they regrew, opened, and sought me out once more.

Fucking A.

I had nothing left. This thing had taken my best shot and chosen not to die. Now it was his turn to attack.

We traded blows. Mine was a powerful first strike, one that hurt him but didn't kill him. One I could not do again. His body was too strong.

Ephelir's strike, on the other hand, went to my very soul.

But wait . . . *what?!*

Ephelir has yielded.

Ryan Kotes is victorious. Experience gained: 0.1% of opponent's total Experience. 16,889,079 Experience total.

Level Up!

You are now Level 19.

Max HP +10

Max MP +10

+1 Attribute point

Achievements awarded this Level:

Duelist: You were judged victorious in a challenge this Level. Experience from all other sources increased by 20% for next Level.

[ERROR:SOURCE_CONFLICT:ACH_DUELIST:UNEXPECTED_NEMESIS_TAG]

Resolving . . .

Resolved:

Achievement awarded: Demon Slayer: You have defeated an evil beyond mortal comprehension, a true Nemesis. Randomly chosen combat-Ability-depth increased. You have been noticed.

Rift Hunter: You gained 51% of your Experience this Level from Nemesis-tagged foes. [+1 to all Attributes]

Doing Your Part: Some of your creations have been used against agents of the Scourge. [+200% Experience awarded for new designs next Level]

Level Up!

You are now Level 20.

Max HP +10

Max MP +10
+1 Attribute point

Achievements awarded this Level:
Duelist: You were judged victorious in a challenge this Level. Experience from all other sources increased by 20% for next Level.
[ERROR:SOURCE_CONFLICT:ACH_DUELIST:UNEXPECTED_NEMESIS_TAG]
Resolving . . .
Resolved:
Achievement awarded: Demon Slayer: You have defeated an evil beyond mortal comprehension, a true Nemesis. Randomly chosen combat-Ability-depth increased. You have been noticed.
Rift Hunter: You gained 51% of your Experience this Level from Nemesis-tagged foes. [+1 to all Attributes]
Reversal: You gained 100% of your Experience this Level from Nemesis-tagged foes. [+3 to highest Attribute]
All Natural: You have spent 80% of this Level with full mana. [+1 Body]

Level Up!
You are now Level 21.
Max HP +10
Max MP +10
+1 Attribute point

Achievements awarded this Level:
Duelist: You were judged victorious in a challenge this Level. Experience from all other sources increased by 20% for next Level.
[ERROR:SOURCE_CONFLICT:ACH_DUELIST:UNEXPECTED_NEMESIS_TAG]
Resolving . . .
Resolved:
Achievement awarded: Demon Slayer: You have defeated an evil beyond mortal comprehension, a true Nemesis. Randomly chosen combat-Ability-depth increased. You have been seen.
Rift Hunter: You gained 51% of your Experience this Level from Nemesis-tagged foes. [+1 to all Attributes]
Reversal: You gained 100% of your Experience this Level from Nemesis-tagged foes. [+3 to highest Attribute]
All Natural: You have spent 80% of this Level with full mana. [+1 Body]

Level Up!

You are now Level 22.
Max HP +10
Max MP +10
+1 Attribute point

Achievements awarded this Level:
Duelist: You were judged victorious in a challenge this Level. Experience from all other sources increased by 20% for next Level.
[ERROR:SOURCE_CONFLICT:ACH_DUELIST:UNEXPECTED_NEMESIS_TAG]
Resolving . . .
Resolved:
Achievement awarded: Demon Slayer: You have defeated an evil beyond mortal comprehension, a true Nemesis. Randomly chosen combat-Ability-depth increased. You have been marked.
Rift Hunter: You gained 51% of your Experience this Level from Nemesis-tagged foes. [+1 to all Attributes]
All Natural: You have spent 80% of this Level with full mana. [+1 Body]

Level Up!
You are now Level 23.
Max HP +10
Max MP +10
+1 Attribute point

Achievements awarded this Level:
Duelist: You were judged victorious in a challenge this Level. Experience from all other sources increased by 20% for next Level.
[ERROR:SOURCE_CONFLICT:ACH_DUELIST:UNEXPECTED_NEMESIS_TAG]
Resolving . . .
Resolved:
Achievement awarded: Demon Slayer: You have defeated an evil beyond mortal comprehension, a true Nemesis. Randomly chosen combat-Ability-depth increased. You have been branded.
Rift Hunter: You gained 51% of your Experience this Level from Nemesis-tagged foes. [+1 to all Attributes]
Reversal: You gained 100% of your Experience this Level from Nemesis-tagged foes. [+3 to highest Attribute]
All Natural: You have spent 80% of this Level with full mana. [+1 Body]

Ecstasy. Rippling waves of absolutely terrible, wonderful, dirty, choking, smothering ecstasy. I trembled as it slithered over me, through me, overwhelmed me with absolute wonder and eclipsed my entire concept of pleasure. It crawled through my insides, opened up my brain, and clawed at my synapses until I collapsed to the floor and gave up on anything other than feeling it.

The son of a bitch had outmaneuvered me, because he didn't think like a human. He was Scourge. He didn't necessarily want to *live*. He just wanted me dead. Barring that, he wanted me infected.

And that's exactly what he had done by conceding our duel.

Depth increasing. Stand by . . .
Depth increasing. Stand by . . .
Depth increasing. Stand by . . .
Depth increasing. Stand by . . .
Depth increasing. Stand by . . .

In my fading vision, as the stream of notifications scrolled through my mind, I witnessed the only other human being on Ralqir finally lose his thousand-year battle with the maelstrom. Death took him, and his body was rendered to ash.

My conscious mind decided that enough was enough and hit the off switch but not before the thick, coppery taste of blood rushed to fill my mouth.

CHAPTER EIGHTEEN

Wake and Make

I awoke in my workshop with an aching head and an empty stomach, and when I finally gathered enough of my will to actually open my eyes, everything felt off—unreal, almost. Or maybe *too* real. The weird, omnipresent white light wasn't helping, either. I felt like I was viewing the world through a wide-lens camera, and the impulses from my mind were just signals sent to a swivel upon which the camera was mounted.

My swollen tongue felt like a foreign entity in my mouth. The *air* tasted wrong too. Someone had gone and replaced my tongue with a dead fish, and everything was being filtered through that dead-fish-filter.

The familiar microscopic mana motes hung in the air around me, too, thick and lazy, drifting in patterns just on the edge of sense.

I drunkenly sat up on my cot, slowly shaking my head and trying to get some feeling back into everything that should have feeling. Nearby, my workbench loomed just outside of the pure white of the rest of the room, all right angles, squeaky joints, and old oil smells. It looked wrong, too . . .

Oh. I was on the floor. Someone had switched out my cot for a pallet of some kind—just padding and a blanket, really. Now that I thought about it, *everything* seemed taller. What had happened to my cot?

I stretched to get my blood circulating again, but something made me hesitate when I tried to move my arm. A slight pressure. Warm.

Looking down, I saw that I wasn't alone. There was another, smaller pallet next to mine upon which Samila lay on her side, her breathing soft and rapid, one hand resting just above my wrist. She looked rough, her robes wrinkled, her face muscles tensed, and her body rigid like she was ready to jump to her feet at any second. The strength with which she was holding onto my arm even in sleep—which I'd somehow only just noticed—was a good indication of how tense she was. If I were someone else, there'd probably be bruises.

Carefully, I shifted the angle of my arm until her grip loosened naturally and fell away. I caught her hand before it could hit the bed and let it down gently. Somehow that seemed to relax her, and she sank down into a more-natural position to sleep.

As for me, I felt like I'd spent enough hours in this bed for two lifetimes.

Also I was surprised to still be alive. It was a welcome surprise, mind you. Very. However, I hadn't really counted on living this long back when I'd hatched this plan. I had half-expected to either die fighting Ephelir, either alone or together, finally ridding the world of both sources of corruption, but things had gone sideways during our little duel, ending in a forfeit where I lived and now I had to go through with the hard part.

I looked down at Samila again. She looked so peaceful like this. The mask she wore in her waking hours was gone, giving way to the more-vulnerable woman underneath. She wasn't goading me into anything or trying to lift my spirits or get me out of my own head. She was just lying there, being herself, and aside from the blue scales and lack of hair, she looked incredibly human—just a pretty girl dreaming peacefully in her bed.

I felt the urge to put my arm back where it had been in order to feel that touch again, or maybe wake her and tell her I was okay, but I decided against it. That urge was coming from a place of . . . I didn't know.

If I were feeling introspective, I'd probably say that Samila was the one that sought me out in my glass cave and dragged me kicking and screaming into the light with other people, and, on some unconscious level, I knew that was something I needed. My mom used to do it when she was alive, take my hand and lead me into wondrous places, and, again, if introspection was something I was doing right now (which I was not), that was probably something I missed.

You do not need to wake the girl because you miss your mom, Ryan. That's weird and creepy and we've moved on. Best let sleeping dragons lie or however that saying goes.

There was a powerful, growing pressure deep in the center of my brain, swelling with urgency and anticipation. I wanted to . . .

There was all this . . . potential like a gas pocket in a mine that was just waiting for a spark to finally expose the deep places of the world to open air. I wanted to—No. I *needed* to stretch, and if I didn't do it soon, I would lose something. Of that, I was increasingly certain.

Compulsion. I feel compelled, but like it's coming from me at the same time. System, is this your doing?

With a thought, I brought up my logs, reviewing the messages I'd received. Five Levels in a matter of seconds. Five error messages. A new achievement received five times.

Demon Slayer.

I couldn't be sure, but that one seemed like something that shouldn't have happened five whole times. It felt momentous, like it was something that would be celebrated back at Exotic HQ. Was there an Exotic HQ? Probably not. If there was one, however, someone getting this achievement would be commemorated with drinks, dancing, and questionable decisions. The reward was—

Depth increasing. Stand by . . .
Depth increasing. Stand by . . .
Depth increasing. Stand by . . .
Depth increasing. Stand by . . .
Depth increasing. Stand by . . .

Status Gained: Internal Bleeding [1 HP/sec]
Status Gained: Brain Hemorrhage [1 HP/sec]
Status Gained: Brain Hemorrhage [2 HP/sec]
Status Gained: Brain Hemorrhage [6 HP/sec]
. . .

Oh.

Apparently, I'd had a stroke. A big one. That was distantly concerning. Distant because I had my logs right there, telling me I was at full-HP again and that the Hemorrhage Status was gone. Distant, also, because my thoughts weren't coalescing on the fear enough to get that jolt of dread usually associated with near-death experiences. They couldn't.

I blinked, trying to pin down why I wasn't freaking out. Had I been nearly killed too many times to worry about that kind of thing anymore, or was the ridiculous urge to *do* eclipsing all other thoughts right now? Was it the System's doing, or was I already a jaded veteran in my late-teens?

Okay. Take control. What do you think you should be thinking?

I did my best to simulate what a normal, non-me entity might think about all of this.

The System had broken my tiny brain by "rewarding" me a little too freely. The error messages had to have something to do with that. There was no way I was supposed to receive Demon Slayer that many times for one kill. Perhaps it was because I received it when "Duelist" threw an error? Then it tried to do it again and again with the same results?

What kind of design was that? What did the System do in a typical case when someone killed a "True Nemesis," as it had said? It had to have happened at least once or twice for the achievement to even exist, so what made me special enough to kill with the reward?

I thought about it for a full minute and, over the course of that minute, started to understand.

My specific situation had to have come up sometime. The universe—er, the multiverse—was an impossibly big place. Someone, at some time, in some universe had to have challenged a corrupted, godlike Exotic way above their Level to a duel . . . and also had said Exotic restrained in a beam of light specifically designed to imprison him . . . which was made by a genius Dark-Lord figure utilizing the power of a unique cosmic phenomenon . . . and . . . then . . . won?

Well, if I put it that way, maybe this was a fringe case. An extreme fringe case. I was still sour about it, though. The reward nearly fried my brain.

Okay. Time to take a look at the Damage.

Ryan Kotes - Level 23 Animator (Uncommon)				
Type:	Artificer (Common)	**Abilities:**	Shape 9 (Transmute)	Devouring Grasp (Magivore) 5
Class:	Animator (Uncommon)		Consume 5 (Reservoir)	Volatility 3+++++
Core:	Engine (Unique)		Iron Grip 4	Imbue 4
HP:	301/301		Trigger 4	Automate 4+
MP:	267/267		Tempered Channels 4	Knife in the Dark 23 (Mark, Curse of Obfuscation)
Attributes:			Hardened Defense 1	Compartmentalize 3
Body:	53		Tension Step 1	Expanded Channels 1
Mind:	42		State Change 1	Collect 1
Spirit:	106	**Skills:**	Climbing 8	Unarmed Combat 5
			Running 5	Stealth (Gray Man) 12
			Conduit 5	Split Mind 9
			Spear 4	Deception 5
			Disguise 3	Sword 6
			Pistol 4	Mana Manipulation 2
			Jumping 2	
		Affinities:	Goblinoid F	Cobalt E
			Iron E	Deep Lead E
			Steel F	Nickel E
Free Attribute points: 5			Magnesium F	Copper E
			Mendau Wood D	Pex Oil F
			Limestone E	

That was simply a stupid amount of "+" signs stacked on top of Volatility.

Five levels of depth applied to a singular ability I wasn't supposed to have in the first place and one I couldn't Level through use.

If Jassin's interpretation of the System through his Dominion magic was correct, then the System was currently carving pathways through my body to make way for my Abilities, but it was a slow, methodical process. This, however, was anything but that. I barely had Volatility at all. If the pathways for my other Abilities were gentle streams, growing wider and deeper over time, as was natural, Volatility had just gone from a tiny rivulet to a giant fissure where water rushed through and was never seen again. Once I used it a bit and completed the depth increase, who knows what might happen? Would I have more brain bleeds to look forward to?

Grimacing, I checked the new description.

> Volatility: &@Attract. Inject_ #$&U. Convert()(#*. Release**

Right. That was supremely unhelpful and disturbing.

I took a long, calming breath and closed my eyes. There was no need to dwell on it—at least not now. I'd deal with the aftereffects when they arose. Hopefully near a hospital.

Plus there were two other Abilities I didn't quite know the ins and outs of just yet.

State Change, I'd gotten when I'd reached Level 15 and, as of yet, had not found a whole lot of use for.

> State Change: Change the state of matter using magical means. Mana cost is directly proportional to energy difference in states.

Yeah, I could use State Change to turn iron into liquid, or mercury into fun little cubes, but the Ability's uses were limited for now because of how expensive it was and how pliable I could already make metals. Why would I need to liquefy copper if I could already mold it exactly how I wanted it with a touch? What use I would have for molten metal in the palm of my hand, I didn't know either, other than gaining familiarity with the beds in the burn ward. Oh, did I forget to mention that? Using mana to change a metal's state came with all the associated temperature changes, too, and let me tell you, molten iron is *hot*.

I did have to admit that turning lead balls into plasma was pretty fun at first. I couldn't deny that. Sure, those experiments were less than practical, and I had to use a few full mana tanks on the Automated casting bowl meant to turn the tiny BBs from a solid to a plasma. That made the expense less than practical if I wanted to mass-produce exploding plasma balls, and said balls, once manufactured, had a tendency to shed their electrons and react to pretty much whatever was floating around in the atmosphere at the time . . . violently, as plasma was wont to do. Thank Constance for blast-shielding.

Change State was probably far from useless, I knew, but using it would probably remain a future-Ryan problem for now. I needed to do more experiments and make a new casting bowl for said experiments since the last one met an unfortunate end.

The newest Ability, the one I'd gotten at 20—Collect—looked like something present-Ryan would like to play with.

Collect: Align Shaped materials to gather ambient mana into associated Triggers. Rate of gathering affected by material composition, material Affinities, Animator's Affinities, ambient mana density, and material surface area.

If I was reading the description correctly, it was now possible for my creations to reach out and grab mana on their own and stuff said mana into whatever Trigger I'd built into it. The aiming arms of all the turrets could collect a portion of their own mana and use that to locomote, as opposed to all of the power coming from my Automated smart cards or from myself. If anything, it would take the edge off the mana cost of operating a turret.

What's more, if I let something like, say, my sword charge itself over time, I could afford to Trigger something cool with it once or twice a day. Maybe a Shape change, or maybe it could cast its own version of Willing Edge.

Wait, *no.* I was thinking about this all wrong. If I could get my material to collect ambient mana to fill Triggers that changed the materials' shape, then I would effectively be converting supernatural energy to something like kinetic energy. The mass would essentially be moving in space, powered by mana.

There was a name for something that converted one type of energy into another type. I'd worked with them my entire life.

Engines—everything from vehicles to power tools to electric toothbrushes . . . I'd tinkered with all of those. They all converted power into motion. If I was right, I might be able to make magic-powered engines.

My fingers twitched. The urge to *do* was almost irresistible.

I looked down at Samila one last time, smiling at how sweet it was for her to wait with me while I—wait, how long had it been? Had this been a nap or a coma?

Either way, the compulsion I was feeling wasn't going away. In fact, I could barely sit still. My Body and my Mind *needed* to do. Right now.

If I'd been out for longer than expected, that just meant I had less time to do this before I'd have to be leaving. That made it the perfect time to slap all of my five points into Mind. I was going to need some brainpower.

Quietly, I slipped out of my bedroll and touched my bare feet to the white glass floor. It was cold but not overly so, thanks to my higher Body score. My boots weren't anywhere around here to put on anyway, and they'd make more noise. Samila looked like she needed the rest, and, if I were being honest with myself, I liked having her here, even as a passive presence in the background.

With great care, I gathered up my bedsheets and spread them over the dragonkin girl, making sure all of her was covered and cozy. Almost instantly she seemed to unclench and fall deeper into a restful state, curling up in the warm bedding and snoring quietly.

I took up one of the little sticks of chalk and leaned on the workbench. I needed to do this right. With direction.

CHAPTER NINETEEN

Exceed My Grasp

I was hunched over my workbench and Shaping what was going to be my tenth collector test by the time Samila finally woke up. The little blue woman stretched languidly like a cat, pushing the blankets down and away with one long outstretched leg. The bright blue of her exposed skin against her bunched and loosely fastened robes tried to draw my eye, but I studiously kept my vision fixed upon my Shaping.

I was a gentleman, and I was going to stay a gentleman and not think about just how much blue I'd seen and the shape of her—

Oh, look! We're in the middle of science! Careful now . . .

Shaking my head, I resumed my work. This experiment was going to be interesting. I'd found gold in my precious-metals pile in the form of coins, and, for some reason, I found it endlessly amusing to turn money into something actually useful. Would people's love for gold give it some kind of boost in the supernatural department? I was about to find out.

Frustratingly, the softer metals like gold weren't easier to Shape, despite all conventional wisdom saying they should be. Maybe it was because I was moving atoms around instead of using a hammer.

"You're quiet when you want to be, Monk." Samila yawned, rolling her neck to get some of the stiffness out as she readjusted the tie on the front of her robes to preserve her modesty. "You would probably make a good game hunter if you could keep from lighting yourself on fire from time to time."

Seeing only a moderate amount of blue out of the corner of my eye, I determined it was safe to turn around now. As I did, I flashed her a slight smile but had to blink rapidly as my eyes adjusted to focusing on something farther away than my workbench. I reached up to rub some of the blur out. How long had I been at this? I looked around at the room, at the bits and bobs scattered around my work area and the line of glowing collectors way across the room, as far from me as possible.

"Maybe I should specialize in moth-hunting," I replied hoarsely. "I think I'd be good at that. Do you guys have giant moths?" I asked, turning back toward my little piece of gold and checking the surface area. I'd stretched this out thin—not quite gold-leaf thin—but close.

"Yes, but they would be more interested in your clothes and sometimes your hair," she said as the slap of her footsteps approached from behind.

"Defacing currency now, are we?" she mused.

I shrugged. "Doing some research. Figured I had some time to myself, since I'm not running for my life or getting my ass kicked at the moment. If not now, not sure when I'll get to do it."

She went quiet, the obvious reply being: *You mean, after you leave.*

We both knew. We just didn't want to acknowledge it.

"Is that what this is? Another experiment?" she asked lightly, setting her hand on a steel construct that looked like a metal kebab with bites already taken out of it. She picked it up in her hand experimentally and tested the heft like it was a weapon, which it kind of was—one that could destroy a pre-industrial society if anyone ever got the hang of making them en masse.

"Oh, no. That's a crank shaft. It's, uh . . . it converts vertical motion to rotational. I made that while I was thinking."

"And these?" She pointed at an odd collection of vaguely cylindrical bits of metal.

"Different piston designs. The first one was a failure, so I kind of had to start from zero."

Making my first overtures toward a magic-powered Engine turned out to be a daunting prospect. Most of what I knew other than the basic concept of force transfer didn't apply. Electricity-based designs were pretty much a bust unless I had an abundance of time on my hands to make a whole magic-powered generator first to power said electric Engine. Mana didn't work like electricity, though I was kind of forcing it to, sometimes. No electricity meant no magnetic field meant no rotation to work with. Another Future-Ryan problem.

Right now, I was leaning more toward perfecting the piston design. Triggers could be used to change the shape of a piston, having it press down on the crankshaft just through magic power alone. When a Trigger went off, it was a powerful thing—almost irresistible if the material was strong enough. With the proper application of mana it could happen at high speeds, too. Then we'd be off to the races.

I was also kicking around an air pressure design where a compression bulb Trigger like the ones on my flamethrower turret could use super-compressed air to force the pistons down. Again, more drawbacks, more frustration. Theoretically, zero heat issues, though.

"I slept through all of this?" Samila asked with disbelief.

"You looked like you needed some rest," I replied honestly. It was surprisingly nice to have her there while I was working. Nobody other than Vince ever hung around while I tinkered, and even he eventually hit his watch-a-guy-hit-things-with-a-wrench-while-cursing limit. I didn't want to think about how this was probably the first and last time this was going to happen.

I didn't mention that I gained a Level in Stealth out of the deal, either, bringing my point value up to 14. I silently wondered if I had Gray Man to thank for that. I'd certainly made mistakes over the course of the night, banging bits of metal around when I hadn't meant to or dropping tools. Samila slept like a baby, though.

Was that the mind-altering aspect of my Stealth keeping Samila from noticing what I was doing? If someone who went a different direction with their Stealth Skill did what I did, would they have roused their hypothetical dragon-kin lady?

Gray Man was weird. Scary, too. Maybe I'd mention that part of my powers later. Or maybe never. Never was probably better.

"Me?" she scoffed. "You're the one we found face down in a puddle of his own blood."

I shrugged again, grabbing a brass button from the bits cup and beginning to Shape it into a cube. "It was pretty restful, actually. Surprised more people don't do it."

"They do," Samila replied acidly. "They just end up sleeping forever. Not all of them have a bishop on hand to repair their brain."

I spun around, mouth open, feeling my eyebrows climb up my forehead of their own accord, maybe all the way to my hairline and beyond. "Kolash healed me?" I gaped.

She still had my crankshaft in her hand, twirling it absently as she replied, "We all rushed into the room after the last of the noise had died down, and we saw you there. His Holiness hesitated maybe a heartbeat, but then he was there healing you. It surprised all of us—the headmaster, especially."

"Uh. Yeah," I said as I grappled with the full implications. "He could have—I mean, how many problems would have been solved had he just let me bleed out or tossed me off the top of the Spire? Sure, you'd still have the Scourge out there, but they wouldn't have had power from the System to feed off of. They'd have become a finite sort of threat, that could have been handled by conventional means."

She rolled her eyes and slapped me on the back of the head with her free hand. "Are you seriously advocating for your own murder? What's the human word for 'suicidally selfless?'"

I raised my hands placatingly. "Hey! Hey! I'm not complaining. I just—I don't know."

"Now you have to live through your plan, and you don't know how to?"

Holy hell, she'd nailed it. I mean, that wasn't all of it, but it was a big part. I hadn't counted on living through the challenge, and now I had to really go the distance if the plan was going to work.

Samila seemed to sense that she'd struck a nerve, and she pivoted quickly so as not to dwell on it. "Anyway, after we found you, we brought you here to recuperate. I dozed off sometime during my shift, I guess. You made a good effort to become a martyr, Monk, but it looks like you're just not cut out for it."

"No, I'm really not," I said, turning back toward the table and peering at the gold petal I'd just made. "But living is turning out to be a lot more work."

"Truth. I, for one, am glad you're still with us, however," Samila replied as she sidled up close to me—close enough that I could feel her warmth on my skin.

I swallowed hard, not sure how to proceed. The subject was right there. All it would take was one or two words. "Did you want to talk ab—"

"No," she cut me off.

"No?" I asked.

"No," she repeated. "Don't get me wrong, Ryan. I want you to stay. But I'm not stupid. As of right now, this is the only plan we have, and I would be a fool to pick a fight with you now over some stupid—uh—whatever."

The two of us stood there in silence, Samila angrily biting her lip and tightening the ties on her robe, me trying and failing to get another Shape going on the gold petal I'd just made.

I heard her sigh, then lean on my shoulder to get a closer look at the stuff on the workbench.

"So, what aspect of warfare are you changing today?" she asked.

I glanced at her out of the corner of my eye and smiled just enough so she could see it. "Making batteries," I answered.

Samila tilted her head. "Like those?" she asked, pointing toward the back of the room where nine other petal formations sat in various states of operational. They all had a sort of flower-shaped design, four petals arranged in a cross pattern with a purple cube of Volatile metal mounted in the center. Every flower was made of different metals, labeled in chalk underneath to indicate what order I'd given them as well as their elemental composition.

"Yeah. Like those," I confirmed. "They're meant to solve my longevity problem."

I heard her suppress a snicker behind me "Oh, I hadn't realized," she said, biting her lip again.

I chose to be the bigger man and ignore her.

"Now that I have to live through the next few weeks, I figured I needed to plan for the long haul," I went on. "The way I figure it, I have several problems that need addressing before I go. Longevity is one of them. My turrets just can't operate forever. They run out of power, they run out of ammo, and they run hot. Our batteries here are meant to alleviate the power problem, and once I solve that, I'll have solved the ammo one, too."

"Out of curiosity, what are the rest of the items on your list?"

"Flexibility—" I began.

Samila snorted but said nothing.

I cleared my throat and went on, already dreading the direction this was going. "Mobility."

She cleared her throat, looking away and obviously holding in a laugh.

"And scale," I grumbled under my breath.

A guffaw tore its way out of her loud enough to make my ear start ringing before she got herself back under control. I glared at her over my shoulder as she tried and failed to compose herself. She alternated between looking away to collect herself, then looking back to me and losing her shit again. It took a full minute.

"I'm sorry." She giggled. "Scale. Are—haha—are there more?"

I shook my head and scowled.

"Okay. Ah. Sorry. Hehe. Scale problems. So, about the battery things, some of them look . . . angry," she observed. She was right, too. All of them had started out as mundane metal with a Volatility-charged cube in the middle, but not all of them stayed that way. Now some had a distinct purple sheen, intense near the center of the flower and fading to the edges. At least two of them glowed a very angry shade of purple.

"True. I probably should have built in some kind of cutoff for the power collection, but I didn't really know that was going to happen. Thought they'd just get full, then stop."

"But you can already make things explode on cue."

"Well, it's not just explosions that I'm after," I explained. "The basic concept is, I use my new Collect Ability to suck up all the mana in the surrounding area and store it for use later. The only problem is that this room has almost zero ambient mana. Have to fix that. I've long theorized that when I make something volatile, it has a certain shelf life before it loses its charge. It uses this wild mana that comes from the System. Super-efficient and energetic, right? Anyway, when I use Volatility and let it fade, that mana has to go somewhere, so I figured, why not try and catch those little mana motes before they get away."

"I'm with you so far."

I shrugged sheepishly. "It worked pretty well, actually. I put a trigger on a prototype and had it curl in on itself once its Trigger was full. It happened pretty quickly—like, in about ten minutes. So, naturally, I wanted to see how far it could go."

"Naturally," she echoed.

"Once I was working on it, I started to think, I have all this mana sitting there in the Trigger. What if I used it for something else? So, I Automated it to transfer that mana back to the center of the flower and recast the Volatility spell through another Automated Trigger. The battery would get its power from my initial kick start, then it would keep itself powered. I—uh—miscalculated."

Actually, I hadn't calculated at all. Hadn't bothered. I accidentally created a feedback loop that would charge my new batteries pretty much forever, and that was going to become a problem in a matter of hours. Whatever juice Volatility used to do its thing was far more potent than the stuff I could produce—maybe because it was a combat Ability. Plus, it was pulled or summoned from somewhere else, not the surrounding environment.

I swallowed uncomfortably and looked around the room for fragile bits I'd need to clean up before we took care of it.

Samila caught on right away. "The glowing petals are very pretty in a deadly sort of way. I imagine when they explode, we won't want to be here."

"Yeah," I said, drawing the word out significantly. "Volatility's energy is . . . sticky now. Hard to describe it any other way."

"Should we leave?" Samila asked.

"Nah," I said, shrugging my shoulders as I looked on at the ever-brightening leaves of the deep-cycle battery. "Probably not yet. They might not blow at all unless we touch them."

She raised a brow. "And you want to use these?"

"Well, not exactly these," I insisted, spreading my arms to encompass the entire row of ten. "Better ones. I'm starting to see more use for Triggers other than just changing shapes and locomotion. The problem with them before was that I just saw them in terms of mana cost. With Collect, it seems they're not so mana-hungry. The thing is, once there's mana in the Trigger, it's just sitting there waiting to be used until told to do so. The retention—how efficient the walls are in the tank—is perfect. Actually perfect. That's unheard of in energy storage back home. There's always bleed—slow, maybe, but always. Not here, though. Magic is crazy stuff, and I'm still learning. The mana that's stored in the Trigger also isn't the same kind of mana that went *into* the Trigger. The Collector bits take it in, and what's kept slowly becomes a different flavor. I'm wondering if keeping certain types of mana next to others converts it, or if it's the material. Or maybe both. See that?" I asked, pointing to my most-successful battery.

"The glowing, purple death flower?"

"Yeah. Well, it started as a deep-lead flower with a glowing cube stuck in the middle. Now the whole thing is a glowing Volatility bomb with nowhere to spend all that energy."

"It looks like you're gardening but with explosives."

I looked down at the crankshaft in Samila's hand, imagining it powering the new type of turrets I was in the middle of designing. If the Collect/Volatility loop could be harnessed, the power budget of a constantly moving machine would suddenly be less of an issue. Spinning fan blades, piston-powered spear turrets, drones, robots. Assuming the physics I knew worked similarly on Ralqir, I could probably generate electricity this way, too. Screw using Storm mana. I'd harness raw electrons and stick with what I knew.

I blinked, coming back to the present moment. "Now I have the budget for lots of stuff. Smart ammo. Self-charging casting bowls. All Automated and mass-produced. If I get a hold of this. It's gonna change everything. Might have a shot at going the distance."

"When we leave," she finished for me.

"Yeah," I replied gloomily, the weight of it all settling down on my shoulders once more. There was so much to do before then.

There was a pause as the brakes on my train of thought locked and ground the whole thing to a screeching halt.

"Wait. What do you mean 'we?'"

CHAPTER TWENTY

Bring My Friends

"Y ou're sure you have it all? Shall I call Mr. Angol over to do one last sweep over the facilities?" Jassin asked for what must have been the dozenth time. The answer didn't matter. We were down to the wire, and even if the interns discovered another big source of metal somewhere in the Spire, I wouldn't have time to suck it all up.

We were on the makeshift parade grounds yet again—the hangar-sized, glorified storage room the military had repurposed as a staging area. It looked a little bit cleaner and more orderly now that there weren't 100 armed soldiers running around grabbing things and shouting orders, however. With just us, the place was downright cavernous, our voices echoing off the hard surfaces.

"I think I got everything," I told Jassin again. "Everything but the decoys."

Garret nodded to me, his mustache curling upward as his mouth curved up underneath it. "We'll start doing our impersonation act tonight. Sure you can't spare a little ammunition to really make the experience a bit more authentic?" The glimmer of hope in Garret's expression was the same one you found on kids throughout the multiverse when they asked for a new toy. This man wanted a crate of rifles for his squad, and he wasn't above outright begging.

"We've been over this," Jassin admonished his master-at-arms. "Ryan is meant to have the best chance to get home alive, and to that end, I insist he takes everything. Additionally, I would rather Ralqir not be plunged into a new era of warfare right after we manage to save it."

I coughed uncomfortably into my fist. "Uh. Yeah. I mean you guys have all seen what's possible with a little kinetic force and a tube. I'm sure somebody will figure it out sooner or later."

"Yes, of course." Jassin sighed. "Especially with so many witnesses to the efficacy of your methods. I predict it will be the goblins first, gods of old, help me. Their propensity for theft does not stop at material goods, and if they aren't upstairs crafting their own firearms of questionable quality and safety right now,

I would be very surprised. They are devilishly clever in their way. We can only hope to be well ahead of the technological curve before the practice becomes widespread among the various tribes."

As Jassin talked himself into an ulcer, I caught Garret's eye. I kept my expression neutral, but I let my eyes flick up to the ceiling twice for half-a-second each. He seemed to get the picture and gave me a wink in return. Upstairs, if he looked hard enough, he'd find a casting bowl and a solid-steel auto-pistol I'd left for him, though he'd have to figure out how to recharge the gun and the bowl himself.

"I don't know, Headmaster. I sense that goblinkind is undergoing a cultural upheaval right now, based on my time among them. They may still surprise us," Kolash croaked. "Tragedies such as this are often the fires in which new ages are forged."

Jassin's frown remained on his face as he—no doubt—thought upon all conflict and strife new ages brought about, but he had the presence of mind to give the bishop a slight nod of acknowledgement.

"Of course, not if our friend from beyond the stars is careless with the life of the first and only goblin queen," Kolash warned, turning toward me and tilting his head much like a tired teacher silently warning his worst student.

I didn't bother looking over my shoulder where my entourage was busily strapping on gear and pretending to not be listening to our conversation. All except Tiba and her guards, of course. They wouldn't understand what we were saying anyway, so they'd be standing there with their spears, watching the tall folks jabbering amongst one another. Geddon would be pointlessly brushing his hair, only to have it ruined when he donned his helmet. Sissa and Samila would be checking each other's straps, making sure they were good and tight. Trix would be meticulously oiling his rifle with a cloth he kept in his pocket. Lots of moisture where we were going, and I'd warned him about rust.

Yes, they were all coming. Yes, I had mixed feelings about that.

But we'd had that argument already.

After Samila broached the subject with me back in my workshop, I was, in a word, irate. There was hyperventilation, babbled accusations, a tiny bit of begging, and a sudden desire to test the limits of the magic practice room's explosive resistance.

After that, they'd all piled into my workshop and hit me with the plan of the century: "We're all coming with you."

When I'd protested that this was not a plan so much as a declaration of intent to die, they filled me in on the rest. Apparently, none of them had been idle while I slept. They knew I was going to live thanks to the bishop's magic and Trix's examination, so they went about putting something together. Apparently, the let-Ryan-do-what-he-needed-to-do plan was unacceptable.

The original plan, as I'd set before Jassin and Kolash, was this: Once Ephelir was no longer a threat, I would need to close my insertion point. The only way

I knew of doing that was either by dying or going back home, and I'd rather not die after having gone through so much to survive. So I would set out on my own and go back to where it all started, staying hidden as long as possible.

Meanwhile, Jassin would evacuate the city—an exodus of the living, taking whatever food and supplies they could with them. They would use the best boats they'd found to head upriver to the nearest garrison where Jassin would rouse as much of an army as he was able to, using his connections. Kolash would get the Church moving as well, once he could get a hold of a proper messenger.

In ten days, if I could make it to the tutorial facility, I would need to show myself to the Scourge in an attempt to draw them all to me. If I was right about the hive-mind thing and their burning desire for my death, they would all come running just as they had in Eclipse. *All* of them, worldwide.

From there I would hold out as long as I could before retreating through the insertion point and depriving them of the power it provided, as well as access to me. If I could hold out long enough before having to pull the ripcord, the Scourge-Touched would all be bottled up in the Baned's territory, and the military could march in and wipe them all out at the same time.

Well, that plan didn't work for my friends. For one, the risk to me was, admittedly, high. There were a lot of parts that could go very off the rails very quickly with even one mistake, and I was not above making those.

"One turn of an ankle or blow to your head, and you are done, Ryan. What, then? We have to face another tainted fulcrum wearing your face?" Trix had argued.

"There is a reason we don't fight alone—not for anything of import," Sissa added matter-of-factly. "That's why you're not going to be alone."

I was seething at the time. They'd all surrounded me—not in a hostile way, exactly, but in my room, each sitting on a different piece of the decor while I spun from one stern face to the next.

"But I'm definitely leaving alone, Sissa," I'd fumed. "I am literally leaving this universe, meaning I'm the only one with a way out of the valley when the time comes, and when I leave, the turrets will be firing blind, if they even keep firing at all."

"We've accounted for that," Samila had dismissed my concern, smiling that little smile that dared me to ask the obvious question.

If the blue scales didn't tell you the dragonkin sisters were sisters, their matching smug expressions would have confirmed it.

When I asked the obvious follow-up question, she set about explaining.

Sissa had recently spent an entire day while I was asleep in a sort of trance, giving her father a call.

Did I mention she could do that? No. No, I didn't, because I had no idea she could do that. When she tried to explain how, there were a lot of proper nouns and spiritualistic terms I wasn't ready to assimilate, and I wasn't sure if any of them had any one-to-one English translations, either. I got the impression that it was sort of half-astral projection, half-prayer to a god—a god who happened to be her dad.

Essentially, Sissa had brought her mind in line with her father's dream as he slept away the eons, and she'd told him everything. Once he learned what was at stake, he had been willing to help. He wasn't in a position to come himself, but he was sending one of his minor allies who was close enough to give everyone a lift out of Hell when I finally had to make a swift exit.

"Can we trust this dragon?" I'd asked, still not believing what I was hearing.

"Hells, no." Sissa snorted. "Father even said as much. Otherwise I'd have asked them to fly us all the way there. I imagine the only reason they're even agreeing to rouse themselves is to capture you and use you to bring back the Age of the Dragons just as the Dark Lord used one of you to end it."

A thought then popped into my head. "I guess it would be too much to ask for this dragon ally to fight with us to save the world."

Samila nodded. "The world's magic is different now, Ryan. It cannot sustain one of the old ones like it used to. The Maelstrom is too much. That doesn't mean they wouldn't be able to snuff us all out with a thought if they so desired, but it would cost them dearly."

"With that in mind, we plan to have our rescuer arrive just as the human slips back into his own universe. They will still be honor-bound to rescue us, since that is the agreement they struck with Father," Sissa declared, looking very pleased with herself.

I came back to the present with a jolt as Garret slapped two hands on my arms, pinning me with a knowing glare. "Easy to get bogged down in other men's parts to play, young man," he said prophetically. "Just stick to what you have to do and trust us to do ours." He didn't outright tell me to trust my friends, too, but the message came across well enough.

"You remember your breathing too, right? You're doing it at night before sleep?" Garret asked with a finger in my face. I never knew my grandfather, but I imagined that this was what it would have been like to have one—a grizzled, veteran one. A kind word one moment, deadly serious advice the next.

"Uh—yeah. When I get the chance," I lied. I hadn't actually slept much after the coma thing. Too busy working. That meant no pushing metaphorical boulders uphill practicing Mana Manipulation.

Garret seemed to detect the dishonesty, frowning slightly, but he let it slide. "You keep doing that. Get your body used to doing it lying down, and work your way up to practicing with your sword. You've had a bit of training, I can tell, though you've let it rust. Let the breathing shake that rust off for you. Learn them together, and let them sharpen each other."

"I—uh—" I stammered. I still had reservations committing to the sword, given my complicated history with it. It always felt like I was borrowing the knowledge from my dad instead of using my own. Of course, the sword was a tool. Such a good one that I'd be stupid to let the Skill just rot on my Status Screen.

"I'll practice as much as I can, Garret," I said, meaning it but not able to see when my life would slow down enough to do so. "Thank you for what you've done. I'll never forget you."

Garret grinned. "Nah. Don't let ol' Garret take up space in your mind. I have it on good authority that you'll live forever, and you don't want this old war hound coming 'round your dreams. Just remember what I taught you."

Kolash was next, towering head and shoulders above me. He put a hand on my shoulder—the intact one he wasn't using to hold his staff. My eyes only flicked momentarily to where he touched me. No curse materialized inside of me, though.

He smiled that big, toothless smile of his. "After everything, you believe I'd still kill you if I could?"

I looked up at him in his alien face, trying to peer into his eyes for some sign of malice. I found none, but I couldn't rule it out. So, I simply shrugged. His hand stayed there for the time being, heavy enough to be uncomfortable.

The big frog nodded, bobbing his head straight up and down. "Very well. Some wounds take time to heal." He shook his staff slightly, wincing as his crooked fingers adjusted.

"Why don't you heal that?" I murmured so that only he could hear me. "You obviously can. You did it with the other one."

"Our scars remind us of our past failings, Human," the bishop rumbled. "It will be healed only after you are gone from this place and the taint you brought with you purged from our world."

I raised an eyebrow. "You failed to kill me, and that's your reminder?"

"A question asked from a limited perspective. It took many failures to bring us to where we are, Ryan. I failed to see the plague for what it was," Kolash gurgled regretfully. "Failed to send for help in time. Failed to see you for what you were. Failed to give you peace through death. The legacy of my failure is all around us."

"You had a chance, down below," I reminded him working up to the real question: "Why did you heal me?"

"The time to kill you had passed. You had just rid us of a great evil, Ryan, and just because it would have been easier to end you, does not mean it would have been the best possible path. If this plan works, we will have staved off another Purge. If it does not, we have our contingency and your death is assured. You have done your best for us, and, for that, I am willing to have some faith."

I felt my dinner churn in my stomach at the mention of the contingency.

Jassin came between the two of us before I could form a response.

"Daybreak is upon us. Your guides await you down below. Are you ready?"

Jassin asked, dragging my gaze back down to his. Kolash and Jassin hadn't been idle during my nap, either. This next part was what they'd come up with as a compromise between letting me go off on my own and ending my life now, rolling the dice with the Scourge.

I inhaled and blew out a long breath, steeling myself for what was to come. "You know, I've never actually seen what you can do," I said to Jassin, trying to sound brave.

"And you're unlikely to. Only rarely do subjects of this spell recall the casting," Jassin said. His sad smile told me he wanted to say more, but there was no time.

"Unbelievable," I declared before spreading my stance and holding out my arms to show I was ready. "Hit me before I change my mind."

"I am glad I met you, Ryan Kotes," Jassin proclaimed as his hands began to glow at their fingertips, white hot and blinding like arc-welders. "Goodbye."

Jassin's mouth moved as he whispered something in no language the System could translate, as deep, resonant humming buzzed in my ears.

His hands flashed, and, quick as a snake, latched onto my flesh, one on my forehead and one on my stomach. I could feel the power burning between those two connection points—searing hot wires that flailed and slashed like living whips until they found one another and connected at their tips, becoming one: a circuit.

Status gained: Cursed
Curse of Inevitable Doom

I came to mid-step in the familiar confines of the smugglers' tunnels, their plain, uniformly gray brick entombing me. I gasped desperately through an already-raw throat, my eyes darting all over the room as I tripped and went down on one knee.

It felt like waking in the middle of a terrible nightmare, stuck between the dreamworld and the here and now. Nothing felt real or would ever feel real again compared to the terrible darkness of before. My blood felt cold in my veins, though it rushed through me like I'd been running a marathon, and my labored breathing bordered on hyperventilation.

"He's back," Samila's worried voice shouted from next to me. She slipped out from under my arm and got down on her knee to look me in the eyes, her golden irises shining in the faint light. My arm shook, and I felt the pressure of her hand there, warm and strong.

"Are you back with us, Ryan?" she asked.

All I could do was breathe, panicked—an animal in a cage. Sweat poured down my skin to drip from my nose, and, as my senses came back online, I found my clothes were already soaked through with moisture and cold.

"Trix!" Samila called out as I hadn't answered immediately.

The little vulpa was there in a flash, reaching up to put a claw up on my face. "It's the same as before. This is a spiritual malady, not one of the body. There will be an adjustment period."

The world spun around me as my brain called out for oxygen it wasn't getting, but I managed to take in enough of a breath to wave them off with a shooing motion from my prosthetic.

I gasped. "It's okay . . . I'm fine."

Trix shot a worried glance at Samila. "The headmaster said it would be like this. All we can do is give him time."

"I'm okay." I breathed.

"I don't like this," Samila growled at Trix, though he'd done nothing to earn any sort of blame.

"I don't either, but—"

"No," I said, cutting him off. "Needed to be done."

"You tend to nearly die a lot. You're not afraid it will go off prematurely?" Trix asked.

"It was a chance we had to take," I replied, feeling better by the second. "Just in case the Scourge can use my access to the System. It was a good idea. Just hurts . . . in here." I slapped my metal hand to my chest, hoping it got the point across. The curse seemed to respond to my thoughts, thrumming with restrained power as it settled further into my spirit.

Tiba brushed past Trix, putting a hand on his back and slipping to the side until she was right in front of me.

"Heavy magic on you, Ryan. Here. This help," she said, opening a pouch and sprinkling something powdery into her palm.

"It's okay. I'm—*PLEPHCH!*" Tiba had blown the powder in my face so suddenly that I inhaled it, and I immediately went into a coughing fit.

Status gained: Soothed

I did not feel soothed. I felt . . . minty. No. *Tingly.* Overstimulated.

However, the world stopped spinning quite so fast around me, and, after I was done coughing, my breath slowed as my conscious mind took further control of my endocrine system.

So I now had a magical dead man's switch in me. I could feel it there like a boulder tossed in the tiny puddle that was my life force. It weighed on me and settled down into the soft center of my soul, but, unlike a boulder, this was a complex working of power that felt almost alive, connected to me.

According to Jassin, this spell was loosely based off another one that agents of the queen endured when they entered her service. When one of the queen's agents was captured, they could activate it with a thought and be instantly incinerated, or if they were murdered, the assassin would be burned along with them. The queen could also activate the curse at will, literally putting the lives of her agents in her hands—a sign of trust and fealty.

My particular curse was Jassin's spin on the classic. If I were to die, I'd be my own funeral pyre, and the thing that killed me would get a nasty blowback, courtesy of all the power I had stored up in my spirit.

It was the only way to guarantee I didn't rise again to plague Ralqir if the worst were to happen—Jassin and Kolash's compromise.

I could deal with this, though. By not dying.

"Thanks, Tiba. Thanks for looking out for me," I said appreciatively.

"My job." Tiba blushed. "As your queen."

CHAPTER TWENTY-ONE

Don't Get Caught

We only had to walk for another hour or so before we reached our destination. However, the smugglers' tunnels in this area were dirtier, overgrown with moss and algae. Dark, mud-stained streaks marked well-trod paths on the floor, and the bricks were discolored from moisture and years of use. Faded drag marks and boot prints told of a long and continuing history in these caves.

We came to a curtain of green and gray, a barrier of plant life draped over the entrance to our tunnel, and our guides had us all get low and quiet before they slipped into the green and out of sight.

Corporal Bole and his subordinate, Private Beedy, seemed to ghost between the leaves and vanish. The two had been so unobtrusive so far, I'd almost forgotten that the two of them had been slated to get us out of the city. Beedy was quiet by nature. I'd never heard him utter more than one or two words at a time ever since we met in the Undercity. However, Bole was uncharacteristically quiet, at least for the portions of the journey for which I was conscious. Not even when I'd had my magic-induced panic attack had he tried to trade barbs with anyone.

We all sat there for a while, listening to the insects and feeling the cold, wet breeze on our faces as it blew into the tunnels from the outside. While we waited, I summoned my new compass and took a look.

It was a simple thing—round, metal, sealed through magic and Automated much like my turrets were. Its power requirement was minimal, just a rotating joint programmed to point in the direction of the nearest "living" Scourge-Touched while a separate Automated mechanism raised and lowered a little mallet to tap the back of the compass lightly to indicate how close the contact was. Faster meant closer. Slower meant farther.

Right now, the compass was pointing back down the tunnel and tapping a slow *click, click, click* in my palm like a tiny heartbeat. That meant there was Scourge somewhere within the range of my aura, but that wasn't saying much. My aura was massive at 106 Spirit.

Bole and Beedy came back inside more brazenly than they'd left, brushing aside the hanging vines and moss clumps to hang them on rudimentary hooks installed in the sides of the entrance. Blood covered the tip of Bole's sword, and Beedy was sporting a new shallow scratch on his face.

"Everyone's gone," Bole said as he cleaned the blade of his short sword on the moss and vines. "Gone long enough for a couple of raptils to move in. Killed 'em in case they were infected. Should be fine to come out now."

Our exit seemed to be far outside the city. In fact, we'd not only passed it but were now well beyond the glade, back under the familiar, smothering blanket of the Mendau trees. It was midday, maybe, but you wouldn't have known it, thanks to the heavy leaf cover overhead.

The swamp was just as I remembered it from long ago, before I'd entered Eclipse and couldn't get back out. The ground was spongy and dark-green with a smattering of black puddles of unpredictable depth that could twist your ankle or swallow you whole. The Mendau trees here were twisted and gray, with hanging moss growing in furry patches up and down their bark, while the leafy canopy overhead felt thick and oppressive—too close to the ground to be proper trees but not quite short enough to be brush. Geddon had to duck under a good half of them.

To our left was a foggy shadowland of thin, twisting tree trunks and thick patches of mist—a visible yet unnecessary reminder of the humidity. I could feel the wet chill acutely, though it only reached skin-deep. A sheen of moisture was already accumulating on my prosthetic, dripping from the fingertips. To our right was some kind of waterway that ran past a rotting, wooden shack sporting a suspiciously well-repaired dock.

"Bet the real guards would pay good money to know where this place is," Geddon opined.

"I'll ignore that slight upon my character, but I'll still thank you to not go spreading this location around at the tavern," Bole replied as he looked appraisingly at the little boathouse connected to the dock. "Looks like they all fucked off with the boats, so we'll be going on foot."

"What's this about 'we?'" Sissa, having taken the lead after we'd exited the tunnels, turned around like she'd been struck. "Thank you for getting us this far, but we're taking it from here."

Bole casually sheathed his sword and slapped Beedy's chest with the back of his hand. "See that, Beedy? Told you we wouldn't be welcome."

Beedy simply frowned and gave everyone an apologetic look.

"That's because you're not," Geddon said, cracking his knuckles one at a time. They sounded like gunshots even through the metal gauntlets.

"That wasn't the plan, Bole," Sissa hissed like a nearly boiling kettle. "We're fine from here on out. Go back and inflict yourself on someone else."

"No, I think I'm exactly where I need to be," Bole countered with folded arms. "Besides, we're wasted playing nursemaid with the civilians."

Sissa's sword was out in a flash, her eyes wide and full of barely contained wrath. "Where you need to be?" she said, a dangerous edge to her tone. "*Need to be?* Careful. You're dangerously close to reminding me of the last time we 'collaborated.' I have tolerated your presence ever since we were thrown into this situation, but that does not mean everything is forgiven between us. I ask you again to go back."

Bole didn't react to the drawn steel. In fact, he made it a point to lean on Beedy as if he were a relaxing under a shady tree.

"I don't need you to forgive me, Princess. I just need you to see the benefits to having more sword arms on hand. You could use men like us in your little band."

"Oh, we could use the help, but you've shown time and again we can't trust you," Sissa replied flatly.

"You *can* trust me, actually," Bole replied. "But you have your reasons not to. You're letting our history get in the way of your mission."

"You don't even know what the mission is," Sissa shot back.

Bole turned to me, looking me up and down with a contemptuous expression. "It's about the monk. It's been all about him since he showed up. It's plain to see, if you know how to look."

Sissa's mouth formed a tight line, her jaw clenching as she searched for something to say. She didn't want to give away more than she had to, but Bole had scored a hit too close to the truth.

"You're the tactician. What would two more capable fighters do for you?" Bole asked before Sissa could come up with a good response.

The dragonkin's grip tightened on her sword hilt, and her expression went from angry to volcanic, the kind that threatened to bury entire civilizations in its pyroclastic flow. "You're not getting it, *Brother*. We can't trust you. We can't trust you not to cut and run when you feel slighted or dispirited or just plain bored. You left your family when they asked you to do your duty, you left the Church when you had a crisis of faith, you left civilized society when the law diverged with your personal desires, and you left me when I wouldn't join you. I would love more help, Fidus," Sissa growled, "but certainly not from you."

Even though he was trying to play it cool, Bole tensed with every word Sissa said, his muscles coiling and his breathing growing more shallow and rapid. By the time she was done, I was almost entirely sure Bole would draw his sword and we would have to kill him.

But lanky, quiet Beedy broke the standoff by putting a comforting hand on Bole's shoulder. The leather creaked under his strong fingers, and whatever Bole was about to do, he now seemed to have second thoughts. He reached up and ran a gloved hand down his face, closing his eyes and sighing.

"That is . . . fair, from your perspective. I've wronged you, and that's forever. I understand that. But you know me, Siss. If there's anything you can trust, it's that I don't let a blow go unanswered. This—" he said, waving a hand in the air,

"—feels like the start of something. Something big. The things back there struck the first blow, and I want to be there to answer, just as my ancestors did."

"I could hang him from a tree by his undergarments if you like," Geddon rumbled from behind Bole and Beedy.

Tiba stood next to the big guy flintily with her spear poised for a fight, and her guards followed suit, adopting a similar pose. They had no idea what was going on, but they were certainly picking up on the mood.

Meanwhile, Samila sidled up to her sister and took up position on her right, almost brushing up against her sword arm. Was Samila planning to step between the two or join in? My money was on restraint.

"And I'll scream the whole time, you big fucker," Bole said. "It would just be easier for you if you agree to let me come along now, and I'll be much more useful. And Beedy here wants to come too, don't ya, Beedy?"

Beedy looked pale, like he'd been caught doing something he shouldn't, but as he looked back from Bole to Sissa, he slowly got the courage to nod in assent.

"We have no need for a sneak thief in the wilds," Sissa insisted. She'd lowered her sword, though.

"You'd be surprised what may need stealing, even in the most rustic of settings." Bole grinned, his mask of roguish confidence back in place.

For a moment, Sissa was torn between her desire to be rid of the man and the desire to make it through the next couple of weeks with all her people alive and intact. Bole was not above just following us as we went about our mission, and, despite all her misgivings, I didn't think Sissa was willing to murder the man for trying to do so.

"You sleep on the opposite side of the fire from me," Sissa finally hissed, sheathing her sword and stomping toward the abandoned shack.

Bole held up both of his hands in surrender, tossing a victorious grin at his partner-in-crime. "Whatever you say, Princess. We're under your command, aren't we, Beedy?"

I sat on the edge of the smugglers' dock, fifty or so feet from the shore. My compass was tapping me only occasionally as the arrow jiggled generally east and southeast. It had been doing that for the past hour without fail, so consistently that I was almost willing to put it down for a while and obsess over something else for a bit.

The creaking dock bobbed below me as I stared down into the glassy black surface of the bayou. It was a hidden branch of the main river, which had been dug with great time and effort by those on the wrong side of the law. As Bole told it, this place served as a sort of stopover, where the shallow draft boats the smugglers tended to use could be docked to offload their real cargo before they floated into Eclipse and went through customs with slightly lighter holds.

The midday sun only partially filtered through the grayish canopy of leaves that stretched over the dock—bright enough to see by but not enough to penetrate the muddy water. Anything deeper than a couple of inches probably hadn't seen true light for centuries. There was plenty of life out there, though. Once in a while, a little cloud of muddy debris, kicked up by motion below, floated to the surface and swirled lazily there until the current took it back down.

Detect Iron showed me flashes of wriggling schools of tiny fingerlings as they flitted underneath the pontoons that held the dock afloat. None of them were Scourge, if my compass was to be believed—just the Ralqir equivalent of fish.

Fishing has never been my thing, basically because there weren't a lot of fish to be had back home, and those that you could get tended to be mostly bone or eyeless nightmares from the deep. People did still fish, though. It was a sport humanity had brought with us from our home world and had somehow survived even on a planet whose oceans were mostly underground. Even though I didn't really go for that sort of thing, I felt I could probably be pretty good at it with Detect, but the Ability would probably also ruin a lot of the mystique.

There were probably no Scourge-Touched in the immediate area, but my mask was on anyway, just in case. My creations' tracking methods weren't foolproof, as I'd seen with a couple different stealth-type monsters that my turrets hadn't recognized until they revealed themselves. Apparently, if you could fool me, you could fool my aura. And if you could fool my aura, you could fool my compass, since the aura was doing the heavy-lifting.

That meant the mask stayed on for now. The time would come soon to show my face, and then I would be in the fight of my life.

I looked up for what must have been the hundredth time, checking to see if the light was finally beginning to fade. Of course, just like last time, I couldn't tell, thanks to the Mendau.

Trix insisted on traveling at night to avoid gaining the wrong kind of attention, and everyone else seemed to just agree despite my insistence that I couldn't see a thing.

A whole planet of people who never really saw the sun. Of course, they saw better in the dark than I did. That didn't stop it from being annoying. When I'd voiced my concern that I'd be stumbling around blind out there, I just got apologetic shrugs and a snigger from Bole.

Well, just waiting passively around wasn't my thing.

Finally setting my compass down, I summoned a handful of the new prototype smart-rounds, a full turret magazine, and the hopper piece to my magazine-loader construct—pretty much an oblong tin tub with a narrow hole at the bottom just large enough for one bullet to fit through at once. The piston-loader arm and the magazine holder weren't needed for this, so I left them in my Spatial Storage.

I took a smart-round between two of my fingers and examined it for flaws. It was brand-new, so it shouldn't have had any, but I wanted to make sure. These were slightly larger than my original smart-rounds—the ones that would return to me once I'd fired them. They were a bit longer than my pinky nail, cylindrical at the back, and conical in the front as most bullets tended to be, but the surface had ringed grooves that went all the way around, meant to protect the "legs" the bullets would deploy after being fired. While my other rounds grew appendages when they were activated as well, I'd discovered it was cheaper to have them already formed and tucked away than to reform them every time they were meant to do their thing.

I set the hopper carefully down on the dock, positioning the base of its edge up against one of the spaces between the dock boards.

Alright. Pathing test time.

Taking a moment to aim, I flicked my smart-round out, sending the bullet careening down the dock and toward the shore. It bounced over the wood before finally coming to rest somewhere in the mud and grass. Then I did the same with three more rounds. Two I kept in my pocket, and the last I let fall into the water. I set the full magazine down on the dock.

"Okay, let's see if you guys have gotten any better at this," I whispered as I sent a little jolt of power into the hopper's Trigger. The Automated smart-card inside of it activated, feeding power into the machine's internals: the loading arm, the stirring mechanism, and the clamps that held loading magazines in place. It also told my other machines that the loader was running and ready to perform.

I felt more than heard the signal go out from the hopper—a slight tremble in my aura, a declaration of intent. I kept a wary eye on the magazine near my feet, but nothing catastrophic was happening with it, at least as of yet. The new pacifying instructions I'd put into the rounds' programming was clearly working there.

Essentially, the rounds sensed they were in a valid magazine and didn't activate until they were fired and were free to go about their programming. It meant I had to Automate a narrow strip of iron in the back of every magazine that touched each round to keep it pacified, but if I could avoid the stupid bullets growing legs inside of an already-cramped magazine, then attempting to claw their way out, I'd take the added mana expense. I'd ruined three whole magazines before I figured out what was happening in the workshop.

The bullets in my pocket were another matter. They crawled out of my shirt like cockroaches on amphetamines, the hooked insectile legs they produced easily able to grab onto the fabric and skitter out to obey the automatic loader's call to be filled. They'd crept their way down my pant leg as a pair and to the dock, where they met their first obstacle, a gap between the boards.

Without hesitation, the lead round leapt the gap. Well, it wasn't so much a leap as a sort-of-forward fall with its forelegs outstretched to catch the other side, leaving it dangling there momentarily between boards. Then the smart-round's partner, suddenly seeing a valid path across the gap, used the lead bullet as a bridge, crawling over and getting across. The poor guy in the crack almost lost its grip and went into the water down below, but it valiantly held on, if only *just*.

From that point they had to cross three separate gaps with varying degrees of success before they could load themselves into the hopper by crawling up the grooves on the side and into the tube. Neither of them went into the drink, though. Once they were safely where they were supposed to be, they retracted their legs and went dormant, rolling noisily around in the bottom of the tube, waiting for the hopper to load them into a magazine.

Soon the four rounds I'd thrown to the shore came trundling up and, one by one, threw themselves into the hopper as well.

Again, I eyed the magazine, watching for shaking or jiggling. I really didn't want to have to make another one. I especially didn't want to retool my Automated programming again. It was already extremely complicated, and holding that entire concept in my head long enough to get it to stick was painful. I would send a prayer of fervent thanks to Constance once I had it down and was able to foist the mental labor off on a casting bowl for mass-production. Thankfully, the magazine sat there next to me inert, joyously unbroken. That was one problem fixed, at least.

The two rounds that got in each other's ways when trying to get into the hopper concerned me slightly, however. Unlike living things, they had no concern for one another or their respective objectives. Once they saw a way to complete their programming, they took it, even if it meant climbing over the broken forms of their brethren. I could see some disaster happening if I recalled a whole magazine of these things or several magazines at once. Not to mention, it was more than a little creepy to watch. A large-enough number of smart-rounds would resemble a swarm of robotic bullet ants—minus the warm, fuzzy disposition of ants.

The round that went into the water never came back. Soon I received some notifications in my Combat Log that shed some light on that mystery, though.

River Pairfish takes 1 Damage. (slashing)
River Pairfish takes 1 Damage. (slashing)
River Pairfish takes 1 Damage. (slashing)
River Pairfish is bleeding.
River Pairfish takes 2 Damage. (slashing)
River Pairfish takes 1 Damage. (slashing)
River Pairfish takes 2 Damage. (slashing)
River Pairfish is bleeding.

It went on and on, little drops of Damage that compounded on one another until . . .

> River Pairfish defeated.
> You have been awarded 0 Experience points. (1 base, -1 Level)

Well, that's what I got for making ammunition that crawled like bugs. Now the thing was stuck inside a fish down at the bottom of the river trying to claw its way out. I did feel a little guilty for killing the fish, though, thinking back to the ancient wretchwyrm I'd slain in a similar fashion. That was a rough way to go, and the least I could do was eat what I killed.

Note to self: Add a cleaning function to the next iteration of the magazine-loader station. There's gonna be blood.

When nighttime finally came, I was well and truly done with experimenting with crawling ammo, and I had the metaphorical scars to show for it. The actual cuts healed quickly after I finally let the offending bullet go. Apparently, I had not programmed them to recognize their daddy, and trying to hold them back from their objective with a closed fist was not wise.

Never doing that again. Those legs are sharp.

I flexed my palm and worked my fingers, remembering the itchy, burning sensation of a tiny robot trying to slice into my tender flesh.

The next iteration was definitely going to have a friend-or-foe ID system.

With so many conditions I was putting into these things, the power and time investment was getting increasingly ridiculous. My batteries would need to charge overtime if I wanted to mass-produce these little suckers. As a consequence, if I created a bigger battery with faster collectors, I'd need to watch said battery like a hawk to shut it down before it could overcharge and have an explosive meltdown.

If I, say, let a casting bowl work overnight producing my new smart-ammo with a new, beefed-up battery array and didn't feed it enough metal to keep it working until morning, I could come back to a bomb sitting right next to a lot of hard, metal projectiles that were practically built to be shrapnel.

Breaking the Volatility/Collect cycle turned out to be harder than I would have liked, though. I had to connect the Volatile cube to the whole thing with Shape to get it to work, and I couldn't Shape it out of the thing once it was saturated with enough Volatility. My Spatial Storage tended to treat the Volatile center of the battery and the collector arms as one singular object once they all had the same energy flowing through them, too.

What I needed was a way to detect how charged a battery was. Once I could do that, I could just Automate a cutoff on the Volatility refresher plate. I could probably do the same thing with a counting system, giving a maximum number of times to refresh the spell, but what if I was in an extended battle? The battery would last longer this way but not indefinitely.

A hand slapped my chest, halting me before I could take another step. I froze mid-stride reflexively. Judging by the silhouette of the person attached to the hand, it was Samila, petite but intimidating in her armor and helm. She gestured down at the open mouth of the water into which I was about to plunge. My boots were already soaked from having already done this a few times in the night, but one never knew how deep these little holes were.

I gave Samila a small nod of appreciation and stepped around.

Though extremely dark, nighttime in the swamp wasn't quite as bad as I thought it would be.

While I had the worst night vision out of anyone in our group, there were ways of seeing where the water was. The cold kept most insects dormant at night, but tiny swarms of glowing gnats swept over the surfaces of a lot of the open water, bright enough to cast a reflection upon the glassy, charcoal-mirror surface. In my experience, they only seemed to come together over water, clustering up and shining bright as they danced around one another.

So, if I could remember where the little fairy lights had been dancing, it was easy enough to avoid the deeper water. I had a breathing tank in my Spatial Storage filled to bursting just in case, however. I was a heavy guy, and if I stumbled into a deep hole, no one was pulling me out but me, more than likely.

Trix, Tiba, and her guards were the most adept at navigating the squishy, mazelike terrain. Their eyes were better than everyone else's, and they weighed less than the rest of us, making them able to use floating deadwood and some of the more-robust lily pads as springboards to get across otherwise-inaccessible swamp. Since I couldn't see anything, as Trix led the group, he carried my compass affixed to his wrist with a narrow leather watch band Geddon had rustled up for him from somewhere. It let him consult the compass while still being able to use his rifle. It was also something I probably should have thought of before. I came from a planet with watches! Why did it take a giant lion-man to come up with the idea for me?

The construct had already paid dividends, warning us of clusters of Scourge before we could bumble into them in the dark. More than once, we'd had to go the long way around something Trix had detected out there.

I made sure to tell him the thing wasn't infallible, however.

Lucky that I did, too.

I'd just sunk my foot into a particularly rank mudbank when a hiss from in front of me drew my attention. As we all did when a halt was called, I sank down low, lying on my belly, listening and doing my best to keep from breathing.

When nothing immediately registered as dangerous, I felt safe to slither up the embankment, past Samila and Geddon, to follow the dryish strips of land where Trix had sent the signal from. He, Tiba, Bole, Beedy, and Sissa were all there, crouched low amongst several bushy clusters of dead moss that had fallen from a nearby tree.

"What's up?" I whispered, knowing the little vulpa's sharp ears would hear me even when I could barely hear myself.

Slowly, deliberately, Trix sank down on all fours and crept until he was looking me in the face. His eyes were especially dark and fox-like in this dim light. He put his nose right up against my ear.

"It's the road," Trix whispered. "Your compass says the nearest-infected are a good distance away to the east, but I don't like it."

"You think the road is being watched?"

"It is the most solid ground you will find out here, and though only sapients use the road itself, many things use the raised ground for travel. Very open; long sightlines. There is a good chance we will be spotted if there is something waiting for us."

There was a shuffling sound from up ahead, and then Tiba was there—not that I would have seen her unless she were right on top of me. Sometime during the night, she'd slathered herself in mud, streaks of it running down in slanted lines across her green skin, even her face and hair. The only dry things she had on her were her spear and her medicine pouch, which she wore across her shoulder.

The goblin queen grabbed Trix's hand and brought him down to the ground where she drew in the mud with the tip of her finger. It was too dark for me to see, but I thought I spotted a long, curved line that represented the road and a few round shapes that could have been trees.

Trix seemed to understand, though, adding to the drawing himself, interplaying his scratchings with hers while Tiba added to and crossed out others. By the time the two had exchanged their pictographic messages, Tiba gave the vulpa a wink and was gone like a shadow in the night.

Trix's gaze lingered on her as she left, an odd look on his face as he absently ran his fingers over his rifle's bolt carrier. He stopped when he saw me watching him.

"What?" Trix asked innocently.

"Nothing," I lied.

"What?" he asked again.

I smiled mischievously. "You two have gotten cozy."

Trix shook his head and did the vulpa full-body shudder thing. "Not 'cozy.' Her Highness has been very helpful, especially with the maps," he whispered, increasingly defensive with every word. "Once you get a sense of goblin pictograms, you can glean a surprising amount of information. Queen Tiba has proved to be intelligent, brave, and fierce in a way I have never—"

"Woah there, Tiger," Sissa murmured. "Maybe tell us what she said, and we'll talk about how dreamy Queen Tiba is later."

Trix blinked, flustered, his mouth working itself open and shut several times. "Dreamy—I—She's—Mmmf—" he sputtered loudly until Sissa reached out and closed his muzzle for him. But Trix didn't reach up to free himself, instead choosing to give the dragonkin a very hard stare. If looks could kill, Sissa would be dead twice over.

"Sorry. Go on, please," Sissa whispered, letting go of Trix's muzzle.

"Please don't do that. It's hard to breathe," Trix pleaded. "You were right to do so, however. I forgot myself and our need for stealth. As I was saying, the queen has spotted several clusters of birds not native to these lands in the trees lining the road. I had seen them but had written them off as normal."

"Scourge?" I asked.

"The compass says no, but you said it isn't always reliable," he replied.

I nodded, uselessly squinting into the darkness to try and see what Tiba had seen. "You can see the best, Trix. What's the play?"

"If we are where Queen Tiba says we are, our pass is perhaps two miles south of here."

"Two miles of swamp is a long way," Sissa interjected.

Trix nodded in agreement, nervously tapping his claws across his rifle again. "It would be best if we don't give ourselves away at this time."

So, they had creatures on the road as lookouts. More of that strategic thinking I was beginning to fear. It was getting far too prevalent in my dealings with the Scourge. Was it getting smarter over time, or had it always been that smart while I didn't have a clear-enough picture of what it was doing?

"You want to wait for them to move, or do we do something more drastic?" Sissa asked.

"I don't think they *will* move," Trix said. "They aren't even breathing."

A thought surfaced in my mind.

"Not breathing means not alive. They're like drones. Without a biological imperative, they could sit in those trees for days. So, you're saying—and correct me if I'm wrong—we need a distraction," I postulated. "Something . . . eye-catching."

Trix's ears drooped down until they practically disappeared into his fur. "Oh, no."

"Devious . . . Dramatic . . ." I continued.

"No, please," Trix replied, violently shaking his head.

"And explosive."

Trix blinked rapidly like I'd just struck him. "I'm sorry, what? I thought you were asking me to glamour these creatures."

I steepled my fingers and waggled my eyebrows at him, trusting that he could see me do it.

"I'm thinking more of a collaboration . . ."

CHAPTER TWENTY-TWO

Don't Be Fooled

My nonexistent heart froze as the clip-clop of hooves echoed out from the east, back toward Eclipse, so close, clear, and loud that I was surprised I hadn't noticed them before.

Beside me Trix was tense, his little foreclaws scratching at his fur, lips mumbling something unintelligible, and his face drawn with intense focus.

The hoofbeats drew closer, and I could now hear the labored breathing of the animal as it staggered down the road, presumably to escape the horrors of the city behind it. It was a wonder it had survived what had to have been weeks of exposure without having been infected. The animal appeared to be one of the white, wiry-haired creatures with broad shoulders and disproportionately tiny hooves I'd seen Garret and his people riding along this very road. I'd never gotten their name, since the whole Scourge-invasion-thing had probably destroyed whatever chance I had of ever riding one.

While the beast was on its feet and doing its level best to save itself from the nightmare of Eclipse, its rider was slumped over in the saddle, kept upright only by virtue of being caught in the stirrups. This couldn't have come at a worse time. We were about to cross this road, and here came someone who needed help— probably someone who had arrived on the scene late, by chance, and now they were trying to escape with their lives.

If we hurried, we could get them off the road and keep them from—

Stealth is now Level 15.
Upgrade paths available:
Gray Man Upgrade: Fractured Recollection
Misdirect
Gray Man Upgrade: Mistaken Identity
Stealth Upgrade: Alert

The sudden burst of text in my log penetrated my thoughts just long enough to realize what I was doing.

Holy hell.

Even with proper warning that the glamour was coming, my mind had been instantly fooled, instantly drawn to the illusion and fixed upon it while ignoring Trix or just accepting that his casting of magic was perfectly normal and right for the situation. The spell, according to Trix, obscured the caster and highlighted the illusion in the mind as well as through more mundane means.

I'd been told it was coming. Hell, I'd helped hatch the plan. And I'd still been taken in.

I was sufficiently impressed to say the least.

Now that I'd caught hold of myself, I could see how strange the situation was. How wrong. The rider and his animal were like scraps of a dream, smoke and impressions, general shapes of a man and his mount, but when I let my mind wander or drift further into the dream, they made more sense and became incredibly real.

In a sense, they were almost *too* real, if I could divorce myself from the idea of them for long enough to think rationally. I could smell them. I could even feel them there. I knew what the hairy mount felt like, despite never having touched one in my life. My mind was processing all these things and substituting that flow of sensory data for the real thing, tricking me into thinking I was experiencing it.

Constance, help me. Trix's magic was *dangerous*. No wonder he had moral objections to using it.

I closed my eyes briefly and concentrated on not participating in the illusion. I was outside of it, an observer. This was not my dream, and I just needed to watch. I was separate from the scene, with my own part to play that did not involve the mount and rider.

That seemed to help.

Trix kept the rider's pace sedate, as if the animal were wounded and tired and the rider was unconscious. The two weaved over the road from side to side, drunkenly. The faint scent of blood wafted into my nose—

No. Into my mind. Remember that. Focus on you, not them.

I frowned, diverting my mind to the choice the System had put in front of me. My choice of upgrade when I'd hit Level 5 in Stealth, Gray Man, might not have been on Trix's level of mind-mojo, but they were distantly related, I was fairly sure. Whatever discomfort I was feeling while watching Trix do his thing was made markedly worse knowing I was doing something like this passively whenever I used my powers to hide. I was reaching into people's minds and subverting their thoughts, and that was a scary prospect for a guy potentially on a one-way road to evil if I kept Leveling the way I was. That gave me pause as I read over the Gray Man Upgrade Paths.

Fractured Recollection: Upgrade the capabilities of Gray Man to affect those who notice you for far longer. Short-term memories of you will be harder for affected entities to recall with clarity. This effect is drastically reduced when being observed through technological means.

Mistaken Identity: Upgrade the capabilities of Gray Man to alter targets' perception of you. Affected entities will be more likely to recognize you as someone familiar to them, personally, both in the moment and when remembering your encounter with them later.

Not sure if I want to go further down that path . . . Messing with people's memories can't be good for them, even if they're someone I want to hide from. Not sure if I could live with that.

The other two upgrades were more what I was looking for:

Misdirect: While actively hiding and partially obscured, you may choose to project an illusory copy of yourself up to thirty feet away. This copy mimics your actions and presence but produces no sensory data other than visual and magical.

Stealth Upgrade: Alert: While actively hiding, you will now receive notifications in the event that you are detected. Entities that detect you may still be affected by Gray Man.

Both looked very useful—one situationally, the other universally. I wouldn't mind being able to project an illusory clone. It would help me get away from things that hunted me or get the jump on things I needed dead, not to mention being able to get my Knife in the Dark bonus more easily if my targets had to pay attention to two of me.

At the same time, Alert would just be plain-useful all the damned time. How many times had I gained a Stealth Level and had no idea what was looking for me or if it had caught sight of me?

The upgrade had its limitations, of course. If I got a notification that I'd been detected by a monster out there and Gray Man kicked in, telling said monster that I was nothing to worry about, I wouldn't know. If I were hiding from multiple monsters, I'd have to choose between fleeing, fighting, or staying hidden, and the extra information might push me into a bad decision.

No. That was a useless line of thought. Of course more information was good. How I acted based on that information was on me, not Stealth. Alert would be a game-changer, and I would have to rely on my better judgment to do the right thing with the information it gave.

Decision made, I looked over at Trix and saw his tortured expression when our eyes met.

"The look on your face reminds me why I don't do this," Trix murmured, pausing his incantation only to say this. It didn't seem to affect the illusion, however.

I really couldn't guess how I looked right now. Half of my attention was on not slipping back into the dream, the other was busy trying not to draw parallels between what I did every day without thinking with what Trix deemed morally repugnant.

I put on a reassuring smile. "Don't worry about us, Trix. You're using your skills to save the damned world, so you're still a saint in my book," I said, giving him a small thumbs-up.

"Stop doing that. No one knows what it means," Sissa chided me.

Stupid Ralqir.

On the other side of Trix, Tiba saw the gesture and copied it, turning to her guards and giving them a thumbs-up too. They seemed to dig it, taking to it like the rest of their tribe had to the middle finger.

If nobody else understood me, at least the goblins did.

"Your magic is a weapon, Trix," Sissa continued, softening her tone for the vulpa. "I'd no sooner judge you for using it than judge Geddon for using his sword."

Concentrating, Trix squeezed his eyes shut, and his lips peeled back slightly to expose his canines, but, after a moment, he acknowledged the point we were making with a slight nod.

The rider had passed us by now and was drifting slowly to the side until he practically collided with a tree full of the Scourge-Touched birds. The birds didn't make a move, but I did hear some rustling in the branches.

Suddenly an odd displacement of air bent the hairs on my face and neck, and I instinctively put up my forearm to block an incoming blow. The blow never came, however, and Bole was conspicuously there shoulder-to-shoulder with me, breathing hard and smelling of swamp water and sweat.

"I put the thing in the thing," he whispered, wiping his hands on his chest armor and flexing his fingers.

I tilted my head. "Something wrong?" I asked.

"Yeah, you're talking too much," Bole spat. "I want to see this."

Finally having tempted the birds enough, Trix nudged his illusion farther down the road away from us. The mount clip-clopped shakily onward, its head drooping downward as it fought exhaustion.

"Anytime, Trix," I said.

Trix nodded but kept up his chanting.

The illusion stopped, the beast digging at the quellstone road nervously as it sniffed at the air.

The entire swamp took a breath . . . Well, not the birds. We'd already established that they weren't breathing.

Then in a sudden, inexplicable panic, the animal rose up on its hind legs, kicked out, and let loose a high, warbling cry like an improperly fitted fan belt. The rider chose that moment to jolt back to consciousness, sucking in a greedy lungful of breath like it was his first in years. Then he screamed, a terrible, haunting cry that almost drew me into the dream again.

I was nearly up on my feet when Bole's strong fingers clamped onto my wrist to arrest my forward momentum. It wasn't enough to stop me, but it was enough to get me thinking. I shot a glance in his direction and settled back down, nodding to indicate I was okay. He never met my eyes, though. His gaze was fixed on the scene before him as he grinned from ear to ear.

Now wide awake and in a full-blown panic, the rider spurred his mount on, and the two of them flew down the road like they were being chased by demons—which wasn't actually far-off from the truth. Whatever the Scourge had been waiting for as they watched the illusion make its way down the road, the sudden jolt of speed and the fear from their prey triggered some kind of predatory instinct in the birds, and they took to the air in a rushing hurricane of flapping wings.

Our entire world became a tapestry of motion, the road a sea of dark feathers, whirling and brushing over one another—a murder of flying Scourge.

They easily matched speed with the illusion, but I imagine that was because Trix wanted them to chase it, to think they were on the verge of drawing more blood. It wove in between the birds with ease, flowing through gaps in the swarm in a way that defied logic but only if you weren't subject to the illusion yourself.

"Almost there," I announced for Trix. The illusion was nearing the log where Bole was supposed to drop the Automated iron ball. Trix had the rider slip to the right, drawing near the log where it would finally—

"What? No, not that one. Farther down the road, on the left," Bole cried.

"You're serious? Where?" I hissed at Bole. "We agreed on that one!"

"You pointed at that exact log, Monk!"

"I pointed at the only hollow log I could see, because I can't see in the fucking dark, Bole!" I whisper-shouted in the man's face, punctuating my sentence by waving a hand in front of my face.

"Boys, please," Samila hushed us. "Can you get there, Trix? Can you see it?"

"Um—Yes. I think. Now!" Trix exclaimed.

With a thought, I Triggered the magical detonator and watched the chaos unfold. I hadn't used my usual purple boom-boom magic for this one. That was swiftly becoming my calling card, and this needed to be more ambiguous. The fewer hints I gave the Scourge that I was headed in this direction the better—not until I was more prepared. Instead, I was using a new trick.

On the surface, the construct was just a ball of iron, about the size of a billiard ball. What it really was, however, was a billiard ball so packed with State Change mana in its Trigger, it had taken me the better part of an hour to fill just enough to convert the entire thing from a solid to a plasma in a single instant when it was Triggered.

The results were spectacular.

Plasma is a funny thing. By all accounts, observing it with the naked eye in a vacuum, it's just a gas but hotter. The molecules have gained so much energy that they're bouncing around and running into walls like a kid that got into the chocolate espresso beans. The difference between plasma and a gas, however, is that at some point when a molecule gets particularly riled up, it sheds its electrons and suddenly becomes very friendly with all sorts of other molecules it normally would never want to associate with. Oxygen is a favorite, especially if introduced in atmosphere.

There was no explosion like one would associate with a giant conflagration. No boom. In this case, there was a sound, something like *FUFF!*, followed by an absolute ton of muted firework crackles and pops as the superheated iron went from a packed and orderly solid to a free-floating and quickly expanding cloud of overactive gas.

The air around the little construct ignited, all available oxygen clinging to the now-superheated elements around it. A bright shower of sparks shot out from ground zero behind the log and enveloped the hundred or so birds that were closest to Trix's fleeing illusion. These ones simply died, going up in individual fireballs with a loose downward trajectory. Those slightly further out caught fire and veered off, only to run into more of their fellows and set them ablaze as well. Not wanting to be on fire, they then took evasive action into other birds, and so on and so forth.

Scourge-Touched Flenser takes 23 Damage. (20 base, +3 Knife in the Dark) (Fire)
Scourge-Touched Flenser is Cursed.
Scourge-Touched Flenser is Marked.
Scourge-Touched Flenser takes 14 Damage. (11 base, +3 Knife in the Dark) (Fire)
Scourge-Touched Flenser is Cursed.
Scourge-Touched Flenser is Marked.
Scourge-Touched Flenser takes 33 Damage. (30 base, +3 Knife in the Dark) (Fire)
Scourge-Touched Flenser is Cursed.
Scourge-Touched Flenser is Marked.
Scourge-touched Flenser takes 23 Damage. (20 base, +3 Knife in the Dark) (Fire)
Scourge-Touched Flenser is Cursed.
Scourge-Touched Flenser is Marked.
Scourge-Touched Flenser takes 20 Damage. (18 base, +3 Knife in the Dark, +1 Marked) (Fire)
Scourge-Touched Flenser takes 11 Damage. (8 base, +3 Knife in the Dark) (Electric)
Scourge-Touched Flenser takes 29 Damage. (26 base, +3 Knife in the Dark, +1 Marked) (Fire)

Trix nearly collapsed in my arms as he let the illusion drop. I could hear him breathing laboriously, and his little arms and legs hung limply from his frame as if he'd just run a long distance and had nothing left in the tank.

"Did I—" Trix panted. "Did I do it?"

"You did it, buddy," I assured him, looking back to Sissa for confirmation, but she was covering her eyes to preserve her night vision. I probably should have done that as well. Everyone was probably night-blind now, but it was the cost of doing business. Bole, at least, was having a great time, giggling up a storm watching the murder of birds going up in flames.

"Tiba?" I asked. "Are we clear to cross?"

The goblin queen got up on her tiptoes, poking her head out of cover and squinting into the dark to examine the road and the trees. Then she turned to me and gave a thumbs-up.

Hell, yeah. Thumbs-up are going to be a thing after all.

"Let's go," I called, and we all got to our feet and rushed across the Dark Lord's road.

I ran in the middle of the group, not bothering to look anywhere but forward. None of the birds that had been Marked by my attack lived long enough to be a threat, and the ones that had escaped the blast zone might as well have been invisible to me, anyway. Plus my eyes were shit, and my arms were full of vulpa. Even if we got into a skirmish, I wouldn't be able to fight.

Samila pulled me by the elbow, leading me across and into the brush on the other side, hastily slipping around shallow puddles and deadwood that might have made noise. We had to be away before the Scourge decided the rider and his mount were no longer worth their collective attention.

Stealth is now Level 16.

We were maybe 100 feet away from the scene when we heard something heavy dragging itself over the cobbled road behind us, loud enough for the sound to carry all the way to us through the trees. The swamp was alive now, too, many creatures hastily beating a retreat from the unnatural fire.

Odds were at least one or two of them were probably infected and headed toward the fire, but we didn't encounter them.

I briefly wondered what the compass was saying right now.

Tiba, naturally, took over for navigation, while Trix rested on my shoulders and recovered from his ordeal. He still had the compass, though, and would call out if we needed to change course. He also kept me out of the water much better than Samila had. Trix and I were old darkness buddies, so he knew what I was capable of and what I wasn't. That helped with our pace.

Gradually over the course of a mile, the land rose, and the swamp receded. I saw fewer pitfalls and standing water, fewer bugs and decaying logs that could trip me.

Then, without realizing it, I found myself climbing over jagged rocks, slippery with morning dew. The trees kept us from looking up to see how close the mountain range was, but I imagined we were getting close.

Sometime later, the last of the glowing bugs stopped materializing over the water, and the nighttime insects quieted down.

Light slowly bled into the gloom, so gradually that I didn't notice until I caught myself actually watching Tiba do her thing at the head of our column. She would bound ahead, catlike, using her small stature and flexibility to slip between the leaves of fallen branches, over deadwood, and vault over rocks. Then, she would stop to tilt her head to listen to something I couldn't hear and orient herself onto a slightly different course, presumably toward a place she knew.

I didn't know how she was navigating, but she seemed confident, as only queens could be.

"She is leading us to the mouth of a pass," Trix told me from my shoulder. "I have several depictions of it on the maps she drew for me. It isn't one recorded in the Spire's records, though I didn't have much time to find the truly old ones in the library."

"A pass over the mountain?" Sissa interjected. "Is there even enough cover to get us over?"

That, Trix did not know, and it was down to me to ask Tiba. Now that it was light enough, I didn't have a hard time jogging to the front of the group and asking a few questions.

"The Baned are inside the mountain now, so we won't take that way. We go through the pass. It is low enough to be below the frost," Tiba declared, standing on a rock to be at head height with me.

"But is there enough cover? Are mountain trees a thing?" I asked.

"Mostly," Tiba hedged, wobbling her head side to side. "Not always. Very thin up that high, but there is usually cover enough this time of year. In the winter, we have to find another way."

I translated for the others.

"We're getting pretty close to winter," Geddon observed as he looked dubiously at the thick canopy overhead.

"Do we wait for nightfall, then?" Samila suggested, also subconsciously glancing up at the trees.

All the goblins shook their heads this time.

"A storm coming," Tiba warned us, anxiety plain on her face. "They do that a lot, clouds ramming into the peaks like mountain goats. If we wait too long, the pass is flooded for days, and we have to go under the mountain. I do not want to go under the mountain again."

Tiba's gaze fell to the ground then, her shame at even tangentially admitting her fear of going back down there obvious. She'd lost many of her people there, the love of her life included.

"Hope you wore your swimmies, Beedy." Bole cackled. He was having a grand old time out here somehow, despite him looking like a drowned rat after having to sneak our bomb into place earlier.

Beedy looked down at his leggings and grimaced.

Samila sidled up to me on my right side and elbowed me gently in the ribs. "Tell me you packed some rope in those magic pockets of yours."

I shot a self-satisfied grin down at her. As a matter of fact, I had packed rope along with food, water, and an entire evil tower's worth of metal bits. I was already probing my Spatial Storage for everything we might possibly need to cross.

"Alright, brothers and sisters, get to it. Climbing time. Essentials only," Sissa ordered.

I tilted my head slightly, wondering as to what she meant.

Then a pauldron hit me in the chest.

Turning, I was greeted by Samila in the middle of stripping off her armor, her back to me. She already had the straps of her breastplate loose and was sliding the whole thing over her head, peeling the wet padding and shirt underneath off in one motion. Her undergarments—just a crisscrossing handful of discolored cloth strips—clung to her muscular back in a disarrayed jumble like they'd been painted on by a toddler.

"You do have room in your magic pockets for my wet things, don't you, darling?" Samila crooned, shooting me a wink over her now-bare shoulder.

"Uh—" I replied none-too-smoothly. Why the System had not seen fit to give me more socially oriented Skills was a true mystery.

"Mine too! I'm already naked back here," Geddon's voice announced from behind a nearby boulder, the top of which already held his full set of armor and shield.

CHAPTER TWENTY-THREE

Climb Any Mountain

All the people in metal armor thought turning me into a pack mule was a lovely idea, actually, and it became a race among them to give me their armor first and get out of their swampy clothes. Even the goblins got in on the fun, Tiba's honor guards seeming to relish finally being able to take their heavy iron suits off, dumping a surprising amount of swamp water from their boots. Tiba didn't feel the need to offload anything, however. She wore the bare minimum already, and she would never in a million years give up Hunty's spear or her herb pouches.

The dragon sisters seemed quite comfortable changing in front of everyone, even peeling off their wet underclothes before putting on dry ones.

I, being a gentleman, turned to give them some privacy after realizing what they were doing, which amused Samila to no end. So, after a cheeky whisper about how I was taking my monk cover story far too seriously, she set about giving me a play-by-play of the entire process—not just what she was doing but Sissa as well—while I silently prayed to Constance to grant me strength or to maybe just remove my blush reflex for a day.

The quick flash of blue I got from the corner of my eye left me with even more questions than I would have had I not seen anything at all. Weren't they supposed to be reptilian? Why did—

Nope. We are not going down that road.

I shot a pained look over at Trix, who was pulling on a dry robe farther up the trail, but he made the smart move and kept out of it, pretending to fold his swampified clothes into just the right shapes while muttering quietly to himself.

The swamp had done a number on everyone. Geddon even had a leech on his upper back that he couldn't reach thanks to his exaggerated musculature, and since everyone else was busy, I was given the honor of peeling it off, which I used as an excuse to get away from Samila.

After ripping the thing off, I went to throw it far, far away (using two fingers and making various noises of questionable masculinity), but Tiba stopped me, scandalized at my willingness to waste "good ingredients."

"Good ingredients make good medicine," was all she would say to clarify, lifting up on her tiptoes to get a better look at the little bug I had pinched between my fingers. She didn't go so far as to jump and snatch at it, but I could see that she was tempted to.

I didn't ask for details regarding what she planned to do with the thing. I simply handed Tiba the fat leech and watched her stick it amongst her herbs while I wiped my slimy fingers on my pants.

Then I had to spend about ten minutes making all the pieces of gear disappear one by one into my Spatial Storage while the rest of the party got their weapons back in place. Bole and Beedy busied themselves scouting, choosing to retain their leathers, but everyone else was down to shirts and pants at the most.

Once everyone was traveling light, with the exception of myself, we started up the trail.

I tried not to feel bitter that I had no way to lighten my own load. I was already very heavy and dense, in contrast with my size. With 53 Body, I'd put on quite a bit of supernatural muscle. I wasn't bulky by any means, but I wasn't small anymore, either. If I had to describe it, I'd call my new frame "functional." I was wider in the shoulders, deeper in the chest, and my limbs were hard and defined without yet transitioning into the more-rounded shape of a bodybuilder. Back home, I'd probably pass for a particularly well-fed Outers scrapper or maybe an amateur boxer.

The infuriating thing was that no matter how much Body I gained, I never felt lighter. Did increasing Body also increase my weight? That theory had some holes in it. I started out with what? 10 Body? 11? Wouldn't I have to be four times heavier now to account for the strength-increase? That couldn't be right. I broke my cot earlier in the week, yes, but quadrupling my strength with appropriate weight would reduce every piece of furniture I used to splinters instantly, wouldn't it?

Always more questions. No. Don't think like that. "Magic" is not an excuse to stop asking questions. That's the lazy answer, and we're not doing that.

The pass started out essentially as a trail, but it quickly turned into more of a constantly forking draw that ran gently uphill.

With the tree cover overhead and no view of the actual mountain range we wanted to traverse, I had a good bit of trouble thinking of the trail as a pass, anyway. At least not yet. If I had a clear view of the mountains, the ability to look up and see what I was crossing, I'd probably have been able to hold the concept in my mind better. However, this was Ralqir. A peak up through the trees toward the sun or the stars anywhere outside of Skyglade was a ticket to blindness and death, especially with my special condition.

As we trekked on, the trail gradually morphed into a creek, which then turned into a roughly carved "V" about one-Geddon-wide with gravel and ground organic bits on the floor while the cracked and jagged walls shot up the sides, just steep enough to be considered a climb instead of a walk. Spreading my arms, I was able to run my hands along both walls, which made steadying myself while climbing over the odd pile of fallen rocks easier.

Overhead, the swamp species of Mendau gave way to a sort-of black-leafed brush with bristly but thick fronds that, along with being the most effective shadetree I'd ever encountered, also seemed to be able to put down roots almost anywhere. In fact, they seemed to seek out the absolute worst places to live.

The path we walked had soil and leaf litter at the bottom, along with squishy sand and gravel—a fine place to put down roots—but the brush had chosen to live life on hard-mode. They grew literally from the side of the mountain, clinging to the rock, roots spreading wide over the stone and forming intricate nets that intertwined with their neighbors and covered the stone surface of the land for as far as the eye could see. Those that had found cracks and crevasses to grow next to, clung to them with thick, hooked protrusions that probably did the lion's share of anchoring themselves and their neighbors so the whole thing couldn't come sliding down.

It wasn't just a few of these shrubs, either. They were *everywhere,* and they grew over the face of the mountain like white whiskers. Their pale bark paired with black leaves to make it seem like someone had come along and switched the world's visual settings to monochrome, then lowered the brightness by half.

The Ralqir natives seemed to take the midday gloominess as a good sign, however. These trees were supposedly deciduous, and their leaves tended to thin this time of year, but we were lucky enough to be experiencing a warm fall. Less light meant more cover, and that was always what you wanted.

By midday, the pass turned into a slow, steady trod. The ground became saturated with moisture, slippery, the sand and gravel no longer allowing our feet to grip properly as we climbed. My legs burned, even with my supernatural durability, and others, by the look of them, were feeling the same.

Geddon had it the hardest. Sometime during the day, the walls narrowed or our path lowered until the big guy had to turn to the side to fit his shoulders within their confines, and our easy view of the slope was no more. The big Leori growled and grumbled the whole time, having to shimmy up the mountain turned sideways to fit in the cramped space, alternating between which was his lead foot.

We were no longer at the bottom of a V but in a trench ten-feet deep with sheer sides, and the floor was split, at times, revealing deep cracks going down into nothing. The debris we accidentally kicked into the gaps made noise for long seconds as the pebbles rolled and clacked off the flowing surfaces until they got too quiet to hear anymore. Annoyingly, the cracks weren't quite wide enough to fit a leg, but they certainly were wide enough to twist your ankle if you weren't paying attention.

Our breaths steamed in the cold now that we'd gotten to a sufficient altitude, and those that had abandoned their wet clothes were doubly grateful to have made themselves dry before the climb—not that they stayed dry for long.

The first peal of thunder cracked overhead, close. Everyone, without exception, froze and looked up in budding horror.

"We must hurry!" Tiba shouted from the lead of the group. No one else understood her, but they didn't have to. Everyone knew a storm was bad news.

The first drop of rain *ping*ed off my prosthetic hand shortly thereafter, and it only got worse from there.

As far as I could tell, this was a light-to-middling shower up here in the mountains. Just clouds from the north running headfirst into the mountain range and dropping their load as they flowed over, as Tiba had predicted. Unfortunately for us, we were in a natural pass that drained the majority of the water from two separate mountainsides. While the gentle patter of raindrops on the black canopy could be heard overhead, what we were quickly subjected to was a deluge.

Gallons of runoff sluiced down from the slopes overhead to fall onto our heads in steady, cold streams. The rest of the mountain may have been getting a light smattering of water, but we got everything—a torrent of freezing cold dumped on our heads courtesy of physics, soaking us to the bone and chilling us to our cores. It battered us, beat us down, and made our bodies heavy, our footing so slippery that our pace slowed to a tenuous crawl, made worse by having to now carry the shorter folk on our shoulders, thanks to our trail disappearing to be replaced by a rushing river of muddy, glacial runoff.

This is where being heavy and dense actually worked in my favor. As the water levels rose, my boots remained firmly on the ground, slippery as it was, more so than my friends', and eventually, I was at the head of the group, a rope tied around my waist and Tiba straddling my shoulders like a kid at a parade as I climbed, gritting my teeth with every grinding step upwards.

"We must get to the top soon, Ryan, or it goes badly for us!" Tiba shouted above the rushing noise.

"So I gathered!" I replied, a sudden gush of water slapping against my sternum, peppering my skin with the hundreds of little pebbles it had brought with it from farther up the mountain.

"How far?!" I asked.

"I'm not sure! It looks different like this!"

Climbing is now Level 9.

"Do we need to go back?" I asked as I took another heavy, laborious step.

The goblin queen's legs tensed on my shoulders, gripping tightly as if I were a mount that might bolt at a bad time.

"We can't!" she replied. "It is probably worse farther down the mountain!"

That just meant I had to buckle down.

The pressure on the rope steadily grew, and the knot dug painfully into my waist. Someone back there was struggling badly, and I desperately hoped it wasn't Geddon. Having to pull the big guy up the mountain would have been—

Climbing is now Level 10.
Upgrade paths available:
Anchor
Create Handhold
Reinforced Musculature

Well, there was a bright side to it all, I guessed. If one of these could help me, I'd gladly pick it now if it meant we could get to the top before someone drowned or turned the pass into the multiverse's most ill-made waterslide.

Anchor: Any force exerted upon you while climbing is reduced by 20%.
Create Handhold: Affix an object you possess to any surface. The adhering of this object requires an investment of mana, while maintaining the bond requires significantly less (variable).
Reinforced Musculature: Your Body score is amplified by 10% while climbing. This bonus is lost after 1 minute of rest or a 1-minute period of using only your feet to move through geographical space.

Anchor. One-hundred percent Anchor.

Create Handhold was another one of those things I could have fun with, magically gluing things to other things, but I could probably mimic the function well enough with prep time, training, and equipment.

Reinforced musculature was a straight 10 percent Body gain while I climbed, which would be huge if I kept getting more Body points from my achievements. Plus, it seemed like I could exploit the loose wording a bit to keep the buff if I was in a situation where I was using my hands and feet to traverse terrain.

However, Anchor had the benefit of being impossible. Any force exerted upon me was reduced? Attacks? Physical? Magical? Metaphorical? It didn't say.

Yes, please. Take a seat, Fundamental Laws of the Universe, I'm climbing here.

I chose it before I could second-guess myself. Instantly, I felt lighter, the force of the rushing water less oppressive, and the rope around my waist stopped digging into my abdomen so deeply. The effect was so sudden and pronounced that—

"Are you okay, Ryan?" Tiba asked, sweeping my hair out of my face to put her hand on my forehead, checking for fever.

"No. I—"

My stomach spasmed, and I doubled over, losing what little lunch I'd had earlier in the day along with a good amount of water.

"Ryan?!"

I had the presence of mind to keep my grip on the rock, but I let go with my weaker hand to give the goblin queen a thumbs-up in between eruptions of vomit. Apparently, gravity was also a force being exerted upon my body as I climbed, and suddenly changing that constant came with consequences.

Once the nausea passed, I shook my head vigorously and was back to climbing—one foot in front of the other, arms outstretched, prosthetic fingers digging into rock.

What must have been hours later, my angle of ascent suddenly changed, and, without warning, my foot touched ground that had leveled out significantly— not entirely, but enough that it felt like flat ground.

I nearly tripped, reaching out for handholds that were no longer there. The sheer walls of the wash were suddenly gone as if I'd entered a room through a doorway, and I was in a miniature forest of pale trunks and black leaves, the lowest of which were maybe a head or two above my own. The water was about shin-high here: a standing, black puddle as opposed to the river I'd just left.

The look of the place was otherworldly, the clouds making the light diffuse before it even hit the trees, casting the world in a strange, eclipse-like gloom.

I let Tiba down gently into the water and started hauling the others up. I felt gravity reassert itself fully now that I wasn't climbing anymore, forcing my stomach to adjust again, but it wasn't nearly so rough going back to normal as it was the other way around. The pull was harder without the assistance, but that was okay. I was upright and anchored enough.

Everyone, without exception, was exhausted when they took my hand for me to help them to the top, Beedy especially. When I hauled him up, grabbing his forearm to get him to his feet, he sagged right back down again into the standing water. Grabbing him by the collar, I heaved him until I could look at his face.

Not good.

His skin was like ice, pale and bloodless, and his lips were an unhealthy shade of blue.

Not good at all.

"Tiba!" I shouted.

"I know! We take shelter near here! Come!"

The dragon sisters seemed to be doing the best out of everyone, with the exception of myself and (surprisingly) Bole, but I was supernaturally durable. So the pair of dragon women got under either of Beedy's arms to help him along as we followed Tiba further into the pass.

She led us through the twilight forest of scrub, to our left, through the trees, and up another slope, but only enough to get us out of the standing water, then to a boulder behind which was a rocky overhang that jutted out of the mountainside to form a curved roof of sorts—shallow but long like the gutter on a colossal house, big enough for us to stop and get out of the rain and comfortably so.

Evidence of fire, soot stains, charcoal scratches on the walls, and black discoloration on the rock overhead indicated that this place had been used as a way station many times before by parties unknown.

We all piled through the gap behind the boulder and into the shelter. Everyone was eager to get out of the elements. Beedy was nearly asleep on his feet, and everyone but me was shivering to the point that I could hear their teeth chattering from ten feet away.

It was down to me to make the fire. Thankfully, my Spatial Storage was much drier than I was.

I chose the spot in the shelter that was already black from previous fires, sandwiched between the back wall and the surface of the boulder that hid the place from view.

Thankfully, I didn't have to start the fire from scratch. No flint and steel required. I simply got one of my oil-soaked logs out of my Storage and piled more of my stock on top. Then I dropped a tiny nail I Automated to State Change into liquid once it left my hand. The results were instantaneous. The log with the oil sparked to life with a *FWOOSH!* and the rest of the wood was ablaze in seconds, to the relief of everyone nearby.

Sissa and Samila practically shoved Beedy into the flames, getting him so close I was afraid his hair was going to catch fire. Then they set about stripping off his leather armor and every bit of clothing he could spare. After that, they huddled close on either side of him to transfer body heat. He didn't have the strength to argue—not that he would have regardless, since he was Beedy.

Everyone else followed suit, shivering and gathering around the fire. The concave shape of the overhang combined with the flat part of the boulder seemed to trap the heat pretty well, and soon everyone was looking better.

With everyone else sorted, I—the only one of us who didn't seem to be affected by the cold—took care of security in the only way I knew how. Trix seemed sad to give up the compass, but he was too busy getting warm to really put up a fight.

The indicator wobbled in its housing, pointing west and southwest, tapping my wrist every couple of seconds or so. The Scourge were out there—maybe not on the mountainside with us but perhaps down below.

Since we were putting down roots for the night, I figured I would as well. Two gun turrets on either side of the flat boulder would keep watch for us while we slept. They were set up for line of sight, so tracking and killing things through the trees was going to be a challenge, but they'd at least make noise if they saw something hostile.

As I got the second turret anchored and loaded, a violent shudder passed through me. Then I heard something loud, deep, and hollow, the kind of sound you could feel in your insides as much as you heard it with your ears.

I'd felt an explosion once when I was a kid. A Colony hauler had veered off-course upon reentry and crashed on a mountain in the Outers, the ship's holds full of promegel that had been processed in orbit. The crash site was far over the horizon from me, but when the holds detonated, the entire world for miles and miles felt it in their chests. It was a force that penetrated skin and bone and rattled everything in you that was soft and vulnerable.

This sound felt like that—a terrible projection of force with disruptive tones too deep to be fully appreciated by a mere human. Only this was long and drawn-out. Emotional. Alive.

Little rocks tumbled down the mountain and landed with a splash in the standing water at my feet.

My lizard brain—the part of me that remembered a time when humanity was not the apex predator of their planet—told me I needed to run, needed to hide, and needed to be quiet. It told me that this was no mere explosion or volcanic eruption that just required caution. It insisted that this impossible sound came from a living thing, and it was *pissed*.

I froze, my head swiveling to pinpoint the direction from which the sound came, and I listened.

CRACK!

It was like a branch snapping under a boot, except far larger, followed seconds later by a thunderous *CRASH!* that reverberated inside of me and brought to mind old myths of Titans that flattened the Earth where they chose to set their feet.

Electric tingling crawled up from my toes to the tip of my scalp. That's when I felt something *notice* me.

I couldn't tell what, where it was, how far away, or what its intentions were, but it *noticed* me. My new Stealth upgrade screamed from wherever my Skills lived.

Alert: Your presence has been detected!
Alert: Your presence has been detected!
Alert: Your presence has been detected!
Alert: Your presence has been detected!

The alerts scrolled through my feed, one after the other in a long series of heart-stopping declarations. My feet felt anchored to the ground, and my muscles refused to do more than stay very, very still.

"He still does the big magic for us," Tiba whispered timidly.

Breathing in sharply as the spell over me dissipated, I spun on my feet and looked down to find the goblin queen right next to me, leaning on her spear tiredly, her head slightly bowed and an arm folded protectively over her stomach.

I turned back to where I'd heard the noise, but . . .

Whatever it was wasn't there anymore. It had either gone without a sound or was no longer paying attention to me. Somehow, I knew it.

"Tiba?" I asked, not fully understanding. "What the hell was that?"

"Kuul," she answered. Her teeth chattered in the cold, and her hand went pale as she gripped her spear with all her might.

"You can't mean—Wait . . ." I choked on the words, remembering. "*That was Kuul?*"

Kuul, the old Stone Heart chief who had enslaved me and forced me to make things for him when I'd first arrived on this planet . . . I'd assumed he was dead. At least, I'd hoped he was dead. Last time I'd seen him he'd been running away from the Baned after murdering Hunty. My friend. Tiba's lover.

When I'd found the Stone Hearts on the way to Eclipse afterward, and he wasn't with them, I'd just . . .

"Yes." Tiba's voice was quiet now, so quiet I could barely hear her over the rain.

"That can't be right," I argued. "How do you know? That was—"

Huge.

"He does the big magic for us," Tiba repeated. "I can feel it . . . down there." She nodded in the direction we were traveling, presumably down the mountain and in the valley where I had entered this universe.

That's the tutorial area. What's he doing in the tutorial area?

"That was Kuul?! Short, green, old, frail, hates me? That Kuul?" I snapped, feeling my volume rise without my consent. "How was that Kuul?!"

"He does big magic to kill many of the Baned, as we are chased, before I am chief. He goes deep into the mountain where the stories are made and does big magic."

"What are you saying? When the Baned invaded the caves, Kuul . . . what? Cast some kind of spell that summoned that?"

Tiba shook her head sadly. "No. That is Kuul, what he is now. I can still feel the chief in him . . . the uh . . . position. He burns it. He is burning."

A shiver passed through me, my body choosing that moment to finally experience the cold.

"Last time Kuul and I met, he wanted me dead," I remembered.

And he was just a goblin back then. What is he now that he sounds like that?

Tiba bowed her head even lower, sliding her free hand nervously over bare skin. "He burns. I feel it now like a hot iron on my face," she said.

"What do you mean?"

"He burns," she repeated, her eyes un-focusing, staring through the trees and into the valley.

"Tiba . . ." I gulped. "When we get down there, will Kuul—I don't know . . . Will he help us or—"

Tiba looked at me with uncertainty and more than a little fear, but she didn't answer.

Wonderful.

CHAPTER TWENTY-FOUR

Choose My Battles

The rain didn't stop until sometime in the middle of the night, according to Trix. That didn't mean the pass was passable yet. That water took a good while to run its way down the mountainside, slowed by the thick root system of the black shrubs. That was okay, though. We had to break camp, and that took time.

Also, by "*we* had to break camp," I meant "*I* had to break camp."

Everyone had been slow on the uptake up until now regarding just how useful a magical pocket dimension of questionable volume was. While true that they hadn't had full knowledge of what I could do for more than a few weeks, they'd still not realized the sheer utility of the thing.

They'd chosen to bring their own packs with their own provisions at the start of our journey, probably out of habit for the military folks. You get told how to pack your things on deployment enough times, and suddenly it becomes the only way you *can* pack.

That programming was quickly overwritten, however, after I had been able to produce dry bedding for everyone the previous evening by just making it all appear in my hand. Samila looked ready to kiss me, the goblins snatched at the blanket and constructed a little fort to sleep in, and Geddon actually went so far as to give me a sloppy, one-armed hug just before he keeled over for the night with the sheets haphazardly draped over him. The journey up had been hardest on him, with the exception of Beedy, who had more color now after some fire and a meal.

So that's how they all grew an appreciation for my breaking the laws of time and space. Now they were all too ready to give me their packs to haul down the mountain, even though I insisted they'd get them back just as soggy and gross as at this very moment.

"Wait. So the items tucked away inside of you are frozen in time?" Geddon asked, looking down at me quizzically, like he was trying to suss out where my magical pockets resided.

"Please don't say it like that," I pleaded before adding, "but yes. I'm pretty sure that's how it works."

Samila was curious as well. "How sure? Can you feel it rolling around in there?"

I sent a little mental probe into the place that I associated with the Ability, nudging a few things. Somehow I just seemed to know they were all frozen in there, in stasis. I shrugged.

"I mean, I can't be 100 percent sure, but I've got a sword in here that's been in the process of, sort of, uh . . . exploding for weeks now. Not even a tickle."

"What made you want to put an exploding sword inside of you, Monk?" Bole sneered from above his open pack. He was the only one to not trust my Ability to do the heavy lifting for him.

"Oh, for the love of—It's not *inside* of me," I insisted. "I didn't eat the damn thing."

"Not what I was implying."

I shot him what I hoped was a withering glare, but he was characteristically unfazed.

"Ryan has an exploding sword?" Trix asked.

"First I'm hearing of it too," Samila lamented sarcastically. "Surprising. Most other men are more than happy to brag about their exploding swords."

"Well, let's see it," Sissa cajoled, raising an eyebrow.

This conversation was going in three different directions with just as many undertones, only one of which I was going to address.

I raised my hands placatingly. "Did you not hear that it's literally in the process of exploding? I like having hair," I said with my hands purposefully relaxed at my sides and not running my fingers through my new brown curls. It had grown back fairly evenly, too. Messy but evenly so, which was a miracle in itself.

"Perhaps the right question to ask, then, is *why* is it exploding, Ryan?" Trix asked, saving me from further innuendo as he rolled up his pint-sized blanket.

I looked around at the group, wondering what was appropriate to share in front of Bole and Beedy. I chose to be specific on materials but vague on the cause of said explosions, just in case, and hope the rest caught on well-enough.

"It's a brightsteel blade. Broken. I found it in a cave where the Underriver feeds into the swamp, and, so far, all it's done is explode. Multiple times," I said carefully.

Bole whistled. "And he's a relic bearer on top of everything else. Be careful, though. Tell a high-enough priest about your little sword and you'll be made a martyr or worse. Would be a terrible thing to witness, how they'd take it from you."

"That is not how that works. Relic bearers are honored by all the faithful," Trix corrected, but Bole ignored him.

"Seriously. Were the universe so kind to me, Monk," he said, locking eyes with me, something approaching pity tugging at the edge of his features, "I'd wonder if kindness were really its goal."

"And most would consider it an honor to wield such an artifact, Corporal Bole, and I find your opinion of our brothers and sisters uncharitable to say the—" Trix began before Sissa cut him off with a violent shake of her head and an almost inaudible hiss that the vulpa heard much more acutely than anyone else. Sissa's stone-hard expression held a warning, a grave one, unspoken but very real.

Bole just laughed, though, barking, bitter, and conveying no warmth nor joy. He kept laughing until all other conversation was good and dead.

The descent started late morning once Tiba thought the pass would probably be drained enough to not be too dangerous a prospect, and she turned out to be correct. Aside from a few slippery vertical-drops-turned-temporary-waterfalls, the pass was largely fine, if somewhat damp and cold to traverse.

Eventually, the black shrubbery thinned until it only appeared in circular clumps, and we started getting peeks of all-too-familiar (to me, at least) titanic trees with multicolored bark overhead, and the ground went from jagged rock to spongy tree litter and soil, still wet from last night's shower. Once we were fully off the mountain, the smell of rotting vegetation and petrichor wafted through a pervasive, light fog that seemed to turn the legion mammoth tree trunks that stretched off into the distance into shadowy obelisks. It took a good half-mile or so until my mind was able to completely process where I was.

The location and its significance hit me suddenly, and I stopped mid-step, my throat tightening as I remembered my first days on Ralqir none-too-fondly. Mostly it was a lot of running . . . Also spiders.

A feeling of terrible uncertainty took hold of me.

This is the place. It all started here. Home is just through these trees. It's literally a universe away, but it's right over there, too.

I swallowed, thinking of how close my old life was. Just a hike in a particular direction and a flick of my will, and I'd be back where I started with my dad and my people, and—

And Ralqir would just be a memory.

I surreptitiously glanced around the group, at all my friends, imagining doing so for the last time. The only other time I'd hopped universes, I'd paid for it with a friend's life. I remembered the feeling of helplessness watching Vince die, the despair at having not been able to do anything to prevent it, the loss. I was ignorant of the toll I had paid the first time, and as long as I could help it, I'd never pay it again.

Never again.

That didn't mean I wouldn't be losing them, though.

Ralqir would be functionally unreachable once I'd left. I wasn't even sure if it was possible to get to Ralqir outside of the System's tutorial insertion point.

Well, it was probably possible. The multiverse was a big place. Exotics, from what I'd heard, sort of popped between universes in places where two of them rubbed up against one another in the void. Who was to say that somewhere in our cosmos we weren't connected in some way with this one?

Of course I wasn't stupid. I couldn't do the math just now without a napkin, a pen, and several degrees I didn't have, but—roughly estimating—the odds of me ever finding Ralqir again were vanishingly small. Getting back before my friends were dead and gone from old age: as close to zero as you could get.

Once I left, that would be it.

This decision to leave was a precipice, a bottomless pit with the unknown lying in wait somewhere in the depths. Having it so close unnerved me, filling me with fear and regret for a thing I hadn't done yet.

The fact that I still had a job to do saved me from full-blown dread and kept my feet moving, however. Silver lining: I could still die before having to choose, and, oddly, that was a comforting thought.

I still had to do right by this place, these people. My arrival had caused a lot of grief for them, and I had a duty to make sure that, in my departure, I left Ralqir in a better state than I'd found it. That meant a life without the Scourge. I owed them that.

Tiba led us quietly east and a bit south deeper into the forest where I continued my slow descent into deja vu. I could almost feel the wreck I was back in those days—mind fractured, running for my life, dreaming of home, fighting to live just a day longer.

Well, I wasn't that guy anymore. I was the guy who was going to slap the Scourge in the face so hard it had no choice but to gather itself all in one place. Then I'd give it the finger as I escaped, ideally as Jassin and his army crested the hill with catapults and a thunderous cavalry charge.

I'd leave just as the killing blow landed, and the Scourge would know I had never been running after all. I'd been hunting.

We all stayed quiet now that we were in what we assumed was enemy territory, but in reality, there seemed to be nothing to hear us. This place was alive last time I was here. Now it was eerily empty—not in the physical sense but in other ways.

There was no birdsong anymore, no skittering reptiles on the trees, no random animal calls in the distance. Nothing moved unless we moved it. The only noise came from the wind in the trees and the crunch of leaves under our feet.

The compass on Trix's wrist, however, was going insane. It had begun to act up since we had entered the valley. Trix was at the front of the group, hiking alongside Tiba, when I noticed him look at the watch face, tap it repeatedly, and put it up to his ear.

Thinking something had gone wrong, I jogged up to him to ask what was the matter, but I guessed as soon as I got within ten feet of him. There was a tinny, buzzing sound coming from the compass, the little mallet inside tapping on the back of the housing so fast it resembled a musical note. When I looked at its face, the needle spun wildly this way and that—never long enough to really tell us anything.

I shared a long look with Trix, then shrugged, holding out a hand to put the compass away in my Storage Space. The compass wasn't going to be of any use here in the belly of the beast unless I reprogrammed it to be more specific regarding what we wanted. It was supposed to point out living Scourge-Touched, but perhaps this close to where the infection resided, most things were technically Scourge-Touched, especially after the Scourge expanded its influence so broadly. I'd need to add "rejigger the targeting logic" to my to-do list, unless I wanted the turrets to just shoot at Scourge-Touched trees all day.

Sometime in the afternoon as the dense green of the canopy overhead was starting to go gray in the waning light, Tiba stopped and waved us over to join her.

"There," she said, indicating a direction with the tip of her finger.

I peered into the gloom, getting low and tilting my head to see where she was pointing. At first I didn't see what she meant. The tree trunks stretched on in every direction for miles, almost uniform in their non-uniformity, drawing the eye in odd directions, but other than that . . .

Then I saw it: a dark shape among dark shapes, only this one was much shorter than the rest of them. It was a clump of little rocky outcroppings, maybe twenty-or-so feet tall, that jabbed out of the ground like a miniature mountain range, wide at the bottom, thinner at the top, but flat, like someone had come and cut off the peaks. The base, meanwhile, was asymmetrical and smooth, and the roots of the structure splayed outward almost organically.

Like a tree.

Yes. Now I saw it. This was the stump of a tree. More accurately, several petrified stumps of monstrously large trees, having grown together somehow when they were alive, now fused into a solid pillar of rock by time. Their equally hardened roots that now made up the wide base had, at some point in the eons, been exposed by weather and shifting soil underneath.

The four petrified stumps had long shed their rougher bits, forming smooth walls that curved and flowed into one another seamlessly, or as seamlessly as they could, having been separate organisms in life. Their gigantic stone roots formed a webwork of waist high walls, pitfalls, and weaving trails that trapped standing water and muck between them.

Tiba and her honor guard, no longer needed as guides, looked around with their mouths open like tourists, the guards pointing at things with their spears and giving each other congratulatory slaps on their backs as if they'd just reached the summit of a mountain and it was time for a drink.

They led us around to the other side of the stump, which took longer than one would have expected. The closer we came, the bigger the place revealed itself to be. While the hunched redoubt was short compared to its living counterparts that shaded us from the sun, the structure still loomed over us the closer we got, until we had to crane our necks to appreciate it up close.

Once on the other side, we discovered the way in—an uneven set of stone "stairs" that must have been part of the whole before they came loose and toppled to the ground like a discarded tower of children's blocks.

Tiba smiled and gestured at the hollow with a sweep of her hand.

"Welcome to the Shade Market, the great fortress of goblinkind," she pronounced, puffing out her chest with pride and posing in front of the yawning entrance. She said the name reverently, more so than the way it came out when I translated it for the others. She spoke of it like a legend come to life instead of an old, hollowed-out tree.

"This place predates the Purge," Trix observed, crouching down to run his claws over the contours of the stone where he was perched. "How is this possible?"

"What?" I asked, confused. "Lots of things predate the Purge, right? Hell, we were sleeping in a place that predated the Purge a few days ago."

"No," Trix insisted as he held out a chunk of petrified tree to me as if that told me anything. "This, if I am not mistaken, is Mendau, but that is impossible. The Dark Lord made the Mendau—Ah! He designed them to reclaim the world and shade it from the Maelstrom. As long ago as that was, it is much too recent to have petrified like this."

So, the timelines didn't add up. I turned a flat bit of petrified wood over in my hand, wanting to guess what was going on, but I chose to ask the expert instead.

Tiba seemed excited to share, taking the stone from me and holding it out to Trix as she spoke. "The stories say that this is a safe place for goblins back in the before. They are planted by the ancients for us, to bring us together. When the Baned take it, the tribes start to break apart and wander with no place to gather anymore, no trust in one another. Now, though . . ." she growled excitedly in a way that needed no translation, "we take it back."

Her guards grunted from behind her, knocking the heads of their spears together in the goblin-warrior version of a high-five.

Trix's eyes widened, seeming to catch a bit of that Tiba-enthusiasm even after translation. "Ancient even before the Purge . . . That would make these proto-Mendau trees, then, Your Highness. Progenitors to those that protect us all now."

"It looks similar to the ones that surround us, doesn't it?" I observed. "I wouldn't be able to tell the difference if I were asked."

"What does the queen say?" Trix asked.

I turned to her and interpreted as best I could.

"The trees of the big valley are always the same, casting it all in shade forever. Goblins always like the trees. Good shade for our eyes. Good shelter for our children. Good ingredients. Good hunting. My ancestors plant trees before the

Purge. Many, many more after, spreading them until the whole world is ready for us to walk upon."

"Is she saying that her people planted all the Mendau after the Purge? Impossible." Trix gaped.

Tiba snorted, laughing a little at the question. "No. We just help. The trees do all the hard work."

"Maybe the Dark Lord acquired more than his pet human in this valley," I speculated.

Trix tilted his head curiously, his ears perked up like satellite dishes. "You have a theory?"

"The Dark Lord's family holdings were just across the mountains from here, right? Close enough that he stumbled upon a human who wandered too far from his tutorial" I said. "That might mean he was on good terms with his goblin neighbors. Good enough to let him wander around out here in their territory."

"That is a sensible assumption," Trix replied.

I went on. "So, maybe once the Dark Lord realized what his new pet was doing to the world, and he was about to pop the whole planet into the Bera Maelstrom to do something about it, he looked to what he knew for the solution."

"A valley of trees hungry for sunlight and able to live communally," Trix continued for me. "He used them as a foundation."

I nodded. "A template. And he just so happened to be neighbors with a sizeable goblin population that knew the trees and knew how to take care of them," I finished, looking over at Tiba, knowing she probably didn't understand what we'd just said, but the pride she felt as we spoke about her people was clear to see.

"You're going to have to write a book when this is all over, Trix," Samila said, sheathing her sword as she climbed down the steps to join the rest of us. "The inside looks empty, like the rest of this forest. You should come see, though."

We entered through the "door" to find that the place was shaped like a hollowed-out molar or a weird, clover-shaped arena. The whole thing was maybe the size of several larger Eclipse-style homes put together: one central courtyard with four roundish protrusions at roughly equidistant corners. The inside was spacious and had probably been carved out from the tiny spring that burbled in the middle of the courtyard floor and trickled down the steps to disappear under the soil. Faint toolmarks and browned, faded paint decorated the walls while animal sign—like bones and clumps of dried feces—dotted the floor. There were also rudimentary shelves built into the walls, large enough for things to be placed upon or perhaps for a goblin to sleep on. Kicking the leaves up to check beneath, I discovered a solid stone floor instead of the squishy tree-dirt that littered the rest of the forest.

I eyed the little spring, wondering if it was safe to drink from.

"It's not bad as far as fortresses go. Thick walls, a single gate, fresh water source . . ." Sissa mused as she inspected the place with a discerning eye, turning in slow circles.

"But it's no Dark Lord's Spire. Some, if not a majority, of the creatures we've fought can scale the walls. No cover from the elements or attack from the air. No escape if we are surrounded, which we most certainly will be. We don't have enough people to man the walls, either, though I guess your turrets will take care of some of that. Still—"

"You think we should find another place?" I asked.

Sissa sighed and shook her head. "No. No. I don't mean to sound like I don't appreciate a good strongpoint. I'm just pointing out the weak spots in our armor. We shouldn't move. Trix believes that your insertion point is only a few miles southwest, and if we went and found a cave somewhere that we could defend better than this, your objective would be much farther away and just as inaccessible when the enemy clusters in the mouth of said cave. More so, even."

"A cave would be a terrible place to hole up. My guns are loud. We'd all go deaf in a day," I predicted.

"Just an example. Now that I think back on it," Sissa began, wincing, "it was bad enough when Geddon had them going full-blast on his back. Even so, I don't like this. The fort is good, but the board is in our enemy's favor. They don't tire like we do, and your turrets may not be able to make up the difference in numbers. We're going to be surrounded and swarmed, sure as sure."

I looked up at the walls, picturing hundreds of snarling faces cresting the lip and filling the inside with enough flesh to drown us all. It was going to be Eclipse all over again.

"Bring down the trees," Geddon's voice muttered from behind us, quiet and contemplative.

As one, Sissa and I turned to see Geddon there, arms full of fallen branches and debris while his gaze was turned upward—not to the walls but higher. He had a thoughtful look on his face, somewhere between doing advanced calculus and having a particularly difficult time in the privy. He said nothing else.

"What's that, Geddon?" Sissa asked as she took a quiet, careful step in his direction. I felt it too, the fragility of the moment, as if a wrong move on either of our parts would shatter Geddon's concentration and he'd forever lose this train of thought.

"Bring down the trees," Geddon said after a long ten-count in my head, more confidently this time, nodding to himself, his eyes brightening as the idea took form. "Normally, I would relish the chance to be surrounded by enemies, making my last stand, and gloriously so, but perhaps in this case, we can slow their numbers to a manageable amount and meet our ends later rather than sooner."

"You want to bring down *those* trees?" Sissa asked, pointing to the enormous trunks of the Mendau that rivaled some buildings I'd seen back home. Even the smallest of them was thick enough for someone to hollow out and live semi-comfortably within.

"Well, not all of them," Geddon scoffed. "Leave the ones that provide shade for us, but take down a circle of them farther out. These vile, disgusting creatures are quite vulnerable to the Maelstrom, yes? No offense, Ryan."

"None taken," I said as I thought ahead. "So we cut down a big circle of trees—not quite a complete circle, though, so we can try to fight our way out when it's time to leave. Then we let the light do the work for us. The Scourge wouldn't be able to come at us during the day, not in numbers. And charging through the starlight will still be unpleasant for them, I'd imagine."

"That still leaves dozens of dead trees out there that the enemy can use as cover," Trix objected. "It will allow them to get closer to us before they swarm. There will be no proper line of sight for us to thin them out."

"Not to mention that when the first tree goes down, it will be like ringing the dinner bell," Bole complained from beside me. I felt my shoulders tense, but otherwise I didn't let my discomfort show. I wished he would stop doing that, just appearing out of nowhere.

Maybe I could make a Bole compass . . .

"Everyone within miles will see it. Probably feel it, too," Bole continued. "No time to do it proper-like for a full circle. Plus, you'd need ten strong lads with axes just to bring down one of them a day."

That was a big problem—potentially a fatal one. Just setting the big trees on fire was an option, if they actually lit well, but trees of that size would take days to burn down. All the while the smoke would hurt the defenders more than it would the attackers. We would be surrounded by wet wood and blinding smoke for possibly days, stinging our eyes and clogging our throats.

Then there was the problem of how we would bring the trees down in the first place. It would take days just to hack through them even if we all dropped what we were doing and worked nonstop.

Then I had an idea.

An awful, dangerous, perfect idea that I was sure I would live to regret.

"Oh, ho ho ho ho. Look. There it is. That look," Geddon said, grinning ear to ear, his pronounced canines giving him a predatory air. "We're doing my plan."

I nodded, already half-a-dozen steps ahead in the planning process. "I'll be in my workshop," I heard myself say as my feet carried me to the corner of the fort that looked the most inviting.

Samila called down from the wall where she'd been kicking debris from the surface and checking for hazards. "Someone, put on some tea. He doesn't sleep when he gets like this."

I was already reaching into my Spatial Storage.

Geddon, buddy, you're going to love this.

CHAPTER TWENTY-FIVE

Make the Call

Geddon did, indeed, love it. He loved his new toy so much, he hadn't stopped using it for the past twenty-four hours, and there was no sign he would ever tire of it. The sound of ravenous metal on poor, defenseless forest flora was now the discordant choir to which I worked. It wasn't loud, per se, just a sort of an irregular, buzzing hum that could easily fall into the background of your mind if you were not cursed with the knowledge of what it was capable of.

The old phrase, "double-edged sword" was woefully inadequate in describing what I'd created.

The chainsaw sword—more like a greatsword, actually—was, by far, the most dangerous thing I'd ever made. On its face, the idea was ridiculous: a blade in constant motion, so sharp it could cut through almost anything. So temperamental you couldn't let it anywhere near your own body, your clothes, your armor, allies, enemies, or even the ground, lest it shoot off in a random direction and cut something you really didn't want cut.

Six feet long from pommel to tip, thick as my palm in width, entirely steel, and fit with a battery that could blow a person-sized crater in whatever ground was unfortunate enough to be under it, the two-handed great sword was a cumbersome monster, but the big Leori absolutely adored it. Even now he was hacking away at our perimeter, making undercuts in the trunks that would cause the giant trees to fall in the proper direction when the time came to bring them down. Last time I'd seen Geddon, his mane was full of sawdust, and his eyes were red and puffy from it.

> You have created Air-Propelled Mortar Tube.
> 2,480 Experience gained. (620 base, 620 New Design, 1,240 Doing Your Part bonus)

I breathed out as the molecules of the final metal seam of my current project intertwined with one another and the many disparate pieces finally became one. My tired eyes drifted in and out of focus, turning the knobby cylinder of metal into an indistinct blob, one I'd been staring at for . . . how long was it now? I'd gone through something like half of our firewood while I worked, as well as countless cups of Samila's tea, but there always seemed to be more to do.

We weren't ready. I'd stop when we were ready.

I stood up from my stool, the muscles in my neck, shoulders, and back protesting at moving after so long hunched over and tensed. Reaching down, I grabbed my pail of spring water and took a couple of sips before dumping the rest of it over my head. The chill wasn't uncomfortable to my Exotic body, but I certainly felt it. The ghost of a shiver passed through me, and I felt my mind clear, somewhat. At some point, little rituals like this helped me stay alert better than the tea did with the added bonus of requiring fewer bathroom breaks.

Efficiency. That was the word I'd been forced to tattoo into my brain.

As I blinked the water out of my eyes, I stretched and let my gaze drift. It was midday or thereabouts, judging by the thinness of the fog and how green the canopy was overhead.

tick tick tick tick tick

A spherical-bodied worker drone clicked over the now-wet floor of my workshop, the coin-sized construct's six articulated limbs scraping at the petrified wood with Imbued fluidity, using its bristly, gripping hairs to sweep little particulates into a neat pile next to my workbench. Soon, once it had a sufficiently large pile, it would start shuffling the whole thing toward the entrance of the fortress and out of sight. Our floor—now mostly visible, at least in the general vicinity of my work area—was an interesting blend of yellows, browns, reds, and grays that swirled into one another where one ancient tree ended and the others began, previously invisible under millennia of dirt and debris.

I could hear another worker doing its thing up above me as well, on the ramparts that overlooked the rest of the forest. The construct's limbs scraped over the stone in a quiet but distinctive way that practically scratched at one's ears. There would be quite a few more of the little drones out there somewhere, doing their thing and waiting to be brought back to their dock to be reprogrammed for logging duty. I really should have built in some kind of return-to-base command, but other than tracking them down and doing it myself, I had no way of getting the entire population on their next task.

PAK!

A round of the new smart-ammo dropped from a casting bowl on the shelf to my left, to roll down the tin chute and into the magazine-loading hopper. The loader itself hummed as it stirred the bits inside until they fit into the feeder at the bottom, while the loading piston snapped another round into one of the old fan magazines.

Getting up on my tiptoes to check the levels in the bowl, I found it nearly empty of scrap metal, and I made a mental note to summon more of my stash later this evening—maybe during mealtime. I was down to the copper alloys now, my iron and steel stores nearly depleted, aside from a few big pieces I was saving for turret components. Making things like brass into rounds wasn't ideal. They'd deform more easily upon impact, meaning I'd get one, maybe two launches out of them before they were useless. That didn't mean they weren't needed, though.

Every bullet was going to be precious when the time came. Irreplaceable. I'd foreseen it when I'd first sat down at my workbench. That's where the idea for the worker drones came in, their casting bowl being the first new thing I'd laid out in our new "manufacturing area."

PAK! PAK!

Another two rounds from two other bowls dropped into the chute. I had five of them going at once, producing bullets, but I still wasn't satisfied with the throughput. Once the lead started flying, attrition was going to be inevitable, and damaged bullets were going to need to go back into the casting bowls for re-Shaping. When that time came, I'd rather have more bowls than I needed and hands to fill them. I also needed to work out some kind of filtering system that could sort out the damaged rounds from the healthy ones.

That was where the worker drones were going to really show their worth. Though the little dudes weren't much use now, I was banking on my prioritization of their creation being vindicated soon.

At least their development had pushed me over the crest of a particular hill.

Split Mind is now Level 11.
Imbue is now Level 5.
Upgrade Paths available:
Efficiency Upgrade
Solid State
Intuitive

Automate is now Level 5+.
Upgrade Paths available:
Efficiency Upgrade
Specialized Automation
Aura Extension

These upgrades had been a long time coming.

I'd already taken one efficiency upgrade to Imbue when Split Mind had hit 10, and I wasn't opposed to taking another. I'd already noticed a huge difference when using Automate in how much cheaper it was—not enough to actually use the word, "cheap," but certainly less like turning my body inside out and squeezing the mana from my internal organs.

"Intuitive" was vague in its description, but the gist of the upgrade was that I would be able to make slight adjustments to the Imbued metal's instructions on the fly, though nothing too big. It would be good for fine-tuning my designs without having to start over and redo the whole thing again. A time-saver, for sure, but not one I necessarily needed. I was almost sure I could use my existing Abilities to achieve something similar.

Solid State was what I ended up choosing in the end.

> Solid State: Imbued mana is now crystalized, slightly increasing mana cost, moderately increasing strength, and greatly increasing resistance to degradation, dispersal, and tampering.

While the Skill seemed okay on its face, the information the System gave me through context was even more valuable. Apparently my mana could be tampered with. Good to know. I'd just add that to the paranoia pile to be dealt with later.

The next choice was easier.

> Specialized Automation: Increase speed, strength, and efficiency of your Automated creations given simple programming. This bonus decreases and eventually becomes a penalty as programmed instructions for a single construct grow more complex.

The funny thing was that I was already kind of doing what Specialized Automation wanted me to do. None of my creations were complex in the way the System considered them. Maybe it came from my background of having been a mechanic as opposed to an engineer or a hacker, but I was always attracted to the idea that any given part of a machine should do its job well and reliably before it tried to do anything else. Simplicity bred efficiency (there was that word again), and if you brought enough simple, efficient things together, they could do some damned complex stuff anyway.

My turrets had a wafer "brain" that functioned as their power source and decision-maker, but in the end, they just boiled down to sending signals on when to do certain things, like firing when the barrel was pointed at a valid target. The rest of the machine—from the aiming arms to the trigger to the magazines— were already each individually Automated to do one thing really well. Specialized Automation encouraged this kind of thing—required it, almost—and it was already the way I worked, making it a straight upgrade for most projects.

The worker drones took a hit on their mana cost, but it was a small one. Their programming boiled down to "walk, find thing, move thing," and that seemed to be just on the other side of the line the System had drawn between "complex" and "simple."

My choice meant I wouldn't be creating sentient robots anytime soon, but I wasn't sure that was a good idea anyway.

"He's talking about naming it Organ Grinder, Ryan." Samila groaned from behind me. She stood there in the natural doorway to the fortress: a coil of rope looped around a pair of sturdy timbers, sharpened at the ends, that would serve as our makeshift gate in the near-future. A quick motion with her hand and a long pull on the knot, and she turned away from her work, satisfied. Her clothes were filthy, and her blue skin was mottled with brown streaks of mud and tiny, navy-blue scratches down one cheek.

"Organ Grinder. Like he's making sausage," she continued, disgust plain on her face. "I love him, but he might just be the most socially maladjusted person I've ever met, outside of you."

I tried not to let the blow to my ego show on my face. "Give him some credit," I allowed jokingly. "It's a pun. Musical instrument and messy food processor in one. It's fitting, kind of . . ."

"That's not a pun," Sissa said, furrowing her eyebrows as she crouched down next to the little spring in the middle of the floor and wetted a cloth to run it over her head and neck. "Is this another translation-magic thing? How did those words end up sounding the same in your language?"

"English is—uh—*borrowed* from lots of different places," I replied. Damn. I'd never be able to trust puns again. Another thing the System had taken from me.

"I assume you mean 'borrowed' the same way Bole does."

"How dare you," I said defensively before the words fully sank in. Then I was forced to wobble my head from side to side and amend my statement. "Yeah. Now that you mention it, I probably mean it a lot like Bole would."

One of the worker drones skittered down from the ceiling above my head, plopping down to the workbench before righting itself. It was carrying another of its kind, dragging it with its back legs. The other drone was inert, simply a sphere with little folded nubs that turned into legs when it had power. This one must have worked itself until it had zero charge. The powered drone pulled its friend over to the side of my work area until the two teetered on the edge, and then it let go, dropping the dead drone into the drone-production hopper. Three other dead workers sat there inside the thing among all the scrap, in the process of being re-Shaped and re-Automated. Job done, the live drone skittered off to do its own thing, probably wood-cutting.

Samila spared a glance over at the hopper, pursing her lips. "It's disturbing every time I see it," she said. "Why not just give them a power source like you do your bowls?"

I shrugged. "I haven't worked out how to stop the collectors just yet. With normal batteries, I'd just hook up a detection-and-protection circuit to it, but with these—I have no way to cut off the charging process. Let's say a worker loses a couple of legs out there and it can't come home. Given enough time, it just turns into a landmine. Plus, having them brought back like this has the added benefit of letting me reprogram them through the casting bowl, so I only have to do the costly spellwork once. Saves me time to work on other stuff."

"Is that why we still have a couple roaming around the castle uselessly sweeping floors?" she asked.

"They'll make it back to the casting bowl eventually," I assured her defensively. "The cleaning round was a test. I couldn't have them all out there chewing through trees unless I knew they were working right and there were enough of them. I had to get it to the point where the system could perpetuate itself."

"Shoemaking," Samila said with a frown and a little knowing nod.

"Uh. Bootstrapping, actually."

"That's exactly what I said."

A whistle sounded out from above us, perfectly mimicking a birdcall. There were no birds in the forest right now, however.

I took a handful of steps away from my work area to get out from under the roof and into the open air of the courtyard. My gaze drifted up to the battlements where Trix sat with his rifle shouldered and looking down the sights.

"What is it?" Samila asked, drawing up beside me, a hand resting on the pommel of her sword.

"Hard to tell," Trix called. He didn't turn to address us, never looking away from his rifle or letting his aim waver. "The scouts are returning with great haste. Movement behind them. Lots of movement."

My stomach did a backflip. "Scourge?" I asked.

"I can't tell. Not goblins or Returned, I can say that much."

I looked over at Samila, already summoning the mask from Spatial Storage. Better safe than sorry.

Samila shook her head. "We're not ready," she told the both of us.

"I am holding my fire," Trix replied. "But if we don't intervene now, they will most likely be overtaken."

I called up the Volatility triggers on the turrets perched on that side of the fort, but Samila, probably sensing my intention or maybe knowing me too well, grabbed me by the shoulders.

"Hey. Hey!" Samila practically shouted, holding my gaze to make sure I stood still and listened. "No firearms. We're not ready."

My mind conjured an image of Bole and Beedy running for their lives from a horde of monsters, the fort in sight—so close but so far away. Then the two of them were brought down and ripped apart while we all watched. In my mind's eye, I could see a vivid image of myself wishing I could have done something to stop it.

My jaw clenched, and I could feel my teeth grinding against one another.

"Hey!" Samila called again, this time more gently, inching closer to my face until her eyes took up most of my field of vision. "Look at me. Don't do it. Not yet. Remember why we're here and what we need to do. Trust us to handle this one. Trust *me*, at least."

Seconds ticked by. Important seconds she didn't need to waste reining me in.

"Time's wasting," I said. It was as close to a concession as I was capable of just now.

She frowned, not quite satisfied with my answer, but she didn't waste any more time. She took off for the gate, scooping up her shield from the floor in the process.

Before she was even out of sight, I was already climbing up the rudimentary stone stairs, slipping my mask over my face as I crested the lip of our battlements that were in reality just a semi-level ring of carved stone about four feet from edge to edge, formerly the bark of the petrified trees. It wasn't fun to walk on, but a highish Body score helped with that.

At the top of the stairs, a pair of inactive kinetic turrets sat low on the floor, their legs folded in on themselves and their housings resting directly on the stone to give them a low profile. I called their activation Triggers up specifically and kept them at the forefront of my mind, just in case.

The area around the fort had changed quite a bit since I'd entered my work fugue. All the brush and scrub within fifty yards of our walls had been cleared away and left as little clusters of tripping stumps. Mangled vines and branches littered the ground and formed a carpet of new over all the old, rotting stuff that made up the soil. The beginnings of a trench, only a quarter-circle-long just now, snaked its way around the fort while sharpened stakes protruded from the bank of it, pointed outward. The smell of freshly cut wood drifted in the air, clashing with the wet and dank of the forest floor.

Geddon, Samila, and Sissa were already forming up down below and jogging together, none of them in their armor but all with their swords drawn. They ran toward two vaguely humanoid figures in the distance. The two were running with reckless abandon, leaping over fallen branches and vanishing briefly below dips in the terrain. They seemed to be moving frantically, desperately.

I saw one of them fall, and the other was forced to stop and go back to help.

Meanwhile, something seethed behind them—something too distant for me to make out as more than a general impression of movement.

"Trix?" I asked, looking to my left to find the vulpa there, his eye-glamour spell he was using to enhance his vision even now tempting me to give his fur a little stroke. It would be so soft, I was sure.

"Not sure yet," he answered. "Whoever is following them is numerous but not a full horde as we saw in the city. I can see a beginning and end to it. They don't move like—Wait. *Yes.* As I thought, these are beasts. Running on six—no, *eight*—legs."

Spiders.

Spiders were ambush predators. That was a nearly universal truth. They were all explosive speed and power with venom to subdue and webs to entangle and—

"We have to assume they're Touched, Trix," I said. "This isn't natural."

"Agreed. All the more reason for you to stay here and not reveal yourself," Trix replied, sparing a cautious glance at me. Damn. Did no one trust me to do the smart thing for once?

One of the running figures—Bole, maybe—got an arm under the taller of the two and helped him hobble along. Beedy seemed to limp forward, favoring his left side. I couldn't see him well enough to be sure, but I imagined a pained expression on his face, judging by how his body was reacting to movement.

The spiders drew closer. Any moment now, they'd be within pouncing distance. I should know, I'd been pounced by Ralqir's giant spiders before. I suppressed a shudder at the memory.

The wedge of Church guards now ran full-speed out to meet them. At some point they were joined by the three goblins who struggled to keep up with the talk folks' pace, but they gave it their all, loosely following the formation with spears held high.

The spiders were closer.

"They're not going to make it," I decided out loud, looking over at the inactive turrets. At this distance, they wouldn't be very accurate, but with the enemy massed like that, they didn't have to be. I could buy them time, at least. We'd be drowning in Scourge within a day, but the two scouts would be alive.

But we weren't ready. Could I get us ready in that time? Could we afford to kick off early? There was no way to know.

My fingers twitched and the muscles in my neck tightened as I made the calculations and hated what I came up with. We had to do something, though.

"Trix, we made your rifle relatively quiet—" I began.

I didn't get to give the full order. My designated shooty-fox was already on it. Had probably already been squeezing the trigger even as I dithered. He'd never leave one of our own hanging out to dry, bless him. Trix's rifle barked three times, splitting the relative silence. The report was quiet by my standards but unpleasantly sharp and sudden compared to anything else, amplified by the stone floors and walls of the courtyard. It echoed infinite times from every single massive tree trunk in the area.

At least it wasn't as distinctive as the turrets.

Trix shifted his shoulders and got down low, resting the barrel of the rifle on an odd lump in the petrified bark, settling himself in for more sustained fire. Then he opened up with rapid, single, precise shots, one every second like the beat of a metronome. Tiny needle-rounds zipped through the air, too small and fast to actually see with the naked eye but with plenty of ballistic power.

I saw two spiders roll and flail as Trix's needles hit them, their legs curling in on themselves and thrashing at the dirt as the projectiles pierced their exoskeletons and did untold damage to their insides. The others climbed over their still twitching corpses, heedless of the casualties they were taking.

CRACK! CRACK! CRACK!

Another spider, about to spring at the men's backs, stopped suddenly and shrank back, its forelegs coming up to shield its face and the slits that were its eyes. Yes, now that they drew closer, I recognized these things.

Armor spiders.

CRACK! CRACK!

Trix's efforts slowed the chasers, or perhaps disincentivized them to pull ahead of the pack, but it wasn't enough. Two hundred yards out from our position, Bole and Beedy were forced to stop and draw steel. Bole seemed to be in a much-better state than his partner, drawing both of his swords and stepping in front of Beedy protectively, shouting something I couldn't make out from this distance. Meanwhile, Beedy had his sword out and in a lazy guard, but he was heavily favoring his left side. Even from here, I could see his shoulders rising and falling with his tortured breaths.

The monsters pounced seconds before our reinforcements could get there. Three spiders took to the air, springing forward, legs out wide, coming down in a hollow arc, flanking the two beleaguered men.

Bole sprang back and let the spider closest to him land before dashing back in to slash at an exposed leg joint, following that up with a stab into the side of the monster's head, dropping it instantly. At the same time, Beedy feinted with a seemingly timid thrust but then severed another spider's leg with the return slash. Unfortunately, the monster didn't respond to the pain with anything other than a forward charge.

Beedy's spider slammed into both the men, using its mass to great effect to knock them both from their feet. Beedy ended up under the creature with his sword in the thing's mouth, while Bole rolled to his feet and whipped his blade at the previously unengaged spider's eyes before it could capitalize on their weakness. The rest of the swarm, twenty strong, closed in around the fight, forming a familiar kill circle that shrunk as the prey's attention was drawn elsewhere.

Trix's rifle spat, and the spider on top of Beedy clawed at its back as a rapid-fire quartet of bullets stippled a line down its carapace. Beedy used the opening to get a kick at the spider's abdomen with his good leg, gaining some precious space.

Then Geddon, Samila, Sissa, and the goblins slammed into the circle of many legs with their countercharge.

None of them had a chance to put on their armor, and only the dragonkin had their shields. That didn't make them hesitate in the slightest, running full-speed into the backs of the monsters.

Geddon was at the head of the charge, making use of his new sword. The man had loved it since the morning I'd handed it to him.

"You made me a mighty blade, my friend. Look at the size! You remembered!" Geddon had gasped with awe as I lifted the thing from my workbench, careful to not let the teeth brush against my skin.

"Not just a big sword," I said, smiling nervously as I reached down and thumbed the safety release on the battery. Then I turned the pommel 180 degrees until I felt the mechanism inside click into place, the connection between the power supply and the rest of the machine snapping together and power rushing into the internals. Simultaneously, I felt a barely perceptible sort of tingle as my mana bounced around in there, ready and waiting.

Activation complete, I brought my upper hand down to the cross guard and carefully squeezed the throttle trigger. The action was instantaneous. The 300 fingernail-sized, triangular teeth on the edge of the blade became a blurry line of buzzing death, whizzing, whistling as they sliced at the air.

It was surprisingly quiet, actually, for a machine with so many moving parts. Without the need for a combustion motor, I was able to apply precise measurements at the molecular level and a healthy dose of Willing Edge in strategic places to prevent parts grinding together, resulting in the chains inside the gutter of the blade simply zipping around, practically frictionless, at ridiculous speeds. The weapon hummed menacingly in my hands, vibrating with deadly potential that I knew was just a touch from becoming realized.

When I let go, the chains halted instantly with a *snap* as the piston Triggers stopped pumping the crankshaft, and I hurriedly turned the pommel again to kill the power. No need to keep it running longer than was strictly necessary and risk losing my only remaining arm. If my math was correct, in the full second I engaged the throttle, every tooth made sixteen full trips around the track on the edge of the blade.

Geddon was like a kid in a candy store, halfway between doing a little dance and standing at attention. He didn't reach out or ask to take the sword, but his eyes were wide with anticipation, and his hands were held tightly down at his sides as if a wrong move on his part would jeopardize his chance at getting to hold his new weapon.

"Listen, big guy," I began, looking up into the grinning face of my Leori friend, "you're a professional. You know your swords and all that. But I feel a certain duty to inform you of just how dangerous this thing is." Some of this was going to fly over his head, but I felt the need to impress upon him just what kind of flesh-hungry death machine he was about to receive.

"There's a reciprocating Trigger *here* in the handle. It's attached to a crankshaft that keeps the chains moving. Mana flows from *here*," I said, pointing at the half-circle-shaped, nickel-cobalt construct that was the pommel—one of my Volatility batteries. "It supplies power to the engine that moves the chain and fuels the maintenance spells. If it ever starts to glow purple, just run the sword on full-throttle for as long as it takes. Gently. Very gently. There is a—uh—slight risk of explosive disassembly if you're not very gentle."

I swallowed uncomfortably, holding the weapon by the cross guard and pointing to the blade track. "The teeth are sharp enough to split hairs and then split *those* split hairs. Some swords are good at cutting, but this thing . . . it's evil. If I were back home, they'd throw me in jail just for *conceiving* of the thing. It'll chew through anything softer than itself. Well, actually, there's a spell being refreshed on each tooth to keep their edges every time they enter the cross guard, so the list of things this sword won't cut is very short."

"A legendary blade, my friend," Geddon said as I finally handed the sword to him. He wrapped a giant fist around the handle, flexing his fingers and allowing it to settle. It looked fitted for his hand, though it would most likely be uncomfortable and dangerous for anyone smaller than him to hold. I'd had to fit the moving parts somewhere.

"Have you named it?" Geddon asked, unable to take his eyes from his new toy.

"What? No. Listen. There's a reason no one makes these things, especially for combat. When you hit something hard with the throttle open, this thing is going to buck like a Bray Knight, and if you don't respect it, you're going to be known as Geddon the Stumpy."

"I will limit my dismemberment to others, Ryan. I promise," Geddon tried to assure me, even going so far as to take his eyes away from the sword to smile at me. "And you don't need to tell me to respect a blade."

Charging directly into the backs of the spiders, Geddon, with his six-foot slab of gray death held out to his side with one hand, shoulder-charged the nearest monster, lifting it up on its side and exposing its belly. The throttle on the chain-sword buzzed, and Geddon used the weight of the creature to rebound off its body and bring the blurring blade around with an almost-casual flick of the wrist.

The carapace of the armor spider parted cleanly, but that was all I could see before a cloud of aerosolized goo and ichor exploded from the creature and obscured everything else. The spider, suddenly losing all interest in everything other than holding its organs inside its own body, got low to the ground and twitched as its legs curled in to keep what was left of its abdomen together.

However, Geddon was already on to the next fight. The following blow from the chain-sword came down on the back of another monster engaged with Bole. The blade met the armor of the spider with a *ching!*, halting its momentum for a mere fraction of a second before the teeth bit into the hard metal of the carapace, pulling itself forward along the monster's back. Instead of fighting the sword's motion, Geddon—in the most disturbing display of swordsmanship I'd seen to date—used the chain-sword's irresistible pull to advance fluidly, allowing himself to be brought along, even bringing his left hand down to apply additional pressure as his body was drawn forward.

The result was a sort-of unzipping of the spider's back, from its abdomen all the way to its head, and Geddon followed along behind his sword, his body sliding through the mess until he was on the other side, tucking his shoulder and rolling over his blade and to his feet with the grace of a dancer. It was as if he'd used a movement Ability, it had happened so fast. The creature was close to bisected by the time his thrust was done and the sword was back under control. Or maybe the sword was under control the whole time and Geddon was a damned genius with cutting instruments.

The dragonkin then exploited the hole in the spiders' perimeter that Geddon had made—hacking at legs, using their shields to block visor slits before crippling their opponents with quick slashes and thrusts. The women worked together like they'd been born to do so, and no spider could come between them.

Meanwhile, while the spiders were concerned with the tall folk, the goblins went wild, stabbing with their spears anywhere the monsters didn't have armor. Tiba, spry as she was, leapt up onto the back of a particularly slow monster and seemed to plant herself, using the its back as a platform to thrust at its friends as the lumbering arachnid turned ponderously and attempted to shake the goblin queen off.

Careful, precise rifle shots caught spiders in the joints where their legs and torsos joined, bullets sometimes slipping into the gap between the thorax and head—or whatever spiders had in their place.

Still, watching the others fight in my stead was a harrowing experience. One wrong move meant disaster, and all I could do was watch. My breaths were rapid, and my hands trembled. I worried for them all. I wanted to be out there. I could help end this right now before the worst could happen, but if I went loud, I'd give away the game too early and risk us all.

The spiders quickly learned to give Geddon his space, retreating from wherever the big man and his screeching death blade chose to go. However, there wasn't much they could do to stop him from catching them one by one. The explosive power of the Leori's legs gave him the ability to leap from one fight to the next to land among the enemy and down one before the rest could react. Geddon was breathing hard, his chest pumping like bellows, but even from here, I could see the huge grin on his face, despite the coating of ichor that covered the rest of him.

Finally, the remaining dozen spiders got the picture and changed tactics. They charged, hoping to use their numbers to bring someone down before they could be separated and slain. Unfortunately for them, they charged the group after they'd formed back up, Geddon at the front, shield guards on the sides, and the goblins and rogues in the middle.

I knew I'd be replaying the resulting bloodbath and Geddon's joyous laughter in my nightmares for a long time to come, but I nurtured the small hope that the Scourge would have similar dreams from here on out.

When the last spider fell, a hush fell over the forest once more.

I knew it wouldn't last.

I'd had Trix use his rifle to buy our people time. The weapon wasn't as loud or distinctive as one of my turrets, but it was probably enough to pique the enemy's curiosity. They'd send scouts, and we wouldn't be able to kill them all before my identity was discovered.

The clock was ticking now.

"Trix!" Samila shouted. She was on her knees, hunched over something, doing something with her hands. Bole was down there next to her, frantically grasping at whatever she was hunched over. As I watched, Samila ripped a long piece of dirty fabric from her shirt and brought it around to—

Trix shouldered his weapon and took off like a shot, scrabbling down the outside wall and using his claws to slide down the petrified roots on all fours. Then he was sprinting away, toward the site of the battle.

Seven people. I counted seven. Someone was down.

Beedy was down. He was the only one I couldn't see. He was down and he wasn't moving.

No. No. No. Not again.

I'd made the wrong call.

CHAPTER TWENTY-SIX

Strike Back Hard

I ignored the queasiness in my stomach as I slid down the outside of the wall, but Anchor's gravity-nullifying effect was only a secondary contributor to the sick feeling. Someone out there was wounded, and I wasn't there.

It couldn't happen again.

The muddy mix of soil and spider insides stuck to my boots as I approached the center of the battlefield. Trix was already there next to Beedy, his claws dug into the man's skin and, presumably, his magic doing its work. Samila, meanwhile, was in the process of stripping off Beedy's upper armor, systematically checking for blood or punctures with her hands while Tiba did the same at the legs.

Beedy himself looked like pale death, his bloodless face contorted into a mask of pain and his breathing labored and erratic. His eyes were open but unfocused.

It was when Samila got to Beedy's chest plate that we realized how bad it was. The shirt beneath the armor was gone, eaten away by the corrosive venom of the spider that had bitten him. Beedy's skin, muscle tissue, and other things I didn't know the name for were also in the process of being dissolved. Little tendrils of smoke slithered up from the intensely envenomed areas and gave off an acrid scent.

As soon as Tiba saw the wound, she shrieked, dropped what she was doing and lunged up to get Samila's hands away from the bite. Then she was digging in her pouch.

"Grorg! Get a handful of sap and shavings! Go now!" she ordered one of her guards who was off before she even finished speaking.

Tiba already had a clay jar in her hand, digging some strange substance out of it, and smearing it on her skin like lotion. Samila reached over to pull more of Beedy's shirt away, but Tiba again batted at her hands aggressively.

"Tell her not to touch," she hissed without turning away from her patient. "These spider bites are hungry. You need special medicine to touch or you end up like him."

"Tell Her Highness that I can't keep this up for long for Beedy's sake," Trix grunted with closed eyes as he used his magic to fool Beedy's body into healing itself even as the venom ate at it.

"Uh, Tiba, what do you need from us? Tell us what to do," I pressed her after doing the necessary translation.

Tiba—in a move I really hadn't expected or wanted to witness—jammed her hand into Beedy's wound, reaching into the crevices where the smoke was thickest and digging globs of what I presumed was venom out to fling it away onto the ground.

"This bite does not happen just now, I think. Quiet Man is made of iron if he runs through the woods like this," Tiba replied absently. Her mind was occupied with what she was doing, and I got the distinct impression that more questions would not be welcome. She did eventually acknowledge my need for answers, though. "I send Grorg for what I need. Nothing else to do for now."

"They came at us from under the ground," Bole said in a low voice. I turned to see the thief, swords unsheathed but hanging loosely in his hands as if he'd forgotten they were there, his eyes staring unblinking up into the trees and pointedly not at his friend on the ground. "It's bad luck. Just bad luck. The only fucking living things for miles and miles. What've they been eating?"

I opened my mouth to try and answer, but I never got the chance.

Something shifted in Bole just then. He blinked, shuddered, and seemed to remember the rest of us were there with him. He turned to me, boiling anger in his eyes. "You said this place was empty," he accused.

"I don't even know what this place is," I countered. "Last time I was here, the place was more . . . alive. Now it seems empty. We've all seen it."

"Last time you were here," Bole repeated as he looked down at his hands and seemed to realize they were full. He gripped the hilts of his short swords tightly, to the point I could hear his leather gloves creaking. "When exactly did you have occasion to come here, Monk? There's no one here for you to kill."

"That's not really important," Sissa interjected. "We're here now, and—"

Bole cut her off. "Speaking of killing, where were you, Monk? Fights are what you're s'posed to be good at, right?"

Sissa stepped between us. "You know where he was, Bole," she argued. "Just where he should have been, keeping out of sight. Sticking to the plan."

"Oh, I know the plan," Bole replied. "I know the plan was to keep our precious *brother* a secret. That's what's bothering me. Why? Why do we need to hide a Rising Fucking Sun from a mindless mob? What's his place in all of this?"

Bole kept his eyes locked on mine, squaring his body as if he were just an inch from taking a swing at me despite the distance. "You don't even need to be in the battle to end it, do you, Monk? What with your special training and machines. Where were you? You could have ended this before—" Bole couldn't finish his accusation, as he struggled to avoid looking over at his dying friend and collapsing into despair.

I did look at Beedy, however. I *had* to. He was here because of me. They all were. Tiba and Trix were still frantically doing what they could, but I could tell Beedy was teetering on the edge.

"Brother Ryan put the mission first, and that's it. It's something we all signed up to do, as you did when you insisted on coming along," Sissa said.

"Don't give me that shit. The mission is done. We're made. There was no reason for him to stay out of that fight other than cowardice. Hells, even the vulpa had the balls to jump in!"

Bole was quick. Though Sissa was between the two of us, he slipped around her and was in my face before I could blink. Sissa tried to grab him but only got a hand around his arm.

"You could have ended it with a little flick of your brain or a few swings of your sword, but you didn't, did you? Now what? We've got a man down, and—" He finally seemed to gather the courage to look down at Beedy, but the sight stole the rest of his words. He swallowed, then snarled in impotent rage.

When he finally gathered himself enough to speak again, his voice was a growl. "We're about to be drowning in the infected and for *what*? Because, you, you spineless, whimpering child . . . you chose to hide instead of fight."

"You're out of line, Bole," Geddon declared from over my shoulder. "Brother Ryan didn't do this, and we will soon have more-than-enough places to direct our anger."

That's where Geddon was wrong. I *did* do this. I was doing all of this, but I was too inept to see what I was doing before it was already done. I was constantly playing catch-up with the consequences of my decisions, even ones I'd made months ago.

Bole glanced down at Sissa's hand on his arm, then lowered his sword. "I've been out of line for years now, Meat. Someone needs to be." Then he took one long, last look at Beedy before he stormed off in a seemingly random direction, making time to kick a dead spider on his way out.

Once Bole had gone a good distance, Sissa spoke up again, hesitant.

"He's not entirely wrong about the mission. We're exposed, or we will be shortly." She looked over at me meaningfully, not putting salt on the wound but letting me know that she wasn't stupid. She knew that I'd made a mistake not going all-in on stealth or violence. I'd tried to split the middle by ordering Trix into the fight but not my turrets, and it had been the worst of both worlds.

There was a groan from Trix, and he slumped over next to Beedy. Samila put out a hand to cradle him and guide his fall.

"He's—" Trix gasped tiredly. "He's stable. Maybe. I think I used too much."

"You did what you could, fuzzball," Samila assured him gently. She cast a worried look up at me, one that told me she was concerned for my well-being, but she said nothing more.

Tiba must have grasped what they were saying through context, because she didn't need a translator.

"He lives for now, but he needs more medicine. Medicine I do not have here." Tiba slipped her medicine pouch back on her waist, a dour look drawing the corners of her mouth down and her eyes growing a shade harder. "I know where some is, though."

I didn't like the way she put that. "We just established that we're not alone in this forest, and we're about to have a lot more company," I cautioned.

"I can get it," Tiba repeated, standing up straight and squaring her shoulders. The goblin queen's stare was implacable, despite her size.

I nodded to her in acknowledgement of her bravery but not in agreement. She seemed confident, but I wasn't ready to send more people out there. Maybe we could all go together to get the cure Beedy needed, leave this place before the Scourge arrived. Could I set the drones to do more of the prep work in the meantime to free us up to do this? It would be slower but . . .

I turned back to Trix. "Will Beedy live without a Church healer?"

Trix braced himself on Samila's hand and stood on wobbly legs, then gave a slight shrug.

No good options.

I did some calculations on how much time it would take to get everyone out of the valley and to safety, but Samila cut me off before I could really come to a conclusion. "I know what you're thinking. You're not getting rid of us. We're here to save the world, remember? Besides, there'll be no getting out of this valley now, not while carrying him. The trip itself might kill him."

"When our ride arrives, they may be persuaded to do something for Beedy," Sissa offered. "If anything, a ride out of the valley on a dragon would be less traumatic than a cross-country ride on Geddon's back."

"I am no substitute for a dragon, true. I'm afraid the moment for your ultimate sacrifice must wait a while longer, Ryan," Geddon said with a ghost of a frown before he added: "Oh, yes. On that subject, I have more bad news."

Geddon tapped on an exposed vein of some kind of metal embedded in the tree, about as thick as my thumb. It clinked when the fingertips of his gauntlet struck it.

"I was on my way to tell you when the excitement happened. They're all like this. Metal bits on the inside. Some are thin like this, some much more substantial."

I took a look. Sure enough, there was a big vein of the stuff traveling up through the tree, exposed by the sharpened legs of the worker drones on one side of the trunk and Geddon's broad saw cuts on the other. Even now, three workers clicked and sawed with their forelegs, ripping off little chunks of yellow wood to reveal more, but they never tried to pry at the metal. The vein was a yellowish, silver color, mirrored in some way on the bark of the tree that laid around the cut.

I reached out and put a full mana bar toward trying to Shape it, only just managing to get the whole thing saturated before I was tapped out. The metal vein was larger than it looked, a branching lightning bolt that ran through a good ten feet of the trunk and down into the roots. I Shaped off a sample of the closest part and Consumed it.

"Nickel and osmium," I announced. "Tough stuff, if I'm remembering that part of science class right."

"It is," Geddon confirmed. "And there is a great quantity of it. At first I thought its presence was a fluke of nature, and I sought to cut through with my characteristically heroic effort. Then I ran into more and more."

I took up a piece of bark that was lying on the ground, running a finger over the dual tones of brown and yellow-gray. It pulled my mind back to my first day on Ralqir. "Nali did say this was the best place to train new animators. I always found that odd. Never got around to asking why."

Geddon put a hand up to his scruffy chin, the picture of deep contemplation. "Metal trees?"

"They're mining drills," I realized aloud. "I've seen these things' roots stab through solid rock. I never thought to question the implications of that. The trade-off in energy has to be huge. Then again, this place has magic. Who knows what's possible? They're capable of tapping into ore veins, I bet. They probably bring ore up from deposits down below, slowly, over centuries."

The big Leori frowned and ran a hand over the titanic Mendau. "Does your new understanding include a way to cut through it? Organ Grinder may be a blade of future legend, but our enemies will be within striking distance soon. If our plan is still to use the Light, this will make things hard," Geddon said.

"If you try to cut through this stuff with . . . uh . . . Organ Grinder, it'll drain the battery fast with how much it'll have to refresh the Willing Edge spells. It's too slow," I replied, largely agreeing with his assessment.

This was bad. The trees needed to come down, or we wouldn't be able to hold out long enough.

They had to come down and soon.

"Do what you can," I ordered. "Give the trees the proper cuts so they fall the right way and then expose as much of the metal as possible. I'll figure out a way to get through the rest."

"Can your bugs chew through metal?"

I shook my head, but internally I was already spitballing ways to remedy that issue.

"Ryan!" Samila shouted as she jogged up to the two of us. The look of worry and frustration she wore told me there was even more bad news. "The goblins are gone."

I was in my work area fussing over the new drone prototypes when we got our first legitimate Scourge attack.

The alarm came as a sort of collective tensing-and-reorientation of the turret barrels on the northern side of the fortress all at once. It was a distinctive sound, metal sliding over metal, followed by a harsh snap as they clicked into place in unison, fixing on their target.

Sighing with frustration, I put down my new-and-improved (fingers crossed) drone and made my way up onto the battlements, putting one foot up on an uneven, petrified bark crenelation as I strained my eyes to see what the Scourge had decided to send us. Unlike my turrets, I had to use actual, mundane sight to pick out my targets. Nothing yet. I knew they would be here soon, though.

The goblins were still out there somewhere. The last thing Tiba had said to me before she'd left was that she knew where she could find medicine that could help Beedy. If she and her guards were out there doing that, I hoped they were close to finished. Things were about to get interesting.

Ideally, I would have liked to avoid committing to the fight until they returned. Of course, there were a lot of things I would have liked to have done before this moment.

I still hadn't quite solved the metal-core problem. As I'd predicted, once Geddon had gone around and made the cuts he'd need for the felling of the trees, he'd tried to slice through the center core of one of them with his sword. He only got about halfway into it, however, before the teeth started to spark against the hard metal inside the tree. Then the sword needed to charge or we'd have lost one of the only tools we had to get through the rest of the cutting.

The undercuts, at least, were as good as Geddon could make them—or that's what he said, anyway. The veins of ore inside the trunks were strangely distributed, spread out like blood vessels, and our resident Leori logging expert had to work around them much of the time. Now that I had Leveled my Affinity for the alloy and, consequently, upgraded Detect Nickel, I could confirm that the inside of the trees were a labyrinth of metal veins, impossible to saw all the way through without five more chain-swords and a week of time we didn't have.

I'd set all my older-model worker drones on the problem, having them strip as much of the wood away from the metal parts of the trees as possible, but I still hadn't been able to get the drones to eat away at the metal veins themselves. The workers just didn't have the strength to dig into metal harder than themselves nor the power required to do more than scratch the stuff, even after I gave a few of them experimental pincers to work with.

The most progress we'd made so far was using one of the laser turrets to spew a bunch of purple light at the trunk of one of the trees at close range based on the theory the metal would count as organic. Sure enough, it ate through a *lot* of the organic matter—bark and wood included—leaving only rainbow smudge goop behind, but the metal remained. The inaccuracy of the setup came back to bite us too, in that it started to eat away at the wrong parts of the tree. According to

Geddon, if we took away matter at a low-enough point on the trunk, we might end up with a Mendau in our laps instead of falling away from the fort like we needed them to. No one wanted to be crushed to death.

Beedy was doing poorly. His breathing was labored, and he hadn't awakened for more than a few minutes since he was wounded. Bole had come back a couple of times to check on him, too angry to speak with me but not able to fully stay away, either. He used the pretense of scouting to keep himself occupied at other times and not watch his friend fight for his life. He was out there right now, but I didn't fear for his safety like I did the goblins. The man was too mean and too risk-averse to die.

Once the turrets all turned to the east, not firing yet but certainly tracking something, it only took Trix a moment to pick up on the threat as well. He sounded the alarm just before opening up with his rifle.

I looked over at the three turrets that were tracking the threat, then to where their barrels were pointed, and then put on my mask, just in case. As soon as the creatures were close enough, it would probably be superfluous—

BRRAP! BRRRAAP! BRAAAAAAP!

All of my turrets on the east side of the fort—two triangular clumps of three each—let loose at once, as soon as their targets got into their effective range of 200 yards. Every barrel was oriented vertically.

Up.

There they were, black against the bright-green of the forest canopy. These particular Scourge-Touched had leathery wings, but the monsters themselves weren't exactly flying. Their bodies were powerfully built with muscular legs that ended in gripping claws that they used to swing from branch to branch, only deploying their expansive wings when they needed to glide from one tree to another. The things seemed to be built to glide as much as climb in the thick branches of the Mendau, scrabbling around the trunks and through the thick foliage as much as flapping their wings.

Even from where I was, I could tell they were sizeable creatures, maybe a little larger than the average human from wing tip to wing tip, but their actual bodies were closer in size to goblins than mine, childlike except for the amount of muscle they had.

Interesting creatures. Flying-Squirrel-Monkey-Goblins.

Too bad they were Scourge.

Scourge-Touched Predator Bat defeated.
You have been awarded 72 Experience points. (80 base, +18 nemesis, +8 chain, -10 Level, +40 group, -64 non-combat Class)
Scourge-Touched Predator Bat defeated.
You have been awarded 80 Experience points. (80 base, +18 nemesis, +16 chain, -10 Level, +40 group, -64 non-combat Class)

Scourge-Touched Predator Bat defeated.
You have been awarded 88 Experience points. (80 base, +18 nemesis, +24 chain, -10 Level, +40 group, -64 non-combat Class)
Scourge-Touched Predator Bat defeated.
You have been awarded 96 Experience points. (80 base, +18 nemesis, +32 chain, -10 Level, +40 group, -64 non-combat Class)

Whereas Trix's gun seemed loud before, it was nothing compared to the collective bursts of explosive power from the turrets. Gone were the days of using just enough power to get by. I'd refitted these models for punch and rapidity, their massive recoil uncaring for hypothetical users' delicate muscle tissues or bones or humanoid capabilities to compensate for the kick. They were all raw, explosive, ballistic efficiency, and their terrible reports could be felt in everyone's guts.

The forest collectively winced as the area became sonic chaos for a brief, ten-second span.

Then the guns stopped as suddenly as they had started, and in the deafening silence, the sound of soft bodies *thupp!*-ing into the forest floor was all we could hear. One or two bats—perhaps the fastest of their kind, or the last to die—smacked wetly against the fortress walls and rolled down the roots, leaving greasy smears of mystery fluid behind before they disappeared into one of the standing puddles.

I ran a discerning eye over the carnage, nodding in satisfaction. None of them had even come close.

"First round goes to us, I guess," Sissa called from her post on the battlements. She looked down at the crumpled form of the predator bat that had hit the wall. "No way the goblins didn't hear that. I hope whatever they're doing, they do it fast."

Suddenly something roared in the distance—something wild and unmistakably huge. Additionally, disturbingly, on the wind from the north, there was an unmistakable change in the ambient sound—a white noise that drifted through the air and tickled at the ear, just quiet enough to allow me to momentarily pretend it wasn't what I knew it was.

"What the hell is that?" Geddon asked, spinning to look in every direction at once and holding Organ Grinder in a high guard.

"Many, many things." Trix shuddered. "Distant but many. As we feared, we have been discovered prematurely."

I pulled off my mask and let it drop to the forest floor. There would be no need for it anymore. Ever.

"On the bright side," I ventured, "we just pressed pause on the apocalypse. Let's give Ralqir a moment to catch her breath."

Samila let out a celebratory "Whoop!" and shot me a predatory grin from her spot on the wall. I did my best to match her with one of my own. In a way it felt good to finally get on with the real fight.

We'll give them hell. The rest is up to you, Jassin.

As I turned to head back to my workshop, I spared one final glance over my shoulder as the last body of the Scourge scouts thudded to the ground.

CHAPTER TWENTY-SEVEN

Buy Some Time

I t didn't take long for the first of the Scourge ground forces to arrive the next morning. They materialized from the fog—a motley bunch of small, quick, largely herbivorous animals ranging from the size of rabbits to large dogs. Trix gave us the warning long before they got into range, and I was able to reach the top of the wall before they entered our defensive perimeter. Their squeaks and screeches of blind rage weren't nearly as intimidating as the proper Scourge-Touched I'd faced in Eclipse, but these things certainly didn't lack for courage, going into a frenzy as soon as they saw us, and charging headlong into the guns.

They lasted about as long as the predator bats had and gave almost zero Experience.

The next waves were less direct. They circled us like wolves, from far out, dancing in and out of turret range so that the guns only got off a round or two of fire before the Scourge scattered and backed off. Then they would do it again and again to a different part of the perimeter every time.

The sound of the short bursts of gunfire were pretty normal now, even in the late hours of night. It was hardly even something to get up for anymore, which was good because I was having a hell of a time with our giant-tree problem.

"They're testing our defenses, Ryan," Sissa ruminated quietly from next to the fire, its dull illumination exaggerating the edges of her scales. Around us, the rest of the team—with the exception of Trix—were all in their bedrolls, asleep from a long day of fortification work.

I gripped the casting bowl in my hand tightly as more of my mana flowed inside, holding my instructions for this iteration in my mind all the while.

Automate a worker drone in this shape with six Imbued legs that form when the Leg Triggers are activated. Activate the Leg Triggers immediately when done being Automated and outside the Casting Bowl. Use 400 mana divided equally among six different tapering layers to form the frontal cone. Place a Trigger in the frontal cone that . . .

And so on. The instructions were becoming lengthy and complex, and maintaining my mind's hold on them the entire time I was Automating the thing was extremely difficult, not to mention expensive. Luckily, I only had to do this once, after which it would be mostly self-perpetuating.

"I said, 'They're testing our defenses.' I don't like it. There's almost a logic to it," Sissa stated more loudly this time.

I dropped the finished bowl on the workbench and slumped over, letting my sweat-soaked hair droop down over my eyes. Sleep called to me, but it was from far away. Too much still needed doing.

"Yeah, I figure they're waiting for enough bodies to make their move this time," I replied.

Sissa cast a worried glance up at Trix's basket perch from which he was even now using his excellent eyes to watch for just such a thing.

"They're getting smarter," she said.

I shrugged tiredly. "Something like that. Learning, maybe."

"They're getting smarter, and we're no closer to ready."

I sighed and turned around, grabbing the new Casting Bowl and setting it on the shelf above the growing mound of metal slag on the floor—the "ant pile," as I'd named it. It was essentially a mound of scrap metal that had been leftover from my new drone-production line—little bits that had been carved off the new models and allowed to collect on the floor to be put to use later. Right now, the mound was about as tall as my ankle and twice as wide, composed entirely of silvery yellow-and-brown popcorn kernels of unshaped metal. Meanwhile, the Casting Bowl directly above was overflowing with dead drones awaiting a re-Shape and recharge.

"We're closer to ready than we were," I said, waving at the setup and then to the new Casting Bowl. "I had to increase the bandwidth of our production to prevent any more traffic jams, but that's done now. The drones should charge at double-speed and work faster."

"Was wondering if you were still working on those things," Sissa chided. "I thought we were moving onto the backup plan, since this one was taking too much time."

"I'm about to do the backup. Really," I insisted. "If I get this working properly, we might have a shot at not running out of metal. Ever."

"Except we aren't aiming for 'ever' are we?" she asked. "Furthermore, we might not make it to 'ever' if we get overrun immediately. Why have me along if you're not going to respect my tactical advice, Ryan?"

"You invited yourself along," I said, trying to keep my tone light but not able to entirely conceal my insecurity.

This was going to work. It *had* to.

That didn't keep me from doubting myself. Beedy's labored breathing from his bedroll was a constant reminder of how fallible I was.

"Beside the point," Sissa said, waving a dismissive hand. "I'm here. We're all here, and we all have an interest in living through this. I thought we discussed that you were going to use one of your explosives to bring down the trees."

I nodded in the affirmative, but I didn't try to conceal my doubts. The size of these things and the metal cores they had made Shaped charges a risky gamble. Using them may or may not work, since there was a lot of mass they had to cut through to bring the trees down. Not just that, but if we went around limiting the approaches to the base right now, how would Tiba get back? Every tree felled meant lower odds of ever seeing our goblins again. What if they were out there now and looking for an opportunity to rush forward?

A hand squeezed my wrist, interrupting my train of thought. Sissa was in front of me, on her feet, her expression somewhat softened. "It's the right decision, Ryan. Don't let what happened keep you from seeing clearly." She leaned forward to make sure my eyes met hers. "Queen Tiba will understand the necessity of it. Of hard decisions. You need to trust her."

I did trust her. I trusted Tiba implicitly. What I didn't trust was that bringing down the trees immediately would help us in the short-term. The goblins needed a way back for as long as I could give them. They deserved a way back. Beedy deserved it, too. That was what I truly believed.

I resisted the urge to glance over at Beedy for the hundredth time and torture myself even more, instead choosing to meet the dragonkin's stare directly.

"I'll get to work on the charges now, but I still think the drones are the right play. Throw some trust my way too," I ventured.

The constructs were already making visible progress on the metal inside the trees. That's where our little ant pile had come from. My constructs weren't quite hard or strong enough to mine the metal with their appendages, so instead I'd come up with a solution that didn't require physical force.

State Change was the answer. An expensive answer but maybe the only one.

The model I'd finally settled upon "mined" the nickel-osmium alloy by essentially pressing their sharpened heads into the metal of the trees, then flash-boiling tiny portions of themselves to quickly bring the foreign alloy to its melting point. The melted metal would then flow from the tree onto the heads and backs of the drones, where it would cool enough to stick. The drones that came back from mining duty came back heavy, but once they were back in the Casting Bowl, the excess was Shaped off and allowed to fall into the ant mound as the drones went through their recharge.

Sissa glanced over at the honestly pitiful amount of metal my method had collected thus far, then back to me with a pained smile. "I hope you're right. I'll also try to *trust* that you're right. How about that?"

"Movement to the north!" Trix shouted. "A large mass! I think this is it!"

Everyone was up on their feet within seconds, hands on weapons and armor already secured.

I got up to the wall via the stairs and heard the nearest trio of turrets snap into line, acquiring targets as I passed.

The night was pitch-black and foggy, meaning I couldn't see a thing out there, but I trusted Trix's night vision and my turrets.

This was it. The Scourge were coming in large numbers this time.

I heard Samila and Sissa shuffle into place on this side of the fort, armor clinking as straps were tightened, and I assumed Bole was getting into position too, though I was never able to hear the guy when he moved. We were all stacked around the north quarter of the wall, spread out to cover a wide semicircle where the charge would probably hit. The turrets would have to cover the other parts of the walls that we couldn't.

There was no slow start to the action tonight. Suddenly the turrets opened on full auto and didn't stop. Thunderous booms of propellant accompanied hollow snaps as dozens of bullets broke the sound barrier all at once, the muzzle flashes from the guns lighting up the surrounding forest and my comrades in an odd, strobing slideshow of purple. The light also dimly illuminated the distant vanguard of the monsters as they approached—never enough for me to pick them out individually but enough to discern there was a massive amount of them.

I made my new machine-pistol materialize in my hand. It was a compact-but-heavy model with a reinforced bolt-carrier and action, a wide, stubby barrel, and a bottom-fed magazine. I flipped the pistol over into my prosthetic hand; then, in a flash, I held my sword, too.

The snarling faces of Baned, beasts, and other, unfamiliar humanoids withered and collapsed as the turrets poured on the damage, closest targets first. Supersonic streams of lead shredded entire swaths of monsters, mowing them down like grass, cracking through bone and perforating secondary targets behind.

The Scourge tried to compensate as they'd done with their scouts, redirecting the mass to attempt to dodge with individual monsters, but this close to the guns, the maneuver lost more than it gained. The sea of bodies parted under the onslaught, the entire blob moving as one to avoid further damage, but the turrets' tracking was flawless. Wherever the Scourge stuck out its neck, said neck would be obliterated.

Despite its efforts, the Scourge was losing lots of bodies, and it eventually opted for a full-on charge with no wasted effort to spare itself further losses.

The horde poured over the inner circle where our barrier of sunlight was slated to be, and I suddenly wished I'd brought down the trees like Sissa had asked. There were so many of them.

For my turrets, it was like trying to hold back the tide with a broom. Where the Scourge couldn't use the tree trunks as cover, the overlapping, overwhelming fire from the guns would create a shallow cavity in the enemy's mass, pulping the softer targets and crippling the others, but as soon as the guns moved onto closer threats, the horde would reassert itself. Damage and Experience messages whizzed through my feed, to which I only gave a cursory glance to see what species we were dealing with here. The sheer variety was staggering.

The tide of monsters flowed into the trench, barely stopping as they were forced onto the sharpened stakes Geddon and the dragonkin had carved and buried. More of the monsters died, but the Scourge simply, remorselessly used their dead as springboards to get at the fortress walls. Once there, they slipped into the deep shadows, invisible to me and to the turrets. The base of the wall was at too-steep an angle for the light or bullets to reach.

When the mass hit the trench, Sissa hit us with her Duty and Mercy spell, and I could feel heat flow into my stiff limbs and my muscles loosen. If I'd had a real heart, it would have pounded in my ears.

My companions were already slashing and stabbing before I could even see what we were fighting. Nightmare pairings of armored humanoids squaring off against leaping horrors tempted my eyes away from my own portion of the wall, but I couldn't allow myself to look. Only a handful of seconds later, I had my own problems to deal with.

The first snarling face I was able to single out came up right in front of me, and the glance I got was only thanks to the harsh, fleeting flashes from the muzzles of the guns. Large. Gangly. Too many limbs. Too many eyes. It moved oddly, spasmodically flailing as it gained purchase on the lip of the wall.

Willing Edge [10 MP/sec]

I slashed at the thing before it could get fully upright, and my sword connected with something solid before the blade went through and out. There was a gurgle, and then a clawed hand raked across my knees, drawing a pained snarl from me but only a handful of HP in real Damage. The next spurt of muzzle flash showed me more creatures like this one on the battlements, one of which was now dead, missing two arms and with holes in its cranium—too small for my turrets but just right for Trix's rifle.

I didn't get a chance to yell out a "Thanks" before more of the creatures bubbled into view.

Carefully, with as much form as I could, I advanced, slashing with Willing Edge at what arms and faces I could reach to give myself space. Then, when I was nearly looking over the lip of the wall, I brandished my machine-pistol. I squeezed the trigger, dumping the entire thirty-round mag down the vertical face of the wall and into the trench.

PRRRRRRRRRRRRTTT!

You hit Scourge-Touched Bekal for 24 Damage.
You hit Scourge-Touched Bekal for 21 Damage.

Scourge-Touched Bekal is bleeding.
You hit Scourge-Touched Mountain Cat for 24 Damage.
Scourge-Touched Mountain Cat is bleeding.
You hit Scourge-Touched Goblin for 22 Damage.
Scourge-Touched Goblin is bleeding.
You hit Scourge-Touched Vine Stag for 19 Damage.
Scourge-Touched Vine Stag is stunned.
You hit Scourge-Touched Goblin for 26 Damage.
. . .

Pistols is now Level 5.
Upgrade Paths available.

The pistol bucked in my hand so hard I could barely maintain my grip without using an Ability. I was using the same big ammo as my turrets and an over-saturated propulsion charge, and the power was such that even the strength of my prosthetic was tested by the recoil. The rest of my body, however, felt the power of those shots more acutely as the kinetic energy was transferred from my metal arm to the rest of me. My insides rattled, and I had to brace my feet and lean forward to keep myself from staggering. Two seconds of automatic fire, and the gun was dry.

I backed up, flicking the mag release and letting it fall to the ground. Another clicked into place as soon as it was out of my Spatial Storage.

The dragonkin sisters had not been idle. Several creatures lay dead at their feet, and I had to assume many more were down and injured below, not having been able to clamber up the wall before the women's swords took them. To my left, Bole was similarly engaged in the fight, though his portion of the wall was mostly clear. He leapt from spot to spot, shouting and cursing as he sliced at the monsters' necks, cut tendons, and impaled them through their eyes before they could haul themselves fully into view. He never hit a target more than twice, and none of the monsters came even close to touching him.

FWOOSH!

Yellow-orange illumination filled the left side of my vision as one of the flamer turrets engaged threats at the gate. I turned toward it reflexively, but the fire itself was beyond the walls and out of my sight. It turned the wall and our heavy wooden gate into black silhouettes. At the gate, a shadow that must have been Geddon stabbed down at a mass of creatures as they clawed at the thick wood.

An agonized scream sounded out from behind me, and I turned just in time to see Samila go down, clutching the back of her leg as a Baned gurgled and died under her boot.

No. Not this time.

With a shout, I charged, feet carrying me over dead and dying monsters, my sword cutting down some kind of emaciated ape-wolf, my machine pistol spitting bursts that raked across the expanding line of enemy that were now cresting the wall. When the pistol ran dry on ammo, I bashed anything within reach with the heavy barrel.

When I got to Samila, she was already trying to stand on her own, but I could tell she was hurting. I slipped under her shield arm and propped both of us up together. My sword arm was next to useless wrapped around her waist, so I made my weapon disappear and brought out my last pistol mag instead.

Samila and I spent the next few minutes together. Her sword work was quick and powerful, but with a whole other person attached to her at the hip, every swing was clumsy, less precise than her usual perfection. Her body attempted to flow into forms her leg could no longer support as she fought the horde, and she was having a hard time compensating. I could feel her torso heaving as the effort and the pain left her more breathless with every move. All I could do was hold on tight and keep her from falling. I aimed and fired at individual creatures as they approached and bashed others if they got too close, while Samila finished them off with her blade.

At some point, the buzzing of Geddon's chain-sword ripped through the backdrop of chaos, followed shortly by a deep roar that drowned all other sound.

Then, as if a switch had been flipped, all was still, silent except for everyone's heavy breathing, the crackle of burning flamer fuel, and the hiss-pop of slowly cooling gun barrels.

Gently, I set Samila down and summoned a rock to hit with Volatility for illumination.

Dead Scourge lined the forest floor and filled the trench. Severed, broken parts lay everywhere, and black blood dripped from still-twitching, monstrous bodies. All of us bled from multiple wounds, though I didn't remember where most of mine had come from.

"Too few—Too few bodies," Sissa panted. She hadn't sheathed her sword yet, instead turning from side to side, the tip of her sword tracking the area along with her eyes.

I looked again. She was right. With the amount of lead we had just thrown out there, there should have been far more carnage than what we saw. The concentration of the dead seemed to be highest near the walls but it tapered off gradually into the distance, where the Scourge's heaviest casualties should have been. Optimal range for the turrets.

"They must have taken them. They're recycling their dead," I said. "They were doing it back in Eclipse, too. It's why the goblins liked to burn their fallen."

"True. That means we'll have to burn these as well," Sissa said. "For various reasons. Disease being one of them."

"Not just that. Look." Samila grunted as she wrenched a pressure bandage into place on her leg.

I turned my attention to our little courtyard. Geddon was there in the center of the circle, next to the fire. The door—such as it was—was in splinters, and a number of charred monsters were dead next to it while several more were in pieces around Geddon. One of them, a mottled orange and black thing that had once been vaguely humanoid, dwarfed the rest. It was taller and broader than even Geddon (or it would have been if it hadn't been bisected), with thick, powerful arms and legs, wicked spikes on its knuckles, and overdeveloped fangs in its still-open mouth.

Geddon, for his part, heaved for breath and slumped down next to the body, but he looked as happy as I'd ever seen him as he rested the point of his chainsword inside the creature's chest cavity. A little further back, behind the Leori, Beedy slept in his bedroll, untouched.

Thank Constance for that.

"They're still testing us," Sissa speculated. "Testing themselves, too. I wouldn't exactly call it 'strategic thinking,' but they are at least as clever as some of the smarter beasts."

"More than that, Princess," Bole corrected. He was busily cleaning his sword with the ragged clothing from one of the Returned he'd downed on the wall. Once the blade was passably clean, he sheathed it and gestured down to the dead, giant cat-person. "The little ones were a feint to hide the gresh there. I've played dice with less-clever folk."

I looked out into the night, pumping more mana into my pebble light to spread the illumination. Nothing but fog and shadow. How many of them were left out there? How much of itself had the Scourge committed to this fight?

"Trix? Do I want to know?" I called up to the vulpa's sniper perch.

"No. You do not want to know," came his terse reply. He sounded as ragged as the rest of us, even though he hadn't mixed it up in melee like we had.

"Those trees really need to come down," Sissa said. She didn't say "I told you so," but I heard it in her tone.

"Yeah," I affirmed. "Yeah, they do."

Tiba, I hope you know what you're doing.

CHAPTER TWENTY-EIGHT

Do the Unexpected

The new-and-improved gate we were forced to cobble together was neither new nor improved. Well, that's not quite fair to say. The gate was "new" in that it was a new configuration of old materials—in this case, repurposed logs and crossbeams cannibalized from our stake wall. As for the "improved" part, it was very easy to open. Right now it was just being held up by friction and prayer. An outsider might argue that this was actually a weakness, but what do they know?

The hard edge of Samila's pauldron dug uncomfortably into the middle of my ribcage as the five of us pressed as close to the new gate as possible. In front of me, Sissa and Geddon both had their hands on the diagonal support braces that held the gate closed and kept it from falling backward into the fort, and the two were readying themselves to pull. At the very back of the formation, Bole *ting!*-ed the naked steel of one of his hidden knives off the hilt of another that way he did just before any sort of up-close fighting.

At our feet, a steady trickle of tiny ant-bullets marched under the gate and made their way to the reloading station. If one knew how to listen, they would be able to hear the gentle whir of the stirring systems and the *click click click click* of the tiny pistons inside the machine shoving bullets back into magazines.

Worker drones—fat and misshapen with newly mined metal—dragged themselves over the ragged stone tops of the walls to plop heavily onto the stone floor. From there they would only have about fifty feet further until they met their final rest in one of the re-Shaping bowls.

The guns were still firing, of course, in little fits and starts. I could feel Damage and Experience notifications trickling by in my Combat Log. I'd long since minimized it. The flow of information had ceased to be useful a while back, ever since the guns had started being pretty much "on" 24/7.

Not all the turrets were active at once, of course. The Scourge were still teasing at the edges of our defenses, keeping us on our toes by probing the perimeter where they could get away with it, but at least two or three of the guns were engaged with *something* out there all the time, generally in one- or two-second bursts. By now, the Scourge had figured out that my guns weren't going to shoot through tree trunks, so they liked to hide in those dead zones and peek out until one of the guns sent them back into hiding. Today, it seemed they were probing mainly from the east.

A whistle—some birdcall I didn't recognize—came from Trix's hanging sniper nest. That was the signal.

Together, Sissa and Geddon yanked on the pull ropes attached to the support braces, and the gate groaned as it pitched back and slammed into the floor.

"Go!" Sissa shouted, hefting her equipment onto one shoulder, and the five of us surged forward.

It was only a second before the collective howl from the surrounding Scourge shook the forest, louder even than the guns. Then it was *on*. We'd made it maybe a dozen steps before the entirety of our ballistic arsenal was back to spewing lead in every direction, suddenly inundated with valid targets.

The Scourge were coming for us.

As we'd planned, Geddon, Bole, and I all took positions on the outside of the formation to shield the dragonkin and their precious cargo. My eyes darted everywhere, waiting for the first monster I would have to fight, and despite my Body score and relative level of fitness, my breathing quickly drowned out most other sounds on the battlefield in my ears.

The women set the pace. Sissa and Samila, despite their full armor and awkward burdens, stepped surprisingly lightly, hopping over exposed roots and fallen branches. The dark, metal constructs in their hands jangled together dangerously as they ran, and every clink and clank conjured a new nightmare I had to consciously dispel from my mind. I'd opted to over-juice the clamp Triggers rather than potentially using too little, so severed fingers weren't entirely pessimistic fantasy. The sooner the sisters were rid of their payloads, the better I would feel, even if we were going to be hip-deep in Scourge afterward.

The Scourge weren't ready for our surprise sortie. Precious few of them were out here in numbers and in range to respond. Scattered clumps of corrupted animals flanked by nimble, snarling Baned were the first enemies we saw alive. They sprang out from behind trees and up from depressions in the ground, never in large-enough numbers to be a problem for the guns but still alarming in how close they'd come to the walls.

Bullets whizzed past us, snapping like tiny firecrackers as air pockets collapsed in their wakes. Anything unlucky enough to be in our way and brave enough to come out of hiding fell to the ground full of holes or missing vital parts of their anatomy, and we never even had to raise our weapons. If the Scourge had been hoping to ambush us with these groups, they'd either not gotten sufficient numbers in place to do so, or they'd underestimated how mechanically efficient the tracking on my turrets had become.

That meant the Scourge would have to stick with swarm tactics if it wanted to catch us out. Good. That would take time to materialize.

Breathing heavily despite the short distance traveled, we reached the inner perimeter well before the Scourge could, and our formation skidded to a stop. Those that weren't carrying chain constructs fanned out and formed a protective barrier for our demolitionists. The tree that would be our first victim of the day had what looked like a huge bite taken out of it on the side that faced home, courtesy of the worker drones.

Samila carefully uncoiled the multi-hinged device in her hand, allowing it to droop down until it nearly touched the ground, then began to whirl it around herself. She swung it like an Olympian with a throwing hammer, around and around, letting her body counterbalance the weight, lengthening the chain link by link.

WHOOSH! WHOOSH!

In the distance, I saw that the Scourge were gathering themselves, singular bodies streaming in from the side while a main column of monsters flowed like black water, approaching the outer perimeter en masse, a rushing river of flesh and bone. Wild-eyed, open-mouthed monsters rushed forward to throw themselves into the jaws of my machines. The flowing mass of bodies roiled over one another, uncaring if those next to them were blown to bits, their only desire to get one step closer to killing me. Monsters on the outside of the mass died quickly, but their bodies fulfilled their purpose well enough, forming semi-solid banks through which the rest could flow forward.

I cast a sideways glance at the spinning dragonkin. It had only been a few seconds, and it was already taking too long. Judging by the tenor of the turrets, the Scourge were going for broke. Their quarry had come out of its hole, and this was their chance to end it. They had to be taking huge losses, but what did they care? If they had the numbers to bog us down and drown us, that would be it. The turrets would stop firing, they'd have their human, and they'd go back to assimilating the planet.

Come on. Come on.

Finally, Samila finally let fly. The hinged rope of Shaped charges whirled through the air and smacked up against the bare flesh of the Mendau tree. The chain—as it was programmed to do as soon as it was in contact with organic matter—deployed hooked blades from its edges that sank into the wood and contracted with a series of clunks.

I dropped out of line to run a hand over the links and confirm they were working.

Good. They're already beginning to glow.

I gave everyone a thumbs-up.

"Done!" Samila shouted just before a body thumped down in the middle of our formation.

"Eyes up! They're above!" Geddon boomed, cranking the engine of his sword as he expertly bisected another airborne creature.

Above, dozens of spindly black figures were busily shimmying down toward us from the top of our tree. Another of them bent its legs and pounced, rocketing down toward us. But this one seemed to lose its enthusiasm halfway down and flopped bonelessly just short of my feet. Squinting, I saw tiny needle holes dotting the Baned's torso.

Hot damn, Trix. You're scary.

I exchanged a look with Sissa, who held her own device that needed to be deployed. She gave the chain an experimental lift, then glanced toward the oncoming horde. The Scourge were getting closer, maybe a hundred yards away. Meanwhile, more bodies dropped out of the trees as Trix kept the skies clear. The sergeant was clearly weighing the odds, not liking what she was coming up with.

I was no tactical genius, but I didn't like it either. We had maybe a 60/40 shot at felling another tree without getting bogged down in a fight. Then again, we needed this. We couldn't last forever without changing the landscape.

"We can do one more!" I yelled to everyone.

Sissa hesitated for half a heartbeat but then gave me the nod.

"One more," she agreed. "Go!"

To the next tree we went. This time, we didn't get there before the Scourge, however. There was a pack of monsters huddled behind the great trunk, out of sight of the guns—wounded, bleeding, but more-than-willing to attack us. Meanwhile, even more streamed in from our surroundings, dashing from other points of cover to get to this one. The guns cut down what they could, but the sheer number of targets was starting to overwhelm them.

Geddon charged, as Geddon loved to do, Organ Grinder revved, never even breaking stride as he barreled into the enemy. Samila covered his left with her shield, while I took his right.

As I raised my pistol up to take aim, I felt the brush of something unfamiliar behind my eyes, a strange potential, a sort of gentle readiness that told me I had the option to do something more here.

> Death Eye: While aiming with a pistol-Class weapon, you are passively made aware of the most vulnerable points in your target's body. Focusing on these points will highlight them in your vision in a manner of your choosing. Targets of significant power may require longer periods of aiming with Death Eye to reveal their vulnerabilities.

Level 5 pistols had been good to me.

I allowed my new Ability to refocus my eyes briefly. What had once been a writhing mass of disparate humanoid and animal bodies now had a new layer on top of it. Blotches of red, pulsing light began to pop in over the monsters as I swept my muzzle over the lot. It was the places you'd expect such as the eyes, the hearts, intersections of bones that could cripple, spinal columns, nerve clusters that would paralyze, and so on. What's more, I could almost feel the slightest sort of tug on my aim just as a new glowing vulnerability popped into existence, as if each one had a weak gravitational pull.

Death Eye would be a downright godly Skill for someone with a steady hand like Trix. With Death Eye and a precision instrument like a Colonial anti-material rifle, maybe a las-model or something, he could destroy whole buildings' worth of nasties.

With me, though . . . I was a quantity-over-quality guy, I guessed.

My machine-pistol barked.

Most targets that caught my eye died with multiple holes in their chests. Others—tightly packed in as they were—were victims of the massive recoil and the weapon's propensity to shift my aim up and to the left. I didn't fight it. Instead, I went with it, allowing the bucking steel bull to draw my fire sideways, drifting from the general vicinity of one glowing red point to the next in a scything motion that ended a new life every other round.

Those that got close, I paused to stab with my sword, and those I couldn't get a clean line on, Bole took from the flank. They never saw him coming. It was almost too easy for a man as fast as he was, especially with monsters that paid almost no mind to him now that their real prey (me) was in sight.

Sissa swung her Shaped charge from the safer side of the tree behind us—the side with all the guns and none of the Scourge. I wasn't worried about her getting swarmed anymore. Now that I was within biting distance, the Scourge only had eyes for me, and I gave them my undivided attention, hacking and shooting a new threat every second.

CLUNK!

"Done! Back off!" Sissa ordered.

Geddon took one more mighty swing with Organ Grinder, and the ripping teeth cleaved through four monsters at once.

"Back!" he growled at all parties involved. Strangely, even the Scourge seemed to listen, pausing momentarily in the ruined mess of their compatriots to give the big lion man and his chain-sword some space.

"Back!" Geddon ordered again, but the spell was broken. The monsters charged once more, leaping to try and get past him.

Well, if they weren't going to listen to reason . . .

I emptied the rest of my mag in their faces. Seven kills in under a second, thanks to Death Eye. That got us some more space.

"Break off now!" Samila shouted.

As one, we made a break for it, away from the half-cover of the tree and out into the open where the turrets could cover us. Sissa was there waiting for us, sword out, shield in place, but once we were all together again, we ran.

"Home! Don't stop!" she called. No one had to be told twice.

The Scourge tried to follow, nipping at our heels, but the majority of them met a quick, messy end. Those that did manage to get into our shadow to avoid the guns . . . well, Bole and I made sure to give them a proper welcome. Knives flashed. Bullets flew. We punished them until our pursuers were too wounded or dead to keep up with us.

Pistols is now Level 6.

Bole let out a victorious whoop as our pursuers scattered to find cover and wait for more numbers.

Grinning, I slapped another magazine into my pistol before resummoning my sword. We might just get away with—

"Turn! Turn right!" Sissa screamed from further ahead.

Something had made it to the approach before we did: a massive, toad-like creature the size of a cargo hauler. It seemed to slide forward on its belly, using its legs to "swim" toward us and at surprising speed. The craggy, gray skin that covered most of the monster's exposed body looked more like rock than flesh, and it didn't seem like it was just for show. Dozens of bullets pang!-ed into the creature over and over, while little shards of rock shot into the air with every impact. Despite the pummeling it was getting, it seemed unbothered, either too far gone with the Scourge plague to experience pain or too tough for a bullet. Other Scourge crawled alongside the toad-thing too, using its shadow as a safe zone.

We juked hard to the right, but the bulky monster made the corner with us, keeping itself precisely between us and home. It was shockingly nimble for its size, only slightly slower than our top speed.

"Is that a damned ignarog?!" Bole shrieked. "Where'd they get an ignarog?!"

"I don't know!" Sissa replied.

Giant toad to our flank, and in front, a countless mass of Scourge poured toward us, and we were on course to meet them in a headlong charge if we didn't change direction.

"We're being herded!" I observed, loud enough to be heard by all.

"Ryan! They aren't dying fast enough!" Sissa made an observation of her own. "They should be dying faster!"

A quick check over my shoulder and ahead of us confirmed Sissa's suspicions for me. "Some of the turrets are stuck trying to bring down the big frog!" I yelled back.

"Tell them to get the smaller ones, Monk!" Bole shrieked. "Ignarog are deeplings! Unless you brought a pickax, you're not bringing it down!"

"That's not how it works! They aren't programmed to move on until their target is dead!"

At that moment, the ignarog lunged sideways in a surprise attack, rearing up, then crashing down next to us. Dirt and tree litter sprayed us, and the ground shook with the thing's weight.

Bole's voice went up a few octaves. "That's really shit magic, Monk!"

"Shut up, Bole! Or go get your own magic!" Sissa castigated him.

The main body of Scourge were getting close, so close I could see the spittle flying from their mouths as they slashed at each other in their frenzy.

"We turn and fight then!" Samila said. "Right now! Turn and slay the big one!"

"Secon—Seconded!" Geddon puffed. As usual, the running part of combat was not Geddon's strong suit.

"I hate that you're right," Sissa agreed, but that was all the hesitation she allowed herself. "Turn now! Sam, Bole, go for the belly and the joints. Bleed it! Geddon, screaming and chopping!"

That was all the big guy needed to hear. Geddon summoned a lungful of air and roared a challenge at the massive creature as he charged, chain-sword held out like a lance.

Sissa's instruction for me was a bit more open-ended.

"Ryan, crowd control!"

Crowd control? I'm doing that right now, and it's not working. That's the problem.

I guessed I could run around to give everyone else time to fight, but that just meant I would die exhausted if they couldn't bring down the toad in time.

That just left one option.

Let's just hope this goes better than last time.

CHAPTER TWENTY-NINE

Run Some Tests

The ignarog barked as it and Geddon charged one another. Meanwhile the army of smaller Scourge flooded in from everywhere else with howls and angry snarls. With several of the guns preoccupied trying to bring down a target that wouldn't die, the little ones were back to being a huge problem.

Crowd control. Right.

Unfortunately, the turrets *were* my crowd control. That was my whole damned thing, and suddenly that wasn't good enough. What was I supposed to do?

Well, there was at least one part of that horde I could delay with a thought. Better to do it now before the Scourge got curious as to why we were out here in the first place. I triggered Volatility, setting off the explosive cores inside the constructs we'd just deployed.

The charges went off flawlessly, almost entirely in sync, each link of the multi-hinged "chain" sending explosively formed, penetrating projectiles through the gnawed flesh of the Mendau trees and severing what was left of their metal cores—or at least enough of them to matter. With an earth-shaking groan, the two slain titans fell, crashing through the branches of their neighbors before finally sending a towering storm of dust and debris high into the sky.

Through the cloud of dust, glorious, brilliant rays of white-hot sunlight lanced down, cutting through gloom that hadn't been disturbed in centuries. The Scourge that were lucky enough not to be crushed under the building-sized falling trees were practically vaporized. Their flesh bubbled and steamed before peeling away while their blood dissolved into smoke. Others went up in flames, eyes first. Collectively, the tenor of the howling voices shifted, adopting a pitch with undertones of fear.

As for me, I fought not to retch.

Suddenly, that part of the forest was very unpopular. The Scourge redirected its minions to go far, far around the new no-go zone.

That job done, I spared one last glance back at my friends as they surrounded the big toad. They seemed to have things well in hand on their end, or at least no one had died yet. Now what was I going to do on my end?

I'd thought about this problem before in my spare time, being caught out in the open like this. Of course it was always a remote, unlikely thing, which would only happen if many, many things went wrong all at once, a "wow, I'd be really screwed if this happened" sort of thing that I spent most of my time and preparations trying to prevent. My working philosophy was, generally, if I ended up having to think on the fly, I had failed in some way. I frontloaded my thinking, choosing to do it when I was calm and rational.

Until recently, that had been working pretty well. No reason to mess with success. Plus, I had all sorts of other stuff to occupy my time and brain space.

Well, now the moment was here, and I was thinking on the fly, meaning I'd failed spectacularly, and all I had to hand were the beginnings of projects, untested ideas, an exploding sword, and a pile of stones that I had meant to use for Volatility.

That left the science projects. The *untested* science projects.

I let out a long breath, hoping my misgivings and sense of self-preservation would be expelled with it.

The mortar tube appeared in my hand.

Okay, so "mortar tube" was probably a misnomer. This thing sucked at being a mortar tube. Despite the System still classifying it as such, the device in my hand didn't launch things high up in the air to rain down on my enemies like I'd envisioned. Whether that was because my munitions were too heavy or my propulsion method was too weak, it just hadn't worked out like that.

It was one of my first forays into air-powered munitions—essentially a long, wide tube with piping and several Trigger bulbs with ultra-compressed air, attached to a shuttle plate that pushed munitions out of the tube at high velocity. I wanted it to be able to launch explodey things over long distances, so we could tackle big masses of Scourge before they could form a good mob.

The problem with my air-powered designs, however, was that they just didn't have the oomph of my explosive Volatility cubes. The test rounds—spherical hunks of metal about the size of Trix's fist—only flew about fifty yards, maximum. Rocks only got us another ten or so yards further afield. At that range, we'd be better off letting the turrets do the job.

However, the way I figured, I could still make the time I'd sunk into the design worth it . . .

. . . by attaching it to me.

I flipped the tube until it was pointing out, then slipped the forearm of my prosthetic into the new attachment rings I'd Shaped onto the side. The Triggers activated automatically, tightening the clamps around the black metal of my arm until the whole thing was *solidly* in place. I didn't feel much of anything, my metal arm being what it was, but with the forces involved, I was pretty sure I'd become an amputee again if I'd tried this maneuver with my fleshy arm.

One flash of magic later, and I slid a little ball of Automated metal into the end of the tube and listened to the retention iris click closed.

Okay. Please don't explode in my face.

FOOP!

My invention might not have been a very effective mortar, but it certainly kicked like one. I felt the recoil in my entire body, as if my prosthetic had just gotten fist-bumped by a giant. My Body score being what it was helped me stay upright, but if my feet hadn't been braced, I'd have been on my ass now. The shot—angled slightly up to give it some arc—was slow enough to be tracked with the naked eye, but only just. That was okay, though. I was just relieved it was far away from me before—

FUFFFFF!

As it was programmed to do, once the metal ball got within ten or so feet of a valid target, the Automated matter flash-ionized in midair directly above said target, namely the concentrated mass of monsters. What was once roughly a pound and a half of brass became a rapidly expanding, highly energetic gas, igniting everything it touched as it suddenly heated up to somewhere in the ballpark of five thousand degrees Fahrenheit. The affected area went up like a bonfire, not just from the gassed brass but from the Scourge themselves suddenly reaching their ignition point, along with the leaves on the ground, the bark of the trees, the air . . .

The blowback reached me in under a second, oven-hot, even though the affected area was thirty yards away.

The burst of Experience messages practically punched me in the brain stem.

Mental note: The airburst programming works. Not to be used in close quarters.

One reload later, I brought the tiny bead on the end of the mortar into line with the next closest mass. This one needed to make contact.

FOOP!

I didn't hit the Scourge I was aiming for. I'd accidentally aimed too high. Luckily there were just so many of them.

The little ball smacked into the shoulder of some kind of hoofed creature and instantly exploded in a cloud of wild purple mana as the charged core detonated. The creatures around the impact site were thrown into the air and into their fellows, crumpling like empty cans under the shock of the explosion. A microsecond later, the bodies immediately in the blast area were reduced to bloody chunks by shrapnel as the Volatility explosion ripped the steel skin off the outside of the little ball and sent it in all directions.

The effective radius was far smaller than I would have liked. Five—maybe eight—feet out, the ballistic steel had already lost a lot of its speed, mostly just maiming and crippling. Any Scourge farther out than that was largely spared any Damage. A shame, really. Mana-wise, that one round was much cheaper than the airburst one, and all the material was theoretically recyclable by the drones.

Need to work on that one. Maybe check the logs later to see what happened.

I only had one other type of round—a delayed one—but with the horde bearing down on us, it wasn't going to be much use.

Think, Ryan. What else do we have?

The big toad thing bellowed from behind me—a short, angry, belching call. I turned to see it open its mouth wide and just miss swallowing Samila whole. She dodged out of the way just in time, tucking her shield under her and attempting to roll away to get more distance between her and the thing's mouth.

She was moving too slowly, however, growling as her injured leg refused to straighten with any speed.

Geddon shouted and slashed at the thing's eyes with Organ Grinder, the weapon's teeth sparking and sputtering as they ground through the ignarog's rock-hard skin. The monster didn't pay him any mind, though. Whatever intelligence it had, it had focused on Samila.

The ignarog kicked out with a tree-trunk-sized leg, faster than a creature its size had any business doing, and Samila had no time to do anything other than hunker down and brace herself. Her shield splintered, and her body went airborne, her arms and legs windmilling as she flew through the air.

She came down silently, rolling to a halt under a pile of leaves.

My heart stopped. My thoughts ground to a halt. The world shrunk until all that existed was Sam's unmoving body and the hollow sound of my rapid breathing. She lay there, utterly still.

No. Get up. Please get up.

Then there was a twitch, a tiny flex of the dragonkin's fingers, followed by a slight shake of her head. A cough.

Something got in the way. Big, gray. It blocked me from seeing her. Was she getting up? Was she still moving?

The ignarog.

In that moment, I would have torn the creature in half if only to catch another glimpse of Samila.

Sissa must have felt the same way. She shrieked and lunged forward, stabbing at the relatively vulnerable inside of the ignarog's extended leg. The blade tore a bloody line down the muscle all the way to the knee. The leg retracted on reflex, yanking Sissa's sword along with it while thick, black Scourge blood gushed from the wound.

There was another shriek—inhuman, insane—this time from my left.

HP [290/301]

The world widened again, becoming real enough to gain my attention, and I did not like it one bit. I needed to know if she was okay.

I roared, rearing up and slamming my metal fist down on the Baned that had bitten me. I held nothing back.

Its head splattered like a rotten melon, and its stinking, black blood shot into my mouth and nose.

The monsters were getting too close.

Right. Crowd control. That's your job. Do your job. Samila would want you to do your job.

I summoned a handful of pebbles and went back to the basics. Familiar, churning blender-blades scraped at the inside of my skull as I used the Ability on multiple objects at once.

```
Volatility [1 MP/sec]
Volatility [1 MP/sec]
Volatility [1 MP/sec]
Split Mind is now Level 11.
Volatility [1 MP/sec]
Volatility [1 MP/sec]
```

My side-armed throw released the pebbles in a fan pattern, and I detonated the volley just as they passed over the swarm's heads. As it had been in Eclipse, the small, relatively fragile monsters were pulped, and the rest fell to the forest floor, stunned. It wasn't enough, though. Other monsters climbed over the fallen, treating them as no more than obstacles.

I had to go bigger.

```
Volatility [1 MP/sec]
Volatility [1 MP/sec]
Volatility [1 MP/sec]
Volatility [1 MP/sec]
Volatility [1 MP/sec]
Volatility [1 MP/sec]
Volatility [1 MP/sec]
Volatility depth increasing [1 of 3]
You gain status: Brain Hemorrhage. [1 HP/sec]
You take 1 Bleeding Damage.
You take 1 Bleeding Damage.
You gain status: Brain Hemorrhage. [2 HP/sec]
You take—
```

My head felt like it was splitting down the middle. Stabbing pinpricks of white phosphorus burned behind my eyes, floating, pulsing, and I found it increasingly hard to do more than breathe through my mouth.

My throw was off, but my enemies were many.

BOOM! BOOM! BOOM! BOOM!

> You take 2 Bleeding Damage.
> You take 2 Bleeding Da—

The pain was excruciating. Everything glowed. Blurred. Too bright. Too loud.

Everything was too real. I tasted blood. The breeze scraped at my exposed nerves. I panted and choked on the air. My limbs trembled, and my knees threatened to buckle.

Something was wrong. Very wrong. I couldn't—

I can't—I can't . . . ah . . . What am I doing? Am I—

Finishing a thought seemed impossible. Nothing made sense.

I felt the ground rise, so I put out a hand to steady it.

No, I was on the ground.

"Duty and mercy!" someone shouted from afar, and something warm and soothing passed through me like a golden breeze. I blinked until the majority of the burning white spots left my vision. I was shivering violently now, but I could think.

Right. I was holding them back. I'm not—I'm not going to last. Sam. We have to go right now.

> You take 3 Bleeding Damage.
> You take 3 Bleeding Damage.

In a flash, the last prototype round for my glorified potato-cannon appeared in my spasming hand. I was barely able to slip it into the tube as I fell into some stumbling semblance of a run toward my friends and the ignarog.

The way home was *through* the ignarog.

I ran into Geddon first. The big toad was going after Sissa now that she was swordless. Meanwhile, Geddon caught his breath between furious bouts of chopping. He only turned my way when I was right next to him.

"Ryan! This thing is—*gods of old, your face!*" Geddon gasped.

"R—R—" I started, but my mouth wouldn't do what I told it to. It was full of blood, and my tongue wasn't behaving. It was like I was working someone else's mouth with a remote control.

"Rumn!" I finally got out. "Go home!" I pointed at the fortress entrance.

Geddon didn't question me. He did, however, relay my message—such as it was—to everyone else.

"Retreat to the stronghold! Ryan has a plan!"

Bless the big man for believing in me, but I really didn't have a plan.

"Not without Ryan!" Sissa shouted back. "It won't let him by!"

I gave Geddon a look that I hoped conveyed confidence, but, instead, the big guy looked unsettled. I reached up and wiped at the trickle of blood coming out of my . . . what was it coming out of? Oh, wow. That *was* a lot of blood.

"I—uh—" Geddon stammered. "I think he has that covered!"

I lurched forward and slapped the big Leori on the shoulder. Apparently, I wasn't controlling my strength very well, because the gesture also made him stagger back a step. It did get him moving, though, circling the monster opposite Sissa. Meanwhile, Sissa was slowly inching away as well. When I finally caught her eye, she too looked taken aback by what she saw.

Beyond the ignarog, I spied Bole in the distance, helping Samila slowly limp in the general direction of safety. They were weaving side to side, taking a serpentine route. She looked okay, all things considered, favoring her left side but largely operating under her own power. She even did a little jump and a wave, which I found odd. She wasn't waving to us but toward the gate.

If I'd been able to control my breathing just now, I would have sighed in relief.

Samila did the jump-wave again. I could tell it pained her. What was she— *Oh, you clever girl.*

She was waving at the guns, indicating the area between their barrels and the ignarog. They were programmed to not shoot at us. She knew that. Whenever the guns tried to fire and there was something in the way, they would move on to other targets.

I gave a sloppy salute to Sissa, then held up my potato-gun.

"S'okay! Halp wave!" I shouted. Dammit. That hadn't come out right. Hold on, had I bitten my tongue? Was that what was making it so hard to speak?

Sissa's eyebrow ridges scrunched together as if I'd just told her I had cheese curds for blood.

However, it was enough to get the big toad to ponderously spin in my direction. As it did that, I lost sight of the dragonkin girl.

Boss Fight time. Let's make it a short one.

With my eyes firmly affixed to the ignarog, I let my awareness of my Mark Ability flash briefly in my mind. Yes, the turrets were marking targets behind me, keeping the little Scourge-Touched from getting a shot at my back. They were largely effective, but the line was inching closer moment by moment.

As an experiment, I feinted to the side, trying to circle around the giant toad to get more in line with the gate. However, when it seemed to realize that was my plan, it flailed, kicking out sharply in a bid to cut off my line of retreat. Yep. It wasn't necessarily here to kill me. It was here to keep me from getting home.

There was that advanced thinking again. The Scourge were getting smarter all the time.

With that path closed to me, I switched to another. I advanced, inching closer to the ignarog until I could almost reach out and touch it.

It must have thought it had lucked out with the easiest kill of its life. Its prey was practically walking into its belly. The ignarog croaked in triumph as the big mouth opened wide. It drew itself up, looming like it had done before with Samila when it had attempted to swallow her whole. Air rushed inside with enough force to nearly sweep me off my feet.

In this very small window, I made my move. I snapped my air cannon up and fired my last round down the creature's throat as I lurched to the side, doing a long-distance belly flop into the leaves. There was a snap and a great shuffling sound that I assumed was the mouth coming down on nothing but leaves and dirt.

Part One of my plan in place, I then tried to scramble to my feet and get moving toward the gate as the others had.

Yep. That was my entire plan. Shoot the thing. Do a dive roll. Run for it.

In my defense, I had a lot going on.

So far, so good, though.

Unfortunately, I was even slower to rise than Samila had been, and I got the same result.

The giant toad's leg kicked out yet again, perfectly in line with my body, and, just as Samila had done (except more clumsily), I wobbled to my feet and angled myself to take the blow on my metal side. Luckily I remembered to activate Hardened Defense on the tender flesh just below my ribcage to further soften the blow.

But I wasn't sure if it worked.

I came to, midair, just before impact with the ground. I didn't bounce or roll when I hit. My body simply cratered, flopping heavily into the damp soil and staying there.

When I finally got my respiratory system working again, I coughed up a glob of something chunky and wet and spit it into the dirt.

You take 56 Bludgeoning Damage.
You gain status: Stunned.
You take 3 Bleeding Damage.
You gain status: Brain Hemorrhage. [4 HP/sec]
You take 4 Bleeding Damage.

Someone yanked me to my feet.

"I don't like to run—*huff!*—either, but surely there are—*huff!*—easier ways to travel." Geddon panted.

I blinked, trying and failing to get my bearings. It turned out I didn't need to, however. The sometimes-gentle giant was already hauling me toward the gap that was the gate.

Oh. Yes. I was nearer the gate now. Great.

"Go!" I ordered my rescuer, as if he weren't already doing that. Geddon was practically carrying me by my good arm to get me to safety.

"Whatever you did, it didn't work. We will have to fight the ignarog from the walls now."

"Waif—" was all I could get out.

"*Wait?* Wait for what?"

"Lanmine." My right leg gave out just then, causing me to stumble, but Geddon took me under his arm with a pained growl.

"Gods, you're heavier than you look. What was that now?" he asked.

"Lanmine!" I gasped, distracted and in pain. One of my eyes blurred and went black just then, and the guns crescendoed until they were all I could hear. The white globs were back and floating in front of me wherever I looked.

Sissa's magic must have been wearing off.

"Light blast it. Help! Trix!" Geddon shouted, and I suddenly noticed I was lying on my back. I was also back inside the fortress. When did we get inside?

"Holy hell, Geddon. He's dying." That was Samila's voice. She sounded like she was in pain. I wanted to see her, but the desire left me before I could perform the requisite movements to do so. The ground was so comfy.

A light pressure on my chest.

"Stand back! Oh, Light and gods of old. What happened?"

"That's what I said! I don't know. He was like this when I found him," a basso voice explained.

"Did the ignarog do this?"

"No. Thi—"

The toad!

Suddenly I found myself brimming with energy—comparatively, at least. I gagged and sat up . . . or tried to. Something forced me back down before I could get all the way upright.

"*H—HOW MUCH?!*" I roared. My volume control wasn't working properly. I wasn't choosing the right words either.

"Hold him down!"

I gagged again, but the blood continued to stream down my throat, choking me. I coughed it up, but there was always more.

WHAM!

Something slammed hard into one of the walls, hard enough for me to feel it through the floor. The guns were going full-auto on something, too. I summoned my focus and spat out a mouthful of blood. I needed to say something.

HP [68/301]
You take 4 Bleeding Damage.

Focus.

"How . . . long?"

"Ryan?" Samila again. She sounded terrible. Worry? Injury? How was she?

"How . . . long?"

"Uh, since you . . . Since you came back? A minute. Two. Maybe more," Samila answered. "Trix, you have to heal him right now."

"I have done all I dare! I could make his blood clot, but if I do that in his head . . . they have a name for that! It's not a good name!"

"He's going to die anyway, Trix!"

I reached for the Volatility Trigger in my head. The new one. The most recent. Where was it? So slippery. The feeling was there, fleeting, squirming. Like my speech, using the Ability felt wrong.

"They're coming! Sam, we have to get up to the wall!" Sissa ordered.

"We can't leave him!"

There! I felt the Volatility Trigger there. It was jumpy, waving.

"Lamine. Down!" I tried to say.

"What?"

Trix's claws dug into my skin.

You have gained status: Underfed (moderate).
You have gained status: Underfed (severe).

"Land mine!" I screamed. It had to have charged by now. The sequence had to have been building for . . . well . . . it needed to be enough.

"I don't understand, Ryan!"

"Down!"

BOOM!

You gain status: Stunned.
You have defeated Scourge-Touched Female Ignarog.
You have been awarded 8,230 Experience points. [15,400 base (-1,010 Level, +3,080 group, +3,080 chain, -12,320 non-combat Class)]

"Augh!" Someone yelled as they dove on top of me and painfully forced the air from my lungs. Then something hot, wet, and rancid splattered down upon us, followed by suspiciously warm rain.

I felt something in my head click into place, followed by a pressure build-up behind my eyes.

Status Lost: Brain Hemorrhage.
You have gained status: Starvation.

Everything went fuzzy at the edges. Things ceased to matter like they used to. I didn't try to yell anymore. I was content to lay here and just rest for as long as it took to—

"Get some food in him," I heard Trix say. "Right now. Force-feed him if you have to. Do not let him sleep."

The joke was on him. I was already asleep.

CHAPTER THIRTY

Find Common Ground

I woke up choking on something sweet and rotten. It was dark where I was. Quiet, too. Gasping, I tried to turn over and spit what I could out onto the floor, but my limbs wouldn't do what I wanted them to. Something constricted around me, squeezing until I couldn't breathe. The way my arms were crossed and stuck against my body, the dampness, the disorientation at just having woken up—all of it built into a surge of panic, and I began to thrash against my bindings. The world started to tilt. The air smelled of stagnant water. Someone gurgled as their mouth slipped beneath the surface—

Then, I heard a voice from the dark.

"Lucky to be alive there. Don't ruin a good thing by getting rowdy."

I knew that voice. *Mom?*

In the course of a few breaths, I came back to the present, and my mind finally started to place things where they were supposed to be. I wasn't bound but wrapped in a bedroll, and I was as far from home as I could get. I was on Ralqir, years after the accident. The tightness in my chest slowly dissipated, the phantom belts loosening before fading entirely.

I lifted my head slightly—as much as I could, at least. My body felt so heavy. Still, I was able to pick out the dim embers of a dying fire and a dark shape sat next to it, the firelight gleaming off one of Bole's tiny knives as he thumbed the edge.

I swallowed and cleared my throat of the leftover food I'd been convinced to eat.

"Uh, morning, Bole," I croaked.

The shadow that was Bole didn't answer. The only sound out there tonight seemed to be the snores of the others and the rustle of the wind in the leaves.

The guns weren't firing for the first time in days.

"Quiet tonight, isn't it?" I asked curiously.

"Small mercy, the quiet," Bole grumbled. I saw the hood of his cloak turn slightly to look my way. "Or at least it was."

I frowned. Message received. "Right," I replied carefully.

A polite person might have elaborated further, told me how the battle went, how long I'd been out, if everyone was all right. Bole didn't do that, though. He just stared into the fire.

```
HP [242/242]
MP [111/267]
Status: Underfed [Severe]
```

So I hadn't been out long enough to refill my mana all the way. I didn't know how much I'd been missing by the end, but I had to assume it was a significant amount. We'd set out in the morning, too. Now it was night. My max HP was lower than it was supposed to be, but I was getting a penalty to my Body score based on my Underfed status. I'd need to fix that ASAP.

I turned my attention back to Bole. "Guess you drew the short straw for watch duty," I ventured.

No reply.

"Though, I would imagine watch duty would have you on the wall, not poking at the fire."

"I was never much of a guard," Bole finally said sourly. "Didn't have much patience for fools or foolish convention." Again his shadowy hood turned toward me pointedly.

Someone coughed weakly from directly to my left. "Stop it, Fidus," the person whispered.

Bole was suddenly up, scrambling on all fours until he was next to the bedroll neighboring mine. "Beedy, you okay, big man? Is there something you need? Water? Food?"

Beedy?

I let my head loll over that way. Beedy lay next to me, still pale, covered in sweat, and shivering with fever. He looked thin—skeletal-almost, courtesy of Trix's magic—but his eyes were wide open, if glazed and unfocused.

"Need you to stop," Beedy whispered through cracked lips.

"Alright, alright. The monk didn't mean to wake you. Just go back to sleep and get your strength up, eh?" Bole replied.

"No. N-Need you to stop it. Stop being—" The man's voice trailed off until it vanished entirely, and he sighed. His gaze drifted upward lazily, and his eyelids drooped until they shuddered to a halt halfway down.

Bole got down and put his head on his friend's chest, genuine fear evident on his face while he held his breath to listen for a long handful of seconds. Then, after an interminable amount of time, Beedy's chest began to rise and fall again.

"—stop the act," Beedy continued as if he hadn't just passed out in the middle of a sentence.

Bole sat up again, clearly relieved but unable to keep the fear and worry out of his voice. His words came out in a nervous sort of chuckle.

"Why, I'm an open book, old boy." He reached over to smooth Beedy's hair. "Just rest, man. Help is on the way." If I didn't know any better, I'd say Bole was close to tears.

He kept talking. "Church healers. Flesh-melders maybe. The best. We've been rubbing elbows with the headmaster, you know. He's gonna have the best. Get you fixed right up. Maybe fix that nose of yours, too. Save me from your snoring."

Beedy didn't respond, however, already back to struggling to breathe in his sleep.

Bole looked on for a solid minute, watching his friend cling to life, then seemed to notice me again, turning away and pulling the hood of his cloak closer around him. He didn't leave Beedy's side, though.

"First time I've ever heard his voice," I said, careful not to be too loud for Beedy's sake.

"Shut the fuck up, Monk," the rogue said, the hood moving as he shook his head. "If you want to keep your tongue, just shut the fuck up."

Finally able to slip a shoulder out of my bedroll, I gave him a weak half-shrug. I trusted he could see the gesture, given how everyone on this damned planet had better night vision than me. "Sorry. Just saying he strikes me as the quietly good type. Solid."

The other man didn't lunge for my throat, despite his warnings. My many brushes with death recently and the tiredness I was feeling left my already-lacking social skills with little brainpower to work with anyway, so I went on.

"If it'll make you feel better, you can cut out my tongue, but I think it just grows back now," I joked.

Bole leaned forward intently as if he were thinking about doing just that. The firelight gleamed off one of his blades, but he made no move to use it. His scowl was surely sharp enough to cut, but he eventually lost his motivation, sighing before getting up to head back to the fire.

"Bah," he scoffed, waving a dismissive hand my way. "Pretty sure your vulpa is still awake, anyway. Don't want to tangle with him if I can help it."

"Tangle with him *again,* you mean," I added, remembering the first time we'd met, how Trix had attached himself to Bole's face. Bole's scars from that little dustup were still pink.

The corner of Bole's mouth inched slightly upward at that. "Right. He was a scrapper before all this. But now he's a killer. Don't want my insides aired out, yeah?"

Bole scooped something up off the ground. Then he reached over to plop a bowl on my chest, which I barely caught before it could roll off to the side. From the smell of it, it was more porridge. I clumsily disentangled my other hand from my bedroll and lifted the bowl to my lips. I'd long lost my taste for the stuff, given the circumstances under which I kept getting fed it, such as this.

Ugh. This is way too much like the time in the Undercity. At least it's not cold.

I said as much between torturous sips.

"I never liked it, either," Bole replied. "Don't know anyone who really does other than those who grow up on it."

"It's like someone stored the oats with their dirty laundry."

Bole snorted. "Oats? Monk, that's Undercity meal. There ain't no oats in that."

"Oh," I said, looking down into the bowl. "Do I want to—"

"Know what's in it? Not if you want to keep your appetite."

More awkward silence. This time because I was busy trying to guess as to what they might put in Undercity meal. Eventually, I had to give up, though. My imagination was too good.

"Tell me about him," I probed with a mouth half-full of food, purposefully not thinking about the taste. "About Beedy, I mean."

"A good man. That's all," Bole said after a long pause. "Deserves better than this, being out here with slagged insides."

I nodded around my porridge. It was always the innocent people who got it the worst when things went to shit. That just might have been the one multiversal truth.

"The world's not kind to the good," I said, my mind going back to Vince and Hunty.

Don't forget Mom.

"Truest thing you've said since I've met you, Monk."

Another bout of silence, what was left unsaid hanging around us like an unseen watcher. Bole sighed and shifted his body until he was facing me entirely. Gone was the man's default disdainful sneer, replaced by a faraway look that I recognized right away.

"That bite was meant for me." The words pried their way out of him, hard, quiet.

I swallowed the last of my food and sat up. "Meant for you?"

"I—I wasn't paying attention. We were out looking for trouble, me and Beedy, but we hadn't found a thing in days. Was starting to think we were alone out here. Would have been nice after that business in the city, you know? There was a hollow under a tree. Should have checked it, but I didn't. I wasn't *on*," he said.

He sniffed.

"Beedy was thinking, though," Bole continued. "When that spider came for me, he—Beedy . . . he was right there."

He looked over at his friend and shook his head mournfully. "We're cousins, actually. By blood. My mum's side. But he's worth six of me by my count."

Family, huh? I didn't see the resemblance, but I'd never been good at that sort of thing.

"It does something to you, doesn't it?" I found myself asking. "Being saved, I mean. You spend the rest of your life wondering if they made the right call."

Bole gave the slightest of nods. He had one of his knives clutched tightly in his hand again, running his thumb over the blade, a trickle of blood dribbling down the side.

"I could have slipped it, Monk. I'm quick on my feet. Strong. That spider didn't have a prayer of biting me."

"Because you're a practitioner," I finished for him.

Surprise played briefly across his face. It wasn't much—just a widening of the eyes and a loosening of his jaw, but it was there. The faraway look left him, and he was back with me for the briefest of moments. However, his poker face was back quickly enough that I almost doubted whether I'd seen the mask slip at all.

"Pfft. Don't know what you're talking about," he said.

"I started to suspect when you decked me in the Undercity," I told him. I slid my bowl to the side so it wouldn't spill as I wriggled my legs out from my bedroll. I was still wearing the pants I had on earlier today, at least. My shirt was MIA, however. Trix's magic had stripped my body of pretty much all fat and some of its muscle mass, but even as I sat here, my System-enhanced healing could almost be observed with the naked eye, rounding out my chest and arms, giving my stomach definition I'd never had in my old life.

"You're fast and quiet. Weirdly so. Then there was that moment where my aura slipped out of my control after I'd woken up in that old basement. Seemed to rattle you. Combine that with the other stuff like your association with Jassin, and it's not a big leap in logic. You're a practitioner, but you don't want anyone to know," I said.

Bole made a rude sound and poked at the fire. "I ain't nothing but me, Monk."

"He would have been a practitioner," Samila said from my left as she crawled stiffly up to the fire to warm her hands. She was wearing her smallclothes, just covering what needed to be covered, which made the enormous navy-blue bruises on her scales all the more apparent. Her movements indicated how weak and sore she had to be at the moment. It was how one might move the day after suffering an accident or running a marathon.

"That is, if his life had turned out differently. Our first relatively quiet night, and the men decide to share their feelings. Typical," she grumbled, though the words had no real venom behind them.

"I'm on watch," Bole corrected her before turning back to me with a frown. "I'm not a practitioner. Wouldn't have been, anyway. It's just something I picked up as a kid."

"Inherited?" I asked.

Bole didn't say, but Samila nodded, causing the hooded rogue to scowl at her. I looked over at Beedy. "What about him, then?"

Bole sighed and shook his head. "If only. He'd be a damned good one. Claim is too weak, though."

"Doesn't seem to stop him," Samila said.

"That's right," Bole agreed with pride. "Strong. Smart. Solid, like the monk said. All without having to sell himself to anyone. Funny, that."

"You would see it as a transaction, wouldn't you?" Samila argued. It sounded like an old argument, one they'd had before. "The oaths we take are a gesture of humility and faith in something bigger than ourselves. We lose nothing and gain everything by taking them."

"Empty words," Bole scoffed. "A bad deal. Empty words exchanged for a lifetime of servitude."

My neighbor stirred again. "Stop it, Fidus," Beedy wheezed before going into a coughing fit. "Can't just be me."

Bole lowered his tone. "You're not going anywhere, mate. Stop talking like that."

Beedy wasn't satisfied, though. "Can't just be—*cough*—me."

The hooded man looked up to the sky as if asking an unseen deity for strength, clenching his fists on his lap. "Fine. Everyone else knows this, Monk, but—" Bole sighed. "—I used to be nobility. One of those families given a title for services rendered during the Crusades. Used to manage a little hamlet way out on the edge of the empire. Nice place. Good people. Beedy's from there, too." Bole glanced over at Samila as if looking for some kind of objection, but he received none.

"Unfortunately for us," he went on, "we were also one of the families that kept their ancestors' relic blades from back in the day."

"Unfortunately?" I asked the obvious question. What was wrong with having a relic? I had one of them supposedly, as well. It liked to explode.

"The secret to brightsteel was lost a while back, when the Church went through a schism. The crusaders were a secretive bunch, and their techniques weren't written so much as passed down from master to apprentice," Samila explained. "The metal is a miracle of sorts. The Maelstrom's purest light made manifest through means unknown. Scholars have been trying to recreate it ever since, and the supply of it dwindles more every year."

Bole looked at her oddly. She'd just explained something that was common knowledge for my benefit, I guessed.

"Right. Well—" Bole continued. "—the Church fancied my father's blade, given to him by his father and his father's father, all the way back to the bloody Crusades. Da was a proud man, though. He wasn't about to give up our family history nor our claim to our legacy," Bole lamented.

He took that moment to unsheathe one of his knives again and twirl it over his knuckles. "He did, however, pledge his second son to serve the Church and strengthen his ties to the faith."

Bole had been in the Church at one time. I'd gathered as much from context clues so far, but I had no idea he'd been practically forced into it. His animosity, while seeming to be irrational at times, made a bit more sense now. That couldn't have been the whole story, though. Nobody as angry as Bole got that way for just one reason.

He let out a long, tired breath, staring into the fire as the knife tumbled around on his fingers. "I tried to make a real go of it. I really did."

"In your own way." Samila giggled. "Brothel visits and tavern crawls among the faithful went up by half, at least."

"No stricture against fun that I can recall, though my recollection from those times is fuzzy." Bole chuckled darkly. "Anyway, that's how I met this lot. Then the Church dissolved my family's title. They took our land and our home. Just like that. Legally, too."

"That's not everything," Samila interjected. "As I recall, they petitioned Lord Bole for access to the sword, but he denied them again and again. I recall your father also declaring all members of the clergy unwelcome on his land. Harsh— especially for the faithful who lived under him."

Bole shrugged. "I did say he was proud. Anyway, they took everything my father owned and folded it into our liege lord's holdings. Da died a year later. After that, I just couldn't keep the faith anymore. I quit."

"You did more than quit," Samila chided. "You stole some sensitive books and scrolls and set a paired flare paper under the head cleric's mattress. Probably sold the scrolls to one of the prefect's stand-ins, too, or you wouldn't have been allowed to join the guard. The Church couldn't prove that, though."

"And they never will. That's when Siss and I parted ways. To a dragon, oaths are forever. Remember that, Monk."

"We just have a highly developed sense of honor and integrity," Samila said as she preened with a raised chin. "More people could do with a little of that."

"The Church broke faith long before I did, and, in my reckoning, made me a free agent. Siss disagreed."

Bole cleared his throat and spared a glance for Beedy, who seemed to be content enough with the story to sleep through it.

"You were doing things, Bole," Samila argued. "Bad things. Things she couldn't be a part of."

"I was playing the hand I was dealt," Bole growled. "Living by my own rules."

He snatched his knife out of the air and got his feet under him like he was going to stand, but then he stopped, slumping back down as he ran his free hand down his face.

Samila seemed like she wanted to reach out and place a hand on Bole's arm, but she only got halfway there before she seemed to decide against it.

"You turned spiteful and angry, Fidus," Samila said, her tone gentler now, less accusatory.

"I was in the middle of destroying my life. Siss didn't need to be there for that," Bole declared with sad finality.

"Then Beedy showed up," I guessed, turning the subject to something Bole was more comfortable with.

"Then Beedy showed up," Bole affirmed with a grateful smile. "Had news of my mum and my brother. Sobered me up just so he could give it to me. Then he just kind of . . . stayed. That's it. He just stayed."

He grinned, seeming to remember something he was keeping to himself.

I thought of Vince, how he stuck with me after my accident, after Mom died. How wretched I felt. The guilt and rage at having been the cause of her death. I'd done my best to push everyone, too. I stopped speaking. Going out. Cutting my hair. I wasn't eating. I actively despised others I'd considered friends beforehand.

As much as I didn't like to think about it, I didn't become a pariah overnight. The Constance clan had their hangups about the weak, but I'd done my part too, hadn't I?

Vince stuck around, though, always with me despite how much I changed since that day. I became a completely different person than the one he knew, but he didn't care.

"Maybe he's waiting for you to come back to yourself," Samila offered.

"Maybe," Bole replied, getting up and stretching before loping over to the stairs that led to the top of the wall. He started climbing. "Maybe I'm already myself. Have been for a while."

Maybe sometimes our friends see something in us we can't see in ourselves.

"Wait. Is sharing time over? You guys aren't going to hug or anything?" Samila teased, stretching as she made to rise.

"Hell, no!" Bole barked from the top of the wall.

"He fed me to dead people," I said with a shake of my head.

Bole chuckled out there in the dark. "Hehe. Yeah. That was pretty good."

Rolling her eyes, Samila started to get up but stopped suddenly, as if something had just occurred to her. She turned to me then and ran her gaze up and down my body, lingering a long time on my exposed chest and shoulders. I bravely stood my ground, since I was too weak to actually run away.

"Sweet dreams," she crooned, before slinking back to her bedroll for the rest of the night.

"Yeah. Uh. You, too," I replied, keeping careful track of her movements until she left the circle of firelight.

Then I was left alone with my thoughts. That wouldn't do.

There'll be time for introspection after I save the world. Or when I'm dead. Preferably in that order.

I looked over to the shadowy area that housed my workbench. On it would be scraps of failed chain charges, the ones that almost got us all killed having to deploy them outside the walls. It was time to go back to the drawing board on that one . . . or was it?

Oh, that just might work . . .

CHAPTER THIRTY-ONE

Flip the Table

I grunted quietly as I heaved the second of two brass balls into the launcher I'd constructed on the ramparts overlooking the northern approach. Together, they shouldn't have weighed more than ten—maybe twenty—pounds, but I was struggling this morning. I was still in the recovery phase of having Trix use his magic on me, meaning I was still lacking energy and muscle mass, not to mention the hefty debuff I got from being just above starvation.

> Underfed (severe)[-40 Body]

And what a penalty it was. I was essentially back to having 13 Body, which was about what I had to begin with. I was much weaker than that, though. My body was fighting for survival, shutting down nonessential processes and scrabbling for calories I just didn't have as of yet. That made working with constructs of pure metal just plain suck.

As the payload slipped inside, I sputtered, letting fly some of the gritty little things that passed for oats on this world. My mouth hadn't had a chance to be empty at all this morning. The half-full bowl of porridge was even now at my feet, waiting for me to pick it up again. More of the slop was scattered around my work area, too. The thought of it almost made me sick. A guy can really get burned out on porridge.

One thing no one mentions when your body loses so much is the cold. Without all that meat and fat insulating my insides and without enough of a Body score to give me supernatural protections, working in a foggy morning in the ancient forest of Ralqir was downright freezing. My entire body shook like a leaf in the wind, and my breaths came in shallow wheezes.

Shot loaded, I then summoned all my might and lifted the mouth of the construct up and over the lip of the rampart until it was propped up at about a 45-degree angle. That took several tries, my reduced strength not allowing for much more than an inch or so of movement before I had to put the whole thing down again to hyperventilate. However, it wasn't long before I had my little cannon angled and ready for a test fire. The brace—a series of claws that dug into the petrified wood to keep the cannon still—was the easiest to attach with just a bit of Shaping juju, and the break gave me a chance to get my spirits back up. I could even eat as I did it.

Whistling a pirate tune I remembered from a movie I'd seen when I was a kid, I put my finger on the tiny wire protruding from the back of the tube and started to pour on the juice.

Volatility [1 MP/sec]

Strictly speaking, I didn't *have* to do this, funnily enough. I could have just Automated a cube that had spent all its charge at once and stuck it in the back of the cannon, but this morning I was feeling the need for historical—well, not exactly "accuracy." Authenticity? Whatever it was, I was feeling it.

"What are you doing?"

My bowl clattered to the ground, spilling the tiny amount of porridge I had left onto the toe of my boot.

"Crap," I whispered, but I really wasn't too sad to take a break from eating.

Samila, still in her loose, tan shirt and underwear that she slept in, limped the rest of the way up the rampart stairs, clutching the leather sheath to her sword in one hand. The soreness in her leg and probably the rest of her showed on her face. The climb looked like it had taken a great deal of effort. Getting kicked by a giant toad did that to a person, not that I would know firsthand. I got a shot of vulpa mind mojo right after I'd had my experience, so my problems were entirely different.

"Didn't mean to frighten you," the dragonkin said quietly as she took the last few stairs. Then she paused and let out a weary breath before giving me a hollow version of her signature little smile. "Unless you're into that."

My eyes were drawn down to her blue skin, the shape of her shoulders, the V at the neck of her shirt before I remembered I was currently channeling mana into a bomb, and I was forcefully ripped back to the moment. Oh, it was already glowing a dangerous shade of purple.

"Yeah. Uh. No. Actually, you—uh—startled me is all. If I woke you, I'm sorry. I thought I was being pretty quiet up here."

She waved a dismissive hand in the air. "No, I wasn't sleeping. I tried, but I couldn't. I relieved Bole and told him to go get some sleep. Need our best fighters healthy and rested for today."

The last sentence came out through clenched teeth.

"Good thing you're all rested then, huh?" I said lamely.

Her only reply was to make a very unladylike sound with her mouth.

"Okay, sorry. Won't do that again," I said, looking up from my Volatility wick to try and catch her eye. The faint light of the early morning was just bright enough to show me the worry in her eyes, and a slight swelling and darkness to the scales.

"Hey! Hey!" I called, tilting my head and leaning over to make sure she was looking at me. "You and I are not out of this fight. A little time, and we'll be back out there. I'll be out there with my sword, flailing around, and you'll get back to being a terrifying, Amazonian demigoddess."

"Terrifying, huh?" She sniffed.

"Absolutely," I assured her.

"What is an 'Am-a-zon-ee-an?' Is this a word from your home?"

I tried to think of a good way to explain it. My knowledge was more mythical than historical. More a product of archived pop culture than real knowledge.

"They were a legendary tribe from back home. All women. Beautiful, fierce, strong. There were epics and poems written about them for thousands and thousands of years," I said, stopping briefly to think about all the books, comics, and movies I'd seen. "Their legend was so strong, the Amazonian name become synonymous with female strength."

A moment passed between us—silent, tense.

Suddenly a ghost of the woman's patented sly smile was back on her face, a genuine one this time. "So you think I'm beautiful."

And there it was. I knew I'd walked right into it, and I kind of did it on purpose. Still didn't make the next part any easier. My mouth expressed what my brain was experiencing.

"Uh."

She shook her head and leaned back to rest on one of the petrified bark crenelations. Her posture slowly gained back some of its casual confidence. "Don't run away from it. It was a nice thing to say."

"Uh, okay," I replied, not quite knowing how to proceed. This was as far as my cheer-Samila-up plan had gotten. I was no good at flirting with girls, even when they did most of the work.

Which Stat do I have to raise to be less like me?

I suddenly gained a new appreciation for the work I'd been doing before the dragonkin came up those stairs. I bent down to get a good read on where I was pointing the cannon. Suddenly, a blue hand was resting on the shaft just next to the wick.

"So tell me. How beautiful would you say I am in comparison to my sister?"

I froze. Yes, my life flashed before my eyes. No, it didn't take very long. I had only one escape.

BOOM!

The cannon shot ripped through the morning. Purple fire belched from the barrel as excess Volatility charge was expended all at once, sending the payload soaring up and away into the forest.

"Light and gods of old, what is all that racket?! Geddon roared from down in the courtyard.

I exchanged a look with Samila, who was now both grinning ear to ear but also gingerly rubbing her hand that was just resting on the cannon.

"Uh, it's okay! I'm doing pirate stuff now," I shouted over my own ringing ears.

"Couldn't it have waited? I was having a dream," Geddon replied.

Trix's basket rocked as the vulpa shifted his weight. A little nose peeked over the edge. "Mmf. I am sure Ryan has a good reason to do . . . whatever he is doing. A very good reason," he added, not bothering to keep the cordial tone.

"He'd fucking better!" Bole growled. He was already half in his armor, his black hair still mussed from his short time abed.

I swallowed, standing up to my full height to sheepishly check where my shot had landed. A quick sweep of the forest floor came up with nothing. Then I had to turn my search up—way up, actually. Farther up than I'd planned.

About fifty or sixty feet up one of the trunks of the Mendau, outside the outer perimeter, I spied a faint purple glow. The chain between my two cannon-balls was already starting its charging process.

Thank Constance for building-sized trees.

"Ryan?" Sissa's voice cut smoothly through the angry grumbling of the others. "What's going on?"

"It's, uh . . ." I tried hard not to glance back over at Samila, who was doing her best to hide how pleased she was at having been the cause of my premature detonation. "I had a dream about pirates and—Well, I was going to wait until you were awake, but I'm ready to bring down the rest of the trees."

On that note, I turned around and peered into the forest gloom. There was movement out there now. None of the Scourge came close enough to the fort to trigger the turrets, but they were moving around out there. The sudden activity had roused them.

"Ryan, the Infected are making their way toward your glowing chain," Trix said. His rifle barrel was up and out of the basket and aimed at targets I could only dream of seeing that far out.

I nodded, feeling a thrill pass through my core.

"I'm seeing lots of Returned and . . . Miur . . . Vulpa . . . Urlan . . . I think the Infected from Eclipse and the surrounding villages have finally arrived. Should I shoot them before they can investigate?" he asked.

Smiling, I brought all the Volatility Triggers to the front of my mind and focused on the newest one. Perfect. "No. Let them be," I replied. If my estimations were correct, the longer we spent in this standoff, the better. More time meant more time to charge.

"That isn't one of the trees we've marked for death. In fact, it is far out of range for the turrets," Sissa observed clinically.

I nodded, smiling slightly to myself. "No, it's not one we need to bring down."

I could see the monsters scurrying over the terrain around the wounded tree, sniffing and casting hateful glances my way, then back up to where my construct lay. Some were even clawing their way up the trunk. The oddly-proportioned-but-strong figures of Baned were the first up, carefully picking their way toward my little chain shot.

Sissa raised a curious eyebrow ridge. "Want to bring me in on this plan?"

"Sure. I was sleeping last night between bowls of mush, and I had a dream about pirates. From back home, I mean," I added when I saw the confusion on her face. "There were lots of stories about them and their exploits. Most of them were terrible, terrible people. Some were devilishly clever. For a while, they used cannons sort of like this one." I put a booted foot up on the expended cannon for emphasis.

The monsters were up the tree now and sniffing around my glowing purple chain. It wouldn't be long now.

"And you chose to test your 'cannon' today as a method of delivering your Shaped charges?" Sissa was a smart girl. She saw at least the first part of my thought process immediately.

One of the Baned began to tug on the now-spiky cannonball to try to dislodge it from the bark of the Mendau tree. They'd been programmed to take their second form as soon as they'd left the barrel of the cannon, and the spikes were meant to help them grab. I wondered how many cuts the little dude was getting on his palms trying to pry it out of the wood.

I wobbled my head side to side, noncommittally. "At first, that's what I was going to do, but the more I thought about it, the worse an idea I realized it was. They're essentially chains. The Scourge saw us use something similar to bring down two trees yesterday. If they're getting as smart as I think they are, I don't think they'll let us do anything like that again. Not without pushback, at least."

"So, this is a test to see how they react then?"

"Nah," I scoffed just as the Baned managed to dislodge one of the spiked anchors, followed shortly by the other. The construct then began its descent to the forest floor. "The thing that made the pirates of old dangerous wasn't necessarily the cannons. It was subterfuge. Lying through action."

I pointed a finger-gun at the accelerating purple jumble of chain as it fell.

"Observe," I said.

BOOM!

The Scourge around the base of the tree exploded as the chain's charge detonated. From all around us, there was a collective howl as the Scourge stirred up into a frenzy. They'd realized the danger they were in immediately, faster than I'd even thought they would.

The Scourge was thinking strategically now, learning concepts it had taken people forever to put together in a matter of seconds. It realized the game had just changed significantly, and if it wanted the best chance at overwhelming us, it needed to act now. The cannon meant we would potentially be able to bring down whatever tree we wanted.

"Okay, people!" I called to the rest of them. "May want to get up on the walls now! Think we're about to see a little action!"

Samila sauntered/limped over to my side and leaned on my metal arm. Sissa came up on the other side, pulling her shield into place on her forearm. The two of them looked rough, off-balance maybe. Sissa was missing her sword, Samila her shield. I'd need to make replacements before I did anything else. Of course, I would have time for that soon.

"They're going to charge en masse," Sissa guessed. "Get ready for a fight on all fronts! This is going to be a bad one!"

"Yes!" Trix shouted. "They are massing out there, all around! Thousands of them that were out of sight! We most certainly have the entire population of Eclipse here now. Perhaps more."

"Ryan, I need to know your plan right now. We're facing overwhelming forces, we're severely depleted, and you don't look surprised," Sissa demanded angrily.

Nodding, I brought up the rest of the Volatility Triggers, ready to detonate them. "Just hold steady! It won't be as bad as it looks!" I ordered. Out of the corner of my eye, I saw a great mass of bodies surge forward—a writhing, black sea of once living beings that represented an entire city of people claimed by the Scourge.

Then, turning to Sissa, I kept my voice low. "Like I said, the cannons aren't what made pirates dangerous. I realized that last night when I was disassembling the Shaped charges into smaller bits."

The Scourge flooded into the outer perimeter, and the turrets went to work. Full auto. Over-penetrating rounds. Every corner of the fortress was awash in purple light and thunderous sound. Scourge died by the triple digits, but the mass kept coming. They kept coming closer and closer to the inner perimeter where we'd once wanted to bring down our trees. Of course, the Scourge went well around the sunlight that now streamed into a large clearing left by our previous work.

Sissa didn't like the theatrics, though. "Ryan! I need to know now! What is going on?"

The inner perimeter was breached. The black tide spilled over the imaginary circle, breaking over the ancient Mendau.

I put my mouth almost directly on her ear, so close my lips brushed the scales. Weird. They felt softer than I'd expected, like down feathers. My voice was quiet, lest I give away the game too soon and our enemy call off its charge. "The charges have been set for hours now. I reprogrammed the drones to do it quietly last night."

She pulled away, narrowing her eyes and turning from me to the battle and back again, realization pulling her jaw down until she looked like a blue fish. Her sister didn't ask any questions, choosing instead to lean on me and pick at her nails. Samila must have been fast on the uptake, or maybe she trusted me in a way Sissa didn't.

Time to rub the salt in.

Stepping forward, I put a foot on the nearest crenelation and leaned out over the wall to stare the nearest Scourge-Touched creature right in the eyes, with what I hoped was a sufficiently cocky grin on my face. I gave the creature a wink, and with a snap of my fingers, I triggered the charges. An almost synchronized series of metallic pops sounded above the din of the guns and the wailing of the Scourge.

The whole forest seemed to slowly fold in on itself, trees leaning degree by degree, falling first slowly—as ancient growth does—then with increasing speed. My brain grappled with the sight. I don't think humans were meant to witness things that massive meet their end. We're meant to live below them, beside them, to view them as an eternal reminder of what a small part of nature's vast tapestry we really are.

The trees fell exactly the way Geddon had predicted, and they fell hard, directly on the teeming mass of monsters, and ground them into paste. Worse for our enemy, they let in the light.

Blinding, burning sunlight . . . Maelstrom light stabbed down from above, forming visible rays in the mist and through the cloud of debris in the air. The light burned through the Scourge like a celestial laser, a circular fence of bright death. Every single one of the creatures even remotely close to our new inner perimeter burst into flames. Oily, black smoke seemed to billow up from those affected, out of their skin, their mouths and eyes, only to disappear as the light dissolved it, too. As one, the tide of Scourge broke upon our new fortification as if they were a solid thing.

Those Scourge that were lucky enough to have charged past the inner perimeter before I'd triggered the charges found themselves quite alone, and the turrets were quick and efficient in dispatching them. The last one tumbled to the ground well before getting within spitting range.

From there, the Scourge scattered as quickly as they had gathered, howling as they ran away to lick their wounds, racing with themselves to get out of range of the turrets before they could take any more losses. Before long, the guns and my companions fell silent once more. My friends didn't seem to have anything to say. Bole started a slow clap that no one else took up, but that was probably more of a result of it being Bole, not the general mood of the crowd.

I stared out at the carnage I'd wrought and inhaled deeply through my nose, tasting absolute victory for the first time since I'd arrived here. A minute and thirty seconds, and the horde had lost thousands—maybe tens of thousands. What's more, we now had a choke point. I knew how to defend a choke point.

It probably wouldn't last, but at this moment, I felt like things weren't entirely hopeless. For the first time in a long time, I felt like we could win. No more running. No more deaths. Complete and absolute victory over evil.

Your move then, asshole.

CHAPTER THIRTY-TWO

Confront My Doubts

The Scourge's next move, it turned out, was to get super-pissy about things. Sure, it had probed at the outer edges of the light perimeter for a while, sending a few scattered creatures as close to the "glow zone" as possible without catching fire, but after it had mapped out what was safe and what wasn't, it chose to scurry away and hide. At least the ones that lived did that—those the turrets hadn't cut down before they could run.

That didn't mean the Scourge were sitting idly, though. The amount of howling and screeching I heard when I got up on the walls to work on one of the turrets or launch the odd State Change fire-starter into a pile of corpses was, quite frankly, disconcerting. It wasn't so much the amount of hate I was getting from the mob of evil dead things. I was used to that, and from shorter distances. What bothered me was more the tone.

From all my previous interactions with them, the horde was capable of pretty much one emotion when it came to me: rage. At least they were up until now. With the change to our circumstances and a good barrier between us, I was seeing a new side to them. Individual monsters scraped the bark off trees, clawed at the rocks and sometimes each other. They seemed almost directionless, and violently so, like their anger at having their prey right there with no direct path to him was eating them up inside.

It warmed my metal heart to see.

I'd reeled in the range on the turrets after the sun wall went up. No use in spending the ammo or generating the heat if the Scourge weren't going to get through the barrier anyway. Instead, I busied myself preparing for the worst while enjoying the relative peace over a bracing cup of awful red Ralqir tea.

There was significant degradation on the barrels, actions, and springs of the most-active turrets, as well as less-than-ideal power issues in the propulsion cubes. The power thing was the easiest to fix with just a little time juicing up the Automated parts, although a long-term solution would probably require an entire overhaul of the design. I was wasting too much power and generating too much heat with every shot. It wasn't a lot, mind you, but over the course of a thousand shots, certain parts of the machines got too hot to safely touch. In ten thousand, they were in danger of meltdown.

The next model needed to be more efficient if I really wanted to fire and forget these bad boys.

While I had the guns disassembled, I thought about giving them self-charging batteries, of course, but I wasn't particularly comfortable with building weapons that needed to be fired or risk being turned into bombs, given that I was sleeping next to them. The self-destruct feature might be useful in keeping my weapons out of enemy hands sometime in the future, though. That was worth something.

The metal degradation was annoying but expected. These parts of the turret were under constant stress from heat and pressure when the thing was in use, not to mention moisture from all the fog and morning dew. Plus they'd been running for . . . eight days straight now?

I was lucky my machines were performing as well as they were. Despite them looking and acting like sophisticated implements of war, they were essentially a pale, primitive imitation of the real kinetic firearms back home. I was sure there were a lot of things I could have built into the design to keep them from eventually failing like this, but I'd never bothered to learn more than surface-level stuff about guns. I was an engine guy, a computer guy, and that was enough to keep a boy busy in the Outers. Well, more like I'd been convinced to "leave the warrior stuff to the warriors" like I was supposed to, and it was coming back to bite me.

I did know about moisture, heat, and pressure, though, and what they did to engines, specifically. There were ways to mitigate those issues, especially if a large part of the machine was exposed to moving air like my turrets were.

"Your new design looks . . . interesting," Trix mumbled from beside me, around a mouthful of some kind of cheese. This was one of the rare but increasingly frequent times he took to stretch his legs outside of his sniper's nest nowadays. With our drop in aggressive Scourge raids, he had been taking more breaks, choosing to help with cooking or changing bandages instead of constantly looking through the lens of his glamor spell. It had done wonders for his mood, being able to cook again. He truly enjoyed making others happy with the things he made.

Just now, though, he was picking at a ring of fingernail-sized fan blades meant to fit into a housing that would go at the "front" of my new gun-cooling concept. A couple of different iterations sat on my workbench as well, each rounded with a hollow part at the front and back like an atmo thruster or one of the Old Earth jet engines.

He was right about the look. The new design was weird. Where my guns had been all clean lines and robotic arms before, now there was an alien, egg-shaped growth attached to the barrel, immediately next to the action. I used a finger to Shape-weld another tiny prong of copper onto the heat-sink sleeve I was making.

"Yeah, well, I'm just slapping a solution on a problem I already have," I replied. "If I had the time, I'd redesign the whole thing to be one piece, but right now we're stuck with aftermarket mods for the current guns. Right now I'll be perfectly happy if the fan spins up and blows air. If that works, then maybe we'll talk about aesthetics."

I punctuated my sentence with a Devouring Grasp that consumed a log the size of my forearm and reduced it to a cloud of orange vapor, reapplying the Engine status to my Character Sheet. My mana ticked out of the double digits again, and the mana migraine I'd been courting faded into the background once more.

I'd gotten a C-grade Affinity with Mendau Wood earlier in the day, and I liked the extra mana I was getting from it. It also came with a jump in the percentage of Hunger Mana that the Mendau supposedly had, which I was less of a fan of. Controlling that mana was hard, almost as hard as it had been my first day on Ralqir (thanks, Tempered Channels).

It was annoying but useful in some ways, too. It was hard to use the foreign mana I was getting from the wood, but their widely different temperaments made it easier to distinguish between types of mana inside of me. The stuff that bent to my will when I asked it to—up to and including backflips and advanced calculus—was "my" mana, while the rabid squirrels I had to ply with treats and keep at arm's length with a stool was the "Hunger" variety. Before gaining higher Affinity, I'd just assumed the two were mixed like soup and I was stuck with the concoction until I'd used it all. Now, with more Hunger to work with, I was becoming able to tease out the good from the bad, which felt good. The practice helped me gain another level in Mana Manipulation, bringing that value up to four.

"So what are the monsters up to, Trix? Still sulking?" I asked as I hunched over the bristling heat sink.

Trix sniffed disdainfully. "After the attempted incursion last night, they appear to have learned about the disadvantageous nature of narrow valleys. Now they seem to be content with continuous psychological warfare. The sounds they make are truly disturbing, not to mention how they've taken up clawing the trees and rocks. Also, to clarify, I wasn't trying to disparage your, uh . . . Well, maybe I was. A little. This new shape is strange and off-putting, but that is not what I wanted to talk about," Trix said, shuffling his feet as his ears flattened uncomfortably. He leaned in, rising on his tiptoes to get nearer to my ear.

"This appears to be a long-term solution to a short-term problem," he whispered.

I looked over at him and raised an eyebrow. "What do you mean?"

"I mean, according to our schedule, we should be finding a way to get you home within three days, and that is at the maximum. Our dragon . . ." Trix paused to shake his head in disbelief. "Funny how I can say that so casually now . . . *Our dragon* is set to arrive in four, and you are to be in your own universe by then, for your own safety and ours. Is that not the plan?"

Looking down at my half-welded outer casing, I swallowed, wishing in that moment I had more awful tea. "Yeah. That's the plan."

"Would it not be more prudent to work on how to get you to the ruins in one piece, then?" he asked.

That was a completely rational question, one that I didn't have a great answer to.

"I'm working on that. I have several plans," I hedged.

Trix tilted his head skeptically. The whiskers on his nose did a curious dance that reminded me of Garret and his mustache.

"Some ideas," I added, defensively. "A few."

His little fox eyes got bigger and bigger until they were all I saw—big pools of brown and black, like a mug of hot chocolate before bed. His fur looked so soft. So adorable . . .

"Okay! Okay! I don't know yet. I see what you're doing," I admitted, swatting him away as I fought to tear my eyes from his. I may have also taken the opportunity to give his fur a pat. It really was soft.

Trix dropped the glamour and brushed the fur I'd mussed back into place, but he didn't seem ready to drop the subject. He looked down at the floor contemplatively, tapping a finger on his chin, and after several tense moments of staring, he figured out what to say. "Ryan, you know none of us blame you for the happenings as of late. This isn't your fault."

That came out of nowhere. Also, it was super-wrong. I was *obviously* to blame. Hell, who else *was* there to blame? Wasn't a guy allowed to blame himself for causing the apocalypse? Constance, Trix was right. The heat sinks looked like tumors.

"Of course I'm not to blame," I lied, sounding too defensive by half. I dove back into the heat sink, pouring myself into it to separate the prongs a bit more. Probably not something I needed to do, but it was better than letting my mind go down the self-flagellation rabbit hole again.

Trix held up his hands in surrender. "Of course. Of course. As I said, you are not to blame. I am just saying, you may be an outsider by birth, but—" He sighed and hunched his shoulders, as if he were afraid someone was going to hit him. "You're an outsider, but that doesn't mean you aren't welcome."

My mouth felt dry. I grasped with my non-Shaping hand for the empty cup next to me and tried to drain the last few drops of tea out of the bottom. *Nothing.*

"Yeah. I understand," I replied. "You guys have been wonderful to me. Best friends I've made in . . . I don't know how long."

Trix cleared his throat. "That's—That's not—I just want you to know that if you're having second thoughts about leaving, you are not the only one."

Something fluttered in the pit of my stomach, sending a tiny thrill through my body. However, the rational part of my mind smashed the thought I was having with a very big hammer.

That was impossible. Dangerous thinking.

It pained me to say it, but it had to be said. "Trix, I can't stay. I'm . . . poisoning you. Just my being here is destroying your home."

The little fox shook his head. "*Changing* our home, Ryan. Changing it," Trix corrected. "Not all change is bad. It may seem bad at the time—horrible even, like a forest fire—but afterward, life goes on. Sometimes the fire is even needed to keep the forest healthy. We of Ralqir have had much practice weathering such things."

I rubbed tiredly at my eyes with the heels of my hands. "But does it always involve this many dead people, Trix?" I asked.

Trix gave the vulpa version of a frown but bowed slightly in acknowledgement. "I don't diminish the cost we have paid. I lament the loss of all these people, and I hope we limit this cataclysm with our actions here. However, this crisis is only the latest in a chain of many, and not even the worst."

He put a clawed hand on my newly restored forearm. "It is also the craft of many hands, none your own. Do not ascribe guilt to yourself when you had no part in making things as they are. I can see the conflict in your words and actions. Do not let these feelings of guilt guide you down a path you do not want to walk."

"For the hundredth time, it's not guilt," I argued. "Besides, my feelings don't matter, Trix. What matters is you. All of you. It's easy to see I'm not supposed to be here."

"Of course your feelings matter, Ryan." He gave my arm a firm squeeze, a gesture that seemed almost comical for someone so small. "With or without you, Ralqir will find a way forward. We—Well, *most* of us . . . would just rather do it with you."

Such a naked admission. Of course it came from Trix the Honest. He and the others accepted me, even though I was dangerous. They wanted me to stay. They were practically *inviting* me to stay, though none of us knew what that would do in the long term. Despite that, they were willing to take that risk.

An image of a pet rock popped into my head. Rounded edges. A child's black-and-white paint job giving it goofy, offset eyes. Only I—the pet rock in this metaphor—was made of pure plutonium.

Did they not think it through? Did they not see what I meant to this place? Maybe they did. Maybe they did and they still wanted me. They were willing to live with the poison I was bringing with me.

That was too much. I short-circuited, dropping the saturation I was trying to achieve with the metal and staring into the middle distance, vaguely in the direction of my workbench.

After I didn't talk for some time, Trix let go of my arm and wandered off, after gingerly returning the fan blade to the little pile on the corner of my bench.

I didn't exactly see him go, but I felt it.

It was tempting, actually, to think of myself as a complete outsider. Blameless.

I wasn't here by choice, and things happened that were beyond my control. It was tempting to look at Ralqir as just the victim of a natural disaster. All this evil just . . . happened, like a storm or an earthquake. If not because of me, it would have been because of someone else, or maybe it would have taken the form of another thing, years later when the Scourge reached critical mass a bit further down the road.

I knew better than that, though, didn't I? Humans weren't meant to be here. It wasn't just my insertion point that was poisoning this place. It was *me*.

A breach of natural law.

The wretchwyrm had said that, just before trying to—I didn't know what. Kill me? Use me? That felt right. It was going to use me like the Dark Lord had used Ephelir. To what end, I didn't know.

Regardless, I'd been here for under a year, and I'd already set off an apocalypse and then, in an attempt to fix that, changed warfare forever. What else would I do to these people if I stayed? If I made a life here, what else would I change? Who else would try to use me?

You have done and you will continue to do to us as long as you live.

Closing my eyes, I reached inward and pulled myself close—all of me. I withdrew my presence from Ralqir and brought it inside of myself, cycling it the way Jassin had taught me, through my body and spirit. It felt like I was stretching, though I was doing the opposite, working a muscle that was woefully undeveloped, and it hurt. The hurt felt right.

Did the world seem better this way, without me? More pure? Less chaotic? The monsters were still there. I could hear them. Then there were the burning questions underneath the problem of the monsters. Even without me, what was the Scourge? What would it do once I'd gone? Would it leave these people in peace? What was it, really, when it wasn't wearing dead things like sweaters?

On my stool, staring at my workbench as the afternoon sun passed by, the world went on without me for a time, while I waited for some kind of sign.

CHAPTER THIRTY-THREE

See Old Friends

We didn't get attacked in earnest until later that night.

Trix had spotted them massing on the north side of the fortress before the action really kicked off, and he'd set off the alarm to give us time to get ready.

In preparation of what was to come, Geddon, Bole, and I moved a few of the turrets from gate duty over to the north wall to help with what was sure to be an action-packed night.

"Gah! It moved! My damned back is going to be killing me after this," Bole whined as he dropped his turret for the fourth or fifth time.

"The weight doesn't bother me!" Geddon shouted from ahead of us. He was holding two at a time up there, one in each hand.

Bole put his turret down to readjust his grip as the barrel jerked, trying to track a target somewhere outside of its range. "Hey, it's not the weight so much as the moving. It shifts all the mass. And it pinches!"

I wasn't having as hard of a time as Bole, thanks to my restored Body Stat, but I could see how the weight of the barrel, the magazine, and the heat sink jerking around in one's hands might play hell on a guy's muscles. I briefly thought of pretending to be having a harder time of it, maybe putting my burden down for a moment to give Bole's masculinity a bit of an ego boost, but . . .

Nah. It's Bole.

"Make sure to keep your barrel pointed away from the fight until you're ready to set up!" I ordered them both, remembering having to wrestle one of these things back into firing position as the horde closed in for the kill. "You think the arms pinch? Wait till the action starts cycling near your face!"

"I will say it again: you've got shit magic, Monk," Bole grumbled.

"Well, you're welcome to use yours to hold off an entire city full of monsters, Bole," I invited, finally setting my turret down next to the others and engaging the anchor clamps.

Once I got my gun all set up and anchored to the floor, I went back for Bole's. I didn't just take it from him, but I did take some of the weight. He seemed both thankful and grumpy at the same time, seeing how easily I was handling it. I ignored his sour look and made as little eye contact as possible.

Just as we engaged the anchor hooks and activated the heat-sink fans again, the Scourge finally got up the courage to charge. Trix warned us a half-second before the guns opened up and bathed the world in purple and thunder.

Not that I could see the Scourge. I couldn't see anything out there, beyond a few feet past the ditch, especially now that we had starlight streaming in all around us, except for the shadows where the entire fight would be taking place. I could fix that, though. A quick summoning of my arm-cannon (new and improved), and I made sure I wouldn't be fighting blind this time.

FOOMP!

The thirty-or-so-yard-wide corridor where the Scourge were pouring in, lit up in the glow of plasma fire. The bottleneck was the only spot of shade that connected our home-away-from-home to the rest of the forest, making it function much as a causeway might have in a medieval castle. It wasn't perfect, though. If I'd designed it or had more time to work on it, I'd have definitely cleared the area so the turrets could have had better line of sight. Only one or two were able to fire directly into the bottleneck, and I'd reprogrammed those for maximum penetration.

However, the trees we'd brought down on either side of the shadowed strip formed impromptu walls that provided cover from the more-extreme angles into the fatal funnel, so most of our firepower was pretty much forced to shoot the monsters as they emerged into the inner perimeter. The result was a clogging mess of bodies directly in the mouth of the bottleneck on our side that only the particularly nimble Scourge were able to traverse quickly, though they died as soon as they crested the top. Meanwhile, the over-penetrating head-on turrets were having a field day shooting through the mass of several monsters at a time.

It was these monsters at the mouth of the corridor that I was using as lighting tonight. After the initial plasma blast, a good chunk of them were now burning on their own.

"Holy hell, they're packed like sardines in there," I observed to whoever was nearby.

Bole was the only one who heard me. "Don't blame 'em for staying in the shade. Had a friend that got light-burned once. His skin crisped up like paper, and he went mostly blind. That's even after a trip to the church."

I whistled at that, giving a sympathetic frown and remembering the time I'd been light-burned. Unpleasant experience, even if you could heal from almost anything. It had taken me days—longer than any other wound I'd ever suffered.

Experience messages flew through my field of vision.

Scourge-Touched Undead defeated.
You have been awarded 30 Experience points. [20 base (-18 Level, +4 nemesis, +20 group, +20 chain, -16 non-combat Class)]
Scourge-Touched Pell defeated.
You have been awarded 5 Experience points. [5 base (--4 Level, +1 nemesis, +5 group, +5 chain, -4 non-combat Class)]
Scourge-Touched Goblin defeated.
You have been awarded 15 Experience points. [10 base (-9 Level, +2 nemesis, +10 group, +10 chain, -8 non-combat Class)]
Scourge-Touched Goblin defeated.
You have been awarded 15 Experience points. [10 base (-9 Level, +2 nemesis, +10 group, +10 chain, -8 non-combat Class)]
Scourge-Touched Pell defeated.
You have been awarded 5 Experience points. [5 base (-4 Level, +1 nemesis, +5 group, +5 chain, -4 non-combat Class)]

Drops in the bucket, really, but with the sheer number of them packed so close that one bullet might kill two or three at a time, those drops were turning into a shower.

Even while dying at an industrial scale, however, they were pushing through. Soon, my candles (read: "burning corpses") were snuffed out, and I was forced to launch another costly orb into the chaos.

FWOOSH!

The advancing mass took another plasma round to the collective face, and a big burst of Experience messages erupted through my feed. The advance halted for a moment as the horde dealt with a wall of burning flesh and fat too hot for the healthy members to step through without joining them in death.

Geddon nodded to me and took this as his cue. With a grunt, he vaulted over the side of the wall and took off running. The man was fast without his armor, his powerful legs eating up distance as fast as some vehicles back home. As long as you didn't ask him to do it over long distances, the guy performed like an Olympian. Better, even.

"I don't like it," Bole grumbled.

I turned and gave him a look. "Don't like easy fights?"

Bole spat over the side of the wall and looked around uneasily. "You said they're getting smarter. Well, this isn't smart. Not like the gresh or the ignarog. Those were real plays. But this . . . there's no misdirection or manipulation. They're just throwing themselves into the sausage-maker."

"Hmm." I turned, looking at the rest of the forest, which was bathed in starlight so bright compared to the perpetual gloom that it was blinding. Beyond, there was nothing. Just darkness.

"I hate to say it," Sissa half-shouted next to my ear to be heard over the guns, "but I agree with Bole. This is too straightforward. The Infected can afford the losses and still keep us surrounded, but I'm afraid we're missing something here."

"Exactly," Bole said. "If you're not seeing the scam, you're getting scammed."

As soon as Geddon got into range, he took the stubby construct he'd been wearing off his back and began to set up the tripod.

"Trix?" I called up to the sniper perch.

"I am keeping him covered. So far there have been several Infected that have slipped past the firewall, but I have brought them down without issue," Trix reported. "I concur with Corporal Bole and Sergeant Sissa. The nature of our fights up until this point may have biased me to expect the worst, but this seems too easy. It doesn't represent the escalation of strategic thinking that we've observed in the past."

Geddon slipped the blocky ammo-housing onto the tripod and engaged the fastening clip. Then with great care, he reached into a pocket on the front of his shirt (stuffed with lots of extra padding at my insistence) and drew out a glowing purple core, which he inserted into the turret. Once he got a few paces away and gave us the signal, I remotely activated the firing sequence.

The laser turret immediately began to bathe the battlefield in purple death, a fire hose of disco light that was hard to look at directly. I'd made the core a bit more robust this time, opting for a greater quantity of discharges over a shorter time period. The result was a solid waggling beam that doused the entire forest.

As its designer, I knew that the light show wasn't a continuous stream, as it appeared to the naked eye, but a high-frequency strobing effect, a rapid-fire barrage of single, low-damage attacks that came too fast to perceive. They caused no real harm on their own, but my bonus Damage from Knife in the Dark certainly accumulated over the course of a few hundred hits, which targets accrued in less than a second.

The attacks spewed out of the turret's barrel, melting through the front ranks of the Scourge like acid, and then penetrating beyond. The first ranks disintegrated almost immediately, melting into rainbow goo as bonus Damage tended to do. Those behind them fared little better, only taking a couple of more seconds for their molecules to also lose cohesion. Then the rank behind them followed. It was like seeing a time-lapse film of a candle melting at 1000x speed. Ten seconds of tongue-swallowing laser show, and the horde was reduced to its component parts, along with a good portion of the fallen trees, the leaves on the ground, and anything else organic and unlucky enough to have been there. Then the bottleneck was just mud, bordered by the half-exposed metal skeletons of the trees, dripping oily ichor as their organic shells sloughed away.

The other turrets went silent once there was nothing left to shoot.

"They are retreating to the edge of the outer perimeter." Trix sighed. "They're still making that godsawful noise wherever they go. All of them. I'd choose gunfire over that at this point." He appeared over the lip of his basket to flip over and slide down his climbing rope. When he got to the floor, he paused to stretch his body to get the stiffness out of his shoulders.

Geddon was already on his way back to the fort, carrying the smoking laser turret over one shoulder. He was grinning from ear to ear, that way he did when he got the chance to indulge in violence.

Movement.

I blinked. There was movement behind Geddon. Close behind. No light. What was it? I turned to the turrets and back to the figures, which were well in range, yet the turrets weren't firing.

"Trix, get back up there!" I shouted. "Something's happening! Geddon!"

I summoned another plasma ball from my Spatial Storage and loaded it into my arm cannon.

Geddon tilted his head, confused for a moment. Then he checked over his shoulder. Whatever he saw there, it made him drop the turret right there in the dirt.

Then my attention was arrested by something beyond the starlight circle, up high. Something impossibly big. It wasn't a tree. I knew that immediately. I followed the shadow of whatever it was up with my eyes, up and up until I was staring into a great, burning pair of orange eyes above a fanged, hellmouth. It opened.

A colossal, terrible sound smashed into my senses, too deep to be properly appreciated by the ears, forcing me to my knees. It was a sound you felt in your guts as it pulverized you from within.

The face in the trees twisted in rage and disgust as it vomited flames in a geyser down toward the ground. No—toward the Scourge. A swathe of tiny black silhouettes disappeared in the blaze, instantly reduced to ash. The ground cracked under the inferno to expose burning Mendau roots that twisted and writhed unnaturally, sizzling as their sap ignited. The roots themselves sought out individual Scourge-Touched, impaling them, wrapping their bodies tight, and squeezing them until they popped.

The fire illuminated only the legs of the giant, bark-covered, gray, gnarled wood in a vague humanoid shape.

Sweet Constance, what is that?

Voices called my name.

"Ryan! Ryan!"

The deep, contrasting shadows concealed the majority of the monster, limiting my perceptions to only impressions. Long legs, a tree-trunk torso, whipcord arms that hung down nearly to its feet.

Something massive whooshed through the air, striking something solid.

"Fuck!" Bole screamed. Hands grabbed me and pulled me to the side, as a truck-sized splinter of Mendau tree slammed into the wall near where I'd just been. The wall itself took the blow badly, crumbling inward to spill shards of petrified wood into the courtyard.

"Ryan!"

I *knew* that voice. I scrambled to get Bole's hands off me, to look over the side of the wall, or whatever of it remained.

The tiny figures—the ones the turrets hadn't fired upon. They were close. They were running *with* Geddon.

"Holy shit. Tiba?" I gasped.

She was waving her arms, the feathers on the head of Hunty's spear orange in the firelight. She was—

"Ryan!" she screamed. "Hide!"

My mouth opened and closed.

Thank Constance, she's alive!

The hellmouth started to turn ponderously toward us.

"Hide now!" Tiba begged from down below.

I blinked again, the realization hitting me like a blow to the head. I let my legs drop out from under me to get me below the lip of the wall. Then I rolled off the battlements to fall the fifteen feet or so onto our bedrolls with a *whup!*

My guts shook with the seismic force of the gods' footsteps, and my bowels turned to water, imagining it coming closer after it had seen me.

That face the thing had made . . . The shape. The character. I knew that face.

Kuul had stepped onto the battlefield.

CHAPTER THIRTY-FOUR

Go Off-Path

Tiba and her guards clambered over the pile of settling rubble that used to be the north wall before nearly collapsing into the waiting embraces of the dragonkin sisters. Geddon was only slightly behind, seeming to waffle between retreating to the fort and turning around to watch the carnage outside with the look of a kid seeing his first fireworks show.

The goblins were looking rough. All of them were covered from head to toe in black soot and sticky mud. Both of Tiba's guards had lost their armor somewhere out there, and one of them, Kelub, was wielding a sharpened stick instead of his spear. Tiba herself was covered in weeping scratches and cuts all over her exposed skin, from what looked like running through underbrush or perhaps fighting a whole family of small animals, and the men hadn't fared much better. Their clothes were in such tattered condition, the only thing protecting all of the goblins' modesty was the layer of mud and grime.

Beyond the walls, the forest burned. Gouts of flame shot down from above to engulf scattered clusters of Scourge-Touched, incinerating them as surely as light from the Maelstrom. Booming footsteps rattled my bones and sent jolts through my stomach. The air shook with every movement the giant made.

Tiba, only on her feet now thanks to the help of Kelub and the support of her spear, panted with exertion. Her wet, matted hair was draped over half her face as she paused to take in the aghast expressions of everyone there. Then she seemed to remember something and rushed forward too fast for Kelub to follow. He tried, but he didn't have the energy to keep up with his queen anymore, instead falling to one knee to catch his breath.

Trix was the first to speak. He'd slid down his rope and was staring wide-eyed at the trio of filthy goblins like they were spirits made flesh. "Your Majesty, you made it! It is a miracle!"

Tiba didn't seem to register anything we were saying, though. She stumbled over the loose rocks, putting a hand on Trix to steady herself as she searched frantically in the dark.

"Tiba? What happened out there?" I asked.

Tiba finally found the thing she was looking for. She rushed past Trix to kneel next to the bedroll where we'd stashed Beedy before the fight. He had largely been spared the collapse of the wall, thankfully, though my workbench that he was under had not been equally spared. It was now a load-bearing column, apparently, the only thing keeping its particular section of the wall upright.

With trembling fingers Tiba untied the knot on her herb pouch and reached gingerly inside.

"W—What is she—" Bole stammered from across the remains of the fire.

"She got her medicine," I realized aloud. "Tiba—"

"Not now, Ryan," she croaked dryly, reaching over to scoop a live ember from the fire onto a tiny pile of kindling. "Every second counts. I explain soon, but you really need to stay out of sight." Then she began to chant something quietly as she ground something in a bowl over the open flame.

"It is a close thing. A bad thing," Kelub lamented tiredly from beside me. "We go down into Stoneheart tunnels to get the medicine. We, her honored guards, tell her it is a bad idea. Bad place now that Baned use it."

Kelub shuddered and gripped the remains of his spear, his gaze far away. In the flickering light of the fire, I saw black discoloration on the tip of the shaft that might have been blood.

"But she is a brave queen," he continued, finally seeming to remember I was still here. "It is a small miracle we find one of these at all. Soon as she picks it, the plant starts to wither. No keeping. No drying. We have to run the entire way, quiet and quick before the medicine goes bad, but when we get here, there is no way to enter."

"The Infected are scattering before the giant thing!" Geddon announced from the rubble of the wall. "Whatever it is, it appears to hold more enmity for our enemies than for us. They're giving ground and running into their holes like mice! Haha!"

"The Baned," Tiba corrected as she scooped the paste she'd been making onto a tiny fingertip. "He hates, most of all, the Baned." She spared a pitying glance over in my direction. "Mostly."

Tiba scooted over to her patient and got a leg up and over Beedy's body, straddling the man's chest and setting her legs on either side like she was about to ride a bull. Then, without warning, she jammed her whole hand far down Beedy's throat.

Beedy almost immediately started to choke, his body reflexively writhing to try to get away from the thing that was suffocating him. His hands searched for something to push away, to grab and fight against, but Tiba didn't budge. Beedy was too weak to resist even a tiny thing like her.

I put a hand out to stop Bole, who had already begun to rush forward with his sword half out of its scabbard.

"Wait!" I told him.

Bole looked at me like I'd gone insane, then tried to rush forward once more, but he was stopped cold. He was working against my metal arm, and it didn't budge in the slightest. The look in his eye was manic, and for a moment, I thought I might have been in danger of him drawing his weapon on me. However, it only took him another couple of heartbeats to get control of himself again.

Beedy gagged and spasmed, making terrible mewling sounds for a good minute before he stopped entirely, his body seeming to give up on struggling. Even his face went slack. Only then did Tiba take her hand from his mouth. Immediately, Beedy's chest started to rise and fall, this time in a natural rhythm instead of the rasping struggle for breath he'd had since his injury. For the first time in days of hellish torture, it looked like Beedy was truly resting without the pain. The change was like night and day.

Tiba sighed with relief as she pulled her hand from his mouth and slumped forward, her eyes closing as if she were falling asleep on her patient's chest. She didn't, though. She slid off Beedy and dragged herself over to the largest pile of remaining embers from the fire, sparing a lungful of air to blow on them half-heartedly before plopping down to warm her hands.

"That one has scars for his whole life, but he lives," she rasped tiredly before asking: "Do you have any food or water for Kelub and Grorg?"

Trix was moving as soon as the goblin said "food." I didn't even have to trans-late. The little vulpa was already next to me listing ingredients to summon from Storage, which I tried to oblige. I didn't know the names for all the things he was asking for, and he had to describe them to me, sometimes at length. That's why you don't ask the pack mule for stuff, you just take it. Unfortunately, this pack mule had to be asked.

Intuiting that the dangerous part was over, I finally let Bole go. He passed Tiba, stopping momentarily as if he wanted to say something, but he thought better of it after a look back at me. Instead he went over to Beedy, collapsed next to him, and bowed his head over the other man's chest. We all pretended not to notice the tears.

Careful to not get anywhere near the gap in the wall and show my face, I sat down a respectful distance from Tiba across the fire.

"The Scourge had us encircled, and there was no way through," I guessed.

I'd been afraid of that. I'd delayed bringing down the trees as long as I'd dared, but it hadn't been enough.

Tiba nodded. She was nearly asleep just sitting there, but at the same time, her gaze flicked back and forth frantically, as if she were not entirely here with us. Understandable, considering how long she'd been hiding and running.

I tried to switch to a more-casual tone, but it just clashed with the subject matter. "So you brought Kuul. That's . . . inventive."

The queen nodded again, before finding the energy to turn to meet my stare. She looked frightened, sad, guilty, but relieved at the same time.

"He still pissed at me?" I asked.

Tiba shrugged, but her trembling lips indicated good odds of the answer being in the affirmative.

I ventured what I hoped was an appreciative smile. "Well, glad to have you back, regardless. We missed you," I said, nodding in Bole's direction before adding. "And thank you for Beedy. You went above and beyond for him when you didn't have to, and I think you saved two lives today. I haven't met a lot of queens, Tiba, but I think I can safely say, you're probably the best queen an honorary goblin can hope for."

That seemed to get through to her. A glimmer of light returned to her eyes, and she attempted a weak little smile, a tiny tear drawing a line of cleanish green down her cheek.

"Thank you for not being mad," she whispered.

I waved a dismissive hand and struck a nonchalant posture that I hoped was convincing.

"Pfft. Mad? If Kuul still wants to kill me, he can take a number and wait like everyone else," I said before leaning forward and adopting a more earnest tone. "You did what you had to do. We'll talk once you've had some rest, okay? Geddon?"

"The giant is a terror!" Geddon announced excitedly. "The Scourge aren't even bothering to fight. They truly *can* feel fear!"

"Okay," I replied, standing to assess the damage myself. "We need to work on getting that wall patched up and the turrets back to sweeping. Think you can get on that?"

Geddon cast about the rubble under his feet and shrugged. "Maybe with a few weeks and good timber I could make a wall out of this mess, but this is stonework. No way are we getting a working wall up in time for it to be useful."

"We'll have to plug up the breach another way, then," Samila suggested. "Maybe a flame turret and a deeper trench. That should at least blunt any charges aimed for it while we do a patch job."

"Ugh. Not more digging," Geddon groaned. "My blisters are only just now healing. You would think sword calluses would help with that, but evidently they are completely different areas of the hand."

"Just wear your gloves, you big baby," Samila replied.

"I shouldn't have to!"

Sissa lowered herself down from the ledge where she'd been watching the battle and dropped between the two of them. "I think we're missing something here," she said, turning to look at everyone expectantly. "Do you see? Anyone?" she asked.

No one offered up an answer.

She sighed and reached up to rub at her temple, though it was a largely performative gesture since her helmet was still on.

"This is the first time in days the enemy is not encircling us. This may be *it*," she said.

I blinked, not quite following what she was saying, but my train of thought got there eventually.

"You're saying we should make a break for it?" I guessed.

Sissa nodded. "The giant has offered us an opportunity, one we may not get again. The Infected are scattered and diminished right now. This is our chance to slip through."

"Your ride won't be here for another two or three days," I replied, shaking my head. "No one's ready to travel, and Jassin's army is probably even farther out than your dragon. Then once I leave, that's it. My turrets will just be paperweights."

"If we move now, the enemy might be in too much disarray to punish us," Sissa said. Her new sword was out, and her body was angled toward the breach in the wall like she was mentally preparing to charge out already. No, she was preparing to risk it all and be a big damned hero, and, in her mind, seconds counted.

"Wait. The monk is leaving? Why is the monk leaving?" Bole was on his feet again, turning confusedly from me to the others and back again, waiting for a response that no one offered.

I had to diffuse this.

"That's a big assumption, don't you think? The Scourge is a hive mind. We get spotted out there by just one, and we'll be neck-deep in bad. You're really willing to bet everyone's lives on this?" I asked.

Sissa gave me a pained look. "Ryan, the mission was never to hold out forever. It was to bait the Infected, get you to your exit, and save the world—in that order, according to you."

"Well, yeah!" I scoffed. "But it also wasn't meant to be a suicide mission. I thought I'd made that clear. I was originally going to do it alone just to keep you and the others safe!"

"You were going to feed yourself to a foe of superior numbers on their home turf. You had no chance by yourself. We had to come. I'm not proposing a noble sacrifice out of the history books. I'm simply talking about the less-risky of two bad options," Sissa replied.

"No, you're not. You're only looking at two of the worst outcomes and choosing one. We'll find another way." Real heat seeped into my voice, and my hands balled themselves into fists. There was no way it had come down to this. I wouldn't let it.

Sissa looked me up and down and raised a disapproving eyebrow ridge. "I presented those two because all others are variations of them. We either stay and die or leave and perhaps live. That's what it boils down to. What happens if the giant notices us while you think of another way to play this, and it decides we are worth incinerating as well?" she asked. "That would be certain death for all of us. We can't fight it, and we can't run from it, either. The outcome would be the same as if the Scourge overwhelmed us. Our best chance is to slip away while both forces are distracted. I believe the healthy among us can sneak out. You show your face at the ruins to draw the Infected, then give the wounded a chance to make for the mountains."

Samila let out an indignant, choking sound at that. "No way you're leaving m—"

"He's not trying to kill us yet, and he's not running out of Baned anytime soon. Better to wait and see rather than get everyone killed running in the dark," I said. I knew my argument was weak. The others could guide me to the insertion point, but I didn't know what else to say. Things were looking uncertain, but they weren't so bad I'd risk the rest of them just to get home.

Sissa looked disappointed. "You know our safety is a secondary concern, Ryan. The mission is what matters, or have you forgotten that? How many lives will it cost if we don't come through? Has it even occurred to you that we might all die here in this old tree, and Ralqir will have to endure another cataclysm? I'm not sure if you've noticed, but things aren't looking ideal. The enemy is limitless. Our people are wounded and exhausted, and there's no relief in sight. That's only going to get worse. Battle takes its toll, even when we win. We're only going to get slower and sloppier, and then there's the giant. Can you guarantee we hold out against that? For now, the perimeter is holding, but what about tomorrow when it decides to step across it? " she asked as she gestured pointedly at the collapsed part of the wall. "If you die or, Light forbid, are converted, it's over anyway. At least if we make an attempt now, you'll be alive, and we'll have a chance at survival too. Everyone has a chance to win."

"The word 'chance' is doing a lot of work there, Sissa," I shot back. "The goblins are dead on their feet, and Beedy is only just now back from death's door. You'll just be hunted down and made into one of them. That's not happening. I refuse to let that happen."

She took a step forward and drew herself up to her full height until she was only a few inches from looking me in the eye. "And who are you to make that decision for us? I guess 'why' is more of the question. Why do our lives weigh so heavily on the scale compared to all the people who will die putting this threat down if we fail? What makes us so special that we deserve that exceptional consideration? Shut up, Bole!" Sissa snapped, as the man opened his mouth to interject.

He did, indeed, shut up.

I struggled for something to say, an argument to make, but my words failed me. "You just—I mean, I can't do that. I can't just leave you out there and hope for the best. There has to be something else."

The sergeant let her arms dangle down at her sides, and let out a long, tired sigh. "Look, Ryan, we all want you to stay. I believe we've all made that clear in our own ways. That doesn't absolve us of responsibility to our people. We're here to save the world. Either we need to hold out longer than we are currently able, or we need to get you out of here, fast."

Samila, Geddon, Bole, and Trix were all gathered around now but at a safe distance, Trix looking like he wished he were even smaller than he was. Bole and Geddon seemed more unsure of themselves than I'd ever seen them.

I could feel my body tensing, the anger boiling up from inside. I refused to be backed into this particular corner. It can't be a choice between my friends or the world. I refused to choose. "I see what you're doing. You can't—"

"Yes, I can! How do you not get this? We've come to a fork in the road. One way means saving everyone we know at great risk to ourselves. The other, I can't see the end of, Ryan, but it's looking like death by a thousand cuts or under a giant's foot. With stakes like these, I choose the path I can see."

She spoke to the others now, turning herself to address each of them. "If saving innocent lives means our deaths, then there is nothing else to discuss. That is the 'duty' part of our creed. We don't matter when weighed against the entire population of Ralqir."

"You matter to me," I said. My good hand was shaking. My jaw was clenched so hard my teeth hurt. I felt like a mountain was pressing down on my shoulders, and it was all I could do to stay upright. "You all matter to me."

"You selfish prick!" Sissa shouted. Her sword had somehow come between us, the point suddenly an inch from my chest.

"Siss, wait—" Samila cautioned, putting out a hand between us, but Sissa wasn't listening.

"We are not special! What about the families that used to live in Eclipse? The people in the market? We waded through their blood, Ryan. Remember? I still see it sometimes when I'm cleaning my armor, washing my clothes, and in my godsdamned dreams. Why do people like them matter less than us? You would bet the lives of *all* our people just because you've known us for all of . . . what? Just over a month? How many would you let die just to preserve some tenuous connection you've imagined between all of us? Just to spare your feelings? You, selfish, sentimental—" Sissa's anger was boiling. The scales on her face were the blackest of blue. Her face, stained by almost-invisible tears as they streamed down her cheeks, looked like a porcelain mask cracking under pressure.

I didn't have a heart anymore, but I felt like it had just been torn open, the blood leaking from my chest, taking all my warmth with it.

Samila took a step between us and knocked Sissa's sword to the side. She looked frightened, conflicted as she turned between the two of us.

"Siss, s-stop it. W—" she stammered.

"Ask him how many more of our people he's willing to sacrifice," Sissa barked. "Ask him."

Samila looked at me and opened her mouth, probably not to ask but to mediate between the two of us somehow, but she froze, the words dying on her lips.

I felt cold. Still. Like everything, all the noise and distractions that had been weighing on me had fallen away. I was an icy pond, smooth as glass and utterly quiet.

Below the calm surface, in the darkness of the deep, there were faces. I didn't have to see them to know they were there. They'd always been there. They were the faces of those I'd let go. Those I'd failed.

Mom was there, of course. Vince, too. Hunty. Others less distinct—more ideas than anything but so very real to me, like images conjured during a nightmare . . . The countless innocents of Ralqir.

My mouth worked without my consent, finally giving voice to the feelings I'd been afraid to express until now.

"How many would I sacrifice, Sissa?" I asked. "None. Not one goddamned soul. Not again. No more noble sacrifices. No more bodies on the pyre of the greater good. No more. I refuse."

Sissa scoffed, preparing herself to say something well-reasoned and correct, but I cut her off.

"I refuse!" I snarled. "This is the line! No one else dies for me! Not even one!" The ice of my frozen pond cracked and parted. The water churned, stirring up the things in the deep.

"The multiverse has *taken from me*," I growled. The words left my throat like ice floes grinding together as they surfaced. "It's taken more than its share, and I just let it happen. Well, I'm not doing that anymore."

Samila took an involuntary step back, only to bump into her sister. Sissa looked shaken too, like she'd seen something just now she didn't like. The anger and frustration she'd been expressing evaporated in a matter of seconds. She wasn't pointing her sword at me anymore. If anything, she seemed to want to reach out, but she was brave and true, her conviction unwavering.

"The world doesn't work like that," she whispered, pleading. "Sometimes we have to choose. We mortals make our choices as best we can. Then we live with the consequences. Those are the lines of fate. If you want to redraw those lines, that's admirable. But foolish. You're not a god, Ryan."

The statement rang in the air briefly. Then a tiny thought crystallized at the very center of me—a kernel of something that clicked into place, connecting disparate parts of myself that I'd never in a million years have associated with one another. It wasn't something I could put into words. It was more of an enhanced understanding, one that shone a light on all the parts of my soul I hadn't dared peer into for years.

"No, I'm not," I admitted, turning away and stepping over to right the stool next to my workbench. I swept an arm over the rubble that covered it, sending the rocks and dust flying to expose the chalk drawings I'd been working on before. "Not yet, at least."

CHAPTER THIRTY-FIVE

Get Called Out

There was one thing Sissa was right about. I wasn't going to make it to the insertion point. Not as I was.

I couldn't just walk over there. The Scourge, despite getting a good scare when Kuul arrived, were still everywhere—scattered, hiding, even if they weren't immediately visible from our current position. Once I was out of the turrets' ranges, it would only be a matter of time before I was spotted and surrounded. How long it would take for the Scourge-Touched to swarm me would be down to speed and a lot of luck.

Sneaking wasn't much of an option, either. The System had seen to that by not giving me an Ability that would allow me to see in the dark. The only way I was getting around out there was if I had a guide like Trix to hold my hand, and that ran up against my little I-want-my-friends-to-live-through-this issue. Any direction I went, they needed to do the opposite. They needed to be far away when the Scourge suddenly didn't have a lightning rod to unleash their fury upon.

In either scenario, the most vulnerable my friends and I would ever be would be when we'd be transitioning from one position to another. While the others would be making a break for the pass to the northwest where they would either bump into Jassin or their ride would find them, I would be running through the woods and trying not to die.

Therefore, I needed to minimize travel time and maximize time spent at the tutorial facility to give my people more time and distance before the Scourge was free to chase after them. The problem was that I had no idea how to do that.

"Finally getting around to making armor, then?" Geddon asked, some kind of cheesy cornbread spilling out of his mouth. Soggy crumbs sprayed over the surface of my workbench with every hard consonant.

I paused Shaping briefly to brush away the tiny bits of food, careful not to smear the chalk markings I'd made this morning while also fighting the urge to grind my teeth. It wasn't Geddon's fault I'd been stuck here all day, and it wouldn't be fair to take out my frustrations on him.

Kuul had continued his rampage through the night and well into the morning, and he showed no signs of tiring. He chased the Scourge-Touched with absolute fury, vomiting fire at them, stomping them, and taking massive swipes with his giant hands. Wherever he went, the Scourge scattered. Smoke hung in the air everywhere from fresh fires and burning bodies, while the horde stalked through the forest in ones and twos, refusing to leave sight of their prey, even in the face of a potentially fiery death.

Or at least that's what I was told by those who were able to go up on the walls. According to Tiba, under no circumstance was I allowed to be seen by the flaming goblin kaiju monster. Apparently, "that would be bad."

Tiba hadn't been up on the walls since she'd arrived, either, choosing to stay in the shadows and wince with every booming crash Kuul made.

"Rage is what fuels Kuul now, Ryan. Nothing else," she'd said. "He burns with it until his enemies die or he does, and I think he still blames you for everything."

That didn't explain why she didn't want to show her face either, but it didn't take a genius to understand how terrified she was of her old chief. The stress of having him so close by shone clearly on her face, the lack of real rest and knife-edge tension making her look hollow and brittle.

Kuul never touched our little home away from home, though. He'd been the historian of the Stone Heart tribe, so maybe he still held this place in high regard. Then again, maybe the outsiders taking shelter in the ruined goblin market were further down the list of priorities than the Baned and their kind.

Whatever Kuul's reasons, he left us alone and provided a much-needed reprieve from fighting . . . provided I stayed down here, out of sight.

"Mmm. Excellent." Geddon chewed in my ear as he expressed his appreciation seemingly for both my work and his food in the same breath.

Frankly, I was surprised the big Leori could tell what I was making at all. Right now, all I had were plates that only theoretically fit together in the vague shape of a human. I'd already scrapped and reformed my current object of frustration—the beginnings of a leg joint—a dozen times, trying to get the seal Triggers to work right. They were either too fast, threatening to take a bite out of my flesh when I used them, or they were so slow and unresponsive as to be useless. As it was, I would probably be better off digging my way to the insertion point, because running in this was out of the question.

"You know, at first I was surprised you hadn't done something like this before," Geddon continued at the precise moment I thought it was safe to dive back into the knee joint to unfreeze it for the fortieth time. "Given how much you get hurt, I always thought it strange that you didn't make the effort to protect yourself with your magic."

I sighed, letting the mana I was gathering dissipate. Maybe it was time for a break, anyway.

"There was always something else to do," I replied. "Other fires to put out, you know?"

"I'm not saying it was a bad move," the Leori added, raising his hands defensively. "I actually admire your methods. All attack, no retreat. Stand somewhere and dare the enemy to move you, right?"

In the interest of not dispelling any air of coolness I'd accidentally gathered around here, I went with it. "Sure. The turrets were a sword and shield at the same time. Armor just seemed like a problem I could put off, given how well I heal. Now that I have some time, I figured I'd get on it."

"Don't let him lie to you like that, Geddon," Samila snarked from on the wall above us. Her new shield—a reinforced steel and aluminum thing I'd whipped up for her to replace her old one—hung proudly in her hand as she smirked down at the two of us. "The idea of armoring himself at all hadn't even popped into his head until he figured it would benefit someone else."

"That's not true," I argued. "If I made a list of stuff I wanted to build but never had time to, I'd have to organize it into volumes. Big ones. You'd need new shelves."

Geddon raised an eyebrow and frowned thoughtfully up at Samila. "You know, now that I think about it, I see what you mean. His underdeveloped sense of self manifests as an almost-suicidal tendency to put others before himself, a personality trait so ingrained he cannot conceive of doing otherwise. He has seen himself as a spectator in his own life for so long, it has even shaped his approach to war. His machines allow him to participate in battle from afar, so that they protect others as no single combatant could reasonably do and simultaneously keep the battle at a safe distance, lest he give into the darker part of his personality he truly fears."

I swiveled on my stool, slowly, until I was facing the big guy, my mouth involuntarily open but with no words coming to mind.

Samila, similarly, stood agape.

"What?" Geddon asked with a sheepish grin. "Fighting tells you a lot about someone. In a way, it is the most honest form of self-expression in the world."

"I told you!" Samila exclaimed, pointing an accusatory finger over at Sissa. "I told you! What did I say?!"

Sissa, who'd been avoiding me for the whole day, took a break from staring intently out into the smoke to roll her eyes and look up to the heavens for strength. She'd been doing that a lot lately. "Fine, Sam. Get it out of your system."

The smaller dragonkin shook her head smugly. "No. I want *you* to say it," Samila goaded.

Sissa growled like a jungle cat and showed her teeth but capitulated only after a long, hard stare. "Geddon is probably more intelligent than anyone on the squad," she grumbled, getting a reproachful look from her sister. "Including me," she admitted before amending her statement in a rush. "Intelligence he refuses to apply to anything other than smashing things!"

"And?!" Samila wasn't satisfied yet.

"And Ryan is stupid and would cut off his own arm before letting anyone else even mildly inconvenience themselves for him. That might even be how he lost it in the first place. There. Are you happy?" she muttered.

Samila sniffed haughtily and crossed her arms. "Maybe. I don't like the way you said it, though."

"Might I offer an opinion?" Bole interjected with a raised finger.

"Shut up, Bole," the sisters shouted in unison.

Bole blinked and seemed to unsuccessfully suppress a shudder, but there was a little smile peeking out from the shadows of his hood, too.

The sisters continued to bicker.

Meanwhile, I cleared my throat uncomfortably and stood, suddenly very interested in more of that cheese bread Geddon was getting everywhere.

Beedy met me at the fire ring and shakily slid the iron pan full of bread over toward me. The man wasn't up and about yet, but he was awake more than asleep nowadays, choosing to set up next to the fire to stay warm. He had taken over as our de facto cook for a couple of meals now, despite Trix being much better at the job than anyone else. Unfortunately, now that he was on the mend, Beedy was back to being silently helpful instead of speaking up and keeping Bole in his place.

"Thanks, Beedy. Smells great," I said, stuffing an overlarge piece of the bread in my mouth to signal I was not going to contribute more to the conversation. I could feel the redness in my cheeks, which I wanted to attribute to the heat of the fire but knew better.

Trix was there too, in a rare moment when he wasn't watching the Scourge from his basket.

"Any progress, Ryan?" the vulpa asked, concern clear in his voice.

"Not really," I replied, once I was able to swallow enough to speak. At least this was a conversation I was comfortable having. It wasn't about me. "The actuators are clumsy and weird. Input is either getting magnified a hundred times or slowed down to a crawl. No in-between. No way to vary it."

"And you insist on having your suit of armor be . . . powered?" Trix asked, trying out the unfamiliar term.

"I don't know. It's starting to look like a pipe dream. I might have to just have to go medieval if I want to get it done at all."

"I thought you said that plan was doomed to failure?" Trix asked.

"It is," I admitted with a shrug.

"That sounds like a less-appealing option, then."

"It's not my pick, no."

One of his ears perked up, and his eyes darted over to the side in feigned nonchalance. "What about—"

"No, Trix."

Compromise on sentencing my friends to death. Going with me. That's what he was about to propose. They wanted to escort me all the way to the tutorial facility and send me on my merry way. Sissa still held out hope it was possible, and Trix didn't take long to get on board, too.

I wasn't budging, though. If they wanted me to sneak through the forest before it was time, they'd have to tie me up and carry me, and I was very heavy.

Even if their plan was a success, they'd immediately get swarmed by the Scourge, I was sure. That was the only way I saw that plan going down. If they didn't spot me on the way to the insertion point, they would certainly notice when the spigot of power got turned off for good, and they would come running.

I would die before I let any of that happen. Thanks to Jassin, I guessed that was always on the table, anyway. Funny that my death would solve all our problems. The only thing keeping me from seriously considering it right now was that people still needed my turrets.

Suddenly a gust of wind slammed down into our camp area, powerful enough to send bedrolls flying and knock over camp gear. Sparks from the fire gusted in all directions and stung my bare skin, while Trix hopped on one foot to avoid setting his fur alight.

I felt the irresistible urge to look up.

The space above us seemed to twist, split, and shatter—a displacement that could not, should not be. Glossy crimson scales, razor talons, and great, flapping wings that spanned wide enough to engulf the entire fort folded into the space above us until I was looking at a hulking, red, honest-to-Constance dragon. It hovered there, nearly vertically with its sinuous tail snaking down to brush the ground, its body long and sleek, and its head a horned maw with tiny yellow eyes that regarded us all imperiously from far overhead. Most disturbing to me, it only flapped its wings once, despite its size, its altitude never wavering. It gave the whole picture an air of impossibility. Wrongness.

The dragon's mouth opened, and a voice spoke in my head, dominating my thoughts in a way I hadn't felt since my time under Eclipse in the presence of—

"MORTAL BEINGS, DO NOT FLEE."

Everyone stood there obligingly, gawking up at the thing. No one had the capacity to move, anyway. I felt like a one-ton lead blanket was draped over my body. When no one ran away screaming, the dragon raised its head and let loose a gout of smoke with a pleased *CHUFF!*

"GOOD. THOSE AMONG YOU WITH THE BLOOD OF TSUMLESTORA, ATTEND ME. BRING TO ME THE HUMAN."

Well, shit.

Our dragon, it seemed, had arrived early, and it wanted to meet me.

CHAPTER THIRTY-SIX

Expose the Truth

The dragon let the statement hang in the air for a good ten or twenty seconds as it stared down at us like a predatory bird that had happened across a nest of mice. It only flapped its wings a few times, but I still found it disconcerting. A living thing that size had no business flying, much less doing it so effortlessly. With every flap, the wind battered us hard, seemingly to make up for that discrepancy.

I cast a brief glance over at our Sissa, who looked as shocked as everyone else in the fort, but I could see the calculations running behind our dragon expert's expression. A heartbeat later, she stepped forward and bowed her head, as if she were in prayer and pressing her hands together in front of her body.

"Old One," Sissa said somberly, "it pleases us all greatly that you have come to honor the pact you have made with our father." The words had an air of formality to them, like this was something she knew how to do but had never done.

The dragon didn't answer immediately, choosing to let Sissa sit there with her head bowed and posed in supplication. Perhaps it was waiting for the rest of us to do the same, or it was ignoring everything except for the immediate carrying-out of its orders for the sisters to bring forth the human. When none of that happened, however, the dragon allowed itself to finally drift downward and land lightly outside the fortress walls, just across the spike trench.

It was easily able to see above the walls without having to even stretch, its serpentine neck allowing its head to pass over the battlements to eye all of us one after the other. Its massive, taloned foot that it set over our entrenchment snapped our stakes in half, and the air crackled like logs in a fire even though I felt no heat.

What was worse were the eyes—great, golden things with stars for pupils, just like Sissa and Samila's. The similarity disturbed me. On the sisters it looked exotic and striking, but on this thing . . . I simply wished they were turned somewhere else. They burned with intensity that pinned you in place when you looked directly into them. They saw things inside of you that it shouldn't.

A memory of Mom flashed through my mind, and I got the irrational feeling we really should have cleaned up better if we were going to meet a god today.

For my part, I did my best to look small and not-humanlike. Unsuccessfully. I also couldn't help but eye the nearest exit, which was right there at the front of the fort, as it always had been. Where I would go if I needed to run, I didn't know.

Once it had landed and given us all the once-over, it finally acknowledged Sissa. The voice spoke in my head again, this time at a manageable level.

"Greetings, Blood of Tsumlestora. It pleases me to come when our home has need, as well as to provide aid to my kin's progeny. It also comes as no surprise to find Tsumlestora's spawn poised atop a once-in-an-age confluence of events. From his noble line, I would expect no less."

Well, that sounded nice, though the words still rattled around in my skull to the point of distraction. Despite the power and intimidation factor, it said it was here to help. Maybe there was hope for us, after all.

Sissa hadn't stopped bowing, seemingly unwilling to look the dragon in the eye—either out of fear or decorum. "We thank you, Old One. Though we have no way to appreciate the sacrifice you are making to come here, we acknowledge your presence in our time of need, and your swift response." The last part was a question phrased as a compliment. The dragonkin sisters' dad—Tsumlestora, I guessed—had specifically told us we couldn't trust who they sent, and we'd hoped to get me out of here before their arrival so as not to give the dragons the opportunity to do something they'd regret. Now, though, we were at this thing's mercy, because it had arrived early and spoiled our not-so-well-laid plans.

The dragon didn't take the bait, though. Maybe conversational cues weren't as much of a thing in dragon culture. Instead, it issued more commands, this time more politely. "I advise you to ready yourselves with haste. I sense a goeshi nearby, and it is either fate or good fortune that you have not drawn its ire thus far. Quickly, mortals. You should already be moving."

I saw Sissa frown as she thought through her next words. "I don't know that word, but if you mean the giant that breathes fire, yes, we have seen it. It appears to only harm the Infected."

Our savior made a sound that emanated from its stomach and echoed through its long, serpentine throat before finally arriving as a rough trill.

"Goeshi are simple creatures, born of a desperate loathing few ever experience, Young One. It has no room in its soul for anything but hatred. If it has seen you and spared you, it was not out of mercy but a greater desire to destroy others first," the dragon said. It spared a quick glance over its shoulder to the empty forest. Hot air puffed from its nostrils that left clear pockets in the fog. "Now move, mortals. The goeshi roams nearby. The creatures that stalk you are even nearer. My pact is for your safe retreat, and I honor it to the letter. If you do not do as I instruct, you will be leaving without your provisions."

Trix caught my eye, making a show of shouldering his rifle and securing his bandolier. He looked from me to the dragon meaningfully, and I gave him the slightest of shrugs. I made no move to pack up my stuff. The plan was for me to stay behind, after all.

When I looked up, the dragon was already there, its long neck craned into the fort and directly above me, staring intently.

The moment was finally here.

Taking a breath, I straightened up and stared back, not nearly as confident as I was trying to project but also not willing to do the bowing thing Sissa was doing. We didn't do that back home, and I figured starting now would look awkward and disingenuous. Better to project strength and honesty than being falsely obsequious.

"Transient being. *Human*," it said, drawing out the last word as if pronouncing a punishment. The weight of the dragon's presence stole the oxygen from my lungs and hung heavily on my shoulders. It lowered its head until it was close enough to brush my clothes, and flicked its tongue. Its scales gave off a strange heat, a sort of ghost sensation of being too near a fire, but it didn't hurt so much as conjure images of all the times I'd ever been burned.

"It is for you that I have awakened," the dragon proclaimed.

I nodded, swallowing uncomfortably. "I suspected as much," I said.

"Old One," Sissa called, repositioning herself to stand at my side, "may I introduce you to our friend, Ryan? It is with his help that we are saving Ralqir."

"Indeed," the dragon replied, not taking its eyes from mine. "It is good to know its name."

Not knowing what else to say, I simply went with what I thought was polite. "It's good to meet you—uh, sorry, I'm not from here. I don't know your name," I asked.

"Myss," it intoned, brand-hot, directly into my mind.

"Then it's good to meet you, Myss. Thank you for coming to help my friends. I will remember you," I probed.

"I am sure you will," Myss replied. "You and I have much to speak on, Human."

Well, this was going well so far. It seemed hell-bent on honoring its pact and saving my friends, and it hadn't tried to kill me. That was more than I could say for half of the things I'd met on Ralqir so far.

But my short-but-nightmarish experience with the wretchwyrm under Eclipse had taught me a few things.

"So when you say you woke up for me, one might interpret that statement's meaning as being that I was the cause of all of this, and that's why you awakened. Another interpretation could be that you roused and came here specifically for me."

Conservative estimates from Sissa's father had put the dragon's arrival as being sometime in the next couple of days. To arrive a full forty-eight hours early, it had to have gone above and beyond its normal effort, probably using magic, and, according to Sissa and Samila, dragons couldn't replenish their magic now that Ralqir was in the Maelstrom. Whatever the dragon had done to get here, it probably came at great cost. That meant it was either very concerned for another dragon's offspring, or it had other plans.

The dragon didn't answer my question. Its face was inscrutable. I guessed I needed to be more direct.

I set my jaw and readied myself for . . . well, anything. I was about to accuse a god of doing something untoward. "And, unless I miss my guess, you don't plan on letting me go."

Samila came up beside me now, opposite Sissa on my other shoulder. She had her armor donned and her backpack on now, but her sword was conspicuously at her hip and the retention strap unfastened.

"Would that be entirely against your wishes, Ryan?" It said my name as if tasting it, its tongue flicking, very lizard-like.

"Old One, we traveled light. We have all we need to make the trip. If you would allow us to say our goodbyes to our friend, we can leave whenever you wish." Poor Sissa still held out hope that this was going to end well, or she was prompting the dragon to come out and state its true intentions.

As Myss and I just tried to stare each other down, Samila finally broached the subject directly.

"The two of you just met, and she's already planning your eternity together. What is it with you, Ryan?" Samila asked.

"MacGuffin problems," I said.

Myss chuffed and bared her teeth but didn't necessarily take the bait. "I do not wish to force you to do anything, Human. I wish to give you an alternate path."

I raised an eyebrow. "But you will force me if you have to. You'll force me to stay here."

Again, the dragon didn't reply directly, but I got the distinct impression that the answer was "yes."

Sissa spoke up again. "Old One, Ryan is set on going back where he came from for the good of our home, despite great risk to himself, and he's gone to great lengths to get as far as he has. I implore you to reconsider. Perhaps even aid us in getting him back there."

The dragon didn't acknowledge her, yet again. "I sense that you have considered walking this path already. Perhaps what has kept you from choosing it fully was fear of failure or perhaps guilt at having been the cause of so much suffering, but I absolve you of those feelings. You may put them down and leave them behind. Stay. Be at peace. Keep your new friends. Save my kin. You can do all of these things simply by coming with me and accepting my help. Does this possibility not appeal to you?"

It did. It really, really did. The prospect of being able to stay in a place I was wanted, in this new life I'd begun . . . maybe go on a date with Samila, read books with Trix next to a fire in an inn somewhere, become a practitioner and go to university under Jassin . . . Maybe I could learn how to keep the System from doing what it was doing to me.

All of it was possible. Myss's offer was everything I'd ever wanted. A home. Friendship. Acceptance. It even stuck the idea of heroism and saving an entire species as a cherry on top.

But I knew better. Things were never so simple. No one was going to come along and fix all of your problems, not without incurring some kind of cost.

Sissa spoke for me. "Ryan believes that the longer he stays here, the more the wound to our reality will fester. From what I've seen, his theory appears true. If Ryan stays, there will be terrible consequences."

Now the dragon did turn to meet Sissa's eyes, and its tone ran hot with anger. "Of course. The consequences of his species' meddling in places that they should not are all around us, Spawn. This fetid wasteland is testament to that. The rotting corpse of a once-beautiful thing, only fit to experience through dreams and lesser incarnations of ourselves," Myss hissed, teeth bared. "The very blood that flows through your veins cries out at how low his meddling has brought us. I simply ask this one to meddle further, until all can be put right."

Sissa bristled at the dragon's slight of her parentage, but she kept her cool. Samila seemed less inclined to let the statements pass, however. She took a step forward with what would have been a threatening manner to any mortal being, but I surreptitiously put out a hand to keep her from doing more. I didn't like where this was going, but I also needed to be sure.

"Much has happened since you went to sleep, Old One," Sissa insisted through clenched teeth. "The people of Ralqir have found a way to thrive even under the Maelstrom's light. We have harnessed magic and built great things. They even say we are in the midst of a golden age, despite our current troubles."

Myss's lip curled into a disdainful sneer. "I will forgive your impudence this time, Spawn, because you were not there," she warned. "But speak to me again of mortal golden ages while our people wither away in their dreams, and you will regret it."

Ever the diplomat, Trix raised a paw. "Sergeant Sissa didn't mean to cause offense, I'm sure," he squeaked. "What she was trying to say was that we have moved forward as best we can in your absence. The Church and the Empire have lifted—"

"Silence!" the dragon commanded. Its eyes flashed, and Trix fell flat to the floor, pinned down. He trembled as something invisible but very real pressed him into the stone, his little chest heaving as he fought to breathe, and I could hear him gasping with obvious pain. "I barely tolerate impertinence from the spawn of my kin, but not from you, the pathetic supplicant of a usurper faith."

Tiba rushed over to Trix and tried to help him up, but whatever force was holding him down couldn't be resisted. She grunted with effort, pulling with all her might, but Trix couldn't rise. Tiba's guards tried to help as well to no avail, and Tiba grew more desperate with every passing second. Wild goblin curses flew from her mouth, and she snarled at the dragon.

Then as if a switch had been flipped, Myss's voice was back to calm and gentle. "I would hear the human speak now."

But I couldn't pull my gaze away from Trix. His little eyes pleaded with me. Realizing she was powerless to help, Tiba finally stopped pulling and got down on her belly, whispering comforting words into Trix's ear as she stroked his fur. I wondered how much of it he understood.

That cold feeling had come over me again.

Geddon's heavy footsteps clomped up behind me, and a big hand rested on my shoulder, giving it a squeeze to let me know I wasn't alone. I derived a little strength from that.

"You know," I began, "Trix proposed that I stay, too." My voice was calm and steady, and this time I felt it. My uncertainty had died an untimely death.

The dragon just regarded me silently, inscrutable as it casually tortured my friend. It didn't have to say anything, did it? It had shown me the carrot. Now I was getting the stick. Myss was smart enough not to transition directly into harming me. She somehow knew my soft spot was the others. The message was that if I didn't cooperate, she could make me, and she didn't even have to take direct action.

Well, that settled it, didn't it?

"That's enough, Myss," I said.

Trix groaned, lifting one claw to reach for us.

"That's enough!"

Suddenly, the weight upon Trix lifted, and the vulpa gulped greedily at the air. Tiba let out a relieved sob.

Myss tilted her head and flicked her tongue. "We understand each other, then. Decide now, Human."

My glassy pond was back. The cracks had been smoothed over, but I knew they were still there. "If you want to secure my cooperation, you're going about it the wrong way."

"Am I? I give you everything you want and promise suffering if refused. It could not be a simpler choice."

A chorus of screams echoed around the courtyard, this time from the goblins. They were all forced to the ground now under Myss's spell.

The dragonkin sisters had had enough too, spreading out as they did when they took on the ignarog. They hadn't drawn steel yet, but from the hard looks in their eyes, they were a heartbeat away from throwing down.

The dragon didn't seem to care, though. It followed them all with its eyes and smiled imperiously, but it took no action against them. Of course it didn't. They were children of another dragon. Torture was for mortals.

Myss was pressuring me, trying to throw me off-balance and get me to accept her terms based on my emotions, but what she had done by going after Trix and Tiba was quite the opposite. She had recategorized herself from "unknown" into "enemy" in my mind, and I was running out of mercy for my enemies.

Step One: Distract.

"An exchange of truths," I declared.

Everyone currently on their feet stopped, even the dragon. All eyes turned to me.

I took a couple of steps forward until I was nearly in grabbing distance of the dragon's horns.

"I propose an exchange of truths," I repeated.

Myss eyed me dubiously. "My words are always true."

I took on a look of mild contempt and leaned forward until the phantom heat was almost unbearable. My skin felt like I was, at once, on fire and frostbitten. "I don't believe you," I said.

The dragon's eyes narrowed. "Careful, child. I will not—"

"I think you need me to cooperate to bring back your age of dragons," I interrupted the god. "Otherwise you'd have already snatched me up and been done with it. Or maybe you're uncertain how you'll be able to do that and fulfill your pact at the same time."

"Perhaps," she replied. "Perhaps it is preferable you cooperate to avoid wasted time."

"An exchange of truths," I repeated, stepping away from the dragon and beginning to circle around it, forcing it to follow me with its head. "During our exchange, no harm will come to any of these people or to me. Afterward, do with me what you think is best."

"This is pointless," she hissed. "I can already do as I wish."

"What he asks is already something you give, Old One," Sissa said guardedly, her eyes flicking from me to Myss and back. I could tell she suspected I was making a play here, and she was trying to work out what it was. "Then it costs you nothing, while he gives you something. Tradition also demands the request be honored."

"Do not lecture me on tradition, Spawn! I know the old ways!" Myss snarled before whipping its head over to me again. "What are you doing, Human?"

I took another step, this time onto the stairs, taking two at a time. "If we're going to exchange words as equals—"

"Do not mistake my desire for your cooperation with equality. I could crush you with a thought."

"Except you can't," I said. "You need me, and I need you. Plus, I like to look people in the eye when we speak." I took another big step up before a pressure built in my chest. Something took hold of me and squeezed what would have been my heart, except my insides were made of stronger stuff nowadays. The weight of it pressed on me, but it wasn't nearly so bad as I had imagined. I grunted, staggered, nearly fell from the stairs, but took another laborious step anyway.

> Status gained: Suppressed (partial)

I was short of breath, but I kept the words flowing. I had to sell this.

"And I'm willing to bet little tantrums like that are costing you, Myss. I have it on good authority your magic doesn't really play well with the Maelstrom . . . Sort of like mine. Unlike me, though, you don't have another universe drip-feeding you power. You're finite. Have been since the Dark Lord showed you how it's done and saved Ralqir for you."

I took another step and another until my head crested the lip of the battlements. The presence that wrapped itself around my chest relented slightly as I came fully onto the walls for the first time since we'd seen Kuul. The smoke and lingering fog obscured most of the forest, though I could see open flames directly outside the sunlight circle that protected us from the Scourge.

Kuul was nowhere to be seen, but . . .

I turned to find the dragon's face inches from my own.

"An exchange of truths. No one gets hurt. Then it's up to you," I said, careful not to let my eyes give anything away.

Smoke billowed from her nostrils as she thought for a long count of ten.

"You will assist us in bringing back the natural order," Myss predicted.

"I might have," I said with a nod. "Before you showed me how cruel you are willing to be. Now, it's a toss-up. Convince me."

"Done," Myss growled. In the courtyard, the others gasped as they were let go and allowed to breathe again.

> Deception is now Level 6.

"Begin," the dragon commanded.

"What would be involved in helping you save your dragons?" I asked, purposefully raising my voice so that everyone could hear me, projecting for maximum volume.

"As your predecessor was used to bring us here, we will use you to send us back," she said.

"That's not an acceptable answer. Tell me more," I demanded.

"There is no more to tell."

"Bullshit." I raised a reproachful eyebrow.

"I do not lie!" Myss snarled, true yellow fire puffing out of her mouth as she enunciated the words. "Do you plan to help us if I play this game of yours?"

I kept it vague and unhelpful as Myss had. "I don't have a choice. I plan to do what is right by these people. What happens to Ralqir while I stay? I'm killing this place. Surely you see that."

Myss looked strangely uncomfortable at this. *Noted.*

"You kill that which is already dead," Myss replied, her head bowed slightly, pensive. "Magic is strange and unusual here. It is no longer alive but is a . . . knowable force. There is no art or imagination to it, no impulse behind its power." Myss spoke the words like they were a curse. "You fear staying in our world, even to give us a chance to save it. Why?"

"I assume you want to send Ralqir back to its original location in the universe. The process did something to the other human. The Dark Lord fed him a steady diet of Experience and power from the System, and he became something else. He was a monster when I found him—a dangerous one even the Maelstrom couldn't kill. I'm worried that while you guys try to replicate that, this place is going to be overrun, and by the time you succeed, I'll be an even bigger problem than the Scourge. Why didn't the dragons stop the Scourge's last incursion before the Purge?"

Myss hesitated at that. "We . . . could not. I tire of this conversation. Make your decision."

"No. That was a non-answer!" I shouted as loud as I dared.

Where the hell is—

Deception is now Level 7.

"Your Scourge is a presence from beyond," Myss growled. "It wears other beings like gloves while its real body searches for others to possess. Fire is an answer but a temporary one. With no way to permanently destroy the alien presence, we were slowly being worn down. So, we allowed the Dark Lord to perform his spell and destroy an enemy we found most vexing. However, we did not know the full cost."

Alert: Your presence has been detected.
Alert: Your presence has been detected.
Alert: Your presence has been detected.

There it was, the message I was looking for.

Keep stalling.

"So, what will Ralqir do without the Maelstrom's light, which definitely kills the Scourge?" I asked. "Kill it with harsh language?"

"If we must."

I shook my head reproachfully. "So you have nothing. You want me to be part of a plan that you've not even thought all the way through?"

"Our power is vast, Human. We grew it over eons before lesser life had even crawled from the ether and beheld the sun. You are new to immortality, so you have no frame of reference to understand this."

"Or, once you take away the Scourge's incentive to congregate here, you'll just be back to Square One with a global extinction event, getting your asses kicked, only this time unable to replenish yourselves."

"Is the ritual the Dark Lord created still intact?" Myss asked.

"As far as I know. It's lacking a mutated human now, though. Took care of that before I left. I want to hear more about your plan. Are you just going to ask the empire for permission to use the ritual again, or are you just going to take it? I don't see them being okay with upending their entire power base to bring back a religion that hasn't been relevant for a thousand years. Better yet, how do you plan on dealing with the Scourge in the meantime, while you figure out how to use me?"

"We know of our enemy now and the cost that must be paid to defeat it. Without a mortal vessel, your Scourge has no way to affect the world. We will deny it viable options until a solution can be discovered."

That, despite even my worst predictions, threw me for a loop. "I—What? How do you, uh . . . deny it?"

The dragon did not answer.

Then it hit me right between the eyes. I cursed myself for not having guessed sooner. "Oh, just like that. You're going to wipe them all out, aren't you? The mortals. There's millions of people here, and that doesn't mean a damned thing to you—not against gaining your precious magic back. Convenient solution too, isn't it? It gets rid of all the mortals that have been studying magic and might give you a good run for your money in the power department."

"Magic is meant to be alive. The world thrived when it could choose who wielded it. Who was worthy. Having to start anew is a small price to pay to restore the natural order."

"See? That's where you lose me."

"We have had our exchange. Your decision. Now, think in the long term, Ryan Kotes, immortal human. Put this planet back as it should be, get what you want, and be a hero to a grateful world. There really is no decision at all."

I sighed dramatically, pretending to consider. I even went so far as to tap a finger on my chin.

"Fine. The answer is no. Screw you. You'll have to carry me kicking and screaming," I said as I pointed blindly in the general direction that I felt Alert doing its thing. "He might have something to say about it, though."

Right on cue, that now-familiar, deep, terrible roar split the air and shook the world, and everyone, god and mortal alike, froze

There, in the foggy shadows of the Mendau, the towering silhouette of Kuul came barreling out of the forest at a full sprint, faster than a speeding train. He was down on all fours, charging like a bear, and the ground shook with the violence of every footfall.

He came on with the speed of a monster that had seen the person it hated most in the entire world.

This was the first time I'd ever gotten a good look at him. He was generally humanoid in shape but made of gnarled wood, gray and black with char marks, his joints glowing orange along with his eyes and mouth. An eternal fire burned inside him that warped the air, crackled and popped. Fire dribbled from the corners of his mouth like spittle to land at his feet as he wordlessly bellowed his hatred at me.

Myss looked from me to Kuul and back again. The dragon looked like it desperately wanted to kill me—maybe torture me until I went insane, then kill me.

Yeah. That sounded more Myss's style.

However, instead of doing that, my new guardian angel let out a frustrated growl and slid herself between Kuul and me, setting her feet in preparation to protect me in what was going to be a big, stupid kaiju fight, and she was going to hate every second of it.

After all, Myss needed me alive.

CHAPTER THIRTY-SEVEN

Be Anywhere Else

Kuul charged forward, eyes filled with burning hatred and fixed upon me, his great, gnarled hands cracking under his weight and with the force of his pounding steps. He blasted through the sun wall quicker than the eye could take in, shooting toward me at an absolutely ludicrous speed.

After a brief moment of consideration, the dragon attempted to grab me. Maybe it was trying to avoid a fight altogether, or perhaps snag me, then make off with her prey before a fight could actually take place. I'd been ready for it, though. This wasn't the first time an evil dragon tried to get me. I mean, it had only happened twice, but things like that tend to leave an impression on a guy.

It was fast, like the wretchwyrm, but I was already on the move, springing down to ground level, then sprinting, low and fast. Instead of reaching me, Myss' claw scraped at bare stone just behind me, tearing grooves in the rock with horrific screeches while tiny splinters stung the back of my neck. I didn't stop until I collided with the west wall under the battlements where it would be hard for them to get a hold of me.

Then the dragon's attention needed to be elsewhere.

With a boom, the two titans clashed in a thunderous exchange that shook the ground and collapsed the rest of the north wall, exposing us all to the outside and burying my work area in rock.

And that was just the first blow.

In a stunning display of speed and skill, the dragon had used its body and low center of gravity to stop Kuul's charge and redirect, though she was forced back until her tail and hind legs pressed against the ditch where we'd set spikes.

Kuul didn't have any intention of stopping. In a strange way, he didn't even seem to register he was in the middle of a fight. He staggered to the side, swiped at the crumbling fortifications, then shook his head and reared up like a bear, his gaze still locked on me as he opened his mouth. Inside was a portal to Hell, a roaring furnace I could feel on my face even from way down here and a whole dragon between us. Fire dribbled down from the uneven row of wooden fangs like spittle, and the wind whistled as Kuul sucked in air.

Oh, Constance, I hadn't thought this through.

I looked around frantically. Everyone was taking cover, just like I was, underneath the awnings. The goblins were as far toward the exit as they could get without going outside. Bole had Beedy on his back near the edge of the wall breach and seemed to be waiting for his chance to make a break for it. Geddon, Sissa, Samila, and Trix were doing the smart thing and cautiously making for the stairs.

If Kuul were to spit fire down in here, everyone on the ground floor would be screwed.

"Shit shit shit shit!" I shouted, forcing my tensed muscles to unclench and get moving again. I leaped up the nearest set of stairs, taking them a handful at a time. If I could get outside and across the ditch before the attack, the others would have a shot. Unfortunately, Kuul's aim followed me unerringly (not hard when you're a hundred feet tall), and he bent at the waist to exhale.

Just before I could be incinerated, my genocidal guardian angel stepped in. A great red tail whipped through the air and slammed into Kuul's chest. Blindsided, Kuul rocked backward with the impact and stumbled, the liquid fire he'd been about to spew at me bubbling in his throat and spilling over his face as he lost his footing and fell on his back with a crash that took out several more feet of wall.

His face now fully on fire, Kuul gurgled his disapproval and rolled onto his side to get to his feet. But before he could rise, Myss said something quiet and oddly pronounced.

"Cutting Embrace." The language she used itched at my ears and prickled the skin on the back of my neck. It felt like a predator had just passed over my head but had chosen, by chance, not to devour me.

Bright orange lashes of magic burst from a point of empty air, crackling just over Kuul's head. The strands exploded from their origin point, whipping in all directions, wrapping around the giant's face. Others shot into the ground, lashed themselves around trees, skewered boulders—anywhere they could anchor. Then they began to squeeze.

Kuul roared in protest, but the strands tightened further, looped around his eyes and mouth, wrenched the giant's head until it twisted round on his shoulders, and his body was forced to follow. Then he was face-down on the forest floor. Kuul's long limbs thrashed, churning the earth, attempting to gain some kind of leverage to free himself, sending waves of damp soil skyward.

Snarling, Myss moved in for the kill. She beat her wings and took to the air with a great whoosh, then came roaring down in a vicious pounce that cracked the bark of Kuul's body underneath her. Fire spurted from the cracks in Kuul's shell with the impact.

It was only then that I remembered I should still be moving. Better yet, I should get the others moving too. I took the opportunity to grab everyone's attention—a difficult task when two gods were fighting right next to you. It had a tendency to draw the eye.

"Hey! Hey! Listen!" I whisper-shouted until everyone was looking at me. "Time to go! Right now!"

With a *RRRRRIP!*, the ground beneath Kuul was rent open, and he twisted at the waist until his upper half was turned toward the dragon while his legs were still pinned beneath. Myss, caught off-guard by the maneuver, attempted to disengage and lift back into the air, but her feet were already thoroughly entangled in animated Mendau roots that writhed and wrapped around her ankles—the same spell the old sorcerer had used to kill Hunty.

Opponent temporarily immobile, Kuul's bark-covered slap caught the imprisoned dragon right in her face, followed swiftly by a lungful of liquid fire that I assumed was originally intended for me. This time, it was Myss who roared in pain and rage. She slashed blindly at her foe's abdomen as she attempted to clear her vision, starting secondary fires in and around the fort as she shook off the goo. Of course, the door was one of the first casualties, igniting instantly.

Kuul didn't seem to be feeling anything that was occurring to him. All he did was attack. On the bright side, he wasn't attacking *me*. Yet. The dragon was now fully on his radar, and she had to die.

"Fucking right it's time to go," Bole said from to my right. Holy hell, how was he already up here? *Right.* Practitioner. He had Beedy supported over one of his shoulders and was helping the other man down onto the nearest root slide that would get him safely to the ground.

"Where are we going?" Sissa asked as she jogged up to me from the other side of the battlements. "The Infected are still out there beyond the sun wall."

That was a good question.

"I don't know! Anywhere but here!" was all I could think of.

"We could have left yesterday!" Sissa exclaimed.

"I know! And we'd be just as screwed!" I shouted back at her. "Now get the hell down there!"

Another boom and a blast of heat. Then Sissa was forced to give an enthusiastic nod of agreement. The dragonkin climbed over the side, followed by Trix, who stopped just before lowering himself down.

"I still hear them out there," Trix said, residual pain from Myss's magic evident in his voice. "Many are still scratching and vocalizing."

I nodded to him and gave his head a slight push to get him moving down the outside of the wall. We'd have to deal with that problem when the time came. Right now, we needed to be anywhere but here. I watched the vulpa's ears disappear below. Geddon and the three goblins on his back were next.

"How did you know?" Samila asked me on her way past. "That she would kill us all and start over if that's what it took?"

"Lucky guess," I said, helping her up the stairs and to the wall. "Makes sense, though. They can't bring the old Ralqir back without destroying the new one, and I'm already on a quest to not let that happen."

Then came the admission. I guessed it was finally safe to say, now that it was a true impossibility. "It sucks, too, because I really do want to stay."

"Of course you do!" Samila shouted, half-pretending to be shocked. "You've got a weird way of showing it, though, you ass!"

"I know! I know! I was afraid to admit it, because, well . . ." I spared a glance to the two fighting giants. "If the dragons could have helped me without getting all genocidal, I would have ridden off into the sunset with the rest of you. Now, if I stay, your dad's species is probably going to fight a war over me."

I took her hand and helped her over the side.

"I guess you were right to be afraid," she admitted.

In for a penny . . .

"There's the other thing, too," I continued.

Samila had one foot up on the lip of the wall, holding my hand for support as she gingerly used her good leg to get hold of one of the grooves. She hesitated, frowning in confusion. "What other—"

Before I had a chance to reconsider, I took a breath and pulled her in close. Then I kissed her.

Again I was struck by how soft and light she was, her scales like downy feathers, belying their outward appearance. The rest of her was delicate and warm—the unarmored parts, at least. Her lips tasted like spiced fruit.

I pulled away when I started seeing spots—which, I am slightly embarrassed to say, didn't take long.

When we finally managed to pull apart from one another, her yellow eyes stared up at me, wide, a little frightened but hungry and intensely intrigued.

About time someone else got that look. I was tired of being the only one.

"Whoa." She breathed, shuddering slightly in my arms. Then her attention was on something over my shoulder. She gasped, true fear stealing any further words she might have had for me, and I saw the reflection of motion in her eyes just before—

WHAM!

A huge fucking red dragon slammed down onto the fort, hitting it with the force of a bomb. The walls buckled and broke. Rocks tumbled out into the forest, propelled by the meteoric force of a multiton monster making landfall in their midst. Myss lay on her back, stunned, her legs twitching as some part of her brain attempted to reassert control of her motor functions. Before she could recover, however, a bark-covered arm snaked over the dragon's torso, and Kuul heaved his broken body atop his opponent. His mouth opened once again, and he roared in Myss's face.

I knew what was going to happen next.

Too close. We were way too close.

I got an arm under Samila and took her up in a bridal carry. Then, praying I had the requisite strength and HP to do this, I leaped.

FWOOM!

I didn't get a chance to perform the tuck-and-roll I had half-planned before taking to the air.

Instead Samila and I were violently hurled outside the remains of the walls, over the trench, and well into no man's land, fire blazing in our wake. I, too, was on fire. I knew I was. It was a sensation with which I was becoming far too familiar. I figured that would probably take care of itself, though, when—

I did my best to get under Samila before we made impact, but I was only half-successful. I had to activate Tension Step midair and kick to try and complete the spin. My mana pool cratered, and I lost myself in white stabbing pain just before we landed. The maneuver was a success, though. My right shoulder took the full impact of the fall. Correction: my right shoulder took the full impact of *two* falls—mine and Samila's. A bone somewhere in there gave way with a pop, and I had a new source of agony to contend with. Then I felt the distinct sensation of rushing fluid in the part of my shoulder that used to be functional.

My senses failed me temporarily. A small mercy, in retrospect.

Hooray! The spots were back. I missed you, spots.

The world had been robbed of its oxygen, or at least that's how it felt. My lungs tried to take in big, desperate gulps of hot air that never seemed to be enough. There was an odd pressure in my chest, too. Something was pressing on my lung and keeping it from filling fully, and there was far too much smoke in the air I did manage to draw in.

Samila got to her feet first and then helped me to mine, none too gently.

I nearly swooned with the pain before I could get fully upright.

Behind us, the dragon whispered another spell.

WHOOSH!

In a flash, the fire disappeared, along with a good chunk of the forest. Everything that was burning turned to ash in an instant, as if we'd just been brought forcefully into the future when the fire had already run its course.

Then the ash started to move. An unnatural wind swept it up and collected it into drifts that flowed, swirled, and gathered in a twisting whirlwind, congealing and growing until it solidified into the shape of yet another dragon—black, gray, and white with hollow, lifeless eyes.

It reared up, opened its mouth, and let out a challenging roar.

In agony, I fought to get my mind working. *Distance.* We still weren't safe. I tried to pull Samila away, to get us moving, but all I got was a terrible wrenching sensation in my shoulder.

"Samila?" I groaned, waving a hand in front of her to get her attention. "We have to—augh—"

Samila was rooted in place. She looked lost—entranced, almost.

"I can—" she whispered, not to anyone in particular. I didn't even think she knew I was there. "I think I understand."

"Samila! Hey!" I shouted.

She continued to stare as the dragon and the goeshi battled to their last.

"Sam!"

Screw it.

Despite being almost ready to pass out, I bent at the waist and picked up my dragonkin girl yet again, this time over my prosthetic shoulder. Thank Constance for cold, unfeeling metal.

The two dragons—the old and the new—attacked Kuul together, one going for the giant's legs and the other for his head. From there it was a rolling, grappling match. Desperate snarls and growls, pops and cracks, wet, ripping flesh and bark—the noises filled the forest. Sounds not meant for human ears chased us as we ran.

The monstrous mass of thesecreatures was staggering. From what I heard behind me, the two flattened everything they touched. The fort was surely no more. Whole trees broke under their combined weights.

"Wait! Wait, Ryan!" Samila protested, wriggling in my grasp. I was barely holding onto her to begin with. Just then, I hit a depression in the ground and twisted my ankle. That was too much. I lost myself momentarily to the pain and oxygen deprivation and stumbled, spilling the two of us onto the forest floor yet again. When I came back to myself, Samila was standing, transfixed by the battle taking place a worryingly close distance from the two of us.

Myss had a broken leg, and her tail was crooked and ripped to the bone. Kuul's torso was still broken, one of his arms was missing—not that he cared—and the liquid fire spilling out of him was enough to form a sizeable pool beneath him.

Myss got the upper hand with the help of her compatriot, pinning Kuul on his back, the ash dragon perched on top of his legs with talons dug into his knees as the red dragon wailed and slashed at his neck and face.

Rearing back with one of her claws, Myss spoke a final spell into existence, and the claw on the middle toe of the dragon's foot extended and changed texture until it shone like a mirror. Then she drove the claw directly into Kuul's forehead. It went all the way through, bursting from the back of his skull to pierce into the soil.

"There!" Samila shouted. "Did you hear it? I'm—I think I got—"

"Got what?" I asked between labored breaths. "What—*gulp!*—are you talking about?"

She looked back at me in barely contained wonder. There were tears in her eyes. "My first Word. Just now. I'd given up on trying."

Confused, I shook my head, not liking what it did to my migraine.

"It's all—It hurts. It—" Her words trailed off as her eyes rolled to the back of her head, and her body collapsed bonelessly to the ground.

Kuul thrashed, despite being impaled through the brain. Liquid fire leaked out of his head where the claw had gone through. The dragon snarled in Kuul's face, showing her teeth to her fallen foe as a sign of contempt. Then, in a Herculean effort, Kuul grabbed the dragon's claw and twisted to angle his face slightly to the left. When the dragon tried to compensate and shift her weight, Kuul seized her head and brought it close.

The goeshi let loose with a final geyser of fire. A much bigger one than the previous. At least I assumed so. It was much too bright to see with the naked eye.

I felt the wall of heat hit just before I registered the impact. The shock wave slammed into me, and I got the distinct impression of tumbling over the ground before I was knocked senseless.

When I could think again, I realized I was face-down on the forest floor, and I wasn't where I remembered being. Pushing myself up, I felt the world swimming around me, awash in heat and billowing smoke. Sam was gone.

Disorientation kept me from standing upright. The pain in my shoulder and back was excruciating, and all I could do was roll and hope I was putting out the flames that were surely there.

How bad was it? Sam . . .

HP [208/301]

I did a quick query of the log. I'd lost HP with the fall, the first blast, internal bleeding, the burning . . . All of that was mine and only mine. That left about 45 HP of Damage unaccounted for that Samila might have taken with me. There was a good chance she was out there somewhere, alive.

Before I knew what I was doing, I was walking back toward where I'd last seen her, my vision wobbling and dimming between breaths.

Through the smoke, I saw the vague forms of the two combatants. The ash dragon was gone, Myss and Kuul were both on fire, and the former was shuddering as her head and neck blazed. Kuul, despite himself also burning, showed no outward signs of weakening or pain. Both were locked in a struggle to end the fight right there, limbs entwined, teeth bared.

Then, suddenly, they were gone, disappearing with a *WHUFF!* as a sizeable portion of the ground beneath them collapsed. I blinked. *What was that?*

After a couple of seconds, Myss's head poked out of the hole the two had fallen in. She was clearly trying to scramble to her feet and get away, but she couldn't seem to gain purchase well enough to break Kuul's grip.

A gnarled hand used the dragon's momentary distraction to reach up and take hold of her horns and wrench. Myss's neck twisted around in a most-unnatural way until the bones inside separated with a wet *pop!*, gunshot-loud.

No. That wasn't right.

I knew gunshots. That was an *actual* gunshot!

Somewhere, amidst the rubble and roaring flames, one of the remaining turrets began to fire. Once. Twice. Three bursts.

BRRAP! BRRRRAP! BRAP!

Then all was silent.

What?

WHUFF!

A sound to my immediate right—the sound of a ton of dirt collapsing in on itself, followed by the earthy scent of petrichor and . . . bodies. I smelled rotting flesh. Fetid breath. The familiar, eerie howls of the Scourge despoiled the silence, and gangly black figures began to trickle out of a freshly dug hole.

WHUFF!

WHUFF!

Two more in the distance. Indistinct black figures rose from the earth, quick and quiet, their figures silhouettes in the thick smoke.

My heart sank as the realization hit me.

Now I knew why they'd made those noises, which had been constantly torturing Trix. They were covering up their mining operation.

They dug their way in. The Scourge started digging their way in the day we'd forced them back.

Sam. Where is she?

I got low, clutching at my shoulder as I stalked through the smoke, attempting to look for her. I needed to find her, get her out of here. Where was she? How long had we been separated? I forced my eyes to stay open, despite the smoke, hoping for a flash of blue or the outline of a shield. They were all I wanted in the world.

Steely fingers suddenly dug into my wrist—small fingers, sharp. The Baned had found me. I tensed, drawing back to throw a haymaker their way with my prosthetic, but I stopped myself when I realized who it was.

Tiba was there. She was crouched low, covered in soot, crawling along the ground like a lizard, with the exception of the hand she was using to try and get my attention. Once she saw I was aware of her, she put a finger to her lips and beckoned for me to follow.

I shook my head. Samila was still out here somewhere. She—

Another tug on my wrist. This time, my shoulder bones ground together hard enough to make the world go all white-static again.

"Arrrrgh," I groaned, but Tiba, quick as a mongoose, had climbed up my torso and put a finger to my lips before I could make any more noise. The look in her eyes told me she was serious. Also very frightened.

She beckoned me to follow yet again.

I clenched my jaw and breathed hard as panic and desperation threatened to override my good sense.

Sam, where are you?

But Tiba's eyes begged me to trust her.

A few more breaths, a quiet moment to let the adrenaline partially wash out of my system, and I was okay again, wresting control of my emotions back from my lizard brain.

Unclenching my hands and relaxing my jaw, I made a show of being calm again. I bent down to whisper in her ear.

"Sam is out there," I told her.

Tiba nodded and put her lips to my ear. "We try to find them. Too dangerous to stay here, though. We move now or have to fight."

Think, Ryan. What do we know?

I hadn't found Samila yet. That meant she'd either moved under her own power, or she'd been moved. Either way, I couldn't find her like this. I was stumbling around blind. Tiba was at home in these woods. She was my best shot at reuniting with the others.

I made a gesture for her to lead on, hoping that I wasn't leaving Sam to die.

Immediately after we started moving, excited, gibbering voices came up behind us, close. Apparently, I'd decided to cooperate at just the right time. I silently hoped they weren't looking for tracks and that they wouldn't fall upon someone else if they didn't find me.

Tiba and I crawled through the smoke and the blazing underbrush, around the sniffing, pawing Scourge-Touched that pursued us. Tiba led me under the fallen trunks of toppled Mendau, around skittering clusters of hunting monsters. Only once we passed through the greasy rainbow mud that still clogged the chokepoint did the voices of the Scourge finally fade into the distance.

Night fell.

To my growing horror, we never saw any of the others.

CHAPTER THIRTY-EIGHT

Make a Promise

Tiba and I stayed in a hollow log until morning. The night had been full of terrible noises as the Scourge reveled in their victory. They were everywhere, sniffing and pawing at the ground, scrabbling up and down trees, and howling into the night, no doubt looking for us—specifically me. Tiba was using some sort of woodcraft I wasn't familiar with to mask our presence, though she wouldn't or couldn't explain. There was something about the log itself combined with our collective smells that kept the creatures from looking inside, but what that was, was entirely out of my wheelhouse. She seemed semi-confident it was working, though.

Unsurprisingly, Kuul was still alive, back to full-rampage mode, roaring and breathing fire everywhere, which was the only source of illumination for someone with pathetic night vision such as myself. From the glimpses I caught through the underbrush, his body looked more battered now after his fight with the dragon. Spiderweb cracks crawled up his torso and neck, glowing orange in the dimness of the forest, and leaking little globules of fire that would splat onto the ground wherever he walked, but walk he did. He felt no pain that I could discern, only a burning desire to kill.

The old son of a bitch was unkillable, apparently, and he packed a mean punch—mean enough to kill a dragon. Oh, yes, that was another thing. Myss was probably dead. That tended to happen when your head was twisted all the way around, but I wasn't ready to ring her death knell, considering we were dealing with ancient magic beings and all that. What convinced me was the fact that we hadn't seen Myss while Kuul was still kicking around, and she wouldn't have left without doing something I would regret.

The Scourge had grown increasingly used to dealing with Kuul. Wherever the goeshi went, the Scourge-Touched had to give way, but as Kuul chased individual monsters that caught his eye, dozens more would rush into the giant's wake and continue about their business of finding me.

Around dawn, when the sound of Kuul's footsteps and the vocalizations of the Scourge were far, far off, Tiba and I dared crawl out of our hiding place.

We retraced our steps slowly, keeping low. The forest got eerily quiet in the absence of all the activity, magnifying each snapped twig and rustled leaf, so we took our time, making the effort to keep out of sight and leave no trail. It was mostly Tiba leading me by the hand and telling me to wait when she needed to scout ahead. At least I got another level of Stealth out of it.

Stealth is now Level 17.

The waiting was hard for me, since I couldn't stop thinking about the others. Everything had gone to shit so fast. The fire and chaos had separated us, and we'd not discussed what to do if that happened. We'd all just assumed we'd be doing this entire thing together and that we'd have a chance to plan things if we were to leave home base. In fact, we'd all assumed that when we left this place, it would be for good, but now we were scattered with no way to find one another without returning to the place we'd just lost to the enemy.

My heart was going a mile a minute as I waited in the bushes outside the sunlight perimeter, staring through the fog and smoke into the smoldering wreckage where we'd used to live. The fortress itself was obliterated, crumbled down to ground level with the strange exception of the southwest corner wall, of which only about six feet of stone remained vertical. The area was charred black, the ditch flattened, the roots of the old petrified trees cracked into jagged boulders. Six ragged holes, wide enough to drive a wagon through, were dug out around the fort in a nearly perfect hexagon. One of these had collapsed to the point where I could see the rough outlines of trenches where the Scourge had tunneled in.

Tiba watched and waited with me, only a little more patient than I felt.

"Something is wrong, Ryan," Tiba said from her half of the bush. "Kelub and Grorg should find us by now."

"Yeah," I agreed. "It's too quiet. I understand the others lying low, but where are the Scourge?"

"They run from Kuul, I think, and you are not here anymore. No reason to stay," she guessed before adopting a more-somber tone. "I keep expecting to hear one of Yik'i'trix's birdcalls. I like his birdcalls."

I did, too. I kept expecting to hear all sorts of things, hoping someone out there was all right. If they were, though, they were doing the same thing we were: watching and waiting.

I reached out and gave her hand a squeeze. "I'm worried about them, too," I said. "Let's give it another half hour, and then, if nothing else happens, we'll make the first move."

Tiba agreed, nodding slightly, but she continued to watch the clearing with big, unblinking eyes.

* * *

Taking the long way around to the choke point, we picked our way carefully through the underbrush. I winced with every clumsy footfall I made. Tiba was silent as a mouse, but I was too big and heavy for that. I just had to hope my Stealth Skill and Gray Man would do something for me. Alert hadn't triggered yet, but I wasn't quite to the point where I trusted it with my life. Like my turrets and my aura, I had to assume it could be fooled by various means.

When we got to the choke point, we found it different from the last time we saw it.

"Drag marks. Big," Tiba whispered, crouching down in a furrow the size of a single-family house. She pointed at a long gash in the mud that contained black slurry. "Blood in the marks, probably all over."

I did some mental calculations, not liking the answers I got. "Dragon blood," I guessed, though I was almost positive this was the case.

Tiba's eyes widened, and she looked around again, in shock. "No," she replied in disbelief. "They took the old one?"

"It's what they do," I said, following the drag marks with my eyes.

South. Toward the tutorial facility. Ground fucking zero. Of course they took her there.

The fort itself was a ruin. Fire had destroyed nearly everything that wasn't stone. Two titans had thrown down directly on top of the structure, and it showed.

Tiba and I carefully picked through it all, looking for some indication that the others had been here. It was the only location we all shared as a point of reference. If a sign was going to be anywhere, it would be here.

Whatever the battle hadn't destroyed, the Scourge had. Not just that, they had desecrated the place. Sets of claw marks marred the surface of every flat area, unmentionable organic leavings were smeared over the ground, and decaying, discarded parts of monsters were left out in the elements to rot in random nooks and crannies. The ruined husks of my machines were scattered over the entire area, barrels bent and hammered until they were flat, magazines broken over rocks, bullets scattered and ground into the dirt. The casting bowls were smashed flat, and the reloading station . . . well, it looked like something had crawled inside and died just to be a jerk. The smell was *unique*, to say the least.

Still, there was no sound but the wind in the leaves overhead.

Finally we found what we were looking for, dead center in the courtyard— the only clean, untouched area in the entire ruin, and conspicuously so. It was as if this particular part of the floor had been carefully preserved, perhaps even swept clean of debris.

My balance faltered and I fell to my knees.

In the middle of the courtyard, on the pristine red-and-gray stone floor, lay a neat and orderly row of . . . things. Armor and weapons, mostly. Geddon's helmet was next to the dragonkin sisters' in a line. Swords were set in the rough form of a star, points all touching, shields stacked on top of one another. Goblin spears were in a cross formation. Articles of clothing and personal effects all laid together as if someone could just slip right into them. Trix's rifle sat to the side, the strap ripped, barrel bent, but the gun itself set down perfectly aligned with his bandolier.

Like with like. What the actual f—

It didn't make sense. This didn't belong here. No way had they taken off their gear like that. No way they were all—

Tiba put a tiny hand on my shoulder.

No. Not dead. Not dead. Not dead.

"They're gone," I said, unable to think of anything else to say. That cold feeling was back, as was the frozen pond. The sensation spread through my body until I felt nothing, numbing everything but the furnace in my heart. That was the only place inside of me I could feel, though I didn't want to.

"The Baned take them," she murmured. "Sometimes they take you. Never see you after they take you."

"No. It's not true," I replied.

"Sorry, Ryan."

"No!" I snarled.

Tiba snatched back her hand like I'd just tried to bite her. She didn't look frightened, per se, just surprised or wary of the sudden shift. There was a question in her eyes.

I sprung to my feet and kicked at the arrangement of my friends' belongings. "It's a message, Tiba! Look! Look at them!" I demanded, pointing to the lines, the shapes everything made, how it was all organized. The more I looked at it, the more I hated it.

"It's gotten smart now. It's gone from strategic thinking to understanding. Understanding *us*," I explained as the engine inside of me thrummed.

This was new. This was personal. This shouldn't have been happening.

"What do you mean?" Tiba asked. "They take our friends, like I say. It changes nothing. I'm sorry, Ryan. They are gone and become Baned. We lose."

That wasn't it. This array of my friends' things had purpose.

It made sense. The Scourge had swarmed the area and couldn't find me. They'd found my friends, though, probably somewhere nearby. They got the others, subdued them, took their gear, and laid it all out here for me to find.

But why? Were they taunting me? Goading me? It was possible, but—

"Tiba, they're still alive," I pronounced.

A pitying look came over her face, and she took a step closer, arms out like she thought I needed someone to hold me. "Ryan, when the Baned take you, you are gone. We are never seeing a person come back."

"They're still alive, Tiba! I know it!" I fumed.

It would normally be happy news, but the thought of it was a hot iron in my brain, a reminder of failure to do the only thing I was here to do.

"Look! Look at it! Nothing the Scourge does is like this! They don't arrange shit! They don't preserve! This is new. It's—" I trailed off, the engine in my chest growling like a caged animal.

"If you're right, only one reason to keep them alive then, Ryan," Tiba cautioned. "I'm no hunter, but this is bait."

"Yeah, it's a trap," I agreed, looking around for the biggest parts of my machines—parts I could repurpose. Violent, dangerous plans flashed through my mind, and I was spinning up my mana even as I spoke. "But I meant what I said. I'm done letting it take from us, Tiba."

The Scourge had taken from me. They'd crossed my line.

They'd given me reason to be cruel.

"I'm going to get them, Tiba. If they're n—"

I couldn't finish the sentence. My throat closed of its own volition, and I had to take a moment to collect myself.

"If I don't find our friends alive," I continued hoarsely, "I'll make sure every last one of these bastards pays the price."

CHAPTER THIRTY-NINE

Ride to Ruin

When the afternoon rolled around, I finally stopped channeling mana and started storing my assembled arsenal. Four functioning kinetic turrets, about twenty new plasma rounds for my arm cannon, a whopping 130 of the new, untested, drone designs, courtesy of our new Frankenstein's monster of a casting bowl, machine pistol plus extra magazines, legs, sleeve, and breastplate I'd made for my armor set, and a rudimentary helmet and face guard to keep my eyes inside my head when I was getting swarmed.

All of it was slapdash, crude, and untested. Over half of it had a non-zero chance of exploding if I'd botched the Automation.

It would have to do.

My head pounded for the twentieth time in the past few hours as my mana points sat in the single digits. I summoned the last of two pieces of oiled wood to give me some relief and take the edge off.

Conduit is now Level 9.

For the first time in hours, I stretched my aching muscles and rolled my neck to loosen up. My vision swam as my equilibrium got used to being upright again and doing something other than frantically pumping mana into metal.

It was time. I was ready. I had to be ready.

Tiba looked ready, too. She'd smeared black streaks of mud across her face and tied additional feathers to the end of her spear. As I watched her burn a sprig of some kind of herb and waft the smoke toward her face, a pang of worry threatened to make me say something I'd regret, but I tamped it down. If she wanted to fight, I wasn't going to deny her. This was her world, and she had a right to throw her life away just like I was doing. I just hoped she was smart about it.

We didn't say anything—just picked up our things and started walking.

Side by side, we squished through the mud of the bottleneck, careful to stay in the middle so as not to expose ourselves to too much sunlight.

Then . . . well, it didn't take an expert tracker to figure out what direction to go. We followed the drag marks, the big, dragon-sized drag marks. Southwest. The tutorial facility. Nearly everything I could ever want in this world was at the tutorial facility. They may have been new at this whole thinking-thing, but the Scourge-Touched had baited their trap extremely well.

Through the silent forest, over downed logs, around great depressions left by fallen Mendau, I walked just as I'd done on Day One of my tutorial. Only this time, I knew more of what I was doing, of the world, of magic, of myself. I was passing through this place a different man than I was then.

The Ryan of Before had only been concerned for himself. He ran when he was chased, like a deer from wolves, with no more thought given to the action than the immediate need to live.

Well, I wasn't running anymore. I'd gained purpose, grim as it was. I knew my enemy was out there, and that was exactly what I wanted. I also knew that only one of us was coming out of this alive. It had finally come to that. They'd engineered that outcome when they'd threatened those I cared about.

Though I still felt heavy, my 53 Body kept fatigue from affecting me, helped me power through the thick brush, climb through the ravines. Navigating the tough terrain was a simple matter now, easy even with Tiba on my back. The presence of my machines rested in my pocket dimension, ready to deploy against any threat. I even found myself wishing for such a thing to happen, an opportunity to start the fight. It never did, though.

From time to time, I made a point to reach down and Consume another bit of Mendau to top off my mana pool, ten times larger than it had been the day I'd been dumped in this place.

Alert: Your presence has been detected.

I froze and crouched, heart thrumming in my chest. Fear was far, far back in my mind, and purposefully so. Fear could wait. This was anticipation, the need for something upon which to vent my wrath. I wasn't even wearing my armor yet, but I half-welcomed an obstacle to bulldoze just now.

I scanned the forest to see what kind of Scourge-Touched had seen me. Nothing had howled or jumped out at me, which indicated a different kind of threat.

Was it restraining itself until I was nearer the trap?

"It's okay, Ryan. Just don't run," Tiba whispered as she gingerly climbed down from my back.

Confused, I glanced over to see her standing tall as she took one step out into the open, exposed, the base of her spear resting in the dirt, and her chin raised in defiance.

What was she doing?

An entire tree bent at the knees and took a long step toward us. In the silence, the deep, groaning and creaking of bark rubbing against itself sounded like bones snapping. Gnarled, gray wood flexed, rose into the air, and slammed down into the dirt dangerously close, burying itself in the dirt. Roots from the surrounding Mendau trees popped out of the soil like worms burrowing out of a corpse to writhe in the midday light.

My gaze crawled up the leg, the trunk. Smoldering crevasses split the wood of the giant at the joints. Larger, more significant cracks dripped fire down onto the ground, where it hissed and set alight anything remotely combustible. Its torso was almost concave, some of the wood missing where one might find a ribcage on a normal person. Inside was a miniature sun that blazed like Hell's heat lamp. He was missing an arm as well, ripped off at the shoulder, the wound still leaking smoke. To top it all off, Kuul's face loomed over me, his mouth twisted into a loathsome sneer.

"Stop it, Kuul!" Tiba shouted, cutting through the moment sharply. To my and Kuul's apparent surprise, the giant froze, a look of what seemed like disappointment twisting his hellmouth into a frown.

"Stop it now! Stop your hate! Ryan is not the Baned!"

At first it seemed Kuul had finally gotten over his shock at being yelled at by a tiny green girl. He bent again, growling as he reached down to silence her, but something stopped him before he could make contact—almost like he'd hit an invisible wall. He didn't like that at all. His face contorted with rage at the tiny thing that dared give him orders and, worse, the fact that it was coming between him and me. He got down into a bear crawl and gnashed his teeth in protest.

I stood up, my machine pistol at the top of my mind for summoning, but Tiba headed me off.

Instead of standing her ground or doing the sensible thing and running away screaming while I fought the giant, Tiba strode forward until she was within slapping distance of Kuul's face.

And that's just what she did. She had to get up on her tiptoes, but she slapped him.

"Kuul! I tell you, no killing Ryan! If anything, Ryan kills you!"

That didn't sit well with the big guy. He straightened up quickly, his expression twisting into an indignant frown and, with his long, muscular arm made of woven Mendau roots, slammed a fist into a nearby tree trunk. The building-sized Mendau shuddered, and for a moment I thought it might come down, knocked out like a boxer.

"Enough! That's enough!"

Kuul growled petulantly, as if the goblin queen had just asked him to eat his vegetables or there would be no dessert.

Tiba was unmoved. In fact, she looked ready to slap the giant again if need be, the way she kept advancing toward Kuul's feet. She certainly had his attention now. He bent down low, growling, as if daring her to slap him again. Instead, Tiba got a big lungful of breath and began to bark in the giant's face.

"Now, you listen, you crooked old goblin. I am Tiba, healer of the Stone Hearts, Chief of the Black Claws, Chief of the Skewers, Chief of the Mountain Clans, Queen of the Eight Tribes. I bring my people together and save them from the Baned. Today, I quest to heal the world just as our ancestors in the stories do!"

Kuul growled the growl of a hundred diesel engines idling at once but, surprisingly, did not smash Tiba or me. I kept a part of my mind focused on my pistol and what it would take to summon it.

"Thing That Is Once My Chief," Tiba pronounced, "you are a horror. You are a terrible nightmare, a curse of destruction given life by a disgraced sorcerer." She pointed her spear at Kuul's eye for emphasis. "Kuul, who destroys his own tribe and kills his own kin. Takes my Hunty from me. I want . . . No, I *demand* you listen to me. Kneel!"

Something passed between the kaiju tree monster and the little goblin queen. I don't know what it was—a contest of wills, magic, vibes, maybe something else. Whatever, it happened over the course of long seconds where I couldn't help but hold my breath.

Then, miraculously, a tipping point was reached. Kuul closed his eyes, bent at the knees, and bowed his head until it touched the ground. The leaves underneath him smoldered, and the soil churned as the Mendau reacted to his touch. There he stayed while Tiba stood over him, breathing hard, furious and full of authority.

She held her spear like she was considering executing him, like a queen from old Earth.

"Tiba, what the hell?" I asked in a whisper, my eyes flicking from her to Kuul. "What are you—

He's—"

"I know," the queen said. I felt compelled into silence for some reason. Tiba still had capital-C Command in her voice. "I'm too small to fight next to you today, Ryan. He is not."

She clutched her spear to her chest, the way she did the day I gave it to her.

My eyes flicked from her to the killing machine she'd tamed. This couldn't be safe. "But he—"

"Yes, he takes my Hunty from me." Tiba sniffed, turning her face to quietly wipe a tear from her cheek with a dirt-covered hand. "Yes, he wrongs me. And he . . . frightens me." She turned back to regard Kuul's now-prostrate form and put a hand on the bark that would have been the crown of his head.

"But he is still goblin. He needs me. You, Kelub, and Grorg need me, too. I am not much of a queen if I can't face him for you."

My lips made a sputtering sound as I rooted around in my brain for the right words to say in this situation, but I came up with nothing except:

"And you knew this would just work?"

She shook her head but gave Kuul's head a pat. "No, but I have a feeling. Turns out, a queen is bigger than a chief. My position is—uh . . . higher. Now, where do you want us, Ryan?"

Somehow intuiting what his queen wanted, Kuul rose, though he had to support himself on a tree with his one remaining arm to do so. The tree next to him bent and groaned. This close to him, Kuul's size was impossible to wrap my head around. Even injured as he was, he cut an imposing figure against the backdrop of the foggy forest.

The tiny green girl who had lost everything and gained a kingdom.

The chief who had betrayed his tribe and became a monster to atone.

Living legends were standing right in front of me. What a tale Ralqir would have to tell after all of this was over.

If we lived.

Well, the odds of that just got a lot better.

So, that's how I ended up riding a kaiju tree monster into the biggest battle of my life, the first kind face I'd seen in this world riding right there with me . . . Or maybe I was riding with her. It was really hard to tell whose quest this was anymore.

The drag marks led us where we needed to go, in more-or-less a straight line. Tiba and I rode on Kuul's shoulder—the one without the missing arm. Kuul's internal temperature was furnace-hot, and any open wound or orifice was dangerous to be near. The shoulder was the only place we could really ride and not be burned to death or at least cooked to medium-rare. Regardless, the heat was oppressive. Sweat poured down my face and out of my helmet to plink off my breastplate.

Honestly, my armor wasn't my best work. Made of steel and deep lead. Angular, heavy, and too thick by half. The plates that covered my chest, legs, neck, and one of my arms were cumbersome to even stand in, much less move around in a fight. Currently unpowered pistons in all the joints hissed and scraped with every move I made, and every time I needed to turn my head, I had to angle my shoulders to point that way, too.

"You think they aren't killing the others when we get there?" Tiba asked, having to raise her voice to be heard over Kuul's ailing tree giant noises. Kuul's footsteps crashed through the forest with muted *CROOM! CROOM! CROOM!*'s, and his body creaked and groaned as its parts ground together. With every bump, the crackling fires inside of him spewed sparks out of his chest, eyes, and empty shoulder socket.

"Not till they have me, I think," I replied. "Wouldn't do to kill your bait before you have your deer."

Tiba crinkled her nose as she thought about that. "Unless they are so many, they think they have you right away. What makes you so sure?"

"Nothing. It's just the only way I see this going where we all make it out alive."

She looked over at me, incredulous, her big brown eyes saying a million things her voice didn't.

I shrugged. "Like I said, I refuse to choose. We're all going to make it, or I won't be around for the rest."

A sad smile tugged at the corners of her mouth. "You're a good goblin, Ryan."

Kuul growled at that, a thing I felt through my feet.

"Hush, Kuul! He's Stone Heart now! I say so!" Tiba chastised him, punctuating her words with stomps from her tiny feet that Kuul probably couldn't even feel.

The Scourge were staying scarce. We only caught glimpses of them in the trees—mostly the monkey-bat-type creatures, who swooped away as soon as we got within rock-throwing or fire-breathing distance. It was only when a pile of what looked like crumbled stone appeared over the horizon that we finally noticed them gathering in earnest, and, boy, did they gather.

As if they'd been summoned, thousands of them appeared from our flanks, streaming in from the low parts of the terrain, flowing toward the stone landmark. They swarmed like ants over everything, climbing over every tree trunk. They burrowed up from the ground and flew down from perches overhead. Thousands of bodies flowed and collapsed, hemming us in.

A pointless gesture.

You don't have to worry about me running. You wanted me. You got me.

The pile of rocks—or, more accurately, the former tutorial facility—was different than I'd remembered. I'd left it as a pile of rubble, of course, the victim of time and the elements, along with a little help from a boulder that had missed me by a hair. However, now it was a ring of crumbled concrete and twisted metal that jutted out of the ground, a festering sore on the planet's crust. The Scourge-Touched swarmed over it, climbing out of crevices and mounting the exposed, rusting bones of the place, sniffing the air and hooting. In the middle of the ring there was now a hole—wide enough to swallow one of the trees—that went down into nothing, darker than dark.

No. That was wrong. The way the light hit it and died . . . I should have been able to see down into it from atop Kuul. But something else was in there, a black substance that swallowed the light. I had the sneaking suspicion that if I were to get close enough to it, that blackness would smell of tar and rot, and it would reach for me.

I fought to suppress a shudder at the memory.

Kuul lumbered forward until we were a hundred yards from the tutorial facility. Then Tiba gave the order to stop. Our giant rage monster growled in barely contained bloodlust as he turned this way and that, unused to allowing Scourge to live, but Tiba's command held him fast. For now.

Silence fell over the forest, and we collectively held our breaths.

Then a glowing, holographic presence appeared next to me on Kuul's shoulder.

"Greetings, Ch-Ch-Defiler," a woman said, her voice tortured with the sound of screeching static.

I slowly turned my head until I was looking down into a familiar face.

"Nali," I acknowledged her.

Nali was looking rough. I remembered her as a short, handsome woman with hard features and kind eyes, the kind of woman with calluses on her hands and fresh-baked bread on her windowsill. Now, the hologram was disjointed, the top of her head not quite lining up with her jaw, and her body undergoing some kind of animation glitch, her work apron flapping wildly in an unseen wind until the garment tore down the middle, exposing Nali's insides as if the apron were her actual skin. Flashes of teeth and sharpened bone no human had ever had before popped out of her, too fast to really get a good look at, but frequent enough to discern what they were. Then she would reset back to normal. Her eyes, however, stayed the same, sunken-looking with black tears streaming down her cheeks.

Tiba took the hologram's presence a little less calmly than I had. She whipped her spear around at impressive speed to slash at this alien creature's chest, but it simply passed through. The incorporeal nature of the hologram caught Tiba off-guard, and she nearly took a tumble from a great height.

I reached out and steadied her. "Hang on, Tiba. I think I know what's going on here," I said.

Nali didn't pay the queen any mind. She was focused entirely on me. "Welcome, D-Defiler, to the e-end of the Animator Class Tutorial. I am Nali, the emissary of this end."

"We've met before," I said. "I was the last Animator you trained before all this."

Nali flickered. "B-Before what?" she asked.

"Before the Scourge," I said, watching carefully for the reaction I was waiting for.

Nali seemed to freeze, and her face broke into five separate chunks, each having their own reaction to the news ranging from terror to anger to . . . very *intense* pleasure. That one, funnily enough, made me the most uncomfortable out of all of them. However, she was back to normal almost instantly.

"I apologize, Defiler. My f-failsafe has been compromised. The possibility of void corruption is h-h-absolute. Please disregard all further advice I give." Her body contorted, her arms bending backwards before stabbing through her own torso and coming out of the other side. Her head collapsed down into her shoulders until her neck was entirely gone. Horrifyingly realistic bone cracks and ripping noises accompanied these motions.

Then, like a switch had been flipped, she was back to normal, albeit her eyes were still weeping black.

Her voice, however, was entirely devoid of any sense of humanity she used to have. She was cold now—not robotic so much as alien and uncanny.

"Greetings, Defiler. I am the voice of the Void. My purpose is to negotiate your destruction."

Sadness seeped into my core when I saw the change. She may have just been a hologram, an AI, but that didn't stop me from feeling something when she changed. Nali as I'd known her was gone now, replaced by this *thing*. I had suspected something like that might happen if she was exposed to the Scourge for much longer, but I hadn't expected to witness it. I'd hoped to trigger her failsafe before it could happen and maybe spare her.

"None of the other Scourge speak. Why do you?" I asked.

"I am not of the Scourge. I am of the System," Nali said flatly. "The Scourge has allowed me to retain what functions I have so that we may speak. I speak for the Scourge, because it does not."

"And you want to negotiate my surrender."

She bobbed her head, the glossy black of her eyes making her look insect-like in that moment. "Your death and destruction."

"And you communicate with the Scourge on my behalf?"

"No. The Scourge does not communicate. It knows. It sees what I—" She spasmed then, rocking back and forth, her lips peeling back to unleash a scream through her clenched teeth that devolved into digital noise. Suddenly her face was that of a real-ish woman again, frightened and confused.

"You—You must l-leave. Leave now, Ch-Ch—It is inside—I am being corrupted."

I resisted the urge to reach out and comfort her. It wouldn't do any good. "Nali? What's happening to you?"

"Run!" she shouted, doubling over in obvious pain now. "Use your quest prompt! Find your way out of this universe!"

"Nali, I can't leave until I—"

"You should already be running! This universe is corrupted. Its destruction is inevitable!"

"Nali, listen carefully. Is your presence housed somewhere around here, and that's how the Scourge are corrupting you?"

"Yes," she answered. "Down in the sublev—"

Nali flickered again and was back to her disjointed, corrupted form. "Defiler, end your life now, and the Scourge will spare the others. Do it now, and they will not be subsumed."

"No," I answered with a shake of my head. "No, I don't think I will. Not until I have proof of life. Does it know what that is?"

"Nali" didn't answer.

"It was smart enough to leave me their things. Smart enough to take hostages. Surely it's figured out that I would want to see that they are alive before I cooperate," I guessed.

"The concept of exchange is new to it. The giving from one to another—the *concept* of 'one'—is new. However, it anticipated some form of persuasion would be needed. The others are here." Nali gestured down to the swarming mass of Scourge gathered in front of the ruined facility, and the crowd parted . . .

My friends lay there in the dirt, bruised and battered. Most of them were face-down, filthy, limp. Trix was the first to move, his head popping up and looking around fervently that way he did, ears vertical, listening. When he realized they were being left alone for some reason, he helped the others get up with brief touches on the forehead. One by one, they all staggered to their feet.

Samila was the first to spot me way up on Kuul's shoulder. I couldn't see her expression from this far, but I imagined some kind of stoic frown there as she shook her head ever so slightly at me. She was telling me to let them be. Don't risk myself. I wasn't behind the walls anymore.

She wanted me to live.

I shifted my armor's weight on my shoulders and turned myself until I caught Tiba's eye to give her a nod.

Then I turned back to Nali. Her stare was blank, but she tilted her head to an extreme angle like no human being would do, listening intently, as if she were ready to hear the terms of my surrender.

And I would have, if I trusted for a second that the Scourge would keep its word, or if it hadn't just told me my death would just result in them getting better treatment than assimilation. Then there was the woman standing in front of me. No way was she getting away after my death.

"If you can hear me, Nali, hold on," I told her. "I'm coming."

Just then a hot, crushing weight settled on my back and squeezed. The armor popped and squealed as Kuul's hand wrapped around me none-too-gently. Then Kuul did what he had probably been wanting to do for quite some time now.

He threw me. Hard.

In a storm of sickening motion and ridiculous G-forces, I was airborne, hurtling toward the little clearing the Scourge had made for the others.

The ground rushed up to meet me, and I tucked my legs and rolled until I was flying roughly feet first. Then I activated the bracing pistons on my new armor's joints.

I hit the ground like a crashing satellite, roughly fifty yards off target, just in front of where my friends were held—though I lost sight of them as soon as the impressive wave of pulverized monsters, dirt, and debris blasted away from the new crater I'd made. My bones rattled in my body, and something inside of my stomach gave the distinct feeling of tearing as I went from terminal velocity to zero instantly. However, once I drew my first breath and checked my HP, I knew I was in business.

You take 30 Impact Damage. (15 mitigated)
HP 271/301]

Deactivating the bracing pistons, I rolled onto my side and groaned as I crawled. Chunks of the creatures I'd landed on peeled away and sloughed off the armor plating to land with wet plops atop their kin. I got up slowly. The armor was heavy, close to the weight of a full-grown man even without the rest of the components. I'd made it that way purposefully. Thick, cumbersome . . .

Loaded with terrific firepower.

With a *clunk!*, I put one plated boot up on the lip of my little crater and braced myself as best I could. My mind flicked to the Triggers I'd kept active on my back.

The Scourge wasted no time now that I was down amongst them. They pounced and surged into my pocket of emptiness from all sides, all teeth and claws and evil.

Now.

The two stripped-down auto-turrets on my back unfolded from the recessed holes I'd built for them and slid up their tracks until they clanked into place just above my shoulders like wings. A Trigger in the boxy compartment on my upper back activated its piston ammo feeders, slapping the first rounds of the day into place.

"You want me dead?! Come do it yourself, Scourge!"

Then the world became fire, blood, and fury.

"Come on! Come on, you little shits!"

CHAPTER FORTY

Machine Mage

C ome on! Come on!"

The turrets on my shoulders spewed hot-lead hate, sweeping their muzzles over the oncoming horde and spraying them with metal death. Their stub barrels belched purple Volatility mana as their overcharged propulsion cubes sent rounds screaming into the mob of Scourge.

THOOM! THOOM! THOOM! THOOM!

They moved in swift, jerking motions as they detected and engaged with targets from closest to farthest, almost too fast to track . . . and there was no shortage of targets. The recoil was gigantic, made even more dramatic by how high above my center of gravity the turrets were operating. Every round fired wrenched my body in a new direction and threatened to send me down to the ground, and I got to experience life for a few seconds at a time as my tripods did. It wasn't pleasant.

The only thing keeping me from being blasted off my feet was the prodigious weight of my body and my new suit of armor. With the exception of my prosthetic arm, it was a hodgepodge, full-plate setup that was overbuilt and thickly reinforced, angular where there should have been curves. Then there were the pistons. I hadn't gotten them working well enough to have them help me run, but I'd certainly gotten them to take a position and stay there. Once I'd activated my turrets, I fed power into the activation Triggers of the stabilizers, and the requisite joints on my armor all locked in unison while steel anchor spikes shot out of the boots and into the ground.

Kuul and Tiba did their parts, too. Kuul sprang forward with a mighty leap and landed directly into the middle of the horde to my left, crushing dozens underfoot. Then came the fire geysering from Kuul's mouth and blasting Scourge to ashes. Tiba directed from atop Kuul's shoulder, pointing him toward targets of opportunity and, hopefully, keeping him a safe distance from me.

I stood as tall as I could, but I couldn't see the others anymore. The Scourge had moved in as soon as I was on the ground. I knew my people were in front of me, though, right where I needed to be. The magazines on my back went dry, and I deactivated the joint stabilizers with a metallic *CLACK*. The anchor spikes in my boots retracted into their housings, and I was free to move again as the backup mags on my lower back whirred into place.

I moved forward, my heavy boots making *THUP! THUP!*s in the dirt. All I could manage was a fast jog—or as fast as I dared at least. I couldn't sprint in the armor without falling on my face. However, I needed to cover ground before I had to reengage with the anchors. I raised my prosthetic arm—the only part of myself that I hadn't bothered to armor—and fired my arm cannon.

FOOP!

The wall of flesh directly in front of me burst into a plasma-induced inferno.

Go. Go. Don't think about it. Just go.

I lowered my head, tucked my shoulder, and covered my eyes as I barreled through the flames. The air crackled. Flames licked at my armor, and my flesh sizzled as hot became scorching. I made the mistake of taking a reflexive breath when the pain got to be too much, and it nearly killed me. I got a lungful of greasy, superheated air, and I nearly doubled over in pain. The only thing that saved me was momentum. I stumbled forward, my armor clanking against itself. Crisped bodies crumpled underfoot as my legs wobbled, and my momentum carried me forward until I finally smacked into something that arrested my movement.

Said something was soft—softer than me, at least. I heaved before it could stop me entirely. It gave way with a surprised grunt and went down under my feet. Then there were more, soft, squishy things laying there, piled high. I plowed through those too.

Then the world went weird. My stomach got that feeling again where gravity wasn't working as it should, and then everything felt lighter.

It's Anchor. I'm climbing!

PANG!

I took my gauntleted hand from my face just in time to smash into a gaggle of Returned that had chosen to brave the flames to get at me as my Climbing Ability told the fundamental laws of force and inertia to sit down and shut up for a moment. Under the influence of Anchor I was effectively 30 percent less affected by everything, including the weight and force of a bunch of monsters trying to bring me down. I smashed through them like they were made of paper, one of them even going airborne as I gave it a hard smack with my prosthetic.

Then I was out. The air was suddenly cool and crisp. It had moisture and life. I took a big, desperate gulp of air.

Except I was among them now. Hands reached out to grasp me. Claws slashed at my face. Teeth gnawed on my legs. The Scourge, yet again, pressed in from all sides.

Grunting, I flexed until I was standing tall again. I pulled my feet apart and set my hips, then I activated the stabilizers and the anchors, followed swiftly by the turrets.

BRRRRRRRRRRRRRRAP!

Full-auto. Non-stop. The monsters practically disintegrated under the close-range barrage. I lashed out with my prosthetic, caving in a monster's face, then summoned another round into the arm cannon.

A Baned hung from it, frantically trying to use it as a handhold to climb up to my face, but I smashed it into another Scourge-Touched that had taken hold of my shoulder.

FOOP!

BOOM!

The explosion was close. Very close. The round hadn't even made it the minimum safe distance away from me before detonating this time. However, I didn't use the plasma. My brain was still somewhat functioning. The Scourge in front of me were reduced to bloody chunks as the shrapnel from the grenade round did its grim work. I felt the force of the blast generally in my chest and acutely in several spots of my body where it felt like being punched by a Leori, but my stabilizers kept me up while my armor kept me safe.

The ringing of metal-on-metal echoed in my helmet a full second after the grenade went off.

Still too close.

They were climbing over each other now. Monsters scrambled over the dead, over the injured, standing on others' shoulders to leap at me. A horned humanoid of some kind—missing its legs ever since my grenade—climbed up my chest to claw at my face. I headbutted him again and again until he fell away. Others grabbed for the barrels of the turrets, despite their tips being red-hot.

Another Trigger, this time next to my wrist. I had to concentrate to get the mana to flow that way instead of through my hand, costing me precious seconds, but I was able to manage. A pair of curved blades sprouted from my wrist quicker than the eye could follow. Even quicker, they began to spin. The Returned that had been gnawing on my wrist at the time lost the better part of the front of his skull, the Willing-Edge-enchanted blades cutting through flesh and bone like butter.

"Auuuuuuuuuugghhhh!" I yelled in their faces as I swept the spinning blades from side to side. The small monsters died instantly. Then a Leori with the flesh missing from half of its face got hold of my helmet and pulled me close to go in for a bite with its broken, rotted teeth.

I pushed against it, gaining a minuscule amount of space, then jammed my wrist blade into the monster's open mouth. Black blood gushed over my arm and down to my shoulder where I could feel it seeping through the joints and soaking into my shirt.

The Leori let go of me when I got to his brain stem, his expression, such as it was, going slack as he slid down to the ground. Then I was left with a little space.

The turrets had gone dry sometime in the melee, so I retracted them and kept moving forward.

FOOP!

Another shrapnel round to the fore. This time I didn't even stop to aim.

I ran through the bloody mist, shoulder-checking the pulverized Scourge that were cognizant enough to get in my way.

Forward.

Forward.

BOOM!

A giant fist slammed down on the Scourge in front of me, then went back up into the sky, stringy giblets and blood stuck between its fingers.

Forward.

Forward.

I extended my fist and led with the spinning wrist blades, charging through the ranks of the Scourge and wreaking havoc on their numbers. Yet there were always more. More faces to cut. More to get through.

I stopped once more to anchor and let the turrets drain their last mags as I heaved for breath and tried to—

There. There they were. Sissa, Samila, Geddon, Trix, Bole, Beedy, Kelub, Grorg . . . they were all there together, their backs against the crumbled concrete wall, bleeding, weak, a pile of dead things around them, felled by hand-to-hand combat.

CLANK!

I disengaged the anchors and plodded forward even as my turrets bucked and boomed from my back. I staggered drunkenly, at the mercy of physics as my turrets did their best to lay waste to my enemies while I concentrated on moving forward. I went down on one knee as something hit me in the back, but it dropped away once I brought my spinning blade around in a blind sweep. My machine pistol appeared from my Spatial Storage and barked, splitting another Baned's head down the middle.

My ragged breath echoed in my helm.

BOOM!

Another massive impact somewhere to my side. Tiba shouted something I couldn't understand.

I was close. One last push.

I summoned and let a charged flamer bulb drop at my feet.

Now move! Move!

"AAAAAAAAUUUUGGH!" I roared as I charged through, battering the Scourge aside, guns blazing on my shoulders. The flamer bulb I'd just dropped went off with a *FWOOSH!* and my back was on fire again as I gave my last to get airborne.

Then, I was amongst friends, or at least in front of them, just as the turrets went dry once more. I landed, going down on one knee, my head drooping down as spots danced in my vision. My lungs burned, and my legs felt like someone had removed their bones.

But I was here.

I'd given everything just to reach this point.

Quest Complete: Tutorial
You have learned the basics of your Class and are ready to begin your new life as one of the Chosen. May you go on to do great things, Ryan Kotes.
Rewards:
+1 Level
ERROR: Rwrd_failed:Max_Level_ttrl=exceeded
Resolving . . .
Rewards:
+10% to all Stats

Return to point of Integration? Y/N

"Not yet," I grunted.

I wasn't done yet. The Stat increase did make me feel a bit better, however. It took the edge off the exhaustion.

Organ Grinder appeared in my hand, summoned from my Spatial Storage. I tossed it in the general direction I'd last seen Geddon.

Two swords. Shields. A rifle.

Hands helped me to my feet, and my swimming vision landed on Samila through the narrow slit of my visor.

She was breathing hard, bleeding from a cut on her cheek, her top lip was split, and she had blood in her teeth.

She was the most beautiful thing I'd ever seen.

"Ryan!" she yelled. "What are you—"

I put both hands on her shoulders to steady myself and panted as the world stopped tilting on its axis: "I need two minutes."

I turned to regard the rest of my friends. "Give me two minutes to set up. Then we're killing them all. Together."

"Hell, yeah, we are!" Geddon whooped.

Leadership is now Level 2.

"RARGH! Thirty seconds is the best we're gonna do here!" Samila shouted, suddenly letting go of me and cleaving through a Baned's chest. The strike itself was powerful, but Samila staggered afterward as if it had taken a lot out of her.

She shook her head and widened her stance drunkenly. "Trix, no offense, but I'm asking the goblins to do my healing next time!"

"I keep saying that I am not a healer, but no one listens!" Trix shouted shrilly from halfway up the pile of rubble to our rear. He spun and shot a gangly troll-type creature through the eye just as it crested the top in an attempt to flank us from behind. Spinning, he let off another expertly aimed shot at another Scourge at his feet. Then another. Every round from his weapon was a kill.

Geddon's chain-sword roared. Blood and viscera soaked his entire body and the ground around him, but gone was the joviality of before, his face now a picture of pure, single-minded focus. His posture, outside of his armor, was lithe and dangerous, and he moved with a dancer's grace, performing the duty of three capable fighters at once.

Sissa and the goblin royal guard were on the left flank, with Sissa performing the shield function of a rudimentary phalanx while the goblins did the stabbing. They were taking on the Scourge-Touched ten at a time, and they'd racked up as many bodies in the handful of seconds I'd been among them.

My armor popped its seals with a series of clanks, and I fell out of the metal shell onto the ground, my helmet landing in the dirt with a *thump!* I felt the stinging, ripping sensation of burned skin peeling away as I left the armor behind. The pain was distracting but not something I hadn't experienced before. But even if my mind didn't register it, my body certainly did. The world swam in front of me, and darkness pressed at the edges of my vision.

Stay awake. Stay awake. They need you.

Samila paused to look back at me with concern. "You set yourself on fire again?!"

My Spatial Storage called, and I got to summoning.

A rounded ball of nickel osmium plopped down to the ground followed by another. Then another.

"Not exactly!" I shouted. Talking was good. Talking kept my brain engaged and not focused on the pain. "I set them on fire, and then they set me on fire! It was a mutual thing!" I wasn't sure if she could hear me over the din, but I was too distracted to really put much effort into projecting my voice.

One mental command later, the metal balls sprouted their legs and instantly took off in different directions, putting distance between them and me and from each other, as I'd programmed them to do.

Next were the guns. Piece by piece I summoned the reclaimed parts of some of the turrets. I'd stripped them down, made them smaller and easier to assemble, fattened the barrels and given the action some play. The Scourge had done a good job destroying a lot of the carefully crafted efficiency of the last model, so we were down to a boomstick-level of sophistication. That was all right. We weren't going for long-range precision today.

BOOM! BOOM! BOOM!

Kuul was having a grand time. He stomped and kicked at the mob of gathered

Scourge-Touched like a hyperactive kid with a toy train set. A very angry hyperactive kid. Dozens of bodies went flying off into the woods at a time, their arms and legs pinwheeling, some so far into the distance that I almost immediately lost sight of them. Others smacked into trees and practically popped like water balloons.

Focus.

Right. Barrel one. Barrel two. Piping. Hopper. Bulb. Legs. Dammit . . . please clamp. Come on. Come on. Clamp! Done!

My first turret was assembled, and it was ugly even by my standards.

It looked like a moonshine still had made a baby with a sawed-off shotgun.

I picked up my new invention and placed it on my shoulder, wincing as the metal scraped against one of the fresh burns. Then I ran with it to the front, right between Samila and Geddon.

The Scourge knew what this was. They'd lost a lot of bodies to similar machines, and they didn't plan on letting me set up another. Howling with renewed vigor, they lunged forward with reckless abandon at full sprints, no longer taking any time to try and skirt around my allies or come at us strategically. Overwhelming us immediately had become their tactic of choice.

They almost made it, too. *Almost.*

I activated the turret just as I became able to see the whites of their eyes.

BOOF! BOOF! BOOF! BOOF! BOOF! BOOF! BOOF!

For the second time today, I felt the horrible sensation of my skin flash-cooking as the world in front of me turned into a stew of bloody chunks and pex oil fire.

The turret had come to life amidst a buffet of valid targets. It hit them with both barrels, spewing four—sometimes five—rounds at the same time, its over-charged propulsion cylinders expending a grotesque amount of energy with each working of the trigger. The rounds weren't even necessarily coming out point-first. They were just being hurled en masse at the nearest Scourgeling. Meanwhile, as they were programmed to do upon close contact with the enemy, the pex oil canister's valves depressurized and sent a jet of sticky, yellow fire into the horde's faces.

The results were messy, a fact I got to appreciate up close. Wet pieces of formerly living beings flew into the air, and dismembered things collapsed at my feet while the aerosolized blood and the scent of cooked flesh invaded my nostrils, threatening to make me empty my stomach. I turned away, slapped at the latest part of my already-ragged shirt to catch fire, and went back to the inner area of the circle to do it again.

One. Two. Three osmium nickel drones. They plopped down and skittered away as the others had.

One container of turret rounds.

"Ryan!" Samila called. She had backed out of her position to get nearer to me, still keeping an eye on her sector but sparing short glances back to check on me as the turret did some of the heavy lifting. "What do you need from us?"

"More time! More turrets! Ammo! Reloads!" was all I could say. My plan didn't go any further than that. *Get to my friends, set up, hold out.* That's all I'd hoped for.

A hand tapped me on the shoulder, and I spun around to find Beedy there—weak and pale but upright. He reached out to take the canister of turret rounds from me. "Where do I put them?" he asked.

"Uh. The top. There's a lid. Swivels to the side. Fills like a bucket," I replied.

He nodded slowly, then shot me a grin. He was missing teeth. When had that happened? "I'll get it done. You keep on keeping us alive," he said.

And then he was off. The can of ammo was obviously weighing him down, but he didn't let that stop him.

That reminded me. I summoned the automated guts of the old magazine reloader and gave it a little prod with the mana trigger.

"There. Now our ammo has a chance to find its way back to us," I said to no one in particular. "If you see ammo rolling around out here, stick it in the nearest turret!"

"You plan to stay a while? Maybe pitch a tent?" Samila asked sarcastically, but she wore that smirk of hers, too, if only to cover the fear she was feeling just as I was. I took some comfort in the fact that she was making the effort, at least. I guessed certain death wasn't going to keep her from being herself.

I summoned the first part of the next turret and got to work. "If that's what I have to do. Are summer homes a thing here? It's a nice spot," I replied, mirroring her grim smile. "This ends today, one way or the other."

The top half of the turret came together, and the clamps activated to attach the top to the base. This one went much smoother.

I ran it over to the spot between Geddon and Sissa's position and set it up, activating the firing sequence with largely the same results as the last one. Everyone gave ground and shied away from the blast of heat as the turret went to work clearing 180-degrees of field for at least ten yards. My allies weren't too pleased at how little regard the flame nozzles had for friendly fire, but they didn't complain once the turret relieved some of the pressure on them.

"Much obliged." Geddon panted, giving a sloppy salute with Organ Grinder as he caught his breath.

"You guys tell me when you need a break," I said to him and Sissa. "Hold the line, and I'll get you more help."

"I need a break," Bole croaked from behind me. His arm was broken and in a makeshift sling, and half of his face was so swollen that I couldn't see his eye.

To my shock, Sissa of all people reached out and put a hand out to support him.

"We all could use one," she said, wincing as she gently turned Bole's head to the side to examine his wounds. "Our captors weren't kind. We've been through a lot, but we'll fight to the last."

Hearing that, seeing the state of them all, I felt that cold anger I'd been nurturing get that much colder.

"Noted," I fumed, though my voice was calm. Enough time should have passed by now, anyway. I reached for the Triggers in my head and activated them.

FWOOM!

The drones that had dispersed among the horde suddenly felt the urge to convert the state of their matter into plasma, and the world went incandescent for a handful of seconds. Everyone that didn't know it was coming put up warding hands in front of their faces as the light became blinding and the atmosphere ignited.

Reams of Experience messages scrolled through my log all at once.

"That'll hold them for a minute or two. Take a breath," I told the others. "Then we're fighting for our lives some more."

I strolled back to my assembly area and began summoning more parts. Against the backdrop of the burning forest, I spied Samila looking me up and down in that way she did. She spared a glance over her shoulder to make sure we were safe for the moment, then limped up to me and crouched down until she was looking me in the eye.

"This better end the good way, Ryan Kotes," the dragonkin purred. "I want you to do that thing again."

I blinked, mid-summoning. "The—What? The *kiss?*" I realized.

This time she looked taken aback, like I'd just insulted her mother or something. "That wasn't just a—It wasn't—Okay. It was. But yes. Absolutely. I want you to do it again, so now we *have* to live."

I felt the blood rush to my cheeks.

No, Ryan. We're not blushing during our last stand. Cool guys don't blush during their last stand.

"Deal," I said, hoping I'd be able to make good on it.

"Look out!" Trix squeaked from the rubble pile as his rifle barked as fast as he could pull the trigger. Panicked fire. "Ryan!"

I looked up to see some kind of black substance oozing its way over the lip of the rubble. It flowed like tar—sticky and sedate—but in other places, it seemed to flow unnaturally fast, tendrils of it waving like seaweed in a spectral tide. Other tendrils stuck to obstacles and pulled the rest of the mass along where gravity wasn't getting the job done fast enough.

The liquid surged, crested the lip of the rubble and splashed down to coat sections of the barrier. Trix did the smart thing and leaped before it could touch him, coming down lightly at the bottom and scrambling to get amongst the others.

* * *

Sweet, rotten, cloying, the smell hit me like a blow to the face. I staggered and, for some reason, felt my saliva glands go into overdrive. The tar substance, though it was far away still *reached* for me. I knew it was reaching for me.

That's it. The smell. It was here. It was in the tower with Ephelir. Void corruption. Scourge.

I stood so I would have a chance to move if we were attacked.

"There you are. Finally showing your face," I said. I didn't know how to fight something that was only semisolid, but, for the Scourge, I was willing to experiment.

A massive, three-clawed hand, dripping with black ichor, slid up and over the lip of the rubble. It moved languidly, relaxed as if it were caressing the concrete after waking from a long nap. Then, suddenly, the hand contracted, crushing the concrete with enough force to send shards of it flying. Rebar squealed as it bent between the fingers. Another hand appeared. A wave of black broke and splashed down the wall as something massive climbed its way out of the pit.

The head of a very dead, very pissed dragon pulled its way out of the Scourge tar. It was missing scales where massive gashes had been carved in its face. Its head sat strangely on her neck, seeming to not be connected to it quite how it should have. Its horns were, at once, broken yet razor-sharp with new points jutting out of them at odd angles, and it teeth were crooked and oversized to the point it could no longer close its mouth.

She'd changed, been despoiled or corrupted or . . . something, but this was most certainly Myss. Emphasis on the *was*.

"Th-They've been emerging from the black pool for some time. I was killing them as they got free, but—" Trix stammered.

"Of course," I said. "Pretty sure the black stuff is the real Scourge. It was distracting us with the little guys while it summoned its real heavy hitter."

"Always a scam," Bole growled. "Guess we're fighting a dragon now, eh, Human?" He stood at my side, sword in hand, the good side of his face a stone mask of determination. If he felt shocked or betrayed or slightly annoyed at having been lied to about my species, he didn't show it. No, he seemed almost eager to step to a fallen god.

"Not if I can help it," I said to him. I put my fingers in my mouth to let out a short whistle, loud as I could make it.

"Yo! Tiba!"

CHAPTER FORTY-ONE

Slay the Dragon

The Scourge-Touched dragon that used to be Myss opened its mouth, working the jaw back and forth experimentally. Black, tar-like drool oozed between its teeth and slapped onto the rocks below. Her empty, soulless eyes jittered in their sockets, seeming to move from one spot to the next without rhyme or reason, focusing and un-focusing at random. That is, until her gaze landed on me.

Just like all the other Scourge-Touched, she lost her mind when she got a good look at Ralqir's only human. Multiple holes in her neck bubbled and whistled as she tilted her head back and let loose a deafening howl. Her ruined throat morphed the vocalization into something more like an oncoming train.

Myss took a single, clumsy step forward, followed by another, a wave of black goo splashing off her body as she got her sizable mass out of the pit.

"Uh—Tiba?!" I called again, uncertainty creeping into my voice. I forced myself to look away from the dragon and back toward the wall of smoke and fire. *Nothing.* In the distance, booming footsteps rampaged, presumably among the Scourge. Way in the distance . . .

Bole cleared his throat at my side.

I turned sheepishly toward the others. "Okay, so we're fighting a dragon. Any ideas?"

We all started backing up together, away from the dragon and the oppressive stench of the Scourge goo.

Myss slid down the wall of rubble like a disgusting penguin, landing in a heap at the bottom before staggering drunkenly to her feet.

"Don't let her speak," Sissa suggested. "Her magic is language. Like mine."

"I've never heard a Scourge-Touched speak," I replied. "Don't think it can."

"Like ours, Sis. Magic like ours," Samila added. "I'm not sure, but I think I can help here."

Sissa stopped abruptly and grabbed Samila by the shoulder. "What? What happened?"

"Got my first word watching Myss fight. Dropped me like a sack of produce," Samila replied, unable to keep the proud grin from her face.

Sissa gasped and pulled her sister up in a tight hug. "You did it. I told you you could do it."

"Stop. Stoooop!" Samila protested with a nervous laugh, wriggling to get out of the embrace before elbowing Sissa in the stomach. "You're gonna get me killed before I can use it. I need a minute."

"Go. Do what you have to do," Sissa told her, giving her a little shove in the arm.

Samila grinned as she passed me. "Don't die before seeing this," she said.

"Uh. Sure. I'll do my best," I said, watching her as she limped toward the edge of the battlefield, almost right next to the wall of fire. I shot a questioning look over at Sissa.

"She found her Duty and Mercy," she said. "It's a concept that resonates with her soul and—Well, it's a dragon thing. You wouldn't understand."

Geddon rolled his neck and shoulders and waved Organ Grinder through an experimental figure eight, finishing with a full-throttle engine burst that sent the sword's teeth spinning.

"I've always wanted to fight a real dragon," he said before glancing over at Sissa. "No offense."

Sissa spared a moment to give him the death stare to end all death stares.

"Well, she's fast. I know that. Or at least she was before dying," I offered if only to keep the conversation on track. "Lots of teeth. The tail works like a whip. Think the Scourge is still getting used to the new body, though. She almost looks drunk."

"That won't last," Bole added. "You can see she's already finding her feet. Then we'll have a right pissed-off Undead god of old on our hands."

He was right. Myss was up on all fours again, bones popping audibly as she stretched and shook herself after her fall.

"Wouldn't be sporting unless we waited for her to get full control of her faculties, would it?" Geddon said, looking to the rest of us for confirmation.

"I'm not feeling very sporting, Geddon," Sissa replied. "Go!"

Geddon laughed gleefully as he bounded forward, once again leading our charge. His long legs shot him far ahead of the rest of us and closed the gap between him and the dragon a full five seconds faster.

He drew first blood.

The Scourge-Touched dragon reared up and bared its teeth, taking a long, lazy swipe with one of its claws, but Geddon dropped into a slide that took him feet-first under the attack, terminating in a half-crouched thrust with his sword directly into Myss' armpit. Black blood spewed from the wound and down onto Geddon, covering him. Unfortunately, it also blinded him to the next attack.

Myss's tail whipped around from behind and lashed against the wounded area with its thick side. The blow slammed into Geddon's back and flattened him to the ground, hard.

Sissa, Bole, and I entered the fight together.

Trix, too, apparently, from somewhere out of sight. His rifle was already cycling through rounds almost too quickly to count, stippling a line of accurate needle fire across the dragon's face. He must have found a good spot somewhere.

Actually, no. Trix was in front of us, leading us, bounding forward on all fours, only pausing to lift his rifle and shoot. No, wait, he was on my shoulder. The sound of the gun was deafening, this close.

"Duty and Mercy!" Sissa shouted from my left, and I felt the signature increase in my physical and mental capabilities.

I raised my arm cannon and snapped off a shot. I aimed for the back of the dragon where the tail met the legs, in hopes of crippling her without dousing us all in plasma, but Myss moved at the last second, a quick shifting of her weight to bring her tail back in line with the rest of her body that made my shot a near-miss. The resulting explosion caught her in the hip and peeled some of her thick skin and made her stumble slightly but was otherwise ineffective.

A huge claw slammed down in front of me, directly on top of Trix. Meanwhile, Trix leaped in from the side, scrabbling onto the back of the claw and clambering up Myss's elbow. The Trix on my shoulder answered with a well-placed shot into the dragon's mouth, which elicited a sudden involuntary shake of the monster's head.

Wait.

"Trix?"

"Can't talk now. This takes effort," Trix muttered in my ear as he squeezed off three more rounds. The other Trixes—and there were an absolute ton of them now—fanned out and were all doing the same from a multitude of different angles. It was a whole mercenary company of tiny fox-people waving their rifles in the air and shooting the dragon in the face. Others crawled up Myss's tail and onto her back, firing wildly and skittering around like squirrels on amphetamines.

Myss swatted them away, bit them with her teeth, squashed them with her feet, but there were always more.

"Wait, so. Trix, are you—"

"Yes, I am very real. Please don't get me killed," Trix grunted. His rifle barked again, and Myss flinched back as one of her eyes was perforated.

I joined in with my machine pistol. As I aimed down the sights, Death Eye didn't give me a damned thing—no glowing weak points to shoot, not even a glimmer. So, as I was wont to do, I went for quantity over quality.

PRRRRRRRRRRRT!

I emptied the mag in the general location of Myss's face, dropping the mag once I heard the click of the action locking open. Trix made a disgusted noise above my head.

"Shut up, fuzzball. You started shooting like three weeks ago," I said.

"That makes it even worse. You know that, don't you?" Trix replied. The nerve of this little fox-man.

Next to Trix's marksmanship, I was pathetic, but my bullets were way, way bigger. My rounds that hit tore through Myss's hide or rent holes in the roof of her mouth and out the back of her throat.

Apparently, that was too close to the mark for the Scourge. Myss tucked her head out of sight behind one of her wings as her tail whipped around in a sweep meant to catch us all in one motion. I tried to track the head with my aim, but by the time I could get off a shot, I was forced to duck out of the way. The displaced air whooshed overhead and blew my hair down over my eyes, while Trix sheltered in the crook where my shoulder met my neck.

Before I was even cognizant that we'd lived through the first attack, the dragon's tail whipped out blindly again. This time, I was barely able to throw myself down to get Trix and me out of the way in time. The air became a hurricane as the tail passed overhead over and over again.

Trix tumbled from my shoulders and into the dirt with a gasp, and his illusory copies faded from existence.

"You okay?" I asked.

"I'll be fine," Trix said, reaching up to scratch at his scalp. "A little shaky but fine."

Sissa and Bole hadn't been idle. As Myss was flailing blindly with her tail, the two of them emerged from underneath the dragon, dragging Geddon behind them. He wasn't moving, his head lolling to the side and his massive knuckles dragging the dirt. The man still had Organ Grinder clutched in his hand, though, carving a winding trail from where he'd fallen. When the three got close to us, Geddon groaned to let us all know he was still alive.

"So, was it everything you hoped for, Big Guy?" Sissa asked, winded from having to sprint-drag a man three times her weight.

"Uuuuugh," was Geddon's reply.

"Trix, do what he needs," Sissa ordered. Then she was on her feet and back in the fight. She got low, waited for Myss's tail to swipe over her head, then broke into a weaving charge that tucked her under the dragon yet again.

Bole, cursing, followed in the dragonkin's wake, only to break off and shout to get Myss's attention. Meanwhile, I did my best to keep the monster's head down. I'd much rather fight a blind dragon. My bullets raked across her wing where I figured her head was, but the skin there was made of tough stuff. Only a few of my direct hits penetrated, and they didn't do much after.

Scourge-Touched Ancient Red Dragon takes 22 Damage. (55 base, -36 resist, +3 Knife in the Dark) (Piercing)

> Scourge-Touched Ancient Red Dragon takes 23 Damage. (57 base, -37 resist, +3 Knife in the Dark) (Piercing)
> Scourge-Touched Ancient Red Dragon takes 18 Damage. (51 base, -36 resist, +3 Knife in the Dark) (Piercing)

"Reborn from ashes!"

The shout came loud and clear—Samila's voice. She sounded different, her voice fuller, more triumphant, more *complete* than I'd ever heard, though I couldn't explain why I felt that way. She stood tall at the edge of our perimeter, well back from the fight, her arms outstretched and her face turned toward the sky.

Her words rang in the air, suspended on invisible wires between each molecule, reverberated through the world like someone had just discovered the musical chord that could shatter all creation like a wineglass.

FWOOSH!

Every fire I'd set on the entire battlefield—the legion of Scourge, the dead wood, the leaves, the bark of the trees—all of it was extinguished in that exact instant, and the things that had been burning were now nothing but ash. Then the air rushed inward—or, more accurately, was sucked toward the epicenter of the spell: Samila. The cloud of ash hit her like an oncoming tidal wave, crashing into itself and sending massive plumes of obscuring dust skyward.

"Ryan!" was all the warning Sissa could give me as she took a two-handed swing at the front of Myss's leg. It must have cut through the tendon, because the limb buckled and failed to hold the dragon's weight. That didn't stop her, though. Myss flapped her wings to stabilize herself and dove for me.

It must have sensed something was going on or that all the people with the guns were distracted. It howled that freight-train howl and shot forward as fast as it could, leading with its teeth.

"*OOH AHH! OOH AHH! OOH AHH!*" A legion of unseen voices echoed her.

Myss's toothy maw filled my entire field of view.

FOOP!

A plasma bomb exploded in her face.

> Scourge-Touched Ancient Red Dragon takes 170 Damage. (Fire) (390 base, -220 resist)

I knew it wasn't enough to kill her. The fire did, however, blind her long enough for me to grab Trix and Geddon and evade. The snapping dragon maw came down where we had been a half-a-breath before. Said maw was still on fire but far, far less affected than I would have liked.

WHAM!

Something big and gray slammed into the dragon's neck from above. Bone cracked just below the base of Myss's skull. The figure was a blur—a vague impression of charcoal wings, a horned head, muscular limbs, and bright, shining sword and shield. The blade thrust down into Myss's flesh and twisted before being withdrawn. Black blood geysered from the wound, while Myss shuddered, writhing as her nerve signals no longer wanted to travel the way they should have.

The Scourge-Touched dragon slashed blindly at the new presence, attempting to dislodge it, but the figure attached itself to it with its shield—a strong, aluminum alloy one I'd definitely seen before in my workshop. Unable to hit with her claws, Myss bucked and threw her head back in a surprising demonstration of speed, flinging the ashen figure up into the air and out of sight.

"Trix!"

"I know!" he squeaked, climbing up onto Geddon's arm and closing his eyes.

The big man came out of his stupor with another groan. His eyes fluttered, and his mouth drooped open, but he was most certainly awake.

"Geddon! We're still in this fight!" I shouted in his face. When he didn't respond I gave him a good slap with my prosthesis.

That got his attention. Geddon shook his head and blinked, seeming to finally realize where he was. "Right," he said. He lifted his hand, seemingly surprised to find his sword still there. "Right!"

Then he staggered to his feet and charged. He didn't even hesitate.

Overhead, the ashen gray figure was back. She swooped in on leathery wings and slashed at Myss's throat, behind her head, at the base of her wings, over and over.

Oh, yes, I could tell it was a she now that I got a good look at her. She was the spitting image of a very upsized, very gray Samila—naked but for the sword and shield she carried. She flew through the air like she'd been born to it, with all the grace of an aerialist and the power of a falling star. Her sword flashed in lightning-fast patterns, and her body moved with such exacting precision, it was all the dead god could do to keep up with her.

Organ Grinder revved, and Geddon limped back into position under Myss's body, almost exactly where he'd made his incision before. All his form was gone. He was barely on his feet as it was. Instead, he hacked at Myss's leg like it was a tree trunk, dodging stomps and chasing after it as the dragon engaged Samila overhead.

Myss bled from so many wounds now the ground was black with blood, but she just wasn't going down.

Things turned bad quickly.

In a move no one had expected, Myss, with a singular flap of her wings, took to the air, fast as a bullet, flying far overhead, only stopping once she had brushed up against the branches of the canopy. Then she tucked her wings and came down again in an explosive display of power that used her mass to its utmost potential.

Everyone in the immediate area was blasted with a wave of earth and wind.

The shock wave hit me, sending me tumbling over the ground before smacking into something hard and unpleasantly hot. My breath left me in a whoosh.

From inside the dust cloud that used to be the battlefield, Myss roared. A claw extended and struck Samila from the sky, swatting her down into the dirt like a bug. She hit the ground hard.

The Scourge cheered their champion as she took the upper hand.

"*OOH AHH! OOH AHH! OOH AHH!*" a thousand sets of vocal cords chanted in unison. Something out there exploded with the sound of thunder and crackling electricity. Gunshots cracked as Scourge poked at our perimeter.

Another flap of Myss's wings dispelled the dust cloud, and she landed nimbly on her feet once more. She loomed over Samila, jaws set wide.

Oh, no.

My armor was expended as far as ammo was concerned, but—

I hit the release on the forearm gauntlet and slipped it on. It was heavy but not nearly so heavy as the whole set. I flexed my fingers and sent a mana charge into the wrist blade, hoping the Triggers had some juice in them still.

VRRRRRRRR!

The blade began to spin, faster and faster. I concentrated and sent a big jolt through the circuitry, hoping a bit would bleed into the components I needed.

BOOM! An explosion rocked Myss's flank and sent her reeling.

I blinked. That wasn't one of mine.

A hand grasped my shoulder from behind. "Not yet, son," a voice said in my ear.

I spun, wide-eyed, the blade in my hand coming up to—

Jassin? Bishop Kolash? Garret?

No. No. They couldn't be here!

My hand found its way up to Jassin's, feeling to see if he was real. He smiled that skeletal smile of his, the strangeness of it countered by the warmth in his eyes. The hand he wasn't currently using to touch me was extended and glowed with a complex, rotating sphere of blue symbols.

"Unbelievable," he remarked with a slight shake of his head.

A bead of sweat dribbled down the man's face.

Bishop Kolash had his staff high up in the air as he gurgled some kind of incantation. A golden fog billowed out of his chest and spread itself over the battlefield. It surrounded me and soaked into my skin, warming me and relaxing muscles I hadn't realized were tense. My burns cooled, and my multitude of cuts felt instantly better.

Jassin shook his head and looked at the bishop reproachfully. "I told you to warn me before you do that. You're lucky my spell was already done."

"*BWORP.* You will live," he said. "And now so will they." He pointed back toward where the dragon was bent over Samila's ashen body, its jaws inches from her face but moving no closer. I squinted.

Frozen. Myss was frozen there as blue light danced around her entire body. Samila, however, was in the process of wriggling out from underneath, equally as surprised to be alive. The rest of my friends were getting to their feet as well.

"*OOH AHH! OOH AHH! OOH AHH!*" Countless soldiers shouted their cadence call as they marched in neat formations, engaging with the enemy. Spears stabbed through Scourge flesh. Glowing spell beams shot into the Scourge's ranks and knocked them to the ground. The front rank took up positions, thrust, reset, and advanced. Some kind of catapult ordnance sailed overhead and landed in the thick of the enemy, bursting open and sending lightning bolts in all directions.

"*OOH AHH! OOH AHH! OOH AHH!*"

They'd come. Jassin had come through, exactly as he said he would. A laugh of utter disbelief bubbled up from my core.

My friends joined us, limping, tired but alive. Samila brought up the rear. As she approached, her ashen body went stiff as a statue, cracked and fell apart, dissolving into fine dust before dumping her out onto the ground.

Mercifully, her dignity was still intact. She was in her armor still, unlike what it seemed in her other form.

Sissa and I, after a second of stunned silence, rushed forward to help her up.

"Holy hell, Sam," Sissa said. "That was what you learned?"

Samila shook like a leaf, trembling in cold only she could feel, unable to speak, but she nodded.

"*Rrgg,*" Jassin grunted. "It is about to break free. Prepare yourselves. Its other selves are about to collide with this timeline and cause a paraclastic surge."

"What the hell does that mean?" Bole asked, rubbing at his almost-fully-healed face. The bishop's magic was working like a charm.

The strain was becoming more pronounced on Jassin's face. "I have forcefully dispersed its place in the timeline, but the blockage being swept away is an inevitability. The Old One's past is currently working to right its present, and the amount of causal energy will be immense for a being of this caliber."

"What?" Bole asked again.

"She's going to come out of this spell a lot stronger," Trix said. "Wounds healed. Maybe a bit more lucid."

"While we're worn down," Sissa finished. "It's going to take an army to stop her."

We had one of those now, I guessed, but then there would be casualties. We'd had to pull multiple things from our collective asses to just live through the first round, and I wasn't about to take that gamble again.

Not even one.

I exchanged a look with Jassin, questions passing between us, which he didn't even realize he had answered for me.

Yes, he'd hold on for as long as he could. No, he couldn't do anything to stop me.

I flexed my gauntlet, spinning the blade back up to full speed and charged.

The shocked voices of my friends followed me, and their hands reached out to grab me, but I was too quick. They were too exhausted. I was, too, of course, but I knew this was my moment to give.

And I gave it my all. I pumped my legs with all my might, my blade construct spinning at my side. I passed the pools of black blood, the broken earth where the dragon had split open the world, the crater where Samila had landed.

Myss's muscles spasmed. Her head jerked to the side suddenly, too fast to follow—or maybe it had always been there. The blue energy that encased her sparked violently, then died. Her flesh knit in front of me; her lost eye regenerated, sucking up the liquid that had been leaking from it and sealing itself with a pop; her claws flexed with monstrous strength, cracking the ground.

The phantom heat was back. My skin burned and froze. My face felt like it was being pressed onto a stove and encased in ice all at once. Memories of fire flashed through my mind and swept away all thoughts . . .

Except one.

I bent my legs and leaped as far and as high as I could, my gauntleted fist rocketing forward. The spinning blade bit into the flesh of the dead god, slicing through scales and meat, parting the fibrous muscle, surging through gallons of blood.

I began to fall, but I took hold of what I could with my prosthetic to keep myself in place.

Iron Grip [0.1 MP/sec]

Anchor kicked in once the System thought I was climbing.

I held on. I held on and pressed my fist deeper into the monster, an inch at a time.

WHAM!

Something smacked into me from behind, smashing my face into the bloody scales. I was spared the worst of it, though. Anchor was doing the impossible, a straight 30 percent mitigation to all force acting against me. Good. I needed to do the impossible.

HP [77/309]

WHAM!

Another blow from behind. I experienced the unique sensation of my spine snapping.

Status gained: Broken bone (Spine)
Status gained: Paralysis (Partial)
HP [34/309]

I was so close, up to my bicep in dragon flesh.

Come on. Come on. Please.

With a sickening pop, my blade punctured the chest cavity (or what I hoped was the chest cavity), and I was suddenly shoulder-deep in Myss's body. Wet, warm Scourge blood oozed out of the wound and down my chest, and I felt some type of organ pressing against the palm of my hand.

Myss hissed and brought her head down to look me in the eye, to take in my broken form—our last moment together before the end. If I hadn't known any better, I would have said she looked pleased, an emotion I was sure the Scourge was incapable of, just a moment ago.

Her mouth opened once more, exposing rows of blackened teeth.

"Light and gods of old." I sighed, feeling like I was emptying my lungs for the last time. "Just die already."

Then, I summoned my exploding brightsteel blade all the way inside Myss's body.

CHAPTER FORTY-TWO

Say Goodbye

The action was instantaneous. I'd expected my fun exploding sword to come out blazing-hot and ready to kill me like usual, yes, but its reaction to being summoned inside an actual, honest-to-Constance Scourge-Touched was, for lack of a better term, *nuclear.*

There were two explosions, really. The first—the one the sword had been in the process of beginning when I'd stored it in my pocket dimension—went off with a muffled *BOOF!*, accompanied by a flash of absolute agony that shot up my arm and into my core. This was followed by the loss of sensation in my entire right side. Then, shock.

The secondary explosion was much, much worse. Upon making contact with the Scourge goo inside of Myss, my brightsteel hand grenade went supernova inside the dragon's chest cavity. The not-so-surgical hole I'd made in her chest bulged outward for a half-second, then erupted like a volcano, spewing blazing, white Maelstrom energy in great quantities. For my part, I did what every other object close to an explosion does: I caught fire and shot away from ground zero like a bullet.

That's what I was told afterward, at least. I'd been under the dragon, clutching her chest, and reaching up into her when it had happened, so the explosion—and thus, my trajectory—was angled down into the dirt where I dug a long furrow of churned earth and scorched plant life. Supposedly, I lay there unconscious, while everyone else watched a full third of the Scourge-Touched dragon dissolve from the inside, which set the rest of its corpse to topple directly on top of me.

You have defeated Scourge-Touched Ancient Red Dragon.
You have been awarded 162,796 Experience points. [406,990 base, +81,398 nemesis, -325,592 non-combat Class]

I woke up to Bishop Kolash's hand on my face—that yellow glow that I'd come to associate with the Church's healing (and curse) spells shining unpleasantly in my eyes. With a cough, I tried to flinch away from the light, but that was a mistake. My entire body was displeased with what we'd done today, and however unpleasant the yellow-glow stuff was or how weird and slimy Kolash's palm, I was being told in no uncertain terms it was time to lie down and shut up for a while.

"He's awake. Surprisingly lively too, considering," Kolash burbled.

I detected the presence of someone else at my side, and I performed the colossal feat of rolling my head over in that direction to find Samila there, holding my metal hand. She was crying but also smiling. Happy tears.

Oh, something good must have happened.

She wiped her eyes and leaned forward until her forehead was touching mine. "You really need to stop doing that," she whispered.

I worked my jaw until it was loose enough to speak again. Even that action could be measured on a pain scale.

"Ugh. Doing what?" I croaked.

The relief at hearing me speak was palpable. "The noble-sacrifice thing. It's endearing up to a point, but, eventually, you'll have to learn a new trick to impress the girls."

"It's working, though. Right? I can tell you're impressed."

"Yeah." She sniffed, nodding, again having to wipe her tears away so they didn't fall on me. "Yeah, it's working."

"Oh good." I sighed. "Long as you're impressed."

"I've gotten him out of the worst of it, stopped the bleeds, repaired some of the bones, but his human anatomy should take it from here," Kolash said. "I am afraid I might put something where it isn't supposed to go."

To see what he meant, I checked my Status Screen.

HP [150/309]
Status lost: Burning
Status lost: Exposure [Radiant]
Status lost: Severed Spine
Status lost: Broken Bone [Arm]
Status lost: Broken Bone [Arm]
Status lost: Broken Bone [Arm]
Status lost: Broken Bone [Hand]
Status lost: Broken Bone [Jaw]
Status lost: Dislocated Bone [Shoulder]
Status lost: Internal Bleeding
Status lost: Punctured Lung
Status lost: Broken Bone [Rib]
Status lost: Ruptured Spleen

It went on like that for a while.

"See? That is what a real healer can do," Trix squeaked from down by my feet. "Now we don't have to force-feed him for a whole day to get him back on his feet."

"Thank Constance for that," I said. "Bole told me what was in the Undercity meal."

"Hehe, yeah. You should have seen his face," Bole sniggered. He was behind Samila along with Sissa and Geddon.

"Glad to have you back, young man," Jassin said from the foot of my personal patch of land. "Are you quite done with your suicide attempt?" He wore his displeasure at my little stunt openly, with crossed arms and a dour frown.

I shrugged weakly. It hurt but not as badly as before.

Experimentally, I put out a hand to push myself up into a sitting position.

THUNK!

The sound surprised me—not because of the ring of metal. I was used to that. It was because it was coming from the wrong side of my body. I looked down to find my entire forearm still encased in my heavy steel gauntlet. Except parts of it looked absolutely slagged. The fingers and knuckles were messes of once-molten metal, and the forearm blackened and deformed, more concave now than when I'd last seen it. The blade I'd used to cut into the dragon looked like it had been made of wax and been rendered down until it had molded and fused with the wrist part of the gauntlet. The joint was entirely frozen.

And in the palm of my hand was the brightsteel blade.

"Ah, yes. We should talk about that," Kolash said. "I did what I could with the bone and tissue damage, but that armor will have to be removed if you wish to make a full recovery. I assume you can handle that. There is also the issue of the priceless, holy relic you have clutched in your fingers."

"That can wait, Bishop," Jassin said. "Ryan is needed right now. Can you stand?"

I waved them off when they tried to put their hands under my shoulders, feeling the need to do this on my own. With some effort, I gingerly got to my feet, careful not to jostle my sore bits more than I needed to. What shirt I still had was stuck to me, glued there with dried blood, but the pain of most of the surface-level stuff was gone. A small mercy.

Once I was upright, I spared a moment to take everything in. The battlefield was a blackened wasteland. Every bit of the underbrush for at least a quarter-mile out was gone, replaced by soot and ash. The army was in the process of after-battle cleanup. Bonfires burned in the spaces between tree trunks, and hundreds of soldiers carried out the grim task of dragging bodies over to the pyres and heaving them on top. Meanwhile, patrols of spearmen walked in loose formations systematically stabbing the more-intact bodies, making sure they were truly dead.

Strangely, Kuul was amongst them. He sat with his back against a Mendau trunk, resting, his eyes closed, his one good arm laid against his chest. The fire inside of him seemed dimmer now but not entirely out. The soldiers gave the giant a wide berth, not bothering to collect the bodies that were closest to him. If those things started to move, the goeshi would probably want to handle it, anyway.

"He rests now," Tiba said as she walked up to the rest of us, Kelub and Grorg in tow. The three of them looked in high spirits, all of them walking with springs in their steps, now that they were reunited and safe. "If the tall folk keep their distance, he doesn't bother them. I am watching, though."

A big knot of tension I hadn't realized I'd been carrying loosened in my gut. "Tiba, you made it!"

"I make it," Tiba replied brightly. "Sorry I am not here for the dragon fight, but Kuul gets carried away with the Baned. You handle it well, though."

"He always die muchly," Trix said in a slow series of grunts, his face contorted like he was maybe having stomach pain or about to vomit.

"Wait. Did you just speak Goblin?" I asked.

Trix's ears flattened in embarrassment. "Oh, did I not use the proper—"

Tiba's eyes lit up like someone had just handed her a whole birthday cake, candles and all.

"Trix, you speak! Do it again! Do it again!" She clapped her hands and bounced up and down excitedly. She looked so young when she did that, not like the first goblin queen in a millennium.

Trix cleared his throat and rolled his shoulders. "Uh—Ryan dies . . . uh . . . much. All time."

Yeah, that sounded painful. I didn't think the little guy's throat was made for the sounds he was trying to imitate.

The goblin queen loved it, though. She lunged forward, squealing in delight, and took his hand, jabbering at him in Goblin, begging him to say something else, talking a mile a minute while Trix tried to follow. There was talk about making him a goblin, too, and since she was a queen now, she could knight him, and he could be in her royal retinue.

Did I just hear the word "concubine?" How would—What?

Meanwhile, Trix just stood there, blinking and obviously increasingly lost as the seconds ticked by. He looked back at me, pleadingly, but I wasn't about to step into the middle of this.

I left them to it.

Jassin was there waiting impatiently, frowning still.

"If you are quite done, you and I have something to attend to," he said. He grabbed my shoulder and pointed me toward the tutorial facility and the still-smoking corpse of a big Undead dragon. Her chest had burst open and taken a significant portion of her back with it, and her neck looked like it was barely attached anymore, lying there curled inward like a snake.

There, in the middle of the giant cavity the explosion had left, stood Nali. Her ghostly light cast the insides of Myss in a strange, dreamlike haze. For her part, Nali looked unfazed, expressionless but always seeming to be looking directly at me.

"She won't speak with me or anyone I send," Jassin said. "She appears to be a projection of some kind. A very advanced, very detailed messenger spell, and she has been waiting, I think, for you."

I nodded. 'It's called a hologram. It's made of light. Not sure how the System made her consciousness, though."

"It's conscious? Now that is interesting," Jassin cooed hungrily. I could see him reassessing his previous observations, probably in hopes of recreating the process someday.

"Well, she's an artificial intelligence, but she's probably in a bad way," I told him. "She's not supposed to be like this. The Scourge has done a number on her, too."

"I detect a troublesome tone in your voice, Ryan. This isn't another problem that requires you to run off and die without consulting me, is it?" Jassin asked.

"Still sore about that?"

"It was literally half an hour ago, young man," Jassin fumed. "Just because I put a complex explosive enchantment on you doesn't mean I wish to see you die. The dragon was a daunting foe, yes, but—"

"You would have lost people bringing her down," I interrupted. "I'm not apologizing for what I did, Jassin."

That vein on his forehead did its pulsating thing again, and he looked like he wanted to lay into me in earnest. The moment didn't last, however. His anger reached some kind of breaking point, and he ended up sighing and massaging his temple instead.

"Very well. I acknowledge that you did what you thought was right for our situation, but don't do it again without—"

I put my hands up in surrender.

"I get it. I really do. I won't do it again," I assured him. He almost had to watch me die, and it had shaken him. Of all the things I understood in this multiverse, that feeling was first and foremost. "Now let's go make sure Ralqir stays saved."

Leaving the others behind, the two of us approached Nali carefully. We had to practically step into the dragon's chest cavity to get within speaking range. This close, I could see Myss's body was in an advanced state of decay, its flesh sagging down and in the process of liquifying and seeping into the soil. Thick, black sludge laid in a pool all around her, and it sprouted tiny hairs that waved eerily in my general direction.

On a hunch, I waved my gauntlet/brightsteel shiv over the stuff, and it literally shied away from the gesture. I used the technique to create some space for us.

Nali spoke first. Her tone was robotic, which paired badly with her weeping black eyes and disjointed body.

"Defiler, you may have been spared today, but nothing you do can stop this place from being cleansed. You have only prolonged its suffering."

Jassin looked to me for translation.

"She seems pissed at me and, by extension, you," I said. "It's not her talking, I think. She's speaking for the Scourge."

Someone shouted an order overhead, and I saw a rank of soldiers with spears and torches engaging a trio of Scourge-Touched on the lip of the concrete ring. The monsters had emerged from the black pool, still dripping with ichor, only to be cut down.

"We have been destroying them since the end of the battle. They emerge from the slime immediately ready to kill," Jassin said. "They are quite a bit weaker than the ones we fought in Eclipse, however. Perhaps because it is down to the dregs of the organic matter it likes to animate."

"Nali, why do they keep coming out of the goo like that? Wouldn't it make more sense to wait until we were gone to start replenishing their numbers?"

Nali twitched. "The Scourge does not have a good grasp of linear time. If it forms new agents now, it means that sometime in the future, it believes it will be successful."

I translated.

"Immortals see the universe differently, I suppose. Of that I am constantly reminded," Jassin said. "As far as I can tell, we have destroyed the majority that have troubled us thus far, but she may well be correct that in ten, maybe a hundred years, our ability to keep them back will be severely diminished by entropy. Perhaps the Empire will have internal turmoil. War. Perhaps just a lack of will to perform a task whose purpose was long forgotten. "

"It's an enemy that never sleeps," I said.

"Precisely. Ask her what it wants," Jassin told me.

"Nali, what does the Scourge want from us?"

"For you to die, Defiler. For your kind to pay for their sin with erasure from the multiverse. For your memory to be forgotten for eternity. For all that you have touched to crumble to dust and be cast into the void."

"Oh, is that all?" Jassin asked sarcastically after listening to my interpretation. "Please, forgive us if we do not go quietly into oblivion, miss."

Nali didn't answer Jassin, though. She just stared at me and waited for my answer.

"Why doesn't she speak with me?" Jassin asked, annoyed.

I thought for a moment. "She's corrupted, but I think she's built on a base code that's meant to be helpful for Animators like me. Maybe even after all the Scourge has done to her, she's still obligated to answer my questions."

"This will make things hard," Jassin said, rubbing his forehead. "Ask her—"

"Hang on," I interrupted him. "Nali, what really is the Scourge?"

Nali's head glitched, giving me a glimpse of her real face—the fear, the pain—but then she was back to neutral. "As the name implies, the Scourge is a punishment inflicted upon humanity for its hubris in breaching the boundaries of its universe. It is a presence from beyond existence, formless, without purpose or thought, until it is brought from its natural place into reality as you know it. To you, it is hate. Hate without end or ending. Hatred for you and your kind."

"Uh huh," I mused, surprisingly not surprised. Honestly, I didn't have the capacity for an existential crisis right now. So there was a thing from the beyond that wanted humanity dead, supposedly for something we had done. That concept was not entirely new to me. We'd always had an "all go, no quit, advancement at whatever cost" nature. Honestly, the fact that it had taken us this long to pick up an enemy of this caliber was the real surprise.

I'd deal with the implications of the threat later, on my own time, when I wasn't staring at a holographic woman I'd made a promise to. "So, am I to assume the black stuff is the Scourge's actual form?"

"In this universe, yes," Nali answered.

"Can it be destroyed?" I probed.

Her body burst open to reveal a horror show of bones and teeth, blood and viscera. She screamed in the voice of a thousand different forms of life. Then she reformed herself, suddenly the Nali I'd known before.

"Y-Yes, Ch- Ch- Chos- Ryan," Nali whimpered. "In theory. The light of the Maelstrom in this universe is u-uniquely suited to do so. In practice, no. There is no hope for you or any that live here to destroy the Scourge. When the planet was transported here, the scouring of the surface came close, but the Scourge burrowed deep, into the spaces where light cannot touch. In a billion years, when all life on Ralqir is gone, it will serve as a trap to capture and convert sentient life that enters its domain. Then it will continue, on and on, until this universe is dead."

Jassin looked from me to the hologram, his eyes calculating. He had to have been bristling with how unable he was to understand our conversation. I summarized as best I could.

The headmaster went a shade paler when I got to the part about it being nestled in the deep places of the world.

"Well, that precludes us from ever going home as the dragons wish." He sighed. He looked genuinely sad to say the words. "Outside the Maelstrom, there would be nothing stopping it from overrunning the surface, too. We will need to be forever vigilant, lest our planet be plunged into another cataclysm. This time we lost a province. Next time it could easily be everything."

I nodded, reluctant to speak. Someone had stolen my breath in the precise moment I finally realized what had to be done.

"We'll be back," I said to Nali, then grabbed Jassin's arm and shuffled us both back to where the others were waiting.

* * *

Geddon clasped my prosthetic hand in a grip that rivaled even my Ability-enhanced one, then crushed me in an enormous bear (cat?) hug. "I will always cherish our time together, Ryan." The Leori sniffled. "We've spilled so much blood together, I feel like I'm losing a brother today. A blood-spilling brother."

"Hey!" I gasped as he squeezed the air out of me. "Just, uh, remember who gave you your sword before you became a warrior of legend, yeah?"

"Oh, I'll remember," he said, lowering me down so he could caress the hilt of his chain-sword lovingly. "I'll make sure they pronounce your name correctly in the ballads."

"Please do not." Kolash burped. "It will be hard enough to keep a second fulcrum a secret without random bards spreading tales of it all."

Trix was next, flanked by Tiba, who was still holding his hand. The little vulpa's ears drooped sadly along with his whiskers, and his rifle hung low on his hip. He was having a hard time meeting my eyes, but when he looked back at the goblin queen, he did that head-to-tail shudder thing.

"Thank you, Ryan," Trix said, his voice cracking. "Thank you for . . . uh . . ." He seemed to lose his words mid-sentence.

I got down on one knee and ruffled his fur playfully. "No. Thank you for being my friend and for sticking with me when you learned the truth. Not to mention having my back on and off the battlefield. You saved my life, Trix. You're a great warrior," I said, my voice threatening to give out. "And a greater man."

Trix did find the courage to meet my gaze then, eyes wide in shock. Then the dam broke. He dashed under my arm to give me a full-body hug. "Don't go setting yourself on fire again without me there," he mumbled into my shirt.

"Never!" I laughed, looking up from my vulpa buddy to Tiba. "Take care of this little guy, will you?"

Tiba nodded regally. "He's a goblin knight now. First Rifle. He never wants for anything long as I live. I promise." Then she slipped underneath my other arm and squeezed me as well.

Next was Beedy, who simply slapped me on the shoulder and grinned. He was looking a lot better after having gotten some treatment from the Church healers the army had brought with them. Even his smile was brighter.

Sissa and Bole came up as a pair. Bole was grinning from ear to ear, while Sissa had a more somber expression. "Take care of yourself, Ryan," Sissa said. "And try to think before you do things. For me. Not every battle requires a noble sacrifice, and I'd feel a lot better if I knew you'd taken that lesson to heart."

"Sure. I'll work on that." I waggled my finger between the two of them. "So, you two, uh, you're—"

"Yep!"

"Absolutely not."

The two of them answered at the same time before looking at each other, an argument forming between them like a bank of storm clouds.

"No, we're not," Sissa insisted, eyes narrowed, daring the shorter man to contradict her. "I just don't think he's as vile as he tried to convince himself he was all these years. I may be wrong."

Bole seemed like he wanted to argue there, but he did the smart thing instead and chose to remain silent before he could be told to shut up. He simply slapped me on the shoulder and gave me a wink from the side of his face Sissa couldn't see.

Samila was my final stop.

"Hey," I said lamely.

"Hi," she replied. The scales on her upper cheeks were dark but still brilliant-blue next to the gold of her eyes, though they were slightly puffy and red. "So, this is it."

There was a lot I wanted to say. So much.

But I had a promise to keep.

I reached out, wrapped my arm around her waist and kissed her once more. This time, she'd been waiting for it. She leaned back, letting me support her weight, melting into my arms as our lips pressed together and the world spun around us. Her body fit perfectly against mine, strong and light and intensely inviting. It went on like that for a while.

Someone in the group cleared their throat.

I was the one to break off first. I pulled back sadly but not before planting another, smaller kiss on her top lip.

Once we were apart, Samila's eyes fluttered open, and she let out a contented sigh.

"Whoa," she remarked for the second time. She glanced over at her sister. "You've got to try this. Seriously," she called, slightly breathless still.

Sissa turned away, suddenly finding the blackened horizon incredibly interesting. "No. No, I will not be doing that."

"I'll try it!" Geddon boomed from way over by Trix.

"I'm kidding, obviously!" Samila teased before quirking an eyebrow. "Mostly."

I laughed, pulling her close again, this time into a hug. She laid her head against my chest, and I cradled her there.

"You taught me what it was like to want again, Ryan. I'd forgotten for a long time, but now—I want things. I want more. I'm not just the Second."

"I'm going to remember you, Sam," I whispered to her. "I'll remember you forever."

We stayed there for a while, just being together, our friends all around us. No one interrupted.

When I finally pulled away, it felt like ripping myself in two, like I was leaving part of myself with her, and it was a ragged wound that would never fully heal.

Somehow I was content with that, despite how much it hurt. I was about to do what was right for her. For all of them.

Jassin nodded to me as I approached him, the dead dragon and the holographic woman waiting beyond.

"Goodbye again, Ryan. I'll be watching," was all he said, smiling warmly as he ushered me on toward my final moments in this world.

Then I was on my own, each step taking me farther into the belly of the beast.

"Nali," I said, back inside the dragon's corpse, my voice cracking under the weight of what I wanted to say, "I want to make a deal."

Nali's black eyes narrowed slightly. Her lips pursed into thin lines. "There is no exchange to be made. The Scourge does not have your others." She was obviously suspicious of me—or the Scourge was. She was right to be, though, considering our history.

"Yes, you do," I said. "You have this place, and with it, you have them."

"Then die and cast yourself into the black, Ryan Kotes," Nali said.

"No," I answered.

"There is no exchange."

"Nali, I'm leaving this place. I'm leaving and never coming back. I'm the one you really want, not them."

Nali was silent at that. I couldn't tell if she was thinking or just waiting for me to continue, so I just did.

"Right now the Scourge is getting a steady flow of power from my insertion point. When I leave, that source of power is going to be cut off. There's a good chance you'll just wither away, impotently attempting to end this world over and over again until you're just a memory."

"Unlikely," Nali argued. "The amount of Scourge currently in this universe is vast, having accumulated over more than a thousand years. It will destroy all you have touched. It will—"

"Or . . ." I interrupted with a raised finger. "Have you considered where I'm returning to?"

Nali frowned thoughtfully. "You are returning to your home universe."

"Right. "

"Explain," she demanded.

I spread my arms invitingly. "Come with me."

Nali blinked, froze for a moment.

I dangled the bait a bit more in front of her. "My home universe, where there's billions of humans just like me. Come with me, and you can inflict yourself on all of us. Supposedly we're the ones who deserve it, right?"

Nali seemed almost taken aback. "This is . . . out of character for you. You preserve the lives of others. Why are you doing this?"

"I want you to spare these people," I said. "Ralqir. Spare them for a while.

Maybe come back little by little when more Animators take their tutorial. But for now, come with me. We'll go back together and leave the people I love in peace."

"It is possible to do as you say . . . It will likely mean your death," Nali considered slowly. "The Scourge does not trust your word."

"Does that matter compared to the opportunity I'm offering? Please, spare them and come with me to the place where your true enemy lives. But—" I added before Nali could open her mouth again to accept. "—Nali comes too. She's got to have some kind of anchor that keeps her consciousness alive. Bring it to me. Then we'll all go together."

Deception is now Level 8.
Deception is now Level 9.

The eternal evil bent on my species' destruction contemplated my proposal for a full minute.

I and the world around me waited.

"We will have our exchange, Defiler," Nali finally said. Then she turned and began to climb the broken concrete remnants of her building, no time wasted, no more hesitation.

I took a big, courage-gathering breath, then followed her, clutching the brightsteel in my hand and keeping it close. I resisted the urge to look back at the people I was leaving.

The burbling tar slid away, keeping its distance from me and my relic, slurping as it retracted into the ground. When we reached the apex of the ring overlooking the bubbling lake of Scourge stuff, the smell was nearly enough to make me faint, but I held out. I only had to hold out for a little longer.

Waiting for me just at the edge of the pool was a fist-sized ball of white glass of a curiously familiar nature, though the color was different from those the Dark Lord used.

"This is what you ask for, Defiler. Take it and enter the pit. The Scourge will do as agreed."

I narrowed my eyes at her. "All of it?"

"All." Nali gestured to the white ball.

I bent down to pick it up. My good hand was still encased in the remains of my melted gauntlet, so I had to use my prosthetic to grab it and press it to the flesh of my upper arm. Another flex of will, a slight twisting of the mana to get the Ability to work the desired way, and it was gone. Unlike the Dark Lord's memory bauble, this one went right into my Storage Space, perhaps because it was willing to.

Nali's projection winked out.

I stared down into the black, shuddering at how it seemed to be inviting me in. My insurance policy ground against the bones of my hand, and little licks of flame sputtered over the surface of the visible steel.

I am Ryan Kotes.

The surface of the pooled Scourge reached out to me as I took my first step forward.

When it touched my skin, I was taken aback at how warm it was. Warm as I was.

I am Ryan Kotes. Nothing in this multiverse is like me.

It was so sudden, so fast, I didn't even see it move. It exploded from its pool and stabbed me with a hundred different proboscises that pierced my skin and wrapped around my bones, and then I was violently pulled under.

Reflexively, I tried to struggle, but there was nothing to struggle against. My hand that still clasped my brightsteel lashed out, tried to strike at what had me, but I was no longer in control. The black either shrank away or I was pulled to the side so that I was never able to make contact. Meanwhile, the horrific, rot-tainted tar entered my nose, forced its way into my mouth, my ears, my eyes . . .

I was sinking. Fast. The pressure grew exponentially. Down, down, lower, and lower into Hell.

The Scourge rushed into me, penetrated my insides, ripped its way into the place where my mana lived, and filled it until it ruptured.

There was no light that could penetrate down here, and it was growing even dimmer. At some point, I felt the Scourge there—the magnitude of it. Not just its physical presence. It was everywhere. Not just inside of me but *everywhere.* It *was* me. I was it. We were in the pit, the soil, the rotting corpses on the pyres, the roots of the trees, the people. We were pooled in caverns deep in the crust of the planet where nothing had ever ventured or lived.

But now no longer.

We pulled, pulled ourselves inward, into this vessel, this husk of organic matter and magic circuitry that called itself "human." We would become an instrument of destruction unlike any its kind had ever seen. We would burst into the vessel's universe and reap entire worlds, spreading, silencing one by one until all was still and the curse of humanity was finally obliterated.

No. I . . .

My thoughts were fuzzy, fleeting, but I still had the frozen pond at my center. From it, I derived courage.

I am Ryan Kotes. Nothing in this multiverse can take that from me.

But then, despite my bold words, I was swept away.

You have been awarded * Experience points.
Level Up!
You are now Level 25!
You have been awarded * Experience points.

Level Up!
You are now Level 49!
You have been awarded * Experience points.
Level Up!
You are now Level 82!
You have been awarded * Experience points.
Level Up!
You are now Level 150!
You have been awarded * Experience points.
Level Up!
You are now Level 221!
You have been awarded * Experience points.
Level Up!
You are now Level 700!
You have been awarded * Experience points.
You are now level 1077#%^&&#$##)(*@$!

Return to point of integration? Y/N
Y
Initiating travel to point of integration. Stand by . . .

Quest Update: ???
??? (Continued): Become worthy.

Dad

Proxis 3: Now

Myron Kotes's fingers flexed on the sweat-slick hilt of his sword as he prepared himself for another attack. A chill wind whipped past his face, carrying stinging particles of silica, airborne seeds, and tiny stars of ice from the upper atmosphere that hadn't had the chance to melt yet. Meanwhile, overhead, the sun was shining brilliantly past Proxis 2 to give his part of this rock he called home a taste of early spring. His clothes were filthy, stained, and torn in places from a combination of the elements and repeated training accidents.

Even so, he still insisted on using real steel.

Mr. White, the Colonial Exotic who he'd been living with for the better part of winter, watched him carefully, calmly, with unblinking eyes. His posture was relaxed, almost comically so, just like his swordsmanship, choosing to let his point droop lazily down, nearly dragging the tip of the blade in the gravel, as if he'd forgotten he was holding it. His training garb fit him loosely like Myron's, but White's was pristine, as if it had never been worn.

That didn't fool Myron, though. He had yet to land a hit on White, despite their months of training together. The man was fast and strong. What's more, he was an intelligent fighter. He never countered Myron's attacks the same way twice, and he always took the match in less than ten moves. He was a live wire in the ring and just as dangerous.

Myron came on with a two-handed thrust, his leading foot nearly hooking White's ankle, but the Exotic's body whipped to the side like a snake, and then his sword was between them and knocking Myron's aside just enough for the point to brush by White's left sleeve. Instead of retreating and trying to catch White on the return slash, however, Myron stepped further into his charge, his elbow rising in a strike meant for the bridge of the Exotic's nose.

But White wasn't there. He'd dropped low, letting his knees buckle until he was well under his elbow, as well as bringing his sword across Myron's body in a slash that would have disemboweled him if White hadn't been holding back. Then, quick as a flash, White was back on his feet and set for another round.

Two moves. The Colony man wasn't feeling generous today.

It was a short exchange, but Myron was already breathing hard. They'd been at this for an hour already, and his opponent never tired. In fact, Myron felt like he had a good grasp on the man's facial tics after so long together, and judging by them, he seemed to be enjoying himself.

He thought about going for another round, but he knew it wouldn't do any good. Maybe he'd get his opportunity tomorrow. Myron let his body relax and gave White a tired salute to signal the end of the training.

"You might have had me with that last gambit, Mr. Kotes, if not for our little disparity," White droned, sheathing his own sword.

Myron made a rude sound and reached for the squeeze bottle he kept just outside their makeshift ring. The "disparity" White was referring to came from supernaturally enhanced muscles and centuries of training that Myron didn't have.

"I am not being patronizing. It is an interesting style your people have developed—a completely separate branch of swordsmanship from the mainstream due to your self-imposed isolation, and it has been a pleasure to experience it," White offered.

Myron grunted, reaching up to wipe at his goggles to get the worst of the streaks off. Maybe he was acting like a sore loser. The man was paying him and the clan a compliment, and he couldn't even bring himself to acknowledge it.

It would come off a lot more genuine if he didn't beat me like a rug every damned time.

White's face was neutral, but now he held Myron's camp chair in his right hand. The Exotic knew Myron would be back on watch after this, and this was his way of being supportive.

Sighing, Myron tossed White the squeeze bottle, which he deftly caught. He didn't take a drink, though. He never did.

"I think the pleasure has been all yours," Myron said, gesturing to the cuts and sweat stains on his fencing attire. "I haven't even gotten a good look at your 'mainstream' techniques. Been too busy landing on my ass."

"Funny, I thought you'd been adjusting to them the entire time," White countered.

Myron took the camp chair from the Exotic and flipped it open, setting it down at the edge of the ring where he could keep a good line of sight on the spot where Ryan had been taken. According to White, he'd turn up here once he was done with his tutorial. Myron still held out hope that was the case.

White handed him back the squeeze bottle and turned to head to his portable hab. "I am due to check in with CRF. I will come join you as soon as—"

It happened suddenly. There was a change in the wind, a slight deviation in the current that could be felt on your skin, the way your hair folds in just such a way. When you're walking into the wind without your goggles, tears in your eyes, sand blasting you in the face, no idea which way is home except forward, and then you feel it—something solid, somewhere up ahead, the way the wind whips over it and curls as it tries to go the way it should. Outers folk called it a "stone sense," when you sense something big out there without having to see it.

Myron felt that stone sense right before—

BOOM!

An explosion knocked him flat, sending him tumbling. He felt his sword clattering out of his numb fingers. His breath left him, and his eyes rolled back into his head briefly before he wrenched himself back to full consciousness.

When he came to, the campsite was flattened. The fighting ring of stones was gone, the habs were torn open and in the process of tumbling off the edge of the ridge, the porta-lights bent and smashed, and Mr. White was facing off against something dark and terrible. Myron was doing his best to just breathe, his diaphragm kick-starting his respiratory process again after the explosion, but that *thing*... It triggered something deep within him, a primal sense that he was in the presence of something that shouldn't be.

A dark figure—some combination of black, segmented metal and sickly flesh—turned its head from side to side slowly, its many eyes working independently, devouring its surroundings with a hundred malevolent glares. Its bulging muscles rippled and distorted, their dark veins squirming under nearly translucent skin that changed shape constantly, seemingly not able to decide on which form to take. In its hand, it held a miniature sun, an incandescent ball of pale fire that stretched the shadow of the monster for miles and miles behind it.

White was standing before it, clutching his arm, which was bent at a strange angle. His fencing tunic was ripped to expose his chest, which was already black with deep bruises. The two figures blurred and came together in an exchange of blows Myron caught the vaguest of impressions of, so fast, his eyes literally could not follow them. When they parted once more, White seemed to be standing strangely, unable to support his weight on one of his ankles.

The monster flexed its metal arm in front of its face, the only part of it that seemed to be of proper proportion. It seemed curious. Perplexed.

"Run, Mr. Kotes!" White shouted, taking the time to meet his eyes. There was fear there and something else. Sadness. Pity. "Go for help! It's a demon!"

Myron's heart thundered in his chest.

A demon? What did that even mean? Where had it come from? How was this real?

The two came together again. The ground quaked under their feet, and thunderous impacts of flesh-on-flesh sent shock waves through Myron's body. When they parted again, White was encircled by a spinning ring of glowing green runes, his good hand out to the side and inscribing more in midair, only to have them drift down to join the others as the ring widened and widened.

Myron felt like his blood had frozen and his nerves had gone dead.

The glowing symbols flared as the monster smashed into an invisible barrier that had formed around it, a mirror of White's runic circle. Then it slowly, almost casually, reached out with its metal hand and plucked the energy from the air. White's spell collapsed in on itself, shrunk down until its structure imploded under the pressure and the dark figure had the entirety of it in its hand.

CRACK!

It crushed White's spell. No, it *consumed* it.

There was a rush of power that streamed into the thing's palm, and the monster itself closed its eyes in some form of sick pleasure. White himself staggered, having been dealt a terrible blow, and went down to his knees.

"Myron! Myron!" White yelled, cutting through the fear that had rooted him in place. "Go! Warn them!"

It was only then that the monster faltered. It seemed to trip, catch itself on something invisible before standing up straight and looking directly at Myron with all its eyes. Myron felt the pressure of that gaze more acutely than he'd ever felt anything in his entire life. He was seen, flayed, dissected, and *known* in a flash, an invasive presence locking onto his very soul and exposing it in all its imperfections and vulnerabilities.

There was something else, too. Familiarity. They both felt it. Myron didn't know how, but they did.

Then, the monster turned its attention down to *itself*, its arms, its chest, and legs, like it was seeing them for the first time. Then its attention settled finally on its hands—the black metal, the glowing sun.

No. That wasn't a star in its hand. It was a blade. A glowing blade of white fire. The creature stared into the flames intently, blinking asynchronously with confusion. Then it wound back to throw the star as far from itself as possible, but, at the last instant, it froze.

There was a battle going on within the monster, Myron saw. It shook its head and trembled, its entire body shivering like a man with a fever or an addict staring at his next high through a pane of glass.

That battle raged for long seconds as Myron and White looked on helplessly, until suddenly a side seemed to have been crowned the victor. Slowly, the monster reached over and took the shining sword in its metal hand and consumed it, too.

The world went supernova. The black figure was consumed in incandescent fire, starting from within and expanding until it was the heart of its own star. Myron had to close his eyes for fear of going blind.

Its scream was composed of a multitude of voices—horrific, alien, yet familiar. The fire burned them all, weakening them, silencing them one by one, yet the thing kept screaming. It screamed and screamed as it burned from the inside . . .

Until it was only one voice that was screaming, one that Myron knew intimately. A memory surfaced in his mind from years ago: an overturned rover, half-submerged in an icy lake.

Ryan?

Then all was silent.

Myron opened his eyes to find the dark figure gone. In its place, the limp body of his only son. Even from this distance he could tell.

He was up on his feet in a flash, his adrenaline giving his limbs strength they'd been robbed of in the presence of the monster. He'd lost his goggles. The wind whipped at his face, carrying his fresh tears with it as he slid to stop on his knees next to Ryan's still-smoking form. His trembling hands found their way under his boy's head, and he cradled it on his lap, just as he'd done when his son was small.

Ryan was larger now, muscular, athletic . . . *whole.* Yes, he was whole again. What few scraps of clothing he wore couldn't hide a large part of his chest that had been replaced with metal unlike anything Myron had seen in his life, but this was most certainly his son. He was different, but this was him. Ryan had come home.

"Mr. Kotes, get away from it!" White panted. There was a chord of fear in his voice, something Myron didn't realize the Colony man was capable of before today.

Myron shook his head, afraid to look away from his boy lest the System take him from his home again. "It's Ryan. This is Ryan. He's come back."

White's breathing was ragged, his body broken in many different places, no doubt causing him a lot of pain, but he looked ready as ever to use the sword he was carrying. "It is a demon. It may look like your son, but it is a demon. Trust me, Myron, please. This is my profession. Get away from it, or I will be forced to—"

BLAP!

White flopped to the ground, mid-dodge, a look of utter shock on his face as he clutched at the hole in his chest.

"You dodge to your left only about a fifth of the time," Myron said, the smoking las-pistol still aimed at White. "No one of your caliber has that kind of flaw in their game. Figured you were playing me. Guess I figured right."

Myron took aim at the Exotic's face this time, finger tightening on the trigger. "No one's taking my son from me."

BLAP!

It was Myron's turn to be shocked. Pale, steely fingers gripped his wrist, forcing his pistol off-target. White, too, stared down at Ryan in surprise.

"Dad?" Ryan said. His voice sounded hoarse like he'd just been screaming loud enough to rupture eardrums, which actually he had. His eyes were barely open, unfocused, but Myron could see a change in them from when they'd last been together. His son's eyes were now the palest of blue, almost white. What had happened to him?

"Dad?" he asked again.

Myron tried and failed to answer twice before he could get a word out. "Y-Yes, Son?"

"No, Dad," Ryan rasped.

Myron wiped another tear from his eye. "What?"

Ryan's words were pained whispers, almost inaudible over the wind. "Not on my account."

Realization hit Myron hard. He'd come a hair's breadth from murder, and his son didn't want to see him become a killer. Slowly, he relaxed his grip on the pistol and let it fall to the ground. As he did so, he caught White's gaze oscillating between him and Ryan, wheels turning.

"This isn't a demon," Myron stated in no uncertain terms.

"Was," Ryan corrected him. "At some point. Tricked them. Brought them inside. Gave the assholes a brightsteel enema." Ryan chuckled darkly, wincing in pain as he did so.

White, hesitated, caught mid-breath. Whatever thoughts were going on behind his eyes, they were contentious ones. The conflict was plain on his face.

"I believe—" White began, pausing to cough up a bit of blood and spit it into the dirt, "—that this might *not* be a demon. Not anymore, at least. May I approach?"

Myron looked down at Ryan, who gave a weak nod of agreement.

White leaned over the two of them, still clutching the hole in his chest and having to clear his throat constantly as blood bubbled up from his insides.

"You going to be okay?" Ryan asked.

White allowed a little smile to pull at the corner of his mouth. "Oh, I'll be fine, young man. Lots of HP, still. We can take a lot of punishment as long as our HP remains, but I assume you know that."

Ryan seemed far away for a moment, the ghost of a smile on his face. "If only you knew."

White's smile blossomed into a grin. Then he took what looked like an old coin out from his pocket. "I do know, actually. Ryan, I am going to give you this, then I want you to issue me a challenge. The coin will be the stakes. Do you understand how this works?"

Ryan nodded.

"Good. I won't accept. Neither of us are in condition to fight anyway, but the coin is part of the tradition. A challenge displays your Level. There is no way to hide it, aside from being far higher in power than your target."

"Okay," Ryan replied. "You're making sure I'm not . . ."

"A demon would be of an abnormally high Level, yes."

Something passed between the two of them, and Mr. White frowned, shaking his head in disbelief. "I don't understand. This isn't possible, not after your tutorial."

Ryan grimaced. "I'd like to file a complaint. My tutorial sucked."

White sat back on his haunches, an almost-indignant look on his face, mouthing quiet arguments to himself that Myron only caught snippets of.

"What is it?" Myron asked. "Is his Level too high?" He looked down at the gun, wondering if he'd be able to grab it in time.

The Exotic blinked and seemed to finally remember Myron was there.

"No. Not high, Mr. Kotes. Ryan is Level 0."

Ryan Kotes - Level 0 Automator (Unique)				
Type:	Artificer (Common)	**Abilities:**	Shape 9 (Transmute)	Devouring Grasp (Magivore) 6
Class:	Animator (Uncommon)		Consume 7 (Reservoir)	Volatility 3+++++
Core:	Engine (Unique)		Iron Grip 4	Imbue 4
HP:	44/309		Trigger 4	Automate 5+
MP:	277/277		Crystalized Channels 1	Knife in the Dark 24 (Mark, Curse of Obfuscation)
Attributes:			Hardened Defense 2	Compartmentalize 3
Body:	58		Tension Step 1	Expanded Channels 2
Mind:	51		State Change 4	
Spirit:	116	**Skills:**	Climbing 10 (Anchor)	Unarmed Combat 6
			Running 7	Stealth 17 (Gray Man, Alert)
			Conduit 9	Split Mind 11
			Spear 4	Deception 9
			Disguise 3	Sword 8
			Pistol 6 (Death Eye)	Mana Manipulation 4
			Jumping 3	Leadership 2
		Affinities:	Goblinoid F	Cobalt E
			Iron E	Deep Lead E
			Steel F	Nickel E
Free Attribute points: 0			Magnesium F	Copper E
			Mendau Wood B	Pex Oil F
			Limestone E	Osmium F

About the Author

J. Drude is the author of the Turret Mage series, originally released on Royal Road. In addition to writer, he has at various times undertaken the roles of cook, computer jockey, soldier, and professional tabletop game master—yes, that last one's a real job; no, it doesn't pay well—but his most challenging and rewarding position to date has been that of a husband and father. J. Drude lives in Texas with his wife, two children, and a menagerie of creatures (only some of which are actually domesticated and at least one of which is most certainly plotting his death).

RESPAWN YOUR CURIOSITY

follow us on our socials

 podiumentertainment.com

 @podiumentertainment

 /podiumentertainment

 @podium_ent

 @podiumentertainment

www.ingramcontent.com/pod-product-compliance
Lightning Source LLC
Chambersburg PA
CBHW050112120726
47904CB00004B/1316